Nineteenth-Century French Short Stories

Contes et Nouvelles Français du XIXe Siècle

A Dual-Language Book

Edited and Translated by

STANLEY APPELBAUM

DOVER PUBLICATIONS, INC.
Mineola, New York

Bibliographical Note

This Dover edition, first published in 2000, consists of a new selection of French stories, reprinted from standard French texts (see the Introduction for dates of first publications in French), accompanied by new English translations prepared for the Dover edition by Stanley Appelbaum, who also made the selection and wrote the Introduction and the numbered explanatory Notes.

Library of Congress Cataloging-in-Publication Data

Nineteenth-century French short stories = Contes et nouvelles français du XIXe siècle : a dual-language book / edited and translated by Stanley Appelbaum.
    p. cm.
    ISBN 0-486-41126-5 (pbk.)
    1. Short stories, French—Translations into English. 2. Short stories, French. 3. French fiction—19th century—Translations into English. 4. French fiction—19th century. I. Title: Contes et nouvelles français du XIXe siècle. II. Title: 19th-century French short stories. III. Appelbaum, Stanley.

PQ1278 .N48 2000
843'.010807—dc21   99-047448

Manufactured in the United States of America
Dover Publications, Inc., 31 East 2nd Street, Mineola, N.Y. 11501

Contents

INTRODUCTION

French Short Stories

The French call short stories *contes* or *nouvelles*. Numerous contradictory attempts have been made to distinguish between the two terms on the basis of themes, complexity, extent of participation by the narrator, and other factors. By the 19th century, at least, the terms were virtually interchangeable, with perhaps a preference for *nouvelle* when referring to a lengthier story.

Storytelling has had a long, glorious history in France, native talents being spurred to greater heights by translations of foreign works at various key periods. In the High Middle Ages, tales were generally written in verse, such as the often satirical and bawdy *fabliaux* (usually concerned with everyday life), the more refined and delicate *Lais* of Marie de France (ca. 1160), and the epics, of various lengths, on Arthurian subjects.

The strong influence of Italian story collections (chief among them, Boccaccio's *Decameron*) brought about a golden age of prose tales in French at the end of the Middle Ages and in the Renaissance. Major collections of this period are the *Cent nouvelles nouvelles* (ca. 1460) and the *Heptaméron* of Marguerite d'Angoulême (1558–1559).

In the 17th century, verse was again the medium for La Fontaine's *Contes et nouvelles,* but a number of Perrault's famous fairy tales were written in prose.

The 18th century was very rich in stories, new specialties being the philosophical and moral tales by men like Voltaire and Diderot, and the flood of exotic tales unleashed by Antoine Galland's epoch-making translation of the *Arabian Nights* (1704 ff.).

Without a doubt, however, the 19th century eclipsed all that had gone before in the genre. Short stories became particularly

fashionable in France; at three points in the course of the century, new vitality was injected into the scene by translations of E. T. A. Hoffmann, Poe (translated by Baudelaire), and Turgenev (translated by Mérimée, among others). Many more authors than ever were supporting themselves (or trying to) by their writing, without wealthy patronage. The great expansion of the short story was chiefly due to the new proliferation of newspapers and magazines in which stories were printed. It became customary for an author to place his story in a periodical before it appeared in volume form (usually within a collection—generally, but not always, all by the same author). In this way, a writer could earn an extra fee, and was also given an opportunity to revise his work before its more formal publication. The drawbacks of first publication in periodicals were the temptation to pad the material unnecessarily (in order to fill up space one would be paid for), and the all-too-real danger of writing too many stories altogether, and becoming trivial and mechanical, or merely anecdotal.

Although obviously too schematic and insufficiently inclusive, one literary historian's breakdown of 19th-century French stories into three classifications is useful: (1) a continuation of the *fabliau* tradition (merry tales told for the sake of amusement); (2) what might be called "reportage," accounts that are true to real life, real events, real people and places; and (3) tales of the fantastic and supernatural.

The present volume assembles six important stories originally published between 1829 and 1886, each by a different author. They are stories that the French themselves regard as highly significant. Various literary trends of the century are represented, including Romanticism, Realism, and Naturalism. In the story by Flaubert, a truly pivotal author, one can also detect strains of Parnassianism (emphasis on form, preference for antique and "archaeological" subjects) and even a foretaste of Symbolism.

Other 19th-century French short-story geniuses who might have been included in a longer volume, and who are highly recommended to the reader, are Chateaubriand, Stendhal, Balzac (a dual-language volume of selected stories by Balzac is available from Dover), Nodier, Gautier, Barbey d'Aurevilly, and Villiers de l'Isle-Adam.

The remainder of this Introduction includes brief biographies of the authors and general background to the stories selected. More specific explanations are given in the notes at the end of the volume, keyed to numbers in the English text.

Prosper Mérimée (1803–1870); "Mateo Falcone" (1829)

Mérimée, son of a prominent drawing teacher, was born in Paris in 1803. After studying law, he worked in various government departments. As inspector general of historical monuments from 1834 to 1860, he traveled all over France, and was instrumental in saving a large number of outstanding medieval buildings. His other travels, many of which he made use of in his stories, took him to Spain, England and Scotland, Italy (together with his friend Stendhal), Greece, Turkey, and the German-speaking lands. In 1845 he became a member of the Académie Française. In 1853, just months after Emperor Napoléon III married Eugénie de Montijo, whose mother Mérimée had known for decades, the writer was made a Senator of France. Mérimée himself remained a bachelor, but was involved in numerous affairs. He died in Cannes in 1870.

As a writer, Mérimée made a name very early. A group of plays, collected in the volume *Théâtre de Clara Gazul*, was first published pseudonymously in 1825. In 1827, continuing to hoodwink the public, he published *La Guzla*, a collection of ballads purporting to be translations from the Illyrian (Slovenian). But it was his short stories that were to bring him his greatest fame, especially the ones collected in the 1833 volume *Mosaïque*, as well as "La Vénus d'Ille" (1837), "Colomba" (1840), and "Carmen" (1845). He also wrote volumes of history and art history, and introduced the French public, by means of translations and essays, to such great Russian writers as Pushkin, Gogol, and Turgenev (a friend).

Mérimée's style, which some of his more exuberant contemporaries found flat, was tightly controlled, admirably terse and matter-of-fact, but laced with sly humor and much local color. Although his language was inspired by 18th-century rationalism, his plots lean toward the violent and the uncanny, the mixture constituting a very personal kind of romanticism.

"Mateo Falcone," which has had several volumes of analysis devoted to it alone, is among Mérimée's greatest stories, one of the two or three that made his reputation when first published. It first appeared in May 1829 in the periodical *La Revue de Paris*—just one month before the publication of his best play, the one-act comedy *Le carrosse du Saint-Sacrement* (The Coach of the Holy Sacrament)—and was then included in the 1833 story collection *Mosaïque*. Opinions are divided as to possible sources Mérimée used for "Mateo Falcone" (he was known not to have made up his stories out of whole cloth).

His knowledge of Corsica, where the story takes place, was derived entirely from books when he wrote the story, but his visit to that island in 1839 led him to make only a few trifling corrections. He then immediately used Corsica as a setting again, in "Colomba" (1840), generally considered his masterpiece, but far too long for inclusion in this anthology.

Corsica had been ceded to France by Genoa in 1768, but was still rather wild and woolly in Mérimée's time, with feuds and rough justice recalling the American Appalachians of a somewhat later day. Of the three towns mentioned, Porto-Vecchio is located in the extreme southeast of the island; Corte, inland in the north-central part, and Bastia on the northwest coast.

Gérard de Nerval (1808–1855); "Sylvie" (1853)

Gérard Labrunie, who later adopted the name Nerval from a family estate, was once dismissed as a "minor Romantic," but is now recognized as one of the most distinctive voices in French literature. "Sylvie," his most perfect story, is universally regarded as a masterpiece of French prose, and thematically a forerunner of both Proust and the Surrealists.

Nerval, born in Paris in 1808, was almost immediately put out to nurse in the country at Loisy, while his mother accompanied her husband, an army surgeon, on Napoleon's campaigns. She died of fever in eastern Germany two years later, and the boy lived in the country with a great-uncle until his father's return to Paris in 1814.

In his early-begun literary career, Nerval first made his mark with a translation of Part One of Goethe's *Faust* in 1827. He became a member of the inner Romantic circle, along with Victor Hugo and Théophile Gautier, and participated in other literary and bohemian groups. An inheritance from his maternal grandfather in 1834 was used up in two years, spent on travel to Italy, expensive antique furnishings, and an unsuccessful luxury magazine.

Next, Nerval turned to journalism, especially theatrical reviewing; he himself wrote verse plays and librettos. From about 1834 until her death in 1842, the chief woman in his life was the stage singer Jenny Colon, who performed at the Théâtre des Variétés and the Opéra-Comique. Between 1838 and 1840, Nerval visited Germany (his mother was buried there; that country's literature and mysticism also attracted him), Austria, and Belgium.

In 1841 Nerval suffered his first serious attack of mental illness and remained in clinics for several months. Late in 1842 he set out for the East, returning a year later after journeys to Egypt, Lebanon, and Turkey. He later combined his travel reminiscences with his own personal fantasies in one of his major works, *Le voyage en Orient* (1851). He continued writing articles, stories, plays, translations (working with Heinrich Heine himself on Heine translations), and poems, some of which are imperishable jewels (such as the sonnet cycle *Les chimères*).

In 1850 he made frequent trips to the Valois countryside of his early childhood, and began using that region as the locale for his writings. In 1852 and 1853 his mental troubles returned, becoming very serious by August 1853. Nerval was in and out of clinics; but he was also producing some of his best work in this trying period, stories in which the walls between dream and reality were broken down and he analyzed his entire life in highly personal terms. Apart from "Sylvie," perhaps the most outstanding story of this final period is "Aurélia," unfortunately left unfinished.

In January 1855 Nerval was found hanged from a grating in the street. From that day to this, the consensus has been that he killed himself, but there have always been voices claiming it was murder, or even an elaborate accident.

"Sylvie" was first published in August 1853 in the *Revue des deux mondes* and inserted in Nerval's 1854 collection *Les filles du feu* (The Daughters of Fire). It brilliantly combines many of the author's chief preoccupations: childhood reminiscences; self-analysis, especially of his love life; interest in French history and culture, as well as ancient Greco-Roman and contemporary German culture and thought; fascination with the uncanny and the occult; appreciation of rural ways and particularly folk songs (in *Les filles du feu,* an article about folk songs Nerval had written earlier was included as a supplement to "Sylvie"). The name of the heroine, of course, comes from Latin, and can be glossed as "woman" (or even "deity") "of the forest."

Geographically (as well as ethically) the story alternates between two poles: sophisticated, metropolitan Paris and the Valois countryside, not far to the northeast of the capital. Before the 1789 Revolution a region within the province Ile-de-France, the Valois plateau—once the appanage of the kings of the house of Valois who ruled France from 1328 to 1589—is now chiefly contained within the Senlis *arrondissement* (roughly equivalent to an American county) of the *département* (roughly, "state") of the Oise. It is an area that

combines agriculture and industry; it contains prehistoric and historic remains from all eras, and still boasts large and small forests well known to Parisian vacationers. Most of the villages, towns, natural features, and historic buildings mentioned in the story are real. The Thève and the Nonette, tributaries of the Oise, are the main streams in the Valois. Chaalis still was spelled with a circumflex (Châalis) in Nerval's time, but now it generally is dispensed with.

The translator's notes (at the end of the volume), though fairly numerous, are merely intended as immediate aids to understanding; it would have been impossible, and surely undesirable, to gloss everything in sight, and so items that the general reader can be expected to know (or that are very easy to look up) have been omitted. The translation is very faithful to the original text, but in two or three places has been slightly expanded interpretively to take special connotations into account.

Alphonse Daudet (1840–1897); "La mule du Pape" (1868)

Daudet was born in the Provençal city of Nîmes in 1840, and spent his childhood in the local countryside. By 1857 his parents' textile business had totally failed (they already had been forced to move to Lyons in 1849), and Daudet's life became very hard; by the end of the year, he was living on his own in Paris. He had started writing at fourteen, and in 1858 his first book, a volume of verse, was published. From 1860 to 1865 he enjoyed a sinecure as private secretary to the Duke of Morny, brother-in-law of Emperor Napoleon III.

Meanwhile: in 1859, Daudet met Frédéric Mistral, who was actively reviving Provençal literature and culture; in 1861, he traveled to Algeria and saw his own first play performed; in 1862, he visited Corsica. It was in 1863 that he spent months in the village of Fontvieille, near Arles, where he saw the windmills that he was to make so famous, and assembled many notes for his forthcoming series of short stories, most of which were published in a periodical in the course of 1866. He added some more in the years that followed, and the first publication in volume form of *Lettres de mon moulin* took place in 1869 (definitive edition, 1879). The fictional framework of the series has the author renting and living in a mill and hearing many of the stories from his neighbors.

In 1867, Daudet married (his sons became writers). In 1868, in addition to more *Windmill* stories, including the one selected for this

anthology, he published his first (highly autobiographical) novel, *Le petit Chose* (Little What's-His-Name). In 1872, there followed both his popular novel on a Provençal subject, *Tartarin de Tarascon* (there were to be two sequels), and his most significant play, *L'Arlésienne* (The Woman of Arles), for which Georges Bizet wrote his memorable incidental music. Another volume of short stories, *Les contes du lundi* (Monday Stories), largely about the Franco-Prussian War, followed in 1873.

Oddly enough, none of his books had been financially successful yet. This situation changed in 1874 with the novel *Fromont jeune et Risler aîné* (Fromont the Younger and Risler the Elder). From then on, Daudet was established and was friendly with the chief Parisian literati of the day. Later important novels were *Jack* (1876), *Numa Roumestan* (1881), and *Sapho* (1884). From 1884 until his sudden death in 1897, Daudet was increasingly tortured by cancer of the spinal cord.

"La mule du Pape" is one of the additional *Windmill* stories Daudet published in 1868 in the newspaper *Le Figaro*. It takes place in Avignon, the historic Provençal city on the Rhône, in the 14th century. (From 1309 to 1378, because of turbulence in Rome, the seat of the papacy was moved to Avignon. In fact, even after the official return of the papacy to Rome, there were still "counter-Popes" or "anti-Popes" in Avignon. This was the period of the Great Schism, which was ended by the Council of Constance. All the Avignon popes were French, and since France was at war with England at the time—Hundred Years' War—the papacy no longer was seen as a truly ecumenical institution, and its prestige diminished.) The Pope in the story is completely fictitious: there were nine Popes altogether who were called Boniface, but none in Avignon. Another thing about the city to which Daudet makes repeated witty references is the famous folk song "Sur le pont d'Avignon, / L'on y danse, l'on y danse" (On the bridge of Avignon, people dance there, people dance there).

The story seems to be based on two French sayings. The first of these is the one about the mule cited in the very first paragraph. There's a complication or a mystification here, though, because in French the Pope's *mule* ordinarily refers to his slipper (the expression *baiser la mule du Pape* is equivalent to "kiss the Pope's toe"): was there never really a proverb about a kicking kind of mule? The other saying can be rendered as "he acts as high and mighty as if he were the chief purveyor of mustard to the Pope"; this is said to refer to an office created by an Avignon pope (John XXII, reigned 1316–1334) for the benefit of his nephew.

Like some others in the *Windmill* series, this story is genuinely funny, employing a kind of nonsense fantasy associated more with English humorists and relatively uncommon in France. Daudet's Avignon is right out of a child's picture book—or one of the more naïve old Hollywood travelogues. The endowment of the mule with human reasoning powers doesn't strike the reader as odd in the midst of the delicious and vivacious goings-on.

Some humorless critics have seen Pope Boniface's guilelessness and the mule's rancor as indicative of the widespread French anticlericalism that was a legacy of the 1789 Revolution. I wholeheartedly disagree—otherwise I never would have selected the story. Fantasy and good-humored banter reign, not malice or denigration; mild jokes about clergymen have been an unchanging, universal element of folklore and popular literature, only taking on an edge at times of particular social distress.

Gustave Flaubert (1821–1880); "Hérodias" (1877)

Flaubert, one of the most respected of all French authors, was born in Rouen in 1821. His father was a surgeon and hospital director. Always interested in writing, Flaubert had works published before he was sixteen. From 1841 to 1843 he studied law in Paris. In 1844 a seizure, of the nature of epilepsy, put an end to his studies, and his domicile was henceforth in the suburbs of Rouen. In the 1830s and '40s he wrote first drafts of novels that were to occupy him for decades to come.

From 1849 to 1851 he traveled extensively in the Levant, Greece, and Italy. From 1851 to 1856 he worked on his most celebrated novel, *Madame Bovary*, which was published in volume form in 1857, but not before Flaubert had been tried for immorality as a writer and acquitted. From 1857 to 1862, he worked on his novel *Salammbô*, set in ancient Carthage, and considered his greatest work by some critics. From 1864 to 1869, he worked on his novel *L'éducation sentimentale*. From 1870 to 1872, he worked on the third and definitive version of the book *La tentation de saint Antoine* (The Temptation of Saint Anthony), which wasn't published in volume form until 1874.

This enumeration of lengthy "periods of gestation" indicates Flaubert's thoroughness of research, whether for local or for exotic subjects, and his unparalleled meticulousness of style; and it explains why his major works are so few, but so rewarding. (His voluminous correspondence is also highly valued.)

In 1875, depressed by financial troubles and personal griefs, Flaubert began writing his *Trois contes* (Three Stories), which might also have been called "Three Saints," because "Hérodias" concerns Saint John the Baptist, "Saint Julien l'Hospitalier" is a medieval-style miracle legend about the saint in the title (Julian the Hospitaler), and in "Un cœur simple" (A Simple Soul), the old servant woman of the title dies believing that her stuffed parrot is the Holy Spirit (Holy Ghost; "Saint-Esprit" in French). "Hérodias" was written between November 1876 and February 1877. The three stories were published, first in newspapers, then in volume form, all in the course of April 1877.

Flaubert died in 1880, leaving unfinished his novel *Bouvard et Pécuchet.*

In "Hérodias" (the name also occurs in French in the form "Hérodiade," as in Massenet's opera), though Flaubert undertook scrupulous research in works of history and archaeology, he didn't hesitate to tinker with chronology in order to bring together in one place, for the space of one day, a number of interesting characters from Rome and the Near East, with the resulting clash of cultures.

New Testament chronology is controversial, but the martyrdom of Saint John the Baptist must have occurred about 28 or 29 A.D. (all dates in the following discussion will be A.D. unless otherwise specified). For about three-quarters of a century, the Romans had been in control of the Holy Land, the ranking official in the area being the legate ("governor") of Syria, with proconsular powers (equality in rank, and emblems of office, to the consuls, the chief magistrates of the city of Rome). Lucius Vitellius, whose great influence was not so entirely dependent on his son's dubious relationships as Flaubert indicates, didn't become the legate of Syria until the year 35. His son, Aulus Vitellius, became emperor for several months in 69, during the turmoil that followed the assassination of Nero and the end of the first, Julio-Claudian, dynasty. (There is no evidence that high-ranking Romans were present at the death of the Baptist, and only the late-1st-century Jewish historian Josephus tells us that it took place in the citadel of Machaerus.)

For some time, the Romans in the area worked with, and through, local rulers, the most outstanding of whom was Herod the Great; his kingdom included (in present-day terms) Israel, much of Jordan, and parts of southern Syria. On his death in 4 B.C., his kingdom was partitioned among three of his sons, who were then called tetrarchs. Archelaus, who was granted what is currently the south and center of

Israel (including Judaea and Samaria), proved so unpopular that he
was deposed in the year 6 and the Romans governed his portion directly, the ranking officer being a "prefect" (the prefect from 26 to 36
was Pontius Pilate). The tetrarch Philip inherited his father's north-
ernmost territory; while Herod Antipas (whom Flaubert calls only
"Antipas," reserving "Hérode" for Herod the Great) inherited Galilee
(where he built the city of Tiberias, naming it after the reigning emperor Tiberius) and Peraea (the area east of the Dead Sea, where
Machaerus was located). Antipas became an enemy of the Nabataeans
of present-day southern Jordan when he divorced their king's daughter in order to marry Herodias. (The Nabataeans, whom Flaubert
merely calls "Arabs" and depicts as wild nomads, were actually highly
cultured.) Herodias had been married to Antipas's half-brother Herod
Philip (not the same as the tetrarch), and Salome (her name supplied
only by Josephus) was the daughter of Herodias and Herod Philip.
Agrippa, Herodias's brother, *was* imprisoned by Tiberius because he
supported Gaius (later the emperor "Caligula") for emperor, but not
until 36, and then only briefly, before rising to new heights.

The Pharisees and Sadducees were the main Jewish parties, both
religious and political. The Pharisees represented that main stream of
Judaism that was to lead to the Talmud; they were guardians of accumulated custom and jurisprudence, in addition to the Law of Moses.
The Sadducees were fundamentalists who believed that only the Law
of Moses counted. The Essenes were an extremist sect living apart in
conditions of rigorous religious purity, and expecting the end of the
world to arrive shortly; they have been identified with the community
at Qumran that kept the Dead Sea Scrolls. The Samaritans, who lived
in what is currently central Israel, developed separately from ordinary
Judaism after the Babylonian captivity (whether they were remnants
of Judaism, as they themselves claimed, or resettled foreigners, as the
Jews claimed). They had their own special cult sites and practices, and
were regarded as outcasts by the followers of the Pharisees and
Sadducees.

The explanations just given, and the three dozen notes at the end
of the volume, are obviously only a "first aid" to understanding the details of the story. A complete annotation, even if expressed concisely,
would be longer than the text itself. Readers not already familiar with
the subject matter are urged to look up further details in a good classical dictionary, a dictionary of the Bible, and a large English dictionary. The translator has used well-known reference sources for the
best English equivalents of proper names. Wherever Flaubert used a

technical term ("velarium," "chlamys," "tympanon," etc.), the precise English equivalent has been used and an explanatory note has been written; the use of glosses (e.g., for the three words cited: "awning," "mantle," "tambourine") would misrepresent Flaubert's very "archaeological" original text.

Salome's dance in the story was inspired both by a medieval sculpture in Rouen cathedral (each of the *Trois contes* is ultimately Rouen-inspired) and by Flaubert's experiences with a belly dancer during his trip to the East. Readers of this Flaubert story will see how closely Oscar Wilde based his play *Salomé* on it.

Emile Zola (1840–1902); "L'attaque du moulin" (1880)

Chiefly celebrated for his numerous novels, such as *Thérèse Raquin* (1867) and the lengthy cycle *Les Rougon-Macquart* (1870–1893), Zola also wrote many short stories, among which "L'attaque du moulin" enjoys particularly high esteem.

Zola was born in Paris in 1840, the son of a civil engineer of Italian origin (the family name was originally Zolla). In 1843, the family moved to Aix-en-Provence, where the elder Zola worked on a dam until his sudden death four years later. In 1858 the future author returned to Paris, where he felt the pinch of poverty until, in 1862, he became advertising manager for the prestigious publisher Hachette and gained entrée into the literary world. Tentative publications (stories) began in 1863, and he also tried his hand at plays.

In 1866, Zola became a book and art reviewer for the daily *L'Evénement* (he had been a close friend of the painter Paul Cézanne ever since their school days in Aix). During the following year, the novel *Thérèse Raquin* was not only a mild success, but also an early manifesto of the "naturalism" in literature that Zola championed. He soon started planning his large cycle of novels, the first of which, *La fortune des Rougon,* was serialized in 1870 and published in volume form in 1871.

Zola's first enormous success was the *Rougon* novel *L'Assommoir* (The Saloon), serialized in 1876, published as a volume in 1877. This book made him famous, and definitively changed his financial status for the better. In 1878 he purchased the country house at Médan (near Versailles) that was to be made famous by the stories written there: six stories, each by a different author, all on the subject of the Franco-Prussian War of 1870–1871, a traumatic defeat for the French, who suffered greatly and lost the Alsace-Lorraine region.

These stories were published in May of 1880, only two and a half months after Zola's second great success (*de scandale*) in the *Rougon* cycle, *Nana*, appeared in volume form. The collective volume of stories was entitled *Les soirées de Médan*, and Zola's contribution—the first item in the book, as was only fitting, because the other authors were younger disciples of his—was "L'attaque du moulin." The second story made *its* thirty-year-old author instantly famous: "Boule de suif" (Ball of Fat; more idiomatically: Butterball) by Guy de Maupassant. One other contributor was to achieve great fame a little later on: Joris-Karl Huysmans, author of the 1884 novel *A rebours* (Against the Grain). *Les soirées de Médan* as a whole also served as a resounding manifesto of naturalism at its peak.

Zola continued writing stories, plays, and articles as the *Rougon* cycle continued with such masterpieces as *Germinal* (1885), *La terre* (1887), and *La bête humaine* (1890). Other novels followed the completion of the *Rougon* cycle, without quite reaching the level of the best of those. Of course, the most famous adventure of Zola's later life was his untiring defense of Captain Alfred Dreyfus between 1897 and 1899, in the course of which the writer himself had to take refuge from the law in England. Zola died in 1902, asphyxiated by gas in his apartment in what may or may not have been an accident.

"L'attaque du moulin" requires little commentary. Its style is extremely lucid and simple, approaching colloquial speech without lapsing into dialect or difficult jargon, though pleasantly tinged with folksy expressions and speech patterns that reflect a peasant mentality. The long, lavish descriptions of nature are characteristic of Zola's painterly eye, but also serve a real purpose in the story: they place the characters more fully within their environment, and the contrast between physical conditions at the beginning and the end of the story is quite consciously achieved. The narrative is crystal clear, moves swiftly, and is full of suspense.

Unlike some of his French contemporaries (especially Maupassant), for whom the invading Germans were sheer subhuman brutes, Zola here displays his customary humaneness and broadmindedness, especially in his references to the unfortunate German sentry, who at one point is practically equated with the young hero of the story. It is war in general that Zola condemns; the French are capable of inflicting just as much grief as the enemy. The multiple ironies of the final words are compounded by the reader's knowledge that France lost the war quite thoroughly.

The place names in the story—other than Lorraine, of course—

seem to be fictitious. In 1893 an opera based on the story, and with the same title, was produced at the Opéra-Comique in Paris. The composer was Zola's friend Alfred Bruneau (1857–1934).

Guy de Maupassant (1850–1893); "Mademoiselle Perle" (1886)

Maupassant was born in Normandy in 1850; the exact place is a matter of dispute. His parents got along badly with each other. A brother, born six years later, eventually died insane (1889). From 1856 on, their mother lived separately with her two boys. After school days in Paris and in Normandy, the future author entered law school in Paris. Beginning in 1871, after the Franco-Prussian War, he worked in various clerical positions in the Navy Department, and later the Department of the Interior; several of his stories deal with the financial difficulties of civil servants who try to keep up with the Joneses. Meanwhile, Maupassant, who had met Flaubert in 1868 and acknowledged him as his spiritual father, was beginning to write, and, through Flaubert, who was not himself a naturalist though he decisively influenced that school, he met Zola in the early 1870s.

Maupassant's first story was published in 1875; he also tried his hand at plays, poems, and journalism. He suffered a serious bout of ill health in 1877, and increasingly severe eye problems in the first years of the 1880s. Meanwhile he achieved his first great success with his long short story "Boule de suif," included in the six-author volume *Les soirées de Médan* (1880; see the section on Zola, immediately preceding). In June of 1880 he left his civil-service post and started to live by his pen.

Hundreds of short stories and six novels were to flow from that pen in the dozen years of intense activity that followed. The stories were first published in periodicals, then collected into volumes. By 1883 Maupassant was able to build a country house in Normandy and to spend his winters in Cannes. He never married—in his stories, marriage usually takes the form of an all-out war between the sexes—but he fathered three children, besides reveling in the pleasures of bordellos, which he described in many of his most famous works.

His health continued to fail, and he was a prey to nervous disorders, either hereditary or due to syphilis, or a combination. After many attempted cures and trips to warm countries, he made a will at the end of 1891 and tried to commit suicide on New Year's Day of 1892. He was institutionalized, and he died the following year.

"Mademoiselle Perle" was included in the collected volume *La petite Roque* in 1886. Technically, it is a very fine piece (many of
Maupassant's short works were written much too hastily; those are
repetitious and mechanical when read in any quantity). The author's
often-used structure of a story within a story has nothing perfunctory
about it in this case, the two chronological levels being exceptionally
well integrated. Maupassant's humor, generally satirical and ironic
when present at all, is more humane and genuinely witty at some moments in the story, which is altogether more likable and upbeat than
much of the author's production. Mister Chantal's narration also
manages to generate some of the menacing feeling of the uncanny
representative of Maupassant's many stories of the supernatural; it's
amazing how many of his characters become frightened stiff at the
slightest out-of-the-way event! Above all, there is no meretricious surprise ending, which is so irritating in many of his stories (especially
when the attempt to surprise fizzles), as it often is in those of his
American imitator O. Henry.

Both sets of events narrated take place on Twelfth Night (Epiphany,
January 6). In many parts of Europe, this day, commemorating the
gifts of the Three Kings (or Wise Men) to the infant Jesus, was celebrated by family parties featuring a cake (twelfth-cake) into which a
single bean, or beanlike object, was baked. Whoever received the slice
containing the bean became king or queen of the feast and could se-
lect a consort on the throne from among the others present. Thus,
Gaston, the narrator, selects Miss Pearl as his queen, and everything
else follows from that . . .

Nineteenth-Century French Short Stories

Contes et Nouvelles Français du XIXe Siècle

PROSPER MÉRIMÉE

Mateo Falcone

En sortant de Porto-Vecchio et se dirigeant au nord-ouest, vers l'intérieur de l'île, on voit le terrain s'élever assez rapidement, et après trois heures de marche par des sentiers tortueux, obstrués par de gros quartiers de rocs, et quelquefois coupés par des ravins, on se trouve sur le bord d'un *maquis* très étendu. Le maquis est la patrie des bergers corses et de quiconque s'est brouillé avec la justice. Il faut savoir que le laboureur corse, pour s'épargner la peine de fumer son champ, met le feu à une certaine étendue de bois: tant pis si la flamme se répand plus loin que besoin n'est; arrive que pourra; on est sûr d'avoir une bonne récolte en semant sur cette terre fertilisée par les cendres des arbres qu'elle portait. Les épis enlevés, car on laisse la paille, qui donnerait de la paine à recueillir, les racines qui sont restées en terre sans se consumer poussent au printemps suivant, des cépées très épaisses qui, en peu d'années, parviennent à une hauteur de sept ou huit pieds. C'est cette manière de taillis fourré que l'on nomme maquis. Différentes espèces d'arbres et d'arbrisseaux le composent, mêlés et confondus comme il plaît à Dieu. Ce n'est que la hache à la main que l'homme s'y ouvrirait un passage, et l'on voit des maquis si épais et si touffus, que les mouflons eux-mêmes ne peuvent y pénétrer.

Si vous avez tué un homme, allez dans le maquis de Porto-Vecchio, et vous y vivrez en sûreté, avec un bon fusil, de la poudre et des balles; n'oubliez pas un manteau brun garni d'un capuchon*, qui sert de couverture et de matelas. Les bergers vous donnent du lait, du fromage et des châtaignes, et vous n'aurez rien à craindre de la justice ou des parents du mort, si ce n'est quand il vous faudra descendre à la ville pour y renouveler vos munitions.

---

*Pilone.

PROSPER MÉRIMÉE

Mateo Falcone

Leaving Porto-Vecchio and heading northwest, toward the interior of the island, you see the terrain rising quite rapidly; and after walking three hours along twisting paths, obstructed by large boulders and sometimes intersected by ravines, you find yourself at the edge of a very extensive area of brushwood. This brush is the home of the Corsican shepherds and of anyone who has fallen afoul of the law. You must know that the Corsican farmer, to save himself the trouble of manuring his field, sets fire to a certain stretch of forest: it's just too bad if the flames spread farther than necessary—let things take their course!—he'll be sure to have a good crop if he sows on that soil fertilized by the ashes of the trees that once grew on it. After the ears of grain are removed—they leave the stalks, which would be bothersome to gather—the roots that have remained in the soil without being burned put out shoots the following spring, very thick clusters that in a very few years reach a height of seven or eight feet. It is this type of dense underbrush that is called *maquis*. It is made up of various species of trees and bushes, mingled and confused as God wishes. A man can only open a passage through it with an axe in his hands, and you can find areas of brush so thick and close that even the wild sheep can't penetrate them.

If you've killed a man, go to the Porto-Vecchio *maquis*, and you'll be safe there with a good rifle, powder, and bullets; don't forget a brown cape furnished with a hood,* which serves as a blanket and a mattress. The shepherds will give you milk, cheese, and chestnuts, and you'll have nothing to fear from the law or the dead man's relatives, except when you have to go down to the town to get more ammunition there.

---

*Pilone. [NOTE: The footnotes with asterisks are by Mérimée himself. The translator's notes, which are numbered, will be found at the end of the volume.]

Mateo Falcone, quand j'étais en Corse en 18—, avait sa maison à une demi-lieue de ce maquis. C'était un homme assez riche pour le pays; vivant noblement, c'est-à-dire sans rien faire, du produit de ses troupeaux, que des bergers, espèces de nomades, menaient paître çà et là sur les montagnes. Lorsque je le vis, deux années après l'événement que je vais raconter, il me parut âgé de cinquante ans tout au plus. Figurez-vous un homme petit, mais robuste, avec des cheveux crépus, noirs comme le jais, un nez aquilin, les lèvres minces, les yeux grands et vifs, et un teint couleur de revers de botte. Son habileté au tir du fusil passait pour extraordinaire, même dans son pays, où il y a tant de bons tireurs. Par exemple, Mateo n'aurait jamais tiré sur un mouflon avec des chevrotines; mais, à cent vingt pas, il l'abattait d'une balle dans la tête ou dans l'épaule, à son choix. La nuit, il se servait de ses armes aussi facilement que le jour, et l'on m'a cité de lui ce trait d'adresse qui paraîtra peut-être incroyable à qui n'a pas voyagé en Corse. A quatre-vingts pas, on plaçait une chandelle allumée derrière un transparent de papier, large comme une assiette. Il mettait en joue, puis on éteignait la chandelle, et, au bout d'une minute dans l'obscurité la plus complète, il tirait et perçait le transparent trois fois sur quatre.

Avec un mérite aussi transcendant Mateo Falcone s'était attiré une grande réputation. On le disait aussi bon ami que dangereux ennemi: d'ailleurs serviable et faisant l'aumône, il vivait en paix avec tout le monde dans le district de Porto-Vecchio. Mais on contait de lui qu'à Corte, où il avait pris femme, il s'était débarrassé fort vigoureusement d'un rival qui passait pour aussi redoutable en guerre qu'en amour: du moins on attribuait à Mateo certain coup de fusil qui surprit ce rival comme il était à se raser devant un petit miroir pendu à sa fenêtre. L'affaire assoupie, Mateo se maria. Sa femme Giuseppa lui avait donné d'abord trois filles (dont il enrageait), et enfin un fils, qu'il nomma Fortunato: c'était l'espoir de sa famille, l'héritier du nom. Les filles étaient bien mariées: leur père pouvait compter au besoin sur les poignards et les escopettes de ses gendres. Le fils n'avait que dix ans, mais il annonçait déjà d'heureuses dispositions.

Un certain jour d'automne, Mateo sortit de bonne heure avec sa femme pour aller visiter un de ses troupeaux dans une clairière du maquis. Le petit Fortunato voulait l'accompagner, mais la clairière était trop loin; d'ailleurs, il fallait bien que quelqu'un restât pour garder la maison; le père refusa donc: on verra s'il n'eut pas lieu de s'en repentir.

Il était absent depuis quelques heures et le petit Fortunato était

When I was in Corsica in 18—, Mateo Falcone's house was located half a league from this *maquis*. He was rather wealthy for that vicinity, living like a nobleman—that is, he did no work himself, but lived off the produce of his flocks, which shepherds of a nomadic type led out to graze here and there in the mountains. When I saw him, two years after the event I'm about to narrate, he seemed to me to be fifty at the very most. Picture a short but robust man with frizzy hair as black as jet, an aquiline nose, thin lips, large, alert eyes, and a complexion the color of boot tops.[1] His skill with a rifle was deemed extraordinary, even in his country, where there are so many good shots. For example, Mateo would never have fired at a wild sheep with buckshot, but, at a hundred twenty paces, he would bring it down with a bullet in the head or shoulder, just as he chose. He used his weapons at night as easily as by day, and I've been told about a feat of his that may seem incredible to those who haven't visited Corsica. At eighty paces, a lighted candle was placed behind a sheet of translucent paper the width of a plate. He took aim, then the candle was extinguished, and after a minute in the most total darkness, he would fire, hitting the paper three times out of four.

With such transcendent merit, Mateo Falcone had acquired a great reputation. He was said to be as good to have as a friend as he was dangerous to have as an enemy: helpful and charitable besides, he lived at peace with everyone in the Porto-Vecchio district. But the story was told of him that, in Corte, where he had taken a wife, he had most vigorously gotten rid of a rival said to be as formidable in war as in love: at least, Mateo was credited with a certain rifle shot that took this rival by surprise as he was shaving in front of a small mirror hanging in his window. When the matter had quieted down, Mateo married. His wife, Giuseppa, had at first given him three daughters (which made him furious), but finally a son, whom he named Fortunato: he was the hope of the family, the heir to his name. The girls had made good marriages: their father could count on the daggers and blunderbusses of his sons-in-law in an emergency. The son was only ten, but he already gave promise of gratifying natural gifts.

On a certain autumn day, Mateo went out early with his wife to visit one of his flocks in a clearing in the *maquis*. Little Fortunato wanted to accompany him, but the clearing was too far; besides, it was necessary for someone to stay and guard the house; thus, his father refused: we shall see whether he didn't have occasion to regret it.

He had been gone for several hours, and little Fortunato was

tranquillement étendu au soleil, regardant les montagnes bleues, et pensant que, le dimanche prochain, il irait dîner à la ville, chez son oncle le *caporal**, quand il fut soudainement interrompu dans ses méditations par l'explosion d'une arme à feu. Il se leva et se tourna du côté de la plaine d'où portait ce bruit. D'autres coups de fusil se succédèrent, tirés à intervalles inégaux, et toujours de plus en plus rapprochés; enfin, dans le sentier qui menait de la plaine à la maison de Mateo parut un homme, coiffé d'un bonnet pointu comme en portent les montagnards, barbu, couvert de haillons, et se traînant avec peine en s'appuyant sur son fusil. Il venait de recevoir un coup de feu dans la cuisse.

Cet homme était un bandit**, qui étant parti de nuit pour aller chercher de la poudre à la ville, était tombé en route dans une embuscade de voltigeurs corses***. Après une vigoureuse défense, il était parvenu à faire sa retraite, vivement poursuivi et tiraillant de rocher en rocher. Mais il avait peu d'avance sur les soldats et sa blessure le mettait hors d'état de gagner le maquis avant d'être rejoint.

Il s'approcha de Fortunato et lui dit:

«Tu es le fils de Mateo Falcone?

— Oui.

— Moi, je suis Gianetto Sanpiero. Je suis poursuivi par les collets jaunes****. Cache-moi, car je ne puis aller plus loin.

— Et que dira mon père si je te cache sans sa permission?

— Il dira que tu as bien fait.

— Qui sait?

— Cache-moi vite; ils viennent.

— Attends que mon père soit revenu.

— Que j'attende? malédiction! Ils seront ici dans cinq minutes. Allons, cache-moi, ou je te tue.»

Fortunato lui répondit avec le plus grand sang-froid:

---

*Les caporaux furent autrefois les chefs que se donnèrent les communes corses quand elles s'insurgèrent contre les seigneurs féodaux. Aujourd'hui, on donne encore quelquefois ce nom à un homme qui, par ses propriétés, ses alliances et sa clientèle, exerce une influence et une sorte de magistrature effective sur une *pieve* ou un canton. Les Corses se divisent, par une ancienne habitude, en cinq castes: les *gentilshommes* (dont les uns sont *magnifiques,* les autres *signori*), les *caporali*, les *citoyens*, les *plébéiens* et les *étrangers*.

**Ce mot est ici synonyme de proscrit.

***C'est un corps levé depuis peu d'années par le gouvernement, et qui sert concurremment avec la gendarmerie au maintien de la police.

****L'uniforme des voltigeurs était alors un habit brun avec un collet jaune.

peacefully stretched out in the sun, looking at the blue mountains and thinking that, on the following Sunday, he would go and dine in town at the home of his uncle the *caporale*,* when he was suddenly interrupted in his meditations by the report of a firearm. He got up and turned toward the direction in the plain from which that sound had come. Other rifle shots followed, fired at unequal intervals, and coming nearer and nearer all the time; at last, on the path that led from the plain to Mateo's house, there appeared a man wearing a pointed cap like those worn by mountaineers; he was bearded, covered with rags, and dragging himself along painfully, using his rifle for support. He had just been shot in the thigh.

This man was a bandit** who had set out at night to get gunpowder in town and, on the way, had fallen into an ambush laid by Corsican light infantryman.*** After defending himself vigorously, he had managed to beat a retreat, eagerly pursued and taking pot shots from one boulder to another. But he wasn't far ahead of the soldiers, and his wound made him incapable of reaching the *maquis* before they caught up with him.

He approached Fortunato and said:

"You're the son of Mateo Falcone?"

"Yes."

"I'm Gianetto Sanpiero. I'm being pursued by the yellow collars.**** Hide me, because I can't go any farther."

"And what will my father say if I hide you without his permission?"

"He'll say you did the right thing."

"Who knows?"

"Hide me fast; they're coming."

"Wait for my father to get back."

"Wait? Damnation! They'll be here in five minutes. Come on, hide me, or I'll kill you."

Fortunato replied with the greatest coolness:

---

*The *caporali* were formerly the chiefs appointed by the Corsican commoners when they revolted against their feudal lords. Today, this name is still sometimes given to a man who, through his property and his connections by marriage and in business, exerts an influence and a sort of *de facto* magistracy over a *pieve* or a canton. By ancient custom, Corsicans are divided into five castes: gentlemen (of whom some are *magnifici*, others *signori*), *caporali*, citizens, plebeians, and foreigners.

**Here this word is synonymous with "outlaw."

***This is a corps formed by the government only a few years ago; it polices the countryside concurrently with the gendarmerie.

****At the time the uniform of these *voltigeurs* was a brown outfit with a yellow collar.

«Ton fusil est déchargé, et il n'y a plus de cartouches dans ta carchera*.

— J'ai mon stylet.

— Mais courras-tu aussi vite que moi?»

Il fit un saut, et se mit hors d'atteinte.

«Tu n'es pas le fils de Mateo Falcone! Me laisseras-tu donc arrêter devant ta maison?»

L'enfant parut touché.

«Que me donneras-tu si je te cache?» dit-il en se rapprochant.

Le bandit fouilla dans une poche de cuir qui pendait à sa ceinture, et il en tira une pièce de cinq francs qu'il avait réservée sans doute pour acheter de la poudre. Fortunato sourit à la vue de la pièce d'argent; il s'en saisit, et dit à Gianetto:

«Ne crains rien.»

Aussitôt il fit un grand trou dans un tas de foin placé auprès de la maison. Gianetto s'y blottit, et l'enfant le recouvrit de manière à lui laisser un peu d'air pour respirer, sans qu'il fût possible cependant de soupçonner que ce foin cachât un homme. Il s'avisa, de plus, d'une finesse de sauvage assez ingénieuse. Il alla prendre une chatte et ses petits, et les établit sur le tas de foin pour faire croire qu'il n'avait pas été remué depuis peu. Ensuite, remarquant des traces de sang sur le sentier près de la maison, il les couvrit de poussière avec soin, et cela fait, il se recoucha au soleil avec la plus grande tranquillité.

Quelques minutes après, six hommes en uniforme brun à collet jaune, et commandés par un adjudant, étaient devant la porte de Mateo. Cet adjudant était quelque peu parent de Falcone. (On sait qu'en Corse on suit les degrés de parenté beaucoup plus loin qu'ailleurs.) Il se nommait Tiodoro Gamba: c'était un homme actif, fort redouté des bandits dont il avait déjà traqué plusieurs.

«Bonjour, petit cousin, dit-il à Fortunato en l'abordant: comme te voilà grandi! As-tu vu passer un homme tout à l'heure?

— Oh! je ne suis pas encore si grand que vous, mon cousin, répondit l'enfant d'un air niais.

— Cela viendra. Mais n'as-tu pas vu passer un homme, dis-moi?

— Si j'ai vu passer un homme?

— Oui, un homme avec un bonnet pointu en velours noir, et une veste brodée de rouge et de jaune?

— Un homme avec un bonnet pointu, et une veste brodée de rouge et de jaune?

---

*Ceinture de cuir qui sert de giberne et de portefeuille.

"Your rifle is unloaded and there are no more cartridges in your *carchera.*"*

"I have my stiletto."

"But will you run as fast as me?"

He made a jump, placing himself out of reach.

"You're not the son of Mateo Falcone! So you'll let me be arrested in front of your house?"

The child seemed to be affected by this.

"What'll you give me if I hide you?" he asked, coming closer.

The bandit groped through a leather pouch that hung from his belt, and pulled out a five-franc piece that he had no doubt kept to buy powder with. Fortunato smiled when he saw the silver coin; he seized it, saying to Gianetto:

"Don't worry about a thing."

At once he made a large hole in a haystack located near the house. Gianetto huddled in it, and the child covered him up in such a way that he left him a little air to breathe, but it was nevertheless impossible to suspect that the hay concealed a man. On top of that, he thought of a primitive ruse that was quite ingenious. He went and got a cat and her kittens and placed them on the haystack to give the impression that it hadn't been touched recently. Next, noticing traces of blood on the path near the house, he carefully covered them with dust; after that, he lay down in the sun again as calmly as could be.

A few minutes later, six men in brown uniforms with yellow collars, commanded by a sergeant-major, stood in front of Mateo's door. This sergeant was very slightly related to Falcone. (As is well known, in Corsica degrees of kinship are traced much further than elsewhere.) His name was Tiodoro Gamba; he was an active man, much dreaded by the bandits, several of whom he had already tracked down.

"Hello, little cousin," he said to Fortunato, coming up to him. "My, but you've grown! Did you see a man go by a little while ago?"

"Oh! I'm still not as big as you, cousin," the child replied, playing the simpleton.

"You'll get there. But, tell me, didn't you see a man go by?"

"Did I see a man go by?"

"Yes, a man with a black-velvet pointed cap and a jacket embroidered in red and yellow."

"A man with a pointed cap and a jacket embroidered in red and yellow?"

---

*A leather belt that serves as a cartridge pouch and wallet.

— Oui, réponds vite, et ne répète pas mes questions.

— Ce matin, M. le curé est passé devant notre porte, sur son cheval Piero. Il m'a demandé comment papa se portait, et je lui ai répondu . . .

— Ah! petit drôle, tu fais le malin! Dis-moi vite par où est passé Gianetto, car c'est lui que nous cherchons; et, j'en suis certain, il a pris par ce sentier.

— Qui sait?

— Qui sait? C'est moi qui sais que tu l'as vu.

— Est-ce qu'on voit les passants quand on dort?

— Tu ne dormais pas, vaurien; les coups de fusil t'ont réveillé.

— Vous croyez donc, mon cousin, que vos fusils font tant de bruit? L'escopette de mon père en fait bien davantage.

— Que le diable te confonde, maudit garnement! Je suis bien sûr que tu as vu le Gianetto. Peut-être même l'as-tu caché. Allons, camarades, entrez dans cette maison, et voyez si notre homme n'y est pas. Il n'allait plus que d'une patte, et il a trop de bon sens, le coquin, pour avoir cherché à gagner le maquis en clopinant. D'ailleurs, les traces de sang s'arrêtent ici.

— Et que dira papa? demanda Fortunato en ricanant; que dira-t-il s'il sait qu'on est entré dans sa maison pendant qu'il était sorti?

— Vaurien! dit l'adjudant Gamba en le prenant par l'oreille, sais-tu qu'il ne tient qu'à moi de te faire changer de note? Peut-être qu'en te donnant une vingtaine de coups de plat de sabre tu parleras enfin.»

Et Fortunato ricanait toujours.

«Mon père est Mateo Falcone! dit-il avec emphase.

— Sais-tu bien, petit drôle, que je puis t'emmener à Corte ou à Bastia. Je te ferai coucher dans un cachot, sur la paille, les fers aux pieds, et je te ferai guillotiner si tu ne dis où est Gianetto Sanpiero.»

L'enfant éclata de rire à cette ridicule menace. Il répéta:

«Mon père est Mateo Falcone!

— Adjudant, dit tout bas un des voltigeurs, ne nous brouillons pas avec Mateo.»

Gamba paraissait évidemment embarrassé. Il causait à voix basse avec ses soldats, qui avaient déjà visité toute la maison. Ce n'était pas une opération fort longue, car la cabane d'un Corse ne consiste qu'en une seule pièce carrée. L'ameublement se compose d'une table, de bancs, de coffres et d'ustensiles de chasse ou de ménage. Cependant le petit Fortunato caressait sa chatte, et semblait jouir malignement de la confusion des voltigeurs et de son cousin. Un soldat s'approcha du tas de foin. Il vit la chatte, et donna un

"Yes, answer fast, and don't repeat my questions."

"This morning the parish priest passed by our door on his horse Piero. He asked me how Papa was feeling, and I told him . . ."

"Ah, you little scamp, you're trying to be smart! Tell me quickly which way Gianetto went—he's the one we're looking for—and I'm sure he took this path."

"Who knows?"

"Who knows? *I* know that you saw him."

"Do you see people pass by when you're sleeping?"

"You weren't sleeping, you scamp; the rifle shots woke you up."

"Cousin, do you really think your rifles make so much noise? My father's blunderbuss makes much more."

"The devil take you, you damned brat! I'm sure you saw Gianetto. Maybe you even hid him. Come on, men, go into this house and see if our man isn't there. He was walking on only one leg and he has too much good sense, the rogue, to have tried to reach the *maquis* hobbling along. Besides, the trail of blood stops here."

"And what will Papa say?" Fortunato asked, snickering. "What will he say if he finds out his house has been entered while he was out?"

"Rascal!" said Sergeant Gamba, taking him by the ear. "Do you realize it's only up to me to make you change your tune? Maybe if I give you twenty blows with the flat of my saber, you'll finally talk."

And Fortunato kept on snickering.

"My father is Mateo Falcone!" he said, significantly.

"Little scamp, do you realize that I can take you to Corte or Bastia? I'll stretch you out in a dungeon, on straw, with irons on your feet, and I'll have you guillotined if you don't tell me where Gianetto Sanpiero is."

The child burst out laughing at that ridiculous threat. He repeated: "My father is Mateo Falcone!"

"Sergeant," one of the infantrymen said quietly, "let's not get on the wrong side of Mateo."

Gamba looked obviously embarrassed. He chatted in a low voice with his soldiers, who had already inspected the whole house. This wasn't a very long procedure, because a Corsican's hut consists of a single square room. The furniture is comprised of a table, benches, chests, and hunting and household utensils. Meanwhile, little Fortunato was petting his cat, seeming to take malicious satisfaction in the embarrassment of the infantrymen and his cousin.

A soldier approached the haystack. He saw the cat, and negligently

coup de baïonnette dans le foin avec négligence, et haussant les épaules, comme s'il sentait que sa précaution était ridicule. Rien ne remua; et le visage de l'enfant ne trahit pas la plus légère émotion.

L'adjudant et sa troupe se donnaient au diable; déjà ils regardaient sérieusement du côté de la plaine, comme disposés à s'en retourner par où ils étaient venus, quand leur chef, convaincu que les menaces ne produiraient aucune impression sur le fils de Falcone, voulut faire un dernier effort et tenter le pouvoir des caresses et des présents.

«Petit cousin, dit-il, tu me parais un gaillard bien éveillé! Tu iras loin. Mais tu joues un vilain jeu avec moi; et, si je ne craignais de faire de la peine à mon cousin Mateo, le diable m'emporte! je t'emmènerais avec moi.

— Bah!

— Mais, quand mon cousin sera revenu, je lui conterai l'affaire, et, pour ta peine d'avoir menti, il te donnera le fouet jusqu'au sang.

— Savoir?

— Tu verras . . . Mais tiens . . . sois brave garçon, et je te donnerai quelque chose.

— Moi, mon cousin, je vous donnerai un avis: c'est que, si vous tardez davantage, le Gianetto sera dans le maquis, et alors il faudra plus d'un luron comme vous pour aller l'y chercher.»

L'adjudant tira de sa poche une montre d'argent qui valait bien dix écus; et, remarquant que les yeux du petit Fortunato étincelaient en la regardant, il lui dit en tenant la montre suspendue au bout de sa chaîne d'acier:

«Fripon! tu voudrais bien avoir une montre comme celle-ci suspendue à ton col, et tu te promènerais dans les rues de Porto-Vecchio, fier comme un paon; et les gens te demanderaient: «Quelle heure est-il?» et tu leur dirais: «Regardez à ma montre.»

— Quand je serai grand, mon oncle le caporal me donnera une montre.

— Oui; mais le fils de ton oncle en a déjà une . . . pas aussi belle que celle-ci, à la vérité . . . Cependant il est plus jeune que toi.»

L'enfant soupira.

«Eh bien, la veux-tu cette montre, petit cousin?»

Fortunato, lorgnant la montre du coin de l'œil, ressemblait à un chat à qui l'on présente un poulet tout entier. Et comme il sent qu'on se moque de lui, il n'ose y porter la griffe, et de temps en temps il détourne les yeux pour ne pas s'exposer à succomber à la tentation; mais il se lèche les babines à tout moment, il a l'air de dire à son maître:

«Que votre plaisanterie est cruelle!»

stabbed the hay with his bayonet, shrugging his shoulders as if he felt his precaution was laughable. Nothing stirred: and the child's face betrayed not the slightest emotion.

The sergeant and his troop were in despair: by this time they were looking seriously in the direction of the plain, as if disposed to go back where they had come from—when their leader, convinced that threats would have no effect on Falcone's son, decided to make one last effort and try out the power of blandishments and presents.

"Little cousin," he said, "you look to me like a really sharp fellow! You'll go places. But the game you're playing with me is a nasty one; and if I weren't afraid of hurting my cousin Mateo, devil take me if I didn't lead you away with me."

"Bah!"

"But when my cousin is back, I'll tell him what happened, and to punish you for lying, he'll whip you till he draws blood."

"How's that?"

"You'll see . . . But wait . . . Be a good boy and I'll give you something."

"As for me, cousin, I'll give you a piece of advice: if you wait any longer, Gianetto will be in the *maquis*, and then it'll take more than one strapping fellow like you to go get him there."

The sergeant drew from his pocket a silver watch that was worth at least thirty francs; and, observing that little Fortunato's eyes sparkled when he looked at it, he dangled the watch from the end of its steel chain, saying:

"Scalawag! You'd surely like to have a watch like this hanging from your neck while you promenaded through the streets of Porto-Vecchio, proud as a peacock, with people asking you, 'What time is it?' and you saying, 'Look at my watch and see.'"

"When I grow up, my uncle the *caporale* will give me a watch."

"Yes, but your uncle's son already has one . . . not as beautiful as this one, it's true . . . But he's younger than you."

The child sighed.

"Well, little cousin, do you want this watch?"

Fortunato, stealing sidelong glances at the watch from the corner of his eye, looked like a cat that was being offered a whole chicken. Since it feels it is being made fun of, it doesn't dare put its claws on it, and from time to time it turns away its eyes to avoid succumbing to the temptation; but every moment it licks its chops, seeming to say to its master:

"How cruel your joke is!"

Cependant l'adjudant Gamba semblait de bonne foi en présentant sa montre. Fortunato n'avança pas la main; mais il lui dit avec un sourire amer:

«Pourquoi vous moquez-vous de moi*?

— Par Dieu! je ne me moque pas. Dis-moi seulement où est Gianetto, et cette montre est à toi.»

Fortunato laissa échapper un sourire d'incrédulité; et, fixant ses yeux noirs sur ceux de l'adjudant, il s'efforçait d'y lire la foi qu'il devait avoir en ses paroles.

«Que je perde mon épaulette, s'écria l'adjudant, si je ne te donne pas la montre à cette condition! Les camarades sont témoins; et je ne puis m'en dédire.»

En parlant ainsi, il approchait toujours la montre, tant qu'elle touchait presque la joue pâle de l'enfant. Celui-ci montrait bien sur sa figure le combat que se livraient en son âme la convoitise et le respect dû à l'hospitalité. Sa poitrine nue se soulevait avec force, et il semblait près d'étouffer. Cependant la montre oscillait, tournait, et quelquefois lui heurtait le bout du nez. Enfin, peu à peu, sa main droite s'éleva vers la montre: le bout de ses doigts la toucha; et elle pesait tout entière dans sa main sans que l'adjudant lâchât pourtant le bout de la chaîne . . . Le cadran était azuré . . . la boîte nouvellement fourbie . . . au soleil, elle paraissait toute de feu . . . La tentation était trop forte.

Fortunato éleva aussi sa main gauche, et indiqua du pouce, par-dessus son épaule, le tas de foin auquel il était adossé. L'adjudant le comprit aussitôt. Il abandonna l'extrémité de la chaîne; Fortunato se sentit seul possesseur de la montre. Il se leva avec l'agilité d'un daim, et s'éloigna de dix pas du tas de foin, que les voltigeurs se mirent aussitôt à culbuter.

On ne tarda pas à voir le foin s'agiter; et un homme sanglant, le poignard à la main, en sortit; mais, comme il essayait de se lever en pied, sa blessure refroidie ne lui permit plus de se tenir debout. Il tomba. L'adjudant se jeta sur lui et lui arracha son stylet. Aussitôt on le garrotta fortement malgré sa résistance.

Gianetto, couché par terre et lié comme un fagot, tourna la tête vers Fortunato qui s'était rapproché.

«Fils de . . .!» lui dit-il avec plus de mépris que de colère.

L'enfant lui jeta la pièce d'argent qu'il en avait reçue, sentant qu'il avait cessé de la mériter; mais le proscrit n'eut pas l'air de faire attention à ce mouvement. Il dit avec beaucoup de sang-froid à l'adjudant:

*Perchè me c . . . ?

And yet Sergeant Gamba appeared to be acting in good faith in offering his watch. Fortunato didn't reach out for it, but he said with a bitter smile:

"Why are you ribbing me?"*

"By God, I'm not ribbing you. Just tell me where Gianetto is, and this watch is yours."

Fortunato emitted a sigh of disbelief, and, with his dark eyes staring directly into the sergeant's, he strove to see how much trust he ought to repose in his words.

"May I lose my epaulets," the sergeant exclaimed, "if I don't give you the watch on those terms! My comrades are witnesses, and I can't go back on my word."

While saying this, he kept moving the watch nearer until it almost touched the child's pale cheek. The boy's face clearly showed the struggle being waged in his soul between greed and respect for the laws of hospitality. His bare chest was heaving mightily, and he seemed close to choking. Meanwhile the watch was swinging, turning, and at times striking the tip of his nose. Finally, little by little, his right hand rose in the direction of the watch; he touched it with his fingertips; and it was resting in his hand with its full weight, although the sergeant didn't release the end of the chain . . . The dial was blue . . . the case newly polished . . . in the sunlight, it seemed to be all ablaze . . . The temptation was too strong.

Fortunato raised his left hand, too, and with his thumb pointed over his shoulder at the haystack on which he was leaning. The sergeant understood him at once. He let go of the end of the chain; Fortunato realized he was sole possessor of the watch. He rose with the agility of a deer and moved ten paces away from the haystack, which the infantrymen immediately began to knock over.

Before long they saw the hay moving, and a bleeding man, dagger in hand, came out; but, when he tried to stand up, his stiffened wound made it impossible to keep his feet any longer. He fell. The sergeant pounced on him and tore his stiletto from him. At once he was tightly bound hand and foot despite his resistance.

Gianetto, lying on the ground, trussed up like a bundle of firewood, turned his head toward Fortunato, who had come up to him.

"Son of a . . .!" he said, with more contempt than anger.

The child threw at him the silver coin he had received from him, feeling that he no longer deserved it; but the outlaw seemed to pay no heed to that action. As calmly as possible he said to the sergeant:

---

*Perchè me c . . .?²

«Mon cher Gamba, je ne puis marcher; vous allez être obligé de me porter à la ville.

— Tu courais tout à l'heure plus vite qu'un chevreuil, repartit le cruel vainqueur; mais sois tranquille: je suis si content de te tenir, que je te porterais une lieue sur mon dos sans être fatigué. Au reste, mon camarade, nous allons te faire une litière avec des branches et ta capote; et à la ferme de Crespoli nous trouverons des chevaux.

— Bien, dit le prisonnier; vous mettrez aussi un peu de paille sur votre litière, pour que je sois plus commodément.»

Pendant que les voltigeurs s'occupaient, les uns à faire une espèce de brancard avec des branches de châtaignier, les autres à panser la blessure de Gianetto, Mateo Falcone et sa femme parurent tout d'un coup au détour d'un sentier qui conduisait au maquis. La femme s'avançait courbée péniblement sous le poids d'un énorme sac de châtaignes, tandis que son mari se prélassait, ne portant qu'un fusil à la main et un autre en bandoulière; car il est indigne d'un homme de porter d'autre fardeau que ses armes.

A la vue des soldats, la première pensée de Mateo fut qu'ils venaient pour l'arrêter. Mais pourquoi cette idée? Mateo avait-il donc quelques démêlés avec la justice? Non. Il jouissait d'une bonne réputation. C'était comme on dit, *un particulier bien famé;* mais il était Corse et montagnard, et il y a peu de Corses montagnards qui, en scrutant bien leur mémoire, n'y trouvent quelque peccadille, telle que coups de fusil, coups de stylet et autres bagatelles. Mateo, plus qu'un autre, avait la conscience nette; car depuis plus de dix ans il n'avait dirigé son fusil contre un homme; mais toutefois il était prudent, et il se mit en posture de faire une belle défense, s'il en était besoin.

«Femme, dit-il à Giuseppa, mets bas ton sac et tiens-toi prête.»

Elle obéit sur-le-champ. Il lui donna le fusil qu'il avait en bandoulière et qui aurait pu le gêner. Il arma celui qu'il avait à la main, et il s'avança lentement vers sa maison, longeant les arbres qui bordaient le chemin, et prêt, à la moindre démonstration hostile, à se jeter derrière le plus gros tronc, d'où il aurait pu faire feu à couvert. Sa femme marchait sur ses talons, tenant son fusil de rechange et sa giberne. L'emploi d'une bonne ménagère, en cas de combat, est de charger les armes de son mari.

D'un autre côté, l'adjudant était fort en peine en voyant Mateo s'avancer ainsi, à pas comptés, le fusil en avant et le doigt sur la détente.

«Si par hasard, pensa-t-il, Mateo se trouvait parent de Gianetto, ou

"My friend Gamba, I can't walk; you're going to have to carry me to town."

"Just a while ago you were running faster than a roebuck," the cruel victor retorted; "but relax: I'm so happy over catching you that I'd carry you a league on my back without getting tired. Anyway, comrade, we're going to make you a litter out of branches and your cloak, and at the Crespoli farm we'll find horses."

"Good," said the prisoner, "and put a little straw on your litter so I'll be more comfortable."

While the infantrymen were busy, some making a sort of stretcher out of chestnut branches, and the others dressing Gianetto's wound, Mateo Falcone and his wife suddenly appeared at the bend of a path that led into the *maquis*. His wife was walking, painfully stooped under the weight of an enormous sack of chestnuts, while her husband was strutting at his ease, carrying nothing but a rifle in his hand and another slung across his back: because it's beneath a man's dignity to carry any burden other than his weapons.

At sight of the soldiers, Mateo's first thought was that they had come to arrest him. But why did he have that idea? Had Mateo had any run-ins with the law, after all? No. He enjoyed a good reputation. He was what is called "an individual of good repute"; but he was a Corsican and a mountaineer, and there are few Corsican mountaineers who, if they racked their memory, wouldn't discover some little peccadillo, in the nature of rifle shots, stiletto stabs, and other trifles. More than many another, Mateo had a clear conscience, because for over ten years he hadn't pointed his rifle at a man; but nevertheless he was cautious, and he now prepared to defend himself bravely if it should prove necessary.

"Wife," he said to Giuseppa, "put down your sack and be prepared."

She obeyed at once. He gave her the rifle he had been carrying on his back; it might have hampered his movements. He cocked the one he had in his hands and proceeded slowly toward his house, keeping close to the trees that lined the road and ready, at the least sign of hostility, to dash behind the thickest trunk and thus be able to fire from a position of cover. His wife was following at his heels, holding his spare rifle and his cartridge pouch. The duty of a good housewife, in times of combat, is to load her husband's guns.

On the other side, the sergeant was most distressed to see Mateo advancing that way, with measured tread, his rifle pointed forward and his finger on the trigger.

"If by chance," he thought, "Mateo was a relative of Gianetto, or if

s'il était son ami, et qu'il voulût le défendre, les bourres de ses deux fusils arriveraient à deux d'entre nous, aussi sûr qu'une lettre à la poste, et s'il me visait, nonobstant la parenté! . . .»

Dans cette perplexité, il prit un parti fort courageux, ce fut de s'avancer seul vers Mateo pour lui conter l'affaire, en l'abordant comme une vieille connaissance; mais le court intervalle qui le séparait de Mateo lui parut terriblement long.

«Holà! eh! mon vieux camarade, criait-il, comment cela va-t-il, mon brave? C'est moi, je suis Gamba, ton cousin.»

Mateo, sans répondre un mot, s'était arrêté, et, à mesure que l'autre parlait, il relevait doucement le canon de son fusil, de sorte qu'il était dirigé vers le ciel au moment où l'adjudant le joignit.

«Bonjour, frère*, dit l'adjudant en lui tendant la main. Il y a bien longtemps que je ne t'ai vu.

— Bonjour, frère!

— J'étais venu pour te dire bonjour en passant, et à ma cousine Pepa. Nous avons fait une longue traite aujourd'hui; mais il ne faut pas plaindre notre fatigue, car nous avons fait une fameuse prise. Nous venons d'empoigner Gianetto Sanpiero.

— Dieu soit loué! s'écria Giuseppa. Il nous a volé une chèvre laitière la semaine passée.»

Ces mots réjouirent Gamba.

«Pauvre diable! dit Mateo, il avait faim.

— Le drôle s'est défendu comme un lion, poursuivit l'adjudant un peu mortifié; il m'a tué un de mes voltigeurs, et, non content de cela, il a cassé le bras au caporal Chardon; mais il n'y a pas grand mal, ce n'était qu'un Français . . . Ensuite, il s'était si bien caché, que le diable ne l'aurait pu découvrir. Sans mon petit cousin Fortunato, je ne l'aurais jamais pu trouver.

— Fortunato! s'écria Mateo.

— Fortunato! répéta Giuseppa.

— Oui, le Gianetto s'était caché sous ce tas de foin là-bas; mais mon petit cousin m'a montré la malice. Aussi je le dirai à son oncle le caporal, afin qu'il lui envoie un beau cadeau pour sa peine. Et son nom et le tien seront dans le rapport que j'enverrai à M. l'avocat général.

— Malédiction!» dit tout bas Mateo.

Ils avaient rejoint le détachement. Gianetto était déjà couché sur la litière et prêt à partir. Quand il vit Mateo en la compagnie de Gamba,

---

*Buon giorno, fratello, salut ordinaire des Corses.

he was his friend, and wanted to defend him, the wads of his two rifles would reach two of us, just as sure as a letter in the mail, and if he
aimed at me, despite our relationship . . .!"

In that perplexity, he made a very courageous decision: he advanced alone toward Mateo to tell him what was going on, greeting
him like an old acquaintance; but the short space separating him from
Mateo seemed terribly long to him.

"Hi there, old comrade!" he shouted. "How's it going, friend? It's
me, it's Gamba, your cousin."

Without a word in reply, Mateo had stopped, and, while the other
man was speaking, he gently raised the barrel of his rifle, so that, by
the time the sergeant reached him, it was pointing to the sky.

"Hello, brother!"* the sergeant said, offering his hand. "I haven't
seen you for quite a while."

"Hello, brother!"

"I had come to say hello to you as I passed by, and to my cousin
Pepa. We've covered a lot of ground today; but you mustn't feel sorry
for our being tired, because we've made a wonderful catch. We've just
laid hands on Gianetto Sanpiero."

"God be praised!" exclaimed Giuseppa. "He stole a milk goat from
us last week."

Those words delighted Gamba.

"Poor devil!" said Mateo. "He was hungry."

"The scamp defended himself like a lion," continued the sergeant,
a little mortified. "He killed one of my infantrymen, and, as if that
wasn't enough, he broke Corporal Chardon's arm; but there's no great
harm in that, he was only a Frenchman . . . After that, he hid so well
that the devil couldn't have detected him. Without my little cousin
Fortunato, I would never have been able to find him."

"Fortunato!" Mateo exclaimed.

"Fortunato!" Giuseppa repeated.

"Yes, Gianetto had concealed himself in that haystack over there;
but my little cousin pointed out the trick to me. I'm also going to tell
his uncle the *caporale* about it, so he'll send him a fine gift for his trouble. And his name and yours will be in the report I'll send to the public prosecutor."

"Damnation!" said Mateo quietly.

They had come up to the detachment. Gianetto was already lying
on his litter and ready to leave. When he saw Mateo in company with

---

Buon giorno, fratello, the customary greeting in Corsica.

il sourit d'un sourire étrange; puis, se tournant vers la porte de la maison, il cracha sur le seuil en disant:

«Maison d'un traître!»

Il n'y avait qu'un homme décidé à mourir qui eût osé prononcer le mot de traître en l'appliquant à Falcone. Un bon coup de stylet, qui n'aurait pas eu besoin d'être répété, aurait immédiatement payé l'insulte. Cependant Mateo ne fit pas d'autre geste que celui de porter sa main à son front comme un homme accablé.

Fortunato était entré dans la maison en voyant arriver son père. Il reparut bientôt avec une jatte de lait, qu'il présenta les yeux baissés à Gianetto.

«Loin de moi!» lui cria le proscrit d'une voix foudroyante.

Puis, se tournant vers un des voltigeurs:

«Camarade, donne-moi à boire», dit-il.

Le soldat remit sa gourde entre ses mains, et le bandit but l'eau que lui donnait un homme avec lequel il venait d'échanger des coups de fusil. Ensuite il demanda qu'on lui attachât les mains de manière qu'il les eût croisées sur sa poitrine, au lieu de les avoir liées derrière le dos.

«J'aime, disait-il, à être couché à mon aise.»

On s'empressa de le satisfaire; puis l'adjudant donna le signal du départ, dit adieu à Mateo, qui ne lui répondit pas, et descendit au pas accéléré vers la plaine.

Il se passa près de dix minutes avant que Mateo ouvrît la bouche. L'enfant regardait d'un œil inquiet tantôt sa mère et tantôt son père, qui, s'appuyant sur son fusil, le considérait avec une expression de colère concentrée.

«Tu commences bien! dit enfin Mateo d'une voix calme, mais effrayante pour qui connaissait l'homme.

— Mon père!» s'écria l'enfant en s'avançant les larmes aux yeux comme pour se jeter à ses genoux.

Mais Mateo lui cria:

«Arrière de moi!»

Et l'enfant s'arrêta et sanglota, immobile, à quelques pas de son père.

Giuseppa s'approcha. Elle venait d'apercevoir la chaîne de la montre, dont un bout sortait de la chemise de Fortunato.

«Qui t'a donné cette montre? demanda-t-elle d'un air sévère.

— Mon cousin l'adjudant.»

Falcone saisit la montre, et, la jetant avec force contre une pierre, il la mit en mille pièces.

«Femme, dit-il, cet enfant est-il de moi?»

Gamba, he smiled a strange smile; then, turning toward the door to the house, he spat on the threshold, saying:

"House of a betrayer!"

Only a man determined to die would have dared pronounce the word "betrayer" with reference to Falcone. A firm stiletto stab, which wouldn't need to be repeated, would have immediately repaid the insult. And yet Mateo made no other gesture than to raise his hand to his forehead like a man overwhelmed.

Fortunato had gone into the house on seeing his father arrive. He soon reappeared with a bowl of milk, which he offered to Gianetto with eyes cast down.

"Get away from me!" the outlaw shouted with a crushing voice.

Then, turning to one of the infantrymen, he said:

"Comrade, give me a drink."

The soldier put his canteen in his hands,[3] and the bandit drank the water given to him by a man with whom he had just been exchanging rifle shots. Then he requested to have his hands tied so that they would be crossed over his chest instead of having them tied behind his back.

"I like to lie comfortably," he said.

They hastened to satisfy him; then the sergeant gave the signal for departure, said good-bye to Mateo, who didn't reply, and descended to the plain in quick time.

Nearly ten minutes went by before Mateo opened his mouth. With nervous eyes, the child was looking now at his mother and now at his father, who, leaning on his rifle, was observing him with an expression of concentrated anger.

"You're making a fine beginning!" Mateo finally said in a voice that was calm but frightening for anyone who knew him well.

"Father!" exclaimed the child, stepping forward with tears in his eyes, as if intending to go down on his knees to him.

But Mateo shouted to him:

"Stand back!"

And the child stopped, sobbing motionlessly a few paces away from his father.

Giuseppa approached. She had just caught sight of the watch chain, one end of which was protruding from Fortunato's shirt.

"Who gave you that watch?" she asked with a severe expression.

"My cousin the sergeant."

Falcone seized the watch and, hurling it violently against a rock, shattered it into bits.

"Wife," he said, "is this child mine?"

Les joues brunes de Giuseppa devinrent d'un rouge de brique.

«Que dis-tu, Mateo? et sais-tu bien à qui tu parles?

— Eh bien, cet enfant est le premier de sa race qui ait fait une trahison.»

Les sanglots et les hoquets de Fortunato redoublèrent, et Falcone tenait ses yeux de lynx toujours attachés sur lui. Enfin il frappa la terre de la crosse de son fusil, puis le jeta sur son épaule et reprit le chemin du maquis en criant à Fortunato de le suivre. L'enfant obéit.

Giuseppa courut après Mateo et lui saisit le bras.

«C'est ton fils, lui dit-elle d'une voix tremblante en attachant ses yeux noirs sur ceux de son mari, comme pour lire ce qui se passait dans son âme.

— Laisse-moi, répondit Mateo: je suis son père.»

Giuseppa embrassa son fils et entra en pleurant dans sa cabane. Elle se jeta à genoux devant une image de la Vierge et pria avec ferveur. Cependant Falcone marcha quelque deux cents pas dans le sentier et ne s'arrêta que dans un petit ravin où il descendit. Il sonda la terre avec la crosse de son fusil et la trouva molle et facile à creuser. L'endroit lui parut convenable pour son dessein.

«Fortunato, va auprès de cette grosse pierre.»

L'enfant fit ce qu'il lui commandait, puis il s'agenouilla.

«Dis tes prières.

— Mon père, mon père, ne me tuez pas.

— Dis tes prières!» répéta Mateo d'une voix terrible.

L'enfant, tout en balbutiant et en sanglotant, récita le *Pater* et le *Credo*. Le père, d'une voix forte, répondait *Amen!* à la fin de chaque prière.

«Sont-ce là toutes les prières que tu sais?

— Mon père, je sais encore l'*Ave Maria* et la litanie que ma tante m'a apprise.

— Elle est bien longue, n'importe.»

L'enfant acheva la litanie d'une voix éteinte.

«As-tu fini?

— Oh! mon père, grâce! pardonnez-moi! Je ne le ferai plus! Je prierai tant mon cousin le caporal qu'on fera grâce au Gianetto!»

Il parlait encore; Mateo avait armé son fusil et le couchait en joue en lui disant:

«Que Dieu te pardonne!»

L'enfant fit un effort désespéré pour se relever et embrasser les genoux de son père; mais il n'en eut pas le temps. Mateo fit feu, et Fortunato tomba roide mort.

Giuseppa's brown cheeks turned brick-red.

"What are you saying, Mateo? And do you realize who you're talking to?"

"Well, then, this child is the first of his line to betray anyone."

Fortunato's sobs and hiccups redoubled, and Falcone kept his lynx eyes fixed on him. Finally he struck the ground with his rifle butt, then threw the rifle over his shoulder, and went back onto the road to the *maquis*, calling to Fortunato to follow him. The child obeyed.

Giuseppa ran after Mateo and took hold of his arm.

"He's your son," she said, her voice trembling and her dark eyes staring into her husband's, as if to detect what was going on in his soul.

"Let me go," Mateo replied. "I'm his father."

Giuseppa kissed her son and entered her hut, weeping. She fell on her knees in front of a statuette of the Virgin and prayed fervently. Meanwhile, Falcone walked some two hundred paces along the path, not stopping until he reached a small ravine, into which he descended. He tested the soil with his rifle butt and found it soft and easy to dig. The spot seemed suitable for his purpose.

"Fortunato, go over to that big rock."

The child did what he was ordered to, then knelt down.

"Say your prayers."

"Father, father, don't kill me!"

"Say your prayers!" Mateo repeated in fearsome tones.

The child, stammering and sobbing, recited the Lord's Prayer and the Apostles' Creed. His father loudly replied "Amen!" at the end of each prayer.

"Are those all the prayers you know?"

"Father, I also know the 'Hail, Mary' and the litany my aunt taught me."

"It's pretty long, but go ahead."

The child completed the litany in a toneless voice.

"Are you done?"

"Oh, father, mercy! Forgive me! I'll never do it again! I'll keep on begging my cousin the *caporale*[4] until Gianetto is pardoned!"

He was still speaking; Mateo had cocked his rifle and was taking aim, saying:

"May God forgive you!"

The child made a desperate effort to get up and clasp his father's knees, but he didn't have the time. Mateo fired, and Fortunato fell down dead.

Sans jeter un coup d'œil sur le cadavre, Mateo reprit le chemin de sa maison pour aller chercher une bêche afin d'enterrer son fils. Il avait fait à peine quelques pas qu'il rencontra Giuseppa, qui accourait alarmée du coup de feu.

«Qu'as-tu fait? s'écria-t-elle.

— Justice.

— Où est-il?

— Dans le ravin. Je vais l'enterrer. Il est mort en chrétien; je lui ferai chanter une messe. Qu'on dise à mon gendre Tiodoro Bianchi de venir demeurer avec nous.»

Without even glancing at the corpse, Mateo went back along the road to his house to fetch a spade so he could bury his son. He had scarcely taken a few steps when he met Giuseppa, who was running up, alarmed at the shot.

"What have you done?" she exclaimed.

"I've dealt out justice."

"Where is he?"

"In the ravine. I'm going to bury him. He died like a Christian; I'll have a Mass sung for him. Have my son-in-law Tiodoro Bianchi told to come and move in with us."

GÉRARD DE NERVAL

Sylvie

Souvenirs du Valois

I. — Nuit perdue

Je sortais d'un théâtre où tous les soirs je paraissais aux avant-scènes en grande tenue de soupirant. Quelquefois tout était plein, quelquefois tout était vide. Peu m'importait d'arrêter mes regards sur un parterre peuplé seulement d'une trentaine d'amateurs forcés, sur des loges garnies de bonnets ou de toilettes surannées, — ou bien de faire partie d'une salle animée et frémissante couronnée à tous ses étages de toilettes fleuries, de bijoux étincelants et de visages radieux. Indifférent au spectacle de la salle, celui du théâtre ne m'arrêtait guère, — excepté lorsqu'á la seconde ou à la troisième scène d'un maussade chef-d'œuvre d'alors, une apparition bien connue illuminait l'espace vide, rendant la vie d'un souffle et d'un mot à ces vaines figures qui m'entouraient.

Je me sentais vivre en elle, et elle vivait pour moi seul. Son sourire me remplissait d'une béatitude infinie; la vibration de sa voix si douce et cependant fortement timbrée me faisait tressaillir de joie et d'amour. Elle avait pour moi toutes les perfections, elle répondait à tous mes enthousiasmes, à tous mes caprices, — belle comme le jour aux feux de la rampe qui l'éclairait d'en bas, pâle, comme la nuit, quand la rampe baissée la laissait éclairée d'en haut sous les rayons du lustre et la montrait plus naturelle, brillant dans l'ombre de sa seule beauté, comme les Heures divines qui se découpent, avec une étoile au front, sur les fonds bruns des fresques d'Herculanum!

Depuis un an, je n'avais pas encore songé à m'informer de ce qu'elle pouvait être d'ailleurs; je craignais de troubler le miroir magique qui me renvoyait son image, — et tout au plus avais-je prêté

GÉRARD DE NERVAL

Sylvie

Memories of the Valois Country

I. A Lost Night

I was leaving a theater in which I was to be seen every evening occupying a stage box in the full finery of a suitor. Sometimes the place was full, sometimes it was empty. I took little interest in turning my glance to an orchestra floor containing only some thirty playgoers there against their better judgment, or to boxes adorned with outmoded bonnets and gowns; and I was equally unconcerned about being part of a lively, bustling audience garlanded at each level with flowery dresses, sparkling jewels, and radiant faces. Just as I was indifferent to the show that the audience provided, the one on stage hardly held my attention—except when, in the second or third scene of one of the sullen masterpieces of the time, a well-known apparition lit up the empty space, giving life, with a breath or a word, to those idle figures that surrounded me.

I felt alive in her, and she lived for me alone. Her smile filled me with infinite bliss; the resonance of her soft, yet strongly sonorous, voice made me quake with joy and love. In my eyes she possessed every perfection, she fulfilled every requirement of my ardors and my caprices—beautiful as the day in the glare of the footlights that illuminated her from below; pale as night when the doused footlights left her illuminated from above in the beams from the chandelier, making her appear more natural, shining within the shadow of her beauty alone, like the godlike Hours, a star on their forehead, who stand out against the brown background of the frescos at Herculaneum.[1]

It had been a year, and I hadn't yet thought about finding out what she was like; I was afraid of clouding the magic mirror that beamed her image at me. At the very most, I had lent my ear to a few remarks

l'oreille à quelques propos concernant non plus l'actrice, mais la femme. Je m'en informais aussi peu que des bruits qui ont pu courir sur la princesse d'Elide ou sur la reine de Trébizonde, — un de mes oncles qui avait vécu dans les avant-dernières années du dix-huitième siècle, comme il fallait y vivre pour le bien connaître, m'ayant prévenu de bonne heure que les actrices n'étaient pas des femmes, et que la nature avait oublié de leur faire un cœur. Il parlait de celles de ce temps-là sans doute; mais il m'avait raconté tant d'histoires de ses illusions, de ses déceptions, et montré tant de portraits sur ivoire, médaillons charmants qu'il utilisait depuis à parer des tabatières, tant de billets jaunis, tant de faveurs fanées, en m'en faisant l'histoire et le compte définitif, que je m'étais habitué à penser mal de toutes sans tenir compte de l'ordre des temps.

Nous vivons alors dans une époque étrange, comme celles qui d'ordinaire succèdent aux révolutions ou aux abaissements des grands règnes. Ce n'était plus la galanterie héroïque comme sous la Fronde, le vice élégant et paré comme sous la Régence, le scepticisme et les folles orgies du Directoire; c'était un mélange d'activité, d'hésitation et de paresse, d'utopies brillantes, d'aspirations philosophiques ou religieuses, d'enthousiasmes vagues, mêlés de certains instincts de renaissance; d'ennuis des discordes passées, d'espoirs incertains, — quelque chose comme l'époque de Pérégrinus et d'Apulée. L'homme matériel aspirait au bouquet du roses qui devait le régénérer par les mains de la belle Isis; la déesse éternellement jeune et pure nous apparaissait dans les nuits, et nous faisait honte de nos heures de jour perdues. L'ambition n'était cependant pas de notre âge, et l'avide curée qui se faisait alors des positions et des honneurs nous éloignait des sphères d'activité possibles. Il ne nous restait pour asile que cette tour d'ivoire des poètes, où nous montions toujours plus haut pour nous isoler de la foule. A ces points élevés où nous guidaient nos maîtres, nous respirions enfin l'air pur des solitudes, nous buvions l'oubli dans la coupe d'or des légendes, nous étions ivres de poésie et d'amour. Amour, hélas! des formes vagues, des teintes roses et bleues, des fantômes métaphysiques! Vue de près, la femme réelle révoltait notre ingénuité; il fallait qu'elle apparût reine ou déesse, et surtout n'en pas approcher.

Quelques-uns d'entre nous néanmoins prisaient peu ces paradoxes platoniques, et à travers nos rêves renouvelés d'Alexandrie agitaient parfois la torche des dieux souterrains, qui éclaire l'ombre un instant de ses traînées d'étincelles. — C'est ainsi que, sortant du théâtre avec l'amère tristesse que laisse un songe évanoui, j'allais volontiers me

that concerned her, not as an actress but as a woman. I sought information about her doings no more than I would have investigated any rumors about the princess of Elis or the queen of Trebizond.[2] One of my uncles, who had lived in the late, but not the last, years of the eighteenth century,[3] as one had to have lived in that century to know it well, had warned me early on that actresses weren't women, and that nature had forgotten to give them a heart. He was no doubt speaking about those of that era; but he had told me so many stories about his illusions and disappointments, he had showed me so many portraits on ivory, charming medallions which he later used for adorning snuff-boxes, so many yellowed love letters, so many faded ribbons once received as love tokens—telling me the story of each one, with its final conclusion—that I had grown accustomed to think badly of all actresses, without keeping the time sequence in mind.

We were then living in a strange era, like those that usually follow revolutions or the humbling of great reigns.[4] We no longer had the heroic lovemaking of the Fronde years, the elegant, decorative vice of the Regency, or the skepticism and wild orgies of the Directoire;[5] instead, we had a mixture of activity, hesitation, and sloth, brilliant utopias, philosophical or religious aspirations, vague enthusiasms mingled with certain presentiments of a renaissance; vexation over past discords, uncertain hopes—something like the era of Peregrinus and Apuleius.[6] Materialistic man yearned for the bunch of roses that would regenerate him at the hands of beautiful Isis; the eternally young and pure goddess appeared to us at night, making us ashamed of the hours we had wasted during the day. But we weren't old enough to be ambitious, and the greedy scramble for places and honors that was then in progress kept us far away from possible spheres of activity. All we had left as a refuge was that ivory tower of the poets, in which we climbed higher and higher to insulate ourselves from the crowd. On these heights to which our masters led us, we could finally breathe the fresh air of solitary places; we drank oblivion from the golden goblet of legends, we were intoxicated with poetry and love. Alas, it was a love for vague shapes, for pink and blue tints, for metaphysical phantoms! Seen up close, real women were a shock to our naïve candor; they had to appear like queens or goddesses; above all, they were not to be approached.

Nevertheless, some of us had little taste for such Platonic paradoxes; and amid our rejuvenated Alexandrian dreams they would sometimes brandish the torch of the underworld gods, which illuminates the darkness for a moment with its trail of sparks. And so, leaving that theater with the bitter sadness left behind by a dream that has vanished, I

joindre à la société d'un cercle où l'on soupait en grand nombre, et où toute mélancolie cédait devant la verve intarissable de quelques esprits éclatants, vifs, orageux, sublimes parfois, — tels qu'il s'en est trouvé toujours dans les époques de rénovation ou de décadence, et dont les discussions se haussaient à ce point, que les plus timides d'entre nous allaient voir parfois aux fenêtres si les Huns, les Turcomans ou les Cosaques n'arrivaient pas enfin pour couper court à ces arguments de rhéteurs et de sophistes.

«Buvons, aimons, c'est la sagesse!» Telle était la seule opinion des plus jeunes. Un de ceux-là me dit: «Voici bien longtemps que je te rencontre dans le même théâtre, et chaque fois que j'y vais. Pour *laquelle* y viens-tu?»

Pour laquelle? . . . Il ne me semblait pas que l'on pût aller là pour une *autre*. Cependant j'avouai un nom. — «Eh bien! dit mon ami avec indulgence, tu vois là-bas l'homme heureux qui vient de la reconduire, et qui, fidèle aux lois de notre cercle, n'ira la retrouver peut-être qu'après la nuit.»

Sans trop d'émotion, je tournai les yeux vers le personnage indiqué. C'était un jeune homme correctement vêtu, d'une figure pâle et nerveuse, ayant des manières convenables et des yeux empreints de mélancolie et de douceur. Il jetait de l'or sur une table de whist et le perdait avec indifférence. — Que m'importe, dis-je, lui ou tout autre? Il fallait qu'il y en eût un, et celui-là me paraît digne d'avoir été choisi. — Et toi? — Moi? C'est une image que je poursuis, rien de plus.

En sortant, je passai par la salle de lecture, et machinalement je regardai un journal. C'était, je crois, pour y voir le cours de la Bourse. Dans les débris de mon opulence se trouvait une somme assez forte en titres étrangers. Le bruit avait couru que, négligés longtemps, ils allaient être reconnus; — ce qui venait d'avoir lieu à la suite d'un changement de ministère. Les fonds se trouvaient déjà cotés très haut; je redevenais riche.

Une seule pensée résulta de ce changement de situation, celle que la femme aimée si longtemps était à moi si je voulais. — Je touchais du doigt mon idéal. N'était-ce pas une illusion encore, une faute d'impression railleuse? Mais les autres feuilles parlaient de même. — La somme gagnée se dressa devant moi comme la statue d'or de Moloch. «Que dirait maintenant, pensais-je, le jeune homme de tout à l'heure, si j'allais prendre sa place près de la femme qu'il a laissée seule? . . .» Je frémis de cette pensée, et mon orgueil se révolta.

gladly went to meet my companions at a club where many of us used to have supper after the performance, and where all melancholy succumbed to the unflagging high spirits of a few intellects that were brilliant, lively, stormy, sometimes sublime—such as have always been found in periods of renewal or decadence. Their arguments used to become so heated that the more timid among us sometimes went over to the windows to see whether the Huns, Turkomans, or Cossacks weren't finally coming to cut short these debates of rhetoricians and sophists.

"Let's drink, let's make love, that's the proper thing to do!" Such was the sole opinion of the younger ones. One of them said to me: "For quite some time now I've been meeting you in the same theater, each time I go there. For which of the women do you come?"

For which one? . . . I couldn't imagine that anyone could go there for anyone else. Nevertheless I confessed who it was. "Well!" said my friend indulgently; "over there you see the lucky man who has just escorted her home, and who, obedient to the rules of our club, perhaps won't go and rejoin her until the night is over."

Without too much emotion, I turned my glance toward the person he had indicated. He was a young man, correctly dressed, with a pale, nervous face, with proper manners, and with eyes filled with melancholy and gentleness. He was tossing gold coins onto a whist table and losing them with unconcern. "What does it matter to me," I said, "whether it's him or anyone else? Necessarily there had to be one, and he seems worthy of having been chosen." "And you?" "Me? What I'm pursuing is an image, nothing more."

On my way out, I passed through the reading room and mechanically glanced at a newspaper. I think I did so to see how the stock market was doing. Among the wreckage of my fortune there was quite a large amount invested in foreign bonds. There had been a rumor that, after being disregarded for a long time, they would now be acknowledged again—and that very thing had just taken place as the result of a change in the ministry. The securities were already quoted at a very high price; I was becoming rich again.

A single thought resulted from this change in my situation: that the woman I had loved for so long was mine if I so wished. I was about to achieve my ideal. But wasn't this just one more illusion, a typographical error to make fun of me? No, the other papers said the same thing. The amount I had earned loomed up before me like the golden statue of Moloch. "What would that young man I just saw say now," I thought, "if I went and took his place beside the woman that he left there alone . . . ?" I was enraged by that thought, and my self-esteem was shocked.

Non! ce n'est pas ainsi, ce n'est pas à mon âge que l'on tue l'amour avec de l'or: je ne serai pas un corrupteur. D'ailleurs ceci est une idée d'un autre temps. Qui me dit aussi que cette femme soit vénale? — Mon regard parcourait vaguement le journal que je tenais encore, et j'y lus ces deux lignes: «*Fête du Bouquet provincial.* — Demain, les archers de Senlis doivent rendre le bouquet à ceux de Loisy.» Ces mots, fort simples, réveillèrent en moi toute une nouvelle série d'impressions: c'était un souvenir de la province depuis longtemps oubliée, un écho lointain des fêtes naïves de la jeunesse. — Le cor et le tambour résonnaient au loin dans les hameaux et dans les bois; les jeunes filles tressaient des guirlandes et assortissaient, en chantant, des bouquets ornés de rubans. — Un lourd chariot, traîné par des bœufs, recevait ces présents sur son passage, et nous, enfants de ces contrées, nous formions le cortège avec nos arcs et nos flèches, nous décorant du titre de chevaliers, — sans savoir alors que nous ne faisions que répéter d'âge en âge une fête druidique survivant aux monarchies et aux religions nouvelles.

II. — Adrienne.

Je regagnai mon lit et je ne pus y trouver le repos. Plongé dans une demi-somnolence, toute ma jeunesse repassait en mes souvenirs. Cet état, où l'esprit résiste encore aux bizarres combinaisons du songe, permet souvent de voir se presser en quelques minutes les tableaux les plus saillants d'une longue période de la vie.

Je me représentais un château du temps de Henri IV avec ses toits pointus couverts d'ardoises et sa face rougeâtre aux encoignures dentelées de pierres jaunies, une grande place verte encadrée d'ormes et de tilleuls, dont le soleil couchant perçait le feuillage de ses traits enflammés. Des jeunes filles dansaient en rond sur la pelouse en chantant de vieux airs transmis par leurs mères, et d'un français si naturellement pur, que l'on se sentait bien exister dans ce vieux pays du Valois, où, pendant plus de mille ans, a battu le cœur de la France.

J'étais le seul garçon dans cette ronde, où j'avais amené ma compagne toute jeune encore, Sylvie, une petite fille du hameau voisin, si vive et si fraîche, avec ses yeux noirs, son profil régulier et sa peau légèrement hâlée! . . . Je n'aimais qu'elle, je ne voyais qu'elle, — jusque-là! A peine avais-je remarqué, dans la ronde où nous dansions, une blonde, grande et belle, qu'on appelait Adrienne. Tout d'un coup, suivant les règles de la danse, Adrienne se trouva placée seule avec moi au milieu du cercle. Nos tailles étaient pareilles. On nous dit de

No! That's not the way, I'm not at the age at which men kill love with gold: I won't buy her affection. Besides, that notion belongs to the past. Also, who says that she would sell herself? I ran my eyes vaguely over the newspaper I was still holding, and I read these two lines: "Festival of the Bouquet of the Province. Tomorrow the archers of Senlis are to hand over the bouquet to those of Loisy." Those very simple words awoke in me a totally new series of impressions: the recollection of the countryside I had forgotten for so long, a distant echo of the ingenuous festivals of my youth. The hunting horn and the snare drum were resounding far and wide in the hamlets and in the woods; the girls were weaving wreaths and arranging bouquets adorned with ribbons as they sang. A heavy farm wagon drawn by oxen was receiving those presents as it passed by, and we, the children of those regions, were forming the procession with our bows and arrows, honoring ourselves with the title of knights—without knowing at the time that we were merely repeating from era to era a Druid festival that had survived the monarchies and the new religions.

II. Adrienne

I went home, got in bed, but couldn't find rest there. I was submerged in a half-slumber, and my entire youth was reviewed in my memory. That mental state, in which the mind still resists the bizarre combinations of the dream state, often allows us to see the most salient scenes of a long stretch of our life compressed into a few minutes.

I pictured a château of the time of Henri IV[7] with its slate-covered pointed roofs and its red-brick facade, with an indentation of yellowed stones along the corners; a large green lawn framed by elms and linden trees, their foliage penetrated by the fiery rays of the setting sun. Girls were performing a round dance on the grass while singing old tunes they had learned from their mothers, in a French so naturally pure that it was clear to you that you were in that old Valois region where the Heart of France has beaten for over a thousand years.

I was the only boy within that dance circle, to which I had brought my companion, still very young, Sylvie, a little girl from the nearby hamlet, so lively and healthy, with her dark eyes, her regular profile, and her lightly tanned skin! . . . I loved only her, I saw only her—until then! In the circle in which we were dancing, I had barely noticed a blond girl, tall and beautiful, whom they called Adrienne. Suddenly, in accordance with the pattern of the dance, Adrienne and I were left alone in the center of the circle. We were of the same height. They

nous embrasser, et la danse et le chœur tournaient plus vivement que jamais. En lui donnant ce baiser, je ne pus m'empêcher de lui presser la main. Les longs anneaux roulés de ses cheveux d'or effleuraient mes joues. De ce moment, un trouble inconnu s'empara de moi. — La belle devait chanter pour avoir le droit de rentrer dans la danse. On s'assit autour d'elle, et aussitôt, d'une voix fraîche et pénétrante, légèrement voilée, comme celles des filles de ce pays brumeux, elle chanta une de ces anciennes romances pleines de mélancolie et d'amour, qui racontent toujours les malheurs d'une princesse enfermée dans sa tour par la volonté d'un père qui la punit d'avoir aimé. La mélodie se terminait à chaque stance par ces trilles chevrotants que font valoir si bien les voix jeunes, quand elles imitent par un frisson modulé la voix tremblante des aïeules.

A mesure qu'elle chantait, l'ombre descendait des grands arbres, et le clair de lune naissant tombait sur elle seule, isolée de notre cercle attentif. — Elle se tut, et personne n'osa rompre le silence. La pelouse était couverte de faibles vapeurs condensées, qui déroulaient leurs blancs flocons sur les pointes des herbes. Nous pensions être en paradis. — Je me levai enfin, courant au parterre du château, où se trouvaient des lauriers, plantés dans de grands vases de faïence peints en camaïeu. Je rapportai deux branches, qui furent tressées en couronne et nouées d'un ruban. Je posai sur la tête d'Adrienne cet ornement, dont les feuilles lustrées éclataient sur ses cheveux blonds aux rayons pâles de la lune. Elle ressemblait à la Béatrice de Dante qui sourit au poète errant sur la lisière des saintes demeures.

Adrienne se leva. Développant sa taille élancée, elle nous fit un salut gracieux, et rentra en courant dans le château. — C'était, nous dit-on, la petite-fille de l'un des descendants d'une famille alliée aux anciens rois de France; le sang des Valois coulait dans ses veines. Pour ce jour de fête, on lui avait permis de se mêler à nos jeux; nous ne devions plus la revoir, car le lendemain elle repartit pour un couvent où elle était pensionnaire.

Quand je revins près de Sylvie, je m'aperçus qu'elle pleurait. La couronne donnée par mes mains à la belle chanteuse était le sujet de ses larmes. Je lui offris d'en aller cueillir une autre, mais elle dit qu'elle n'y tenait nullement, ne la méritant pas. Je voulus en vain me défendre, elle ne me dit plus un seul mot pendant que je la reconduisais chez ses parents.

Rappelé moi-même à Paris pour y reprendre mes études, j'emportai cette double image d'une amitié tendre tristement rompue, — puis

told us to kiss, and the dance and chorus spun around more quickly than ever. As I gave her that kiss, I couldn't keep from squeezing her hand. The long, curly ringlets of her golden hair brushed my cheeks. From that moment on, an unfamiliar disquiet took hold of me. The beautiful girl had to sing to have the right to reenter the dance. We sat down around her and immediately, with a clear, penetrating voice, slightly veiled, like those of the daughters of that misty region, she sang one of those old ballads, full of melancholy and love, which always tell of the misfortunes of a princess locked in a tower by the orders of her father, punishing her for being in love. In each stanza, the melody ended in those quavering trills that are set off to such good advantage by young voices when they imitate in a modulated tremolo the shaky voice of old women.

While she was singing, darkness was descending from the great trees, and the nascent moonlight was falling on her alone, isolated as she was from our attentive circle. She fell silent, but no one ventured to break the silence. The lawn was covered with light, condensing vapors that unfurled their white foam-flakes on the tips of the grass blades. We thought we were in heaven. Finally I stood up and ran to the château garden, where laurels were planted in large faience pots painted in monochrome. I brought back two branches, which were then woven into a wreath and tied with a ribbon. I placed this decoration on Adrienne's head; its shiny leaves glittered on her blond hair in the pale moonbeams. She looked like Dante's Beatrice smiling at the poet who was wandering on the outskirts of the holy dwelling places.

Adrienne rose. Drawing herself up to her full height, tall and slender, she said good-bye to us gracefully, and ran back into the château. We were told that she was the granddaughter of one of the descendants of a family connected by marriage to the old kings of France; the blood of the Valois flowed in her veins. For that holiday she had been allowed to take part in our games; we were not to see her again, because the next day she returned to a convent boarding school.

When I went back to Sylvie, I noticed that she was crying. The wreath I had given to the beautiful singer with my own hands was the reason for her tears. I offered to pick another one for her, but she said that she definitely didn't want it, since she didn't deserve it. It was in vain that I tried to defend myself; she didn't say another word to me while I took her home to her parents.

When I myself was called back to Paris to resume my studies, I carried away that double image of a tender friendship sadly broken, and

d'un amour impossible et vague, source de pensées douloureuses que la philosophie de collège était impuissante à calmer.

La figure d'Adrienne resta seule triomphante, — mirage de la gloire et de la beauté, adoucissant ou partageant les heures des sévères études. Aux vacances de l'année suivante, j'appris que cette belle à peine entrevue était consacrée par sa famille à la vie religieuse.

III. — Résolution.

Tout m'était expliqué par ce souvenir à demi rêvé. Cet amour vague et sans espoir, conçu pour une femme de théâtre, qui tous les soirs me prenait à l'heure du spectacle, pour ne me quitter qu'à l'heure du sommeil, avait son germe dans le souvenir d'Adrienne, fleur de la nuit éclose à la pâle clarté de la lune, fantôme rose et blond glissant sur l'herbe verte à demi baignée de blanches vapeurs. — La ressemblance d'une figure oubliée depuis des années se dessinait désormais avec une netteté singulière; c'était un crayon estompé par le temps qui se faisait peinture, comme ces vieux croquis de maîtres admirés dans un musée, dont on retrouve ailleurs l'original éblouissant.

Aimer une religieuse sous la forme d'une actrice! ... et si c'était la même! — Il y a de quoi devenir fou! c'est un entraînement fatal où l'inconnu vous attire comme le feu follet fuyant sur les joncs d'une eau morte ... Reprenons pied sur le réel.

Et Sylvie que j'aimais tant, pourquoi l'ai-je oubliée depuis trois ans? ... C'était une bien jolie fille, et la plus belle de Loisy!

Elle existe, elle, bonne et pure de cœur sans doute. Je revois sa fenêtre où le pampre s'enlace au rosier, la cage de fauvettes suspendue à gauche; j'entends le bruit de ses fuseaux sonores et sa chanson favorite:

> La belle était assise
> Près du ruisseau coulant ...

Elle m'attend encore ... Qui l'aurait épousée? elle est si pauvre!

Dans son village et dans ceux qui l'entourent, de bons paysans en blouse, aux mains rudes, à la face amaigrie, au teint hâlé! Elle m'aimait seul, moi le petit Parisien, quand j'allais voir près de Loisy mon pauvre oncle, mort aujourd'hui. Depuis trois ans, je dissipe en seigneur le bien modeste qu'il m'a laissé et qui pouvait suffire à ma vie. Avec Sylvie, je l'aurais conservé. Le hasard m'en rend une partie. Il est temps encore.

of an impossible, vague love, the source of painful thoughts that the philosophy taught in school was powerless to soothe.

The figure of Adrienne remained the only triumphant one—a mirage of glory and beauty, comforting or sharing in my hours of serious study. During the next year's vacation I learned that that beauty I had merely glimpsed had been dedicated by her family to the life of a nun.

III. Resolution

Everything was explained to me by that recollection I had half-dreamt. That vague, hopeless love conceived for an actress, which seized upon me every evening at the hour of the performance and didn't release me until bedtime, had its roots in my memory of Adrienne, that nocturnal flower opening in the pale moonlight, a pink and blond phantom gliding over the green grass that was half-drenched with white vapors. Her similarity to a figure forgotten for years was now delineated with enormous clarity; it was a chalk drawing, blurred by time, turning into a painting, like those old-master sketches admired in a museum, the dazzling original of which you discover somewhere else.

To love a nun in the guise of an actress! . . . And what if it were the same woman!—That could drive a man crazy! It's a fatal allurement into which the unknown draws you like a will-o'-the-wisp flying from you over the reeds of a stagnant pool . . . Let's set our feet back on solid, real ground.

And Sylvie, whom I loved so much, why have I forgotten her for three years now? . . . She was a really pretty girl, the most beautiful one in Loisy!

She exists, and is no doubt kind and pure in heart. I see once more her window, where the grapevine twines around the rosebush, the cage of warblers hanging on the left side; I hear the clicking of her noisy lace bobbins and her favorite song:

> The beautiful girl was seated
> By the side of the flowing brook . . .

She's still waiting for me . . . Who would have married her? She's so poor!

In her village and those around it, there are good peasants in smocks, with rough hands, emaciated faces, sunburned complexions! She loved only me, the little Parisian, when I went to see my poor uncle, now dead, near Loisy. For three years I've been squandering like a lord the modest inheritance he left me, which could have satisfied me for life. With Sylvie, I would have held on to it. Chance has restored a part of it to me. There's still time.

A cette heure, que fait-elle? Elle dort . . . Non, elle ne dort pas; c'est aujourd'hui la fête de l'arc, la seule de l'année où l'on danse toute la nuit. — Elle est à la fête . . .

Quelle heure est-il?

Je n'avais pas de montre.

Au milieu de toutes les splendeurs de bric-à-brac qu'il était d'usage de réunir à cette époque pour restaurer dans sa couleur locale un appartement d'autrefois, brillait d'un éclat rafraîchi une de ces pendules d'écaille de la Renaissance, dont le dôme doré surmonté de la figure du Temps est supporté par des cariatides du style Médicis, reposant à leur tour sur des chevaux à demi cabrés. La Diane historique, accoudée sur son cerf, est en bas-relief sous le cadran, où s'étalent sur un fond niellé les chiffres émaillés des heures. Le mouvement, excellent sans doute, n'avait pas été remonté depuis deux siècles. — Ce n'était pas pour savoir l'heure que j'avais acheté cette pendule en Touraine.

Je descendis chez le concierge. Son coucou marquait une heure du matin. — En quatre heures, me dis-je, je puis arriver au bal de Loisy. Il y avait encore sur la place du Palais-Royal cinq ou six fiacres stationnant pour les habitués des cercles et des maisons de jeu: — A Loisy! dis-je au plus apparent. — Où cela est-il? — Près de Senlis, à huit lieues. — Je vais vous conduire à la poste, dit le cocher, moins préoccupé que moi.

Quelle triste route, la nuit, que cette route de Flandres, qui ne devient belle qu'en atteignant la zone des forêts! Toujours ces deux files d'arbres monotones qui grimacent des formes vagues; au-delà, des carrés de verdure et de terres remuées, bornés à gauche par les collines bleuâtres de Montmorency, d'Ecouen, de Luzarches. Voici Gonesse, le bourg vulgaire plein des souvenirs de la Ligue et de la Fronde . . .

Plus loin que Louvres est un chemin bordé de pommiers dont j'ai vu bien des fois les fleurs éclater dans la nuit comme des étoiles de la terre: c'était le plus court pour gagner les hameaux. — Pendant que la voiture monte les côtes, recomposons les souvenirs du temps où j'y venais si souvent.

IV. — Un Voyage à Cythère.

Quelques années s'étaient écoulées: l'époque où j'avais rencontré Adrienne devant le château n'était plus déjà qu'un souvenir d'enfance. Je me retrouvai à Loisy au moment de la fête patronale. J'allai

At this hour, what is she doing? She's sleeping . . . No, she's not sleeping; today is the archery festival, the only one in the year when you dance all night long. She's at the festival . . .

What time is it?

I didn't have a watch.

In the midst of all the wonderful bric-a-brac it was customary at that time to assemble in order to restore an old apartment to its period style, there shone with renewed brilliance one of those Renaissance tortoise-shell clocks whose gilded dome, topped by the figure of Time, is supported by caryatids in Medici style, which themselves rest on half-rearing horses. The historical Diana,[8] her elbow on her stag, is in bas-relief below the dial, on which the enameled numbers of the hours are displayed against a niello background. The works, no doubt excellent, hadn't been rewound for two centuries.—It wasn't to know the time that I had bought that clock in Touraine.

I went downstairs to the concierge. His cuckoo clock was sounding one A.M. In four hours, I told myself, I can arrive at the dance in Loisy. On the Palais-Royal square five or six hackney carriages were still standing and waiting for the habitués of the clubs and the gambling houses. "To Loisy!" I said to the most conspicuous one. "Where's that?" "Near Senlis, eight leagues from here." "I'll drive you to the stagecoach station," said the coachman, who was less eager than I was.

What a dismal road at night that Flanders road is! It doesn't become beautiful until you reach the forest zone. On and on, those two rows of monotonous trees grimacing with their vague shapes; beyond them, patches of greenery and dug-up fields, bordered at the left by the bluish hills of Montmorency, Ecouen, Luzarches. Here is Gonesse, a vulgar market town filled with memories of the Ligue[9] and the Fronde . . .

Past Louvres there's a road lined with apple trees whose blossoms I've often seen shining in the night like stars on earth: it was the shortest way to reach the hamlets. While the coach is climbing the slopes, let's reassemble the memories of the time when I came here so frequently.

IV. A Voyage to Cythera

A few years had gone by: the time when I had met Adrienne in front of the château was already no more than a childhood memory. I found myself in Loisy at the moment of the patron saint's day. Again I went and

de nouveau me joindre aux chevaliers de l'arc, prenant place dans la compagnie dont j'avais fait partie déjà. Des jeunes gens appartenant aux vieilles familles qui possèdent encore là plusieurs de ces châteaux perdus dans les forêts, qui ont plus souffert du temps que des révolutions, avaient organisé la fête. De Chantilly, de Compiègne et de Senlis accouraient de joyeuses cavalcades qui prenaient place dans le cortège rustique des compagnies de l'arc. Après la longue promenade à travers les villages et les bourgs, après la messe à l'église, les luttes d'adresse et la distribution des prix, les vainqueurs avaient été conviés à un repas qui se donnait dans une île ombragée de peupliers et de tilleuls, au milieu de l'un des étangs alimentés par la Nonette et la Thève. Des barques pavoisées nous conduisirent à l'île, — dont le choix avait été déterminé par l'existence d'un temple ovale à colonnes qui devait servir de salle pour le festin. — Là, comme à Ermenonville, le pays est semé de ces édifices légers de la fin du dix-huitième siècle, où des millionnaires philosophes se sont inspirés dans leurs plans du goût dominant d'alors. Je crois bien que ce temple avait dû être primitivement dédié à Uranie. Trois colonnes avaient succombé emportant dans leur chute une partie de l'architrave; mais on avait déblayé l'intérieur de la salle, suspendu des guirlandes entre les colonnes, on avait rajeuni cette ruine moderne, — qui appartenait au paganisme de Bouffleurs ou de Chaulieu plutôt qu'à celui d'Horace.

La traversée du lac avait été imaginée peut-être pour rappeler le *Voyage à Cythère* de Watteau. Nos costumes modernes dérangeaient seuls l'illusion. L'immense bouquet de la fête, enlevé du char qui le portait, avait été placé sur une grande barque; le cortège des jeunes filles vêtues de blanc qui l'accompagnent selon l'usage avait pris place sur les bancs, et cette gracieuse *théorie* renouvelée des jours antiques se reflétait dans les eaux calmes de l'étang qui la séparait du bord de l'île si vermeil aux rayons du soir avec ses halliers d'épine, sa colonnade et ses clairs feuillages. Toutes les barques abordèrent en peu de temps. La corbeille portée en cérémonie occupa le centre de la table, et chacun prit place, les plus favorisés auprès des jeunes filles: il suffisait pour cela d'être connu de leurs parents. Ce fut la cause qui fit que je me retrouvai près de Sylvie. Son frère m'avait déjà rejoint dans la fête, il me fit la guerre de n'avoir pas depuis longtemps rendu visite à sa famille. Je m'excusai sur mes études, qui me retenaient à Paris, et l'assurai que j'étais venu dans cette intention. «Non, c'est moi qu'il a oubliée, dit Sylvie. Nous sommes des gens de village, et Paris est si au-dessus!» Je voulus l'embrasser pour lui fermer la bouche; mais elle me boudait

joined the knights of the bow, taking my place in the company I had already been a member of. Young men belonging to the old families that still own several of those châteaux lost in the forests there, buildings that have suffered more from time than from revolutions, had organized the festival. From Chantilly, Compiègne, and Senlis there arrived joyful cavalcades that took their place in the rustic procession of the companies of archers. After the long promenade through the villages and market towns, after the Mass in church, the contests, and the awarding of prizes, the victors had been invited to a meal being given on an island shaded by poplars and linden trees, in the center of one of those ponds fed by the Nonette and the Thève. Boats decked with flags carried us to the island, which had been selected because it contained an oval temple with columns, which was to serve as the banqueting hall. There, as in Ermenonville, the countryside is dotted with those small-scale buildings from the end of the eighteenth century, for the plans of which the millionaire *philosophes* were inspired by the prevailing taste of the time. I think that this temple must have originally been dedicated to Urania. Three columns had collapsed, carrying along with them a part of the architrave; but the interior of the room had been cleared, garlands had been hung between the columns; they had rejuvenated this modern ruin, which belonged more to the paganism of Boufflers or Chaulieu than to that of Horace.[10]

The crossing of the lake had perhaps been conceived as a reminiscence of Watteau's painting *The Voyage to Cythera*. Only our modern clothing was an impediment to the illusion. The immense bouquet of the festival, removed from the wagon that was carrying it, had been placed on a large boat; the girls dressed in white, who accompany it in procession according to custom, had taken their seats on the benches, and that graceful *theoria*[11] recalling the days of antiquity was reflected in the calm waters of the pond that separated it from the banks of the island, so vermilion in the rays of the evening sun, with its thornbush thickets, its colonnade, and its bright foliage. All the boats touched shore very soon. The ceremoniously carried basket occupied the center of the table, and everyone was seated, the more favored young men near the girls: for that, they merely needed to be known to their parents. That was the reason I found myself next to Sylvie. Her brother already had caught up with me during the festival, and had reproached me for not having visited his family for so long. My excuse was my studies, which detained me in Paris, and I assured him I had come with precisely that in mind. "No, it's me that he's forgotten," said Sylvie. "We're only villagers, and Paris is so far above us!" I tried to kiss her to

encore, et il fallut que son frère intervînt pour qu'elle m'offrît sa joue d'un air indifférent. Je n'eus aucune joie de ce baiser dont bien d'autres obtenaient la faveur, car dans ce pays patriarcal où l'on salue tout homme qui passe, un baiser n'est autre chose qu'une politesse entre bonnes gens.

Une surprise avait été arrangée par les ordonnateurs de la fête. A la fin du repas, on vit s'envoler du fond de la vaste corbeille un cygne sauvage, jusque-là captif sous les fleurs, qui de ses fortes ailes, soulevant des lacis de guirlandes et de couronnes, finit par les disperser de tous côtés. Pendant qu'il s'élançait joyeux vers les dernières lueurs du soleil, nous rattrapions au hasard les couronnes, dont chacun parait aussitôt le front de sa voisine. J'eus le bonheur de saisir une des plus belles, et Sylvie souriante se laissa embrasser cette fois plus tendrement que l'autre. Je compris que j'effaçais ainsi le souvenir d'un autre temps. Je l'admirai cette fois sans partage, elle était devenue si belle! Ce n'était plus cette petite fille de village que j'avais dédaignée pour une plus grande et plus faite aux grâces du monde. Tout en elle avait gagné: le charme de ses yeux noirs, si séduisants dès son enfance, était devenue irrésistible; sous l'orbite arquée de ses sourcils, son sourire, éclairant tout à coup des traits réguliers et placides, avait quelque chose d'athénien. J'admirais cette physionomie digne de l'art antique au milieu des minois chiffonnés de ses compagnes. Ses mains délicatement allongées, ses bras qui avaient blanchi en s'arrondissant, sa taille dégagée, la faisaient tout autre que je ne l'avais vue. Je ne pus m'empêcher de lui dire combien je la trouvais différente d'elle-même, espérant couvrir ainsi mon ancienne et rapide infidélité.

Tout me favorisait d'ailleurs, l'amitié de son frère, l'impression charmante de cette fête, l'heure du soir et le lieu même où, par une fantaisie pleine de goût, on avait reproduit une image des galantes solennités d'autrefois. Tant que nous pouvions, nous échappions à la danse pour causer de nos souvenirs d'enfance et pour admirer en rêvant à deux les reflets du ciel sur les ombrages et sur les eaux. Il fallut que le frère de Sylvie nous arrachât à cette contemplation en disant qu'il était temps de retourner au village assez éloigné qu'habitaient ses parents.

V. — Le Village.

C'était à Loisy, dans l'ancienne maison du garde. Je les conduisis jusque-là, puis je retournai à Montagny, où je demeurais chez mon

keep her quiet, but she was still cross with me, and her brother had to intervene to get her to offer me her cheek in an unconcerned manner. I had no joy in that kiss, which many others were favored with, because in that patriarchal region where you greet every passer-by, a kiss is nothing but an act of courtesy among well-meaning people.

A surprise had been arranged by the organizers of the festival. At the end of the meal, we saw flying out of the bottom of the enormous basket a wild swan, which till then had been kept prisoner beneath the flowers; with its strong wings, it lifted up entangled garlands and wreaths and finally scattered them on all sides. While the bird was happily soaring toward the final gleams of sunlight, we caught the garlands that came our way, and each young man immediately adorned the brow of the girl next to him. I was lucky enough to seize one of the prettiest, and this time Sylvie smiled and let me kiss her more tenderly than before. I realized that I was thereby erasing the past memory. This time I admired her wholeheartedly; she had grown so beautiful! She was no longer the little village girl I had disdained in favor of one who was taller and more endowed with worldly graces. Everything about her had improved: the charm of her dark eyes, so seductive since her childhood, had become irresistible; below the arcs of her eyebrows, her smile, suddenly illuminating her placid, regular features, had something Athenian in it. I admired that face, worthy of ancient art, in the midst of her companions' sweet, but irregular features. Her hands, long and delicate; her arms, which had rounded out and grown whiter; her pliant shape—all made her quite different from what I had seen in her before. I couldn't keep from telling her how changed I found her from her old self, hoping in that way to make up for my short-lived infidelity in the past.

Moreover, everything was in my favor: her brother's friendship, the charming impression of that festival, the evening hour and the location itself, where, with a most tasteful imagination, they had reproduced an image of the amatory ceremonies of long ago. To the extent that we could, we kept slipping away from the dance to talk about our childhood memories and, as we dreamt together, to admire the reflections of the sky on the shade trees and the waters. Sylvie's brother had to come and tear us away from that contemplation, saying it was time to return to the quite distant village where his parents lived.

V. The Village

It was at Loisy, in the former gamekeeper's lodge. I accompanied them there, then I returned to Montagny, where I was staying with my uncle.

oncle. En quittant le chemin pour traverser un petit bois qui sépare Loisy de Saint-S . . ., je ne tardai pas à m'engager dans une *sente* profonde qui longe la forêt d'Ermenonville; je m'attendais ensuite à rencontrer les murs d'un couvent qu'il fallait suivre pendant un quart de lieue. La lune se cachait de temps à autre sous les nuages, éclairant à peine les roches de grès sombre et les bruyères qui se multipliaient sous mes pas. A droite et à gauche, des lisières de forêts sans routes tracées, et toujours devant moi ces roches druidiques de la contrée qui gardent le souvenir des fils d'Armen exterminés par les Romains! Du haut de ces entassements sublimes, je voyais les étangs lointains se découper comme des miroirs sur la plaine brumeuse, sans pouvoir distinguer celui même où s'était passée la fête.

L'air était tiède et embaumé; je résolus de ne pas aller plus loin et d'attendre le matin, en me couchant sur des touffes de bruyères. — En me réveillant, je reconnus peu à peu les points voisins du lieu où je m'étais égaré dans la nuit. A ma gauche, je vis se dessiner la longue ligne des murs du couvent de Saint-S . . ., puis de l'autre côté de la vallée, la butte aux Gens-d'Armes, avec les ruines ébréchées de l'antique résidence carlovingienne. Près de là, au-dessus des touffes de bois, les hautes masures de l'abbaye de Thiers découpaient sur l'horizon leurs pans de muraille percés de trèfles et d'ogives. Au-delà, le manoir gothique de Pontarmé, entouré d'eau comme autrefois, refléta bientôt les premiers feux du jour, tandis qu'on voyait se dresser au midi le haut donjon de la Tournelle et les quatre tours de Bertrand-Fosse sur les premiers coteaux de Montméliant.

Cette nuit m'avait été douce, et je ne songeais qu'à Sylvie; cependant l'aspect du couvent me donna un instant l'idée que c'était celui peut-être qu'habitait Adrienne. Le tintement de la cloche du matin était encore dans mon oreille et m'avait sans doute réveillé. J'eus un instant l'idée de jeter un coup d'œil pardessus les murs en gravissant la plus haute pointe des rochers; mais en y réfléchissant, je m'en gardai comme d'une profanation. Le jour en grandissant chassa de ma pensée ce vain souvenir et n'y laissa plus que les traits rosés de Sylvie. «Allons la réveiller,» me dis-je, et je repris le chemin de Loisy.

Voici le village au bout de la sente qui côtoie la forêt: vingt chaumières dont la vigne et les roses grimpantes festonnent les murs. Des fileuses matinales, coiffées de mouchoirs rouges, travaillent réunies devant une ferme. Sylvie n'est point avec elles. C'est presque une demoiselle depuis qu'elle exécute de fines dentelles, tandis que ses parents sont restés de bons villageois. — Je suis monté à sa chambre sans étonner personne; déjà levée depuis longtemps, elle agitait les

Leaving the road to cross a small wood that separates Loisy from Saint-S—,[12] it wasn't long before I was following a low-lying footpath that borders the Forest of Ermenonville; after that, I expected to come across the walls of a convent that I needed to follow for a quarter-league. From time to time the moon concealed itself behind the clouds, barely illuminating the dark sandstone rocks and the heather, which was becoming denser beneath my feet. To the right and left, the edges of forests without beaten paths, and constantly ahead of me those druidic rocks of the region that preserve the memory of the sons of Armen[13] wiped out by the Romans! From the top of these sublime heaps of stone, I saw the distant ponds standing out like mirrors on the misty plain, although I couldn't make out the one where the festival had been held.

The air was warm and fragrant; I decided to go no further but to await the morning there, sleeping on tufts of heather. When I awoke, I gradually recognized the spots close to the place where I had become lost during the night. To my left, I saw delineated the long line of walls of the convent of Saint-S—, then, on the other side of the valley, the Hill of the Men-at-Arms, with the jagged ruins of the old Carolingian residence. Near to that, above the tufts of forest, the high remains of the Abbey of Thiers outlined on the horizon their sections of wall pierced with trefoils and ogives. Beyond that, the Gothic manor house of Pontarmé, surrounded by water as in the past, soon reflected the first rays of sunshine, while one could see rising to the south the tall castle keep of La Tournelle and the four towers of Bertrand-Fosse on the nearest slopes of Montméliant.

That night had been sweet to me, and I was thinking only of Sylvie; but the sight of the convent gave me the idea for a moment that it might be the one where Adrienne lived. The ringing of the morning bell was still in my ears and had no doubt awakened me. For a moment I had the idea of taking a look over the walls, climbing up the highest extension of the rocks; but when I thought it over, I refrained, as if it were a profanation. As the daylight increased, it drove that futile memory from my thoughts, leaving only the rosy features of Sylvie. "Let's go wake her up," I said to myself, taking the road to Loisy again.

Here is the village at the end of the footpath that edges the forest: twenty thatched cottages whose walls are festooned with grapevines and rambling roses. Women out early spinning, with red kerchiefs on their heads, were working together in front of one farmhouse. Sylvie isn't with them. She is practically a young lady of a higher class, because she makes fine lace, while her relatives have remained simple villagers. I went upstairs to her room without anyone being surprised;

fuseaux de sa dentelle, qui claquaient avec un doux bruit sur le carreau vert que soutenaient ses genoux. «Vous voilà, paresseux, dit-elle avec son sourire divin, je suis sûre que vous sortez seulement de votre lit!» Je lui racontai ma nuit passée sans sommeil, mes courses égarées à travers les bois et les roches. Elle voulut bien me plaindre un instant. «Si vous n'êtes pas fatigué, je vais vous faire courir encore. Nous irons voir ma grand'tante à Othys.» J'avais à peine répondu qu'elle se leva joyeusement, arrangea ses cheveux devant un miroir et se coiffa d'un chapeau de paille rustique. L'innocence et la joie éclataient dans ses yeux. Nous partîmes en suivant les bords de la Thève à travers les prés semés de marguerites et de boutons d'or, puis le long des bois de Saint-Laurent, franchissant parfois les ruisseaux et les halliers pour abréger la route. Les merles sifflaient dans les arbres, et les mésanges s'échappaient joyeusement des buissons frôlés par notre marche.

Parfois nous rencontrions sous nos pas les pervenches si chères à Rousseau, ouvrant leurs corolles bleues parmi ces longs rameaux de feuilles accouplées, lianes modestes qui arrêtaient les pieds furtifs de ma compagne. Indifférente aux souvenirs du philosophe genevois, elle cherchait çà et là les fraises parfumées, et moi, je lui parlais de *la Nouvelle Héloïse*, dont je récitais par cœur quelques passages. «Est-ce que c'est joli? dit-elle. — C'est sublime. — Est-ce mieux qu'Auguste Lafontaine? — C'est plus tendre. — Oh! bien, dit-elle, il faut que je lise cela. Je dirai à mon frère de me l'apporter la première fois qu'il ira à Senlis.» Et je continuais à réciter des fragments de l'*Héloïse* pendant que Sylvie cueillait des fraises.

VI. — Othys.

Au sortir du bois, nous rencontrâmes de grandes touffes de digitale pourprée; elle en fit un énorme bouquet en me disant: «C'est pour ma tante; elle sera si heureuse d'avoir ces belles fleurs dans sa chambre.» Nous n'avions plus qu'un bout de plaine à traverser pour gagner Othys. Le clocher du village pointait sur les coteaux bleuâtres qui vont de Montméliant à Dammartin. La Thève bruissait de nouveau parmi les grès et les cailloux, s'amincissant au voisinage de sa source, où elle se repose dans les prés, formant un petit lac au milieu des glaïeuls et des iris. Bientôt nous gagnâmes les premières maisons. La tante de Sylvie habitait une petite chaumière bâtie en pierres de grès inégales que revêtaient des treillages de houblon et de vigne-vierge; elle vivait seule de quelques carrés de terre que les gens du village cultivaient pour elle depuis la mort de son mari. Sa nièce arrivant, c'était le feu

already up for some time, she was moving the bobbins of her lace, which clicked softly on the green cushion she held on her lap. "There you are, lazybones," she said with her divine smile; "I'm sure you're just now getting out of bed!" I told her about my sleepless night, my random wanderings through woods and over rocks. For a moment she was good enough to take pity on me. "If you aren't tired, I'll make you run around some more. We'll go see my great-aunt at Othys." I had scarcely replied when she stood up joyfully, arranged her hair in front of a mirror, and put on a rustic straw hat. Innocence and joy shone in her eyes. We set out, following the banks of the Thève across meadows dotted with daisies and buttercups, then along the Saint-Laurent woods, at times crossing brooks and thickets to take shortcuts. The blackbirds were whistling in the trees, and the titmice flew merrily out of the bushes that we brushed as we walked.

At times we found beneath our feet the periwinkles so dear to Rousseau, opening their blue petals among those long branches with paired leaves, modest vines that caught my companion's furtive feet. Indifferent to the reminiscences of the Genevan philosopher, she was looking here and there for fragrant strawberries, while I spoke to her about the *Nouvelle Héloïse*, reciting some passages by heart. "Is that pretty?" she said. "It's sublime." "Is it better than August Lafontaine?"[14] "It's more tender." "Oh, well," she said, "I must read that. I'll tell my brother to bring me a copy the next time he goes to Senlis." And I continued to recite excerpts of the *Héloïse* while Sylvie picked strawberries.

VI. Othys

Emerging from the woods, we came across large tufts of foxgloves; she made an enormous bouquet of them, saying: "It's for my aunt; she'll be so happy to have these beautiful flowers in her room." We had only a small stretch of plain to cross to reach Othys. The village belfry stood out on the bluish slopes that extend from Montméliant to Dammartin. The Thève was again flowing noisily amid the sandstone rocks and the pebbles, growing narrower as we approached its source, where it reposes in the meadows, forming a little lake in the midst of the gladioli and the irises. Soon we reached the nearest houses. Sylvie's aunt lived in a little thatched cottage built of sandstone blocks of differing sizes, covered with trellises of hops and Virginia creepers; she lived alone, deriving her income from a few patches of land that the village folk had cultivated for her ever since her husband's death. Her niece's arrival

dans la maison. «Bonjour, la tante! Voici vos enfants! dit Sylvie; nous avons bien faim!» Elle l'embrassa tendrement, lui mit dans les bras la botte de fleurs, puis songea enfin à me présenter, en disant: «C'est mon amoureux!»

J'embrassai à mon tour la tante, qui dit: «Il est gentil . . . C'est donc un blond! . . . — Il a de jolis cheveux fins, dit Sylvie. —Cela ne dure pas, dit la tante; mais vous avez du temps devant vous, et toi qui es brune, cela t'assortit bien. — Il faut le faire déjeuner, la tante, dit Sylvie.» Et elle alla cherchant dans les armoires, dans la huche, trouvant du lait, du pain bis, du sucre, étalant sans trop de soin sur la table les assiettes et les plats de faïence émaillés de larges fleurs et de coqs au vif plumage. Une jatte en porcelaine de Creil, pleine de lait, où nageaient les fraises, devint le centre du service, et après avoir dépouillé le jardin de quelques poignées de cerises et de groseilles, elle disposa deux vases de fleurs aux deux bouts de la nappe. Mais la tante avait dit ces belles paroles: «Tout cela, ce n'est que du dessert. Il faut me laisser faire à présent.» Et elle avait décroché la poêle et jeté un fagot dans la haute cheminée. «Je ne veux pas que tu touches à cela! dit-elle à Sylvie, qui voulait l'aider; abîmer tes jolis doigts qui font de la dentelle plus belle qu'à Chantilly! tu m'en as donné, et je m'y connais. — Ah! oui, la tante! . . . Dites donc, si vous en avez, des morceaux de l'ancienne, cela me fera des modèles. — Eh bien! va voir là-haut, dit la tante, il y en a peut-être dans ma commode. — Donnez-moi les clefs, reprit Sylvie. — Bah! dit la tante, les tiroirs sont ouverts. — Ce n'est pas vrai, il y en a un qui est toujours fermé.» Et pendant que la bonne femme nettoyait la poêle après l'avoir passée au feu, Sylvie dénouait des pendants de sa ceinture une petite clef d'un acier ouvragé qu'elle me fit voir avec triomphe.

Je la suivis, montant rapidement l'escalier de bois qui conduisait à la chambre. — O jeunesse, ô vieillesse saintes! — qui donc eût songé à ternir la pureté d'un premier amour dans ce sanctuaire des souvenirs fidèles? Le portrait d'un jeune homme du bon vieux temps souriait avec ses yeux noirs et sa bouche rose, dans un ovale au cadre doré, suspendu à la tête du lit rustique. Il portait l'uniforme des gardes-chasse de la maison de Condé; son attitude à demi martiale, sa figure rose et bienveillante, son front pur sous ses cheveux poudrés, relevaient ce pastel, médiocre peut-être, des grâces de la jeunesse et de la simplicité. Quelque artiste modeste invité aux chasses princières s'était appliqué à le pourtraire de son mieux, ainsi que sa jeune épouse, qu'on voyait dans un autre médaillon, attrayante, maligne, élancée dans son corsage ouvert à échelle de rubans, agaçant de sa

brought a spurt of activity to the house. "Hello, Aunt! Here are your children!" Sylvie said. "We're good and hungry!" She kissed her tenderly, placed the bunch of flowers in her hands, then finally thought about introducing me, saying: "This is my sweetheart!"

I kissed her aunt, too, and she said: "He's nice . . . So he's blond . . . !" "He has fine, pretty hair," said Sylvie. "That doesn't last," said her aunt, "but you have time ahead of you, and you, Sylvie, you're a brunette and that makes a nice match." "We have to give him some breakfast, Aunt," said Sylvie. And she went looking through the cupboards, the bread bin, finding milk, whole-wheat bread, sugar, spreading out on the table without much ceremony dishes and plates of faience painted with large flowers and roosters with bright plumage. A basin of Creil porcelain, filled with milk in which strawberries were floating, became the centerpiece, and after stripping the garden of a few handfuls of cherries and currants, she placed two vases of flowers at the two ends of the cloth. But her aunt had spoken these fine words: "All that is merely dessert. You've got to let me go to work now." And she had taken the frying pan off its hook and thrown a bundle of wood into the tall hearth. "I don't want you to touch this!" she said to Sylvie, who wanted to help her. "To ruin your pretty fingers, which make lace more beautiful than in Chantilly! You've given me some, and I'm an expert." "Oh, yes, Aunt! . . . Tell me if you have any pieces of old lace, I can use them as models." "All right, go look upstairs," her aunt said; "there may be some in my commode." "Give me the keys," Sylvie replied. "Bah!" said her aunt; "the drawers are open." "That's not so, there's one that's always locked." And while the good woman was cleaning the frying pan after passing it through the fire, Sylvie detached from the pendants of her belt a little key of worked steel, which she showed me triumphantly.

I followed her, rapidly climbing the wooden staircase that led to the bedroom. O sacred youth and old age! Who would have thought of sullying the purity of his first love in that sanctuary of faithful mementos? The portrait of a young man of the good old days was smiling with his dark eyes and pink lips, in an oval with a gilded frame hanging at the head of the rustic bed. He wore the uniform of the gamekeepers of the house of Condé; his semimilitary attitude, his pink, benevolent face, his unclouded brow beneath his powdered hair, exalted that pastel, which may have been mediocre artistically, with the graces of youth and simplicity. Some unassuming artist invited to the princely hunts had attempted to portray him as well as he could, as well as his young wife, who was to be seen in another medallion, attractive, mischievous, slender in her open bodice with a ladder of ribbons, teasing with the

mine retroussée un oiseau posé sur son doigt. C'était pourtant la même bonne vieille qui cuisinait en ce moment, courbée sur le feu de l'âtre. Cela me fit penser aux fées des Funambules qui cachent, sous leur masque ridé, un visage attrayant, qu'elles révèlent au dénouement, lorsqu'apparaît le temple de l'Amour et son soleil tournant qui rayonne de feux magiques. «O bonne tante, m'écriai-je, que vous étiez jolie! — Et moi donc?» dit Sylvie, qui était parvenue à ouvrir le fameux tiroir. Elle y avait trouvé une grande robe en taffetas flambé, qui criait du froissement de ses plis. «Je veux essayer si cela m'ira, dit-elle. Ah! je vais avoir l'air d'une vieille fée!»

«La fée des légendes éternellement jeune!...» dis-je en moi-même. — Et déjà Sylvie avait dégrafé sa robe d'indienne et la laissait tomber à ses pieds. La robe étoffée de la vieille tante s'ajusta parfaitement sur la taille mince de Sylvie, qui me dit de l'agrafer. «Oh! les manches plates, que c'est ridicule!» dit-elle. Et cependant les sabots garnis de dentelles découvraient admirablement ses bras nus, la gorge s'encadrait dans le pur corsage aux tulles jaunis, aux rubans passés, qui n'avait serré que bien peu les charmes évanouis de la tante. «Mais finissez-en! Vous ne savez donc pas agrafer une robe?» me disait Sylvie. Elle avait l'air de l'accordée de village de Greuze. «Il faudrait de la poudre, dis-je. — Nous allons en trouver.» Elle fureta de nouveau dans les tiroirs. Oh! que de richesses! que cela sentait bon, comme cela brillait, comme cela chatoyait de vives couleurs et de modeste clinquant! deux éventails de nacre un peu cassés, des boîtes de pâte à sujets chinois, un collier d'ambre et mille fanfreluches, parmi lesquelles éclataient deux petits souliers de droguet blanc avec des boucles incrustées de diamants d'Irlande! «Oh! je veux les mettre, dit Sylvie, si je trouve les bas brodés!»

Un instant après, nous déroulions des bas de soie rose tendre à coins verts; mais la voix de la tante, accompagnée du frémissement de la poêle, nous rappela soudain à la réalité. «Descendez vite!» dit Sylvie, et quoi que je pusse dire, elle ne me permit pas de l'aider à se chausser. Cependant la tante venait de verser dans un plat le contenu de la poêle, une tranche de lard frite avec des œufs. La voix de Sylvie me rappela bientôt. «Habillez-vous vite!» dit-elle, et entièrement vêtue elle-même, elle me montra les habits de noces du garde-chasse réunis sur la commode. En un instant, je me transformai en marié de l'autre siècle. Sylvie m'attendait sur l'escalier, et nous descendîmes tous deux en nous tenant par la main. La tante poussa un cri en se retournant: «O mes enfants!» dit-elle, et elle se mit à

expression on her snub-nosed face a bird that was perched on her finger. And yet this was the same good old lady who was doing the cooking at that very moment, stooping over the fire in the hearth. That made me think of the fairies at the Funambules[15] who conceal beneath a wrinkled mask an attractive face, which they reveal at the climax, when the temple of Love appears with its rotating sun and its magical rays. "O good aunt," I exclaimed, "how pretty you were!" "And what about me?" said Sylvie, who had managed to open that special drawer. In it she had found a large gown of taffeta with a wave pattern, the pleats of which rustled loudly. "I want to try it on and see if it fits me," she said. "Ah, I'm going to look like an old fairy godmother!"

"The fairy in the legends who is eternally young!" I said to myself. And Sylvie had already unfastened her calico dress and was letting it fall around her feet. Her old aunt's ample gown fitted perfectly on Sylvie's slender shape, and she asked me to do it up. "Oh, these flat sleeves, how ridiculous they are!" she said. And yet the short, wide sleeves trimmed with lace left her arms enchantingly bare, her bosom was framed by the pure bodice with its yellowed tulle and faded ribbons, a bodice that hadn't clung very tightly to the vanished charms of her aunt. "Come on and finish! Don't you know how to hook up a dress?" Sylvie said. She looked like the betrothed village girl in Greuze's painting. "You need some powder," I said. "We'll go find some." She rummaged through the drawers again. Oh, what riches! How good it smelled, how it shone, how it flashed with bright colors and inexpensive finery!—two partially broken mother-of-pearl fans, almond-paste boxes with Chinese themes, an amber necklace, and a thousand other baubles, among which there gleamed two little slippers of white drugget, their buckles encrusted with rock crystal! "Oh, I want to put them on," Sylvie said, "if I find the embroidered stockings!"

A moment later, we were unrolling silk stockings of a pale pink with green clocks; but her aunt's voice, accompanied by the hissing of the frying pan, suddenly brought us back to reality. "Go downstairs fast!" said Sylvie, and, despite all I said, she wouldn't let me help her on with the shoes and stockings. Meanwhile her aunt had just emptied the contents of the frying pan onto a platter, a slice of bacon fried with eggs. Sylvie's voice soon called me back. "Get dressed fast!" she said, and, fully dressed herself, she showed me the gamekeeper's wedding outfit gathered together on the commode. In an instant I transformed myself into a bridegroom of the past century. Sylvie was waiting for me on the stairs, and we both came down holding hands. Her aunt gave a cry when she turned around. "Oh, my children," she said, and she started weeping, then smiled through her

pleurer, puis sourit à travers ses larmes. — C'était l'image de sa jeunesse, — cruelle et charmante apparition! Nous nous assîmes auprès d'elle, attendris et presque graves, puis la gaieté nous revint bientôt, car, le premier moment passé, la bonne vieille ne songea plus qu'à se rappeler les fêtes pompeuses de sa noce. Elle retrouva même dans sa mémoire les chants alternés, d'usage alors, qui se répondaient d'un bout à l'autre de la table nuptiale, et le naïf épithalame qui accompagnait les mariés rentrant après la danse. Nous répétions ces strophes si simplement rhythmées, avec les hiatus et les assonances du temps; amoureuses et fleuries comme le cantique de l'Ecclésiaste; — nous étions l'époux et l'épouse pour tout un beau matin d'été.

VII. — Châalis.

Il est quatre heures du matin; la route plonge dans un pli de terrain; elle remonte. La voiture va passer à Orry, puis à La Chapelle. A gauche, il y a une route qui longe le bois d'Halatte. C'est par là qu'un soir le frère de Sylvie m'a conduit dans sa carriole à une solennité du pays. C'était, je crois, le soir de la Saint-Barthélemy. A travers les bois, par des routes peu frayées, son petit cheval volait comme au sabbat. Nous rattrapâmes le pavé à Mont-Lévêque, et quelques minutes plus tard nous nous arrêtions à la maison du garde, à l'ancienne abbaye de Châalis. — Châalis, encore un souvenir!

Cette vieille retraite des empereurs n'offre plus à l'admiration que les ruines de son cloître aux arcades byzantines, dont la dernière rangée se découpe encore sur les étangs, — reste oublié des fondations pieuses comprises parmi ces domaines qu'on appelait autrefois les métairies de Charlemagne. La religion, dans ce pays isolé du mouvement des routes et des villes, a conservé des traces particulières du long séjour qu'y ont fait les cardinaux de la maison d'Este à l'époque des Médicis: ses attributs et ses usages ont encore quelque chose de galant et de poétique, et l'on respire un parfum de la Renaissance sous les arcs des chapelles à fines nervures, décorées par les artistes de l'Italie. Les figures des saints et des anges se profilent en rose sur les voûtes peintes d'un bleu tendre, avec des airs d'allégorie païenne qui font songer aux sentimentalités de Pétrarque et au mysticisme fabuleux de Francesco Colonna.

Nous étions des intrus, le frère de Sylvie et moi, dans la fête particulière qui avait lieu cette nuit-là. Une personne de très illustre naissance, qui possédait alors ce domaine, avait eu l'idée d'inviter quelques

tears. It was the image of her youth—cruel and charming apparition! We sat down beside her, touched and almost solemn; then our merry mood soon returned, because, after the first moment had passed, the good old lady could do nothing but recall the pompous celebration of her wedding. She even found in her memory the response songs that were then customary, sung in alternation from one end of the wedding table to the other, and the naïve epithalamium that accompanied the new couple as they came home after the dance. We repeated those stanzas with their very simple rhythms, with the hiatus between vowels and the assonance instead of pure rhymes so characteristic of the time; stanzas as loving and flowery as the Song of Songs of the Ecclesiast. We were the bride and groom for all of one beautiful summer morning.

VII. — Chaalis

It's four in the morning; the road sinks into a dip in the terrain; it rises again. The coach is going to go through Orry, then La Chapelle. To the left, there's a road that runs along the Forest of Halatte. It was along that road that Sylvie's brother took me one evening in his cart to a local celebration. I think it was Saint Bartholomew's Eve. Through the woods, over infrequently used paths, his little horse flew as if to a witches' sabbath. We rejoined the paved road at Mont-Lévêque, and a few minutes later we stopped at the gamekeeper's lodge at the old abbey of Chaalis. Chaalis, another memory!

That ancient retreat of emperors has nothing left to offer to our admiration but the ruins of its cloister with its Byzantine arcades, the last row of which still stands out against the background of the ponds—the forgotten remains of the religious building projects located in these domains that were once called Charlemagne's dairy farms. Religion, in this area remote from the hubbub of roads and cities, has preserved special traces of the long sojourn made there by the cardinals of the house of Este at the time of the Medici: its characteristics and customs still retain something romantic and poetic, and the air carries a fragrance of the Renaissance beneath the arches of the chapels with their fine tracery, decorated by artists from Italy. The figures of saints and angels are outlined in pink against the vaults painted pale blue, with a semblance of pagan allegory recalling the sentimental poems of Petrarch and the fabulous mysticism of Francesco Colonna.[16]

We were uninvited guests, Sylvie's brother and I, at the private party being held that night. A person of very illustrious birth, the owner of that domain at the time, had had the idea of inviting a few local families

familles du pays à une sorte de représentation allégorique où devaient
figurer quelques pensionnaires d'un couvent voisin. Ce n'était pas une
réminiscence des tragédies de Saint-Cyr, cela remontait aux premiers
essais lyriques importés en France du temps des Valois. Ce que je vis
jouer était comme un mystère des anciens temps. Les costumes, com-
posés de longues robes, n'étaient variés que par les couleurs de l'azur,
de l'hyacinthe ou de l'aurore. La scène se passait entre les anges, sur
les débris du monde détruit. Chaque voix chantait une des splendeurs
de ce globe éteint, et l'ange de la mort définissait les causes de sa destruction. Un esprit montait de l'abîme, tenant en main l'épée flam-
boyante, et convoquait les autres à venir admirer la gloire du Christ
vainqueur des enfers. Cet esprit, c'était Adrienne transfigurée par son
costume, comme elle l'était déjà par sa vocation. Le nimbe de carton
doré qui ceignait sa tête angélique nous paraissait bien naturellement
un cercle de lumière; sa voix avait gagné en force et en étendue, et les
fioritures infinies du chant italien brodaient de leurs gazouillements
d'oiseau les phrases sévères d'un récitatif pompeux.

En me retraçant ces détails, j'en suis à me demander s'ils sont réels,
ou bien si je les ai rêvés. Le frère de Sylvie était un peu gris ce soir-là.
Nous nous étions arrêtés quelques instants dans la maison du garde, —
où, ce qui m'a frappé beaucoup, il y avait un cygne éployé sur la porte,
puis au dedans de hautes armoires en noyer sculpté, une grande hor-
loge dans sa gaîne, et des trophées d'arcs et de flèches d'honneur au-
dessus d'une carte de tir rouge et verte. Un nain bizarre, coiffé d'un
bonnet chinois, tenant d'une main une bouteille et de l'autre une
bague, semblait inviter les tireurs à viser juste. Ce nain, je le crois bien,
était en tôle découpée. Mais l'apparition d'Adrienne est-elle aussi vraie
que ces détails et que l'existence incontestable de l'abbaye de Châalis?
Pourtant c'est bien le fils du garde qui nous avait introduits dans la salle
où avait lieu la représentation; nous étions près de la porte, derrière
une nombreuse compagnie assise et gravement émue. C'était le jour
de la Saint-Barthélemy, — singulièrement lié au souvenir des Médicis,
dont les armes accolées à celles de la maison d'Este décoraient ces
vieilles murailles . . . Ce souvenir est une obsession peut-être! —
Heureusement voici la voiture qui s'arrête sur la route du Plessis;
j'échappe au monde des rêveries, et je n'ai plus qu'un quart d'heure de
marche pour gagner Loisy par des routes bien peu frayées.

VIII. — Le bal de Loisy.

Je suis entré au bal de Loisy à cette heure mélancolique et douce encore où les lumières pâlissent et tremblent aux approches du jour. Les

to a sort of allegorical performance in which a few pupils from a nearby convent were to take part. It wasn't a reminiscence of the tragedies of Saint-Cyr;[17] rather, it went back to the first lyrical experiments imported into France in the time of the Valois. What I saw them act was like a mystery play of long ago. The costumes, long robes, differed only in their colors: azure, hyacinth, and saffron yellow. The action took place among the angels, amid the wreckage of the world, which had been destroyed. Each voice sang of one of the splendors of this extinguished globe, and the angel of death enumerated the reasons for its destruction. A spirit rose from the abyss, holding in its hands a flaming sword, and called upon the others to come and admire the glory of Christ, Who had triumphed over hell. That spirit was Adrienne, transfigured by her costume, as she had already been by her religious calling. The halo of gilded cardboard that enframed her angelic head seemed to us quite naturally to be a circle of light; her voice had taken on greater strength and range, and the endless fioriture of Italian bel canto embroidered the austere text of the pompous recitativo with their birdlike warbling.

As I retrace these details, I wonder to myself whether they're real or whether I have merely dreamed them. Sylvie's brother was a little drunk that evening. We had stopped for a few moments in the gamekeeper's lodge, where—and this made a great impression on me—there was a swan with outstretched wings on the door, and then, inside, tall armoires of carved walnut, a big grandfather's clock in its case, and trophies of bows and arrows of honor above a red and green target. A bizarre dwarf, with a Chinese cap on his head, holding a bottle in one hand and a ring in the other, seemed to be inviting the marksmen to aim accurately. I think this dwarf was cut out of sheet metal. But is the apparition of Adrienne as true as these details and as the indisputable existence of the abbey of Chaalis? And yet it was definitely the gamekeeper's son who had ushered us into the hall where the performance took place; we were near the door, in back of a large audience seated there and solemnly affected by the play. It was Saint Bartholomew's Day—peculiarly connected to the memory of the Medici, whose arms, conjoined with those of the house of Este, decorated those old walls . . .[18] That memory may be an obsession! Fortunately, my coach is now stopping on the road to Le Plessis; I escape from the world of daydreams, and I have only a fifteen-minute walk left to reach Loisy by very infrequently used paths.

VIII. The Dance at Loisy

I arrived at the Loisy dance at that still melancholy and sweet hour when the lights grow dim and tremble at the approach of day. The

tilleuls, assombris par en bas, prenaient à leurs cimes une teinte bleuâtre. La flûte champêtre ne luttait plus si vivement avec les trilles du rossignol. Tout le monde était pâle, et dans les groupes dégarnis j'eus peine à rencontrer des figures connues. Enfin j'aperçus la grande Lise, une amie de Sylvie. Elle m'embrassa. «Il y a longtemps qu'on ne t'a vu, Parisien! dit-elle. — Oh! oui, longtemps. — Et tu arrives à cette heure-ci? — Par la poste. — Et pas trop vite! — Je voulais voir Sylvie; est-elle encore au bal? — Elle ne sort qu'au matin; elle aime tant à danser.»

En un instant, j'étais à ses côtés. Sa figure était fatiguée; cependant son œil noir brillait toujours du sourire athénien d'autrefois. Un jeune homme se tenait près d'elle. Elle lui fit signe qu'elle renonçait à la contredanse suivante. Il se retira en saluant.

Le jour commençait à se faire. Nous sortîmes du bal, nous tenant par la main. Les fleurs de la chevelure de Sylvie se penchaient dans ses cheveux dénoués; le bouquet de son corsage s'effeuillait aussi sur les dentelles fripées, savant ouvrage de sa main. Je lui offris de l'accompagner chez elle. Il faisait grand jour, mais le temps était sombre. La Thève bruissait à notre gauche, laissant à ses coudes des remous d'eau stagnante où s'épanouissaient les nénuphars jaunes et blancs, où éclatait comme des pâquerettes la frêle broderie des étoiles d'eau. Les plaines étaient couvertes de javelles et de meules de foin, dont l'odeur me portait à la tête sans m'enivrer, comme faisait autrefois la fraîche senteur des bois et des halliers d'épines fleuries.

Nous n'eûmes pas l'idée de les traverser de nouveau. — Sylvie, lui dis-je, vous ne m'aimez plus! — Elle soupira. — Mon ami, me dit-elle, il faut se faire une raison; les choses ne vont pas comme nous voulons dans la vie. Vous m'avez parlé autrefois de *La Nouvelle Héloïse*, je l'ai lue, et j'ai frémi en tombant d'abord sur cette phrase: «Toute jeune fille qui lira ce livre est perdue.» Cependant j'ai passé outre, me fiant sur ma raison. Vous souvenez-vous du jour où nous avons revêtu les habits de noces de la tante? . . . Les gravures du livre présentaient aussi les amoureux sous de vieux costumes du temps passé, de sorte que pour moi vous étiez Saint-Preux, et je me retrouvais dans Julie. Ah! que n'êtes-vous revenu alors! Mais vous étiez, disait-on, en Italie. Vous en avez vu là de bien plus jolies que moi! — Aucune, Sylvie, qui ait votre regard et les traits purs de votre visage. Vous êtes une nymphe antique qui vous ignorez. D'ailleurs les bois de cette contrée sont aussi beaux que ceux de la campagne romaine. Il y a là-bas des masses de granit non moins sublimes, et une cascade qui tombe du

linden trees, dark at the bottom, were taking on a bluish tint at their tops. The rustic flute was no longer fighting so hard against the nightingale's trills. Everyone was pale, and in the thinned-out groups I had trouble finding faces I knew. Finally I caught sight of Big Lise, a friend of Sylvie's. She kissed me. "It's a long time since we've seen you, Parisian!" she said. "Oh, yes, a long time." "And you're arriving at this hour?" "By stagecoach." "And none too quickly!" "I wanted to see Sylvie; is she still at the dance?" "She won't leave until morning, she likes dancing so much."

In an instant I was at her side. Her face was tired, but her dark eyes were still shining with that Athenian smile of the past. A young man was standing near her. She made a sign to him that she would sit out the next quadrille. He bowed and withdrew.

Day was beginning to break. We left the dance floor, holding hands. The flowers in Sylvie's hair were drooping over her tresses, which were coming undone; the bouquet on her bosom was also shedding its petals onto the crumpled laces, her own clever handiwork. I offered to escort her home. It was broad daylight, but the weather was overcast. The Thève was noisily flowing to the left of us; where it made bends, it left behind swirls of stagnant water in which yellow and white water lilies were opening wide, and in which the delicate embroidery of the water starworts was shining like daisies. The plains were covered with loose sheaves and haystacks, whose fragrance was going to my head without intoxicating me, just as the fresh smell of the woods and thickets of blossoming thorn had done in the past.

We didn't consider crossing them again. "Sylvie," I said, "you don't love me anymore!" She sighed. "My friend," she said, "you must resign yourself; things in life don't go the way we'd like them to. Once you told me about *La nouvelle Héloïse*; I read it, and I got a shock when I came upon this sentence right at the beginning: 'Any girl who reads this book is ruined.' And yet I kept on going, trusting in my powers of reason. Do you remember the day when we put on the clothes from my aunt's wedding? . . . The engravings in the book also showed the lovers in old costumes of long ago, so that, for me, you were Saint-Preux and I imagined myself as Julie. Oh, why didn't you come back then? But I was told you were in Italy. You saw much prettier girls than me there!" "Not one, Sylvie, who has your eyes and the fine features of your face. You are an ancient nymph, and you don't even know it. Besides, the woods in this region are just as beautiful as those in the Roman campagna. There are masses of granite over yonder that are no less sublime, and a cascade that falls from the top of the cliffs

haut des rochers comme celle de Terni. Je n'ai rien vu là-bas que je puisse regretter ici. — Et à Paris? dit-elle. — A Paris . . . Je secouai la tête sans répondre.

Tout à coup je pensai à l'image vaine qui m'avait égaré si longtemps.

— Sylvie, dis-je, arrêtons-nous ici, le voulez-vous?

Je me jetai à ses pieds; je confessai en pleurant à chaudes larmes mes irrésolutions, mes caprices; j'évoquai le spectre funeste qui traversait ma vie.

— Sauvez-moi! ajoutai-je, je reviens à vous pour toujours.

Elle tourna vers moi ses regards attendris . . .

En ce moment, notre entretien fut interrompu par de violents éclats de rire. C'était le frère de Sylvie qui nous rejoignait avec cette bonne gaieté rustique, suite obligée d'une nuit de fête, que des rafraîchissements nombreux avaient développée outre mesure. Il appelait le galant du bal, perdu au loin dans les buissons d'épines et qui ne tarda pas à nous rejoindre. Ce garçon n'était guère plus solide sur ses pieds que son compagnon, il paraissait plus embarrassé encore de la présence d'un Parisien que de celle de Sylvie. Sa figure candide, sa déférence mêlée d'embarras, m'empêchaient de lui en vouloir d'avoir été le danseur pour lequel on était resté si tard à la fête. Je le jugeais peu dangereux.

— Il faut rentrer à la maison, dit Sylvie à son frère. A tantôt! me dit-elle en me tendant la joue.

L'amoureux ne s'offensa pas.

IX. — Ermenonville.

Je n'avais nulle envie de dormir. J'allai à Montagny pour revoir la maison de mon oncle. Une grande tristesse me gagna dès que j'en entrevis la façade jaune et les contrevents verts. Tout semblait dans le même état qu'autrefois; seulement il fallut aller chez le fermier pour avoir la clef de la porte. Une fois les volets ouverts, je revis avec attendrissement les vieux meubles conservés dans le même état et qu'on frottait de temps en temps, la haute armoire de noyer, deux tableaux flamands qu'on disait l'ouvrage d'un ancien peintre, notre aïeul; de grandes estampes d'après Boucher, et toute une série encadrée de gravures de l'*Emile* et de *La Nouvelle Héloïse*, par Moreau; sur la table, un chien empaillé que j'avais connu vivant, ancien compagnon de mes courses dans les bois, le dernier carlin peut-être, car il appartenait à cette race perdue.

like the one at Terni. I saw nothing there that I miss here." "And in Paris?" she said. "In Paris . . ."

I shook my head without answering.

Suddenly I thought of the futile image that had led me astray for so long.

"Sylvie," I said, "let's stop here, all right?"

I threw myself at her feet; shedding hot tears, I confessed my lack of resolve, my caprices; I mentioned the deadly specter that stalked through my life.

"Save me!" I added. "I'm coming back to you for good."

She turned her compassionate eyes toward me . . .

At that moment, our conversation was interrupted by violent bursts of laughter. It was Sylvie's brother, who was coming up to us with that wholesome rustic gaiety, the indispensable result of a night of merry-making, but now increased beyond measure by numerous potations. He was calling to Sylvie's partner at the dance, who was lost far off in the thorn bushes, but who overtook us before long. That lad was no steadier on his feet than his companion; he seemed even more embarrassed by the presence of a Parisian than by Sylvie's. His candid face, his deference mingled with confusion, prevented me from getting angry with him for being the partner in whose honor she had stayed so late at the party. I didn't consider him much of a threat.

"We must go home," Sylvie said to her brother. "See you soon!" she said to me, offering me her cheek to kiss.

Her suitor didn't mind.

IX. Ermenonville

I didn't feel at all like sleeping. I went to Montagny to see my uncle's house again. A great sadness came over me as soon as I glimpsed its yellow facade and green shutters. Everything seemed to be in the same condition as before; only, I had to go to the tenant farmer to get the key to the door. Once the shutters were open, I saw once more, with emotion, the old furniture preserved in the same condition and polished from time to time, the tall walnut armoire, two Flemish pictures that were said to be the work of an old painter, an ancestor of ours; large prints after paintings by Boucher, and an entire framed series of engravings by Moreau of scenes from *Emile* and *La nouvelle Héloïse*; on the table, a stuffed dog that I had known when it was alive, an old companion of my walks in the woods, perhaps the last *carlin* pug, for it belonged to that extinct breed.

— Quant au perroquet, me dit le fermier, il vit toujours; je l'ai retiré chez moi.

Le jardin présentait un magnifique tableau de végétation sauvage.
J'y reconnus, dans un angle, un jardin d'enfant que j'avais tracé jadis.
J'entrai tout frémissant dans le cabinet, où se voyait encore la petite
bibliothèque pleine de livres choisis, vieux amis de celui qui n'était
plus, et sur le bureau quelques débris antiques trouvés dans son
jardin, des vases, des médailles romaines, collection locale qui le
rendait heureux.

— Allons voir le perroquet, dis-je au fermier. — Le perroquet de-
mandait à déjeuner comme en ses plus beaux jours, et me regarda de
cet œil rond, bordé d'une peau chargée de rides, qui fait penser au regard expérimenté des vieillards.

Plein des idées tristes qu'amenait ce retour tardif en des lieux si
aimés, je sentis le besoin de revoir Sylvie, seule figure vivante et jeune
encore qui me rattachât à ce pays. Je repris la route de Loisy. C'était
au milieu du jour; tout le monde dormait fatigué de la fête. Il me vint
l'idée de me distraire par une promenade à Ermenonville, distant
d'une lieue par le chemin de la forêt. C'était par un beau temps d'été.
Je pris plaisir d'abord à la fraîcheur de cette route qui semble l'allée
d'un parc. Les grands chênes d'un vert uniforme n'étaient variés que
par les troncs blancs des bouleaux au feuillage frissonnant. Les
oiseaux se taisaient, et j'entendais seulement le bruit que fait le pivert
en frappant les arbres pour y creuser son nid. Un instant, je risquai de
me perdre, car les poteaux dont les palettes annoncent diverses routes
n'offrent plus, par endroits, que des caractères effacés. Enfin, laissant
le *Désert* à gauche, j'arrivai au rond-point de la danse, où subsiste encore le banc des vieillards. Tous les souvenirs de l'antiquité
philosophique, ressuscités par l'ancien possesseur du domaine, me
revenaient en foule devant cette réalisation pittoresque de
l'*Anacharsis* et de l'*Emile*.

Lorsque je vis briller les eaux du lac à travers les branches des
saules et des coudriers, je reconnus tout à fait un lieu où mon oncle,
dans ses promenades, m'avait conduit bien des fois: c'est le *Temple de
la philosophie*, que son fondateur n'a pas eu le bonheur de terminer.
Il a la forme du temple de la sibylle Tiburtine, et, debout encore, sous
l'abri d'un bouquet de pins, il étale tous ces grands noms de la pensée
qui commencent par Montaigne et Descartes, et qui s'arrêtent à
Rousseau. Cet édifice inachevé n'est déjà plus qu'une ruine, le lierre
le festonne avec grâce, la ronce envahit les marches disjointes. Là,
tout enfant, j'ai vu des fêtes où les jeunes filles vêtues de blanc

"As for the parrot," the tenant farmer said, "it's still living; I've taken it to my house."

The garden offered a magnificent picture of wild vegetation. In one corner I recognized a child's garden I had once laid out. Filled with emotion, I entered the study, where there could still be seen the small bookcase full of selected books, the old friends of the man who was no more, and on the desk some remains of antiquity found in his garden, vases, Roman medals, a local collection that used to make him happy.

"Let's go see the parrot," I said to the tenant farmer. The parrot asked for food just as in his palmiest days, and looked at me with those round eyes, encircled with heavily wrinkled skin, which make me think of the knowing eyes of old men.

Full of the melancholy thoughts that were evoked by this belated return to places I had loved so well, I felt the need to see Sylvie again, the only living and still young figure that tied me to that region. Once more I took the road to Loisy. It was in the middle of the day; everyone was asleep, tired out by the party. I got the idea of amusing myself with a walk to Ermenonville, a league away by the forest road. It was beautiful summer weather. At first I was pleased by the freshness of this path, which resembles the tree-lined avenue of a manorial park. The uniform green of the tall oaks was only interrupted by the white trunks of the birches with their trembling leaves. The birds were silent, and I heard only the sound made by the woodpecker striking the trees to hollow out its nest. For a moment I was in danger of getting lost, because in spots the posts carrying signs indicating the various directions have only obliterated lettering. Finally, leaving the Desert to my left, I arrived at the dancing intersection, where the old men's bench still remains. All the reminiscences of ancient philosophy, revived by the former owner of the domain, came rushing back to me as I stood before that picturesque embodiment of *Anacharsis* and *Emile*.[19]

When I saw the waters of the lake shining through the branches of the willows and the hazels, I completely recognized a spot where my uncle had taken me many times on his walks: it was the Temple of Philosophy, which its founder was not lucky enough to finish. It has the form of the temple of the Sibyl in Tivoli, and, still standing, in the shelter of a cluster of pines, it lists all the great names in the realm of thought beginning with Montaigne and Descartes and concluding with Rousseau. This unfinished building is by now no more than a ruin; ivy festoons it gracefully, brambles invade its disjointed steps. There, as a child, I saw celebrations in which girls dressed in white

venaient recevoir des prix d'étude et de sagesse. Où sont les buissons
de roses qui entouraient la colline? L'églantier et le framboisier en
cachent les derniers plants, qui retournent à l'état sauvage. — Quant
aux lauriers, les a-t-on coupés, comme le dit la chanson des jeunes
filles qui ne veulent plus aller au bois? Non, ces arbustes de la douce
Italie ont péri sous notre ciel brumeux. Heureusement le troëne de
Virgile fleurit encore, comme pour apuyer la parole du maître inscrite
au-dessus de la porte: *Rerum cognoscere causas!* — Oui, ce temple
tombe comme tant d'autres, les hommes oublieux ou fatigués se dé-
tourneront de ses abords, la nature indifférente reprendra le terrain
que l'art lui disputait; mais la soif de connaître restera éternelle, mo-
bile de toute force et de toute activité!

Voici les peupliers de l'île, et la tombe de Rousseau, vide de ses
cendres. O sage! tu nous avais donné le lait des forts, et nous étions
trop faibles pour qu'il pût nous profiter. Nous avons oublié tes leçons
que savaient nos pères, et nous avons perdu le sens de ta parole,
dernier écho des sagesses antiques. Pourtant ne désespérons pas, et
comme tu fis à ton suprême instant, tournons nous yeux vers le soleil!

J'ai revu le château, les eaux paisibles qui le bordent, la cascade qui
gémit dans les roches, et cette chaussée réunissant les deux parties du
village, dont quatre colombiers marquent les angles, la pelouse qui
s'étend au-delà comme une savane, dominée par des coteaux om-
breux; la tour de Gabrielle se reflète de loin sur les eaux d'un lac fac-
tice étoilé de fleurs éphémères; l'écume bouillonne, l'insecte bruit . . .
Il faut échapper à l'air perfide qui s'exhale en gagnant les grès
poudreux du désert et les landes où la bruyère rose relève le vert des
fougères. Que tout cela est solitaire et triste! Le regard enchanté de
Sylvie, ses courses folles, ses cris joyeux, donnaient autrefois tant de
charme aux lieux que je viens de parcourir! C'était encore une enfant
sauvage, ses pieds étaient nus, sa peau hâlée, malgré son chapeau de
paille, dont le large ruban flottait pêle-mêle avec ses tresses de
cheveux noirs. Nous allions boire du lait à la ferme suisse, et l'on me
disait: «Qu'elle est jolie, ton amoureuse, petit Parisien!» Oh! ce n'est
pas alors qu'un paysan aurait dansé avec elle! Elle ne dansait qu'avec
moi, une fois par an, à la fête de l'arc.

X. — Le grand frisé.

J'ai repris le chemin de Loisy; tout le monde était réveillé. Sylvie
avait une toilette de demoiselle, presque dans le goût de la ville. Elle
me fit monter à sa chambre avec toute l'ingénuité d'autrefois. Son œil

received prizes for schoolwork and good behavior. Where are the rose bushes that surrounded the hill? Dog roses and raspberry bushes conceal the last ones, which are reverting to the wild state. As for the laurels, have they been cut down, as said in the song about the girls who no longer want to go to the woods?[20] No, those shrubs from gentle Italy have perished in our misty climate. Fortunately, Vergil's privet still flourishes, as if to lend support to the words of the master inscribed above the doorway: *Rerum cognoscere causas!*[21] Yes, this temple is falling like so many others; men, forgetful or weary, will turn away from its vicinity; indifferent nature will resume sway over the plot of ground that art had laid claim to; but the thirst for knowledge will remain eternal, the moving force of all strength and all activity!

Here are the poplars of the island and the tomb of Rousseau, no longer containing his ashes.[22] O sage, you had given us the milk of the strong, and we were too weak to make use of it. We have forgotten your lessons, which our fathers knew, and we have lost the meaning of your words, the last echo of ancient wisdom. And yet, let us not despair, and, as you did in your final moments, let us turn our eyes toward the sun!

I saw once again the château, the peaceful waters that border it, the cascade that moans among the rocks, and that roadway joining together the two parts of the village, whose corners are marked by four dovecotes; the lawn that extends beyond it like a savanna, dominated by shady slopes; Gabrielle's[23] tower is reflected far off in the waters of an artificial lake studded with short-lived flowers; the foam froths, the insects buzz . . . You must escape from the treacherous air that it gives off by reaching the powdery sandstone of the desert and the sandy moors, where the pink of the heather augments the green of the ferns. How solitary and sad it all is! Sylvie's magical eyes, her madcap dashes, her joyful cries, once lent so much charm to the places I have just been walking through! She was still a wild child, her feet were bare, her skin tanned in spite of her straw hat, whose wide floating ribbon would get entangled in the tresses of her black hair. We would go to drink milk at the Swiss farm, and people would say to me: "How pretty your sweetheart is, little Parisian!" Oh, a peasant wouldn't have danced with her *then!* She would dance only with me, once a year, at the archery festival.

X. Big Curly

I took the road back to Loisy; everyone was now awake. Sylvie was dressed like a well-born young lady, almost in Parisian style. She asked me up to her room with all the candor of the past. Her eyes still

étincelait toujours dans un sourire plein de charme, mais l'arc prononcé de ses sourcils lui donnait par instants un air sérieux. La chambre était décorée avec simplicité, pourtant les meubles étaient modernes, une glace à bordure dorée avait remplacé l'antique trumeau, où se voyait un berger d'idylle offrant un nid à une bergère bleue et rose. Le lit à colonnes chastement drapé de vieille perse à ramage était remplacé par une couchette de noyer garnie du rideau à flèche; à la fenêtre, dans la cage où jadis étaient les fauvettes, il y avait des canaris. J'étais pressé de sortir de cette chambre où je ne trouvais rien du passé. — Vous ne travaillerez point à votre dentelle aujourd'hui? . . . dis-je à Sylvie. — Oh! je ne fais plus de dentelle, on n'en demande plus dans le pays; même à Chantilly, la fabrique est fermée. — Que faites-vous donc? — Elle alla chercher dans un coin de la chambre un instrument en fer qui ressemblait à une longue pince. — Qu'est-ce que c'est que cela? — C'est ce qu'on appelle la mécanique; c'est pour maintenir la peau des gants afin de les coudre. — Ah! vous êtes gantière, Sylvie? — Oui, nous travaillons ici pour Dammartin, cela donne beaucoup dans ce moment; mais je ne fais rien aujourd'hui; allons où vous voudrez. Je tournais les yeux vers la route d'Othys: elle secoua la tête; je compris que la vieille tante n'existait plus. Sylvie appela un petit garçon et lui fit seller un âne. — Je suis encore fatiguée d'hier, dit-elle, mais la promenade me fera du bien; allons à Châalis.» Et nous voilà traversant le forêt, suivis du petit garçon armé d'une branche. Bientôt Sylvie voulut s'arrêter, et je l'embrassai en l'engageant à s'asseoir. La conversation entre nous ne pouvait plus être bien intime. Il fallut lui raconter ma vie à Paris, mes voyages . . . — Comment peut-on aller si loin? dit-elle. — Je m'en étonne en vous revoyant. — Oh! cela se dit! — Et convenez que vous étiez moins jolie autrefois. — Je n'en sais rien. — Vous souvenez-vous du temps où nous étions enfants et vous la plus grande? — Et vous le plus sage! — Oh! Sylvie! — On nous mettait sur l'âne chacun dans un panier. — Et nous ne nous disions pas *vous* . . . Te rappelles-tu que tu m'apprenais à pêcher des écrevisses sous les ponts de la Thève et de la Nonette? — Et toi, te souviens-tu de ton frère de lait qui t'a un jour retiré *de l'ieau*. — Le *grand frisé!* c'est lui qui m'avait dit qu'on pouvait la passer . . . *l'ieau!*

Je me hâtai de changer la conversation. Ce souvenir m'avait vivement rappelé l'époque où je venais dans le pays, vêtu d'un petit habit à l'anglaise qui faisait rire les paysans. Sylvie seule me trouvait bien mis; mais je n'osais lui rappeler cette opinion d'un temps si ancien. Je ne sais pourquoi ma pensée se porta sur les habits de noces que nous

sparkled with a smile full of charm, but the pronounced arch of her eyebrows gave her a serious air at moments. Her room was decorated simply, but the furniture was recent; a mirror in a gilded frame had replaced the old pier glass, which had depicted an idyllic shepherd offering a nest to a blue-and-pink shepherdess. The four-poster bed, with its chaste curtains of old floral chintz, was replaced by a small walnut plank bed with a curtain on a rod; at the window, in the cage where the warblers used to be, there were canaries. I was impatient to leave that room, in which I found nothing from the past. "Aren't you going to work on your lace today?" I asked Sylvie. "Oh, I don't make lace anymore, there's no more local demand for it; even in Chantilly, the workshop is closed down." "What do you do, then?" She went over to a corner of the room to get an iron instrument that looked like a long pair of pliers. "What's that?" "They just call it the machine; it's to hold the leather of gloves steady so you can sew them." "Oh, you're a glovemaker, Sylvie?" "Yes, here we work for a firm in Dammartin; it's very profitable just now; but I won't do any work today; we can go wherever you like." I turned my eyes toward the road to Othys: she shook her head; I understood that her old aunt was no longer living. Sylvie called over a little boy and asked him to saddle a donkey. "I'm still tired from yesterday," she said, "but the outing will do me good; let's go to Chaalis." And there we were, crossing the forest, followed by the little boy, who was wielding a branch. Soon Sylvie wanted to stop, and I kissed her, urging her to sit down. Conversation between us could no longer be very intimate. I had to tell her about my life in Paris, my travels . . . "How can anyone travel so far?" she said. "Seeing you again, I'm surprised at it myself!" "Oh, you're just saying that!" "But admit that, long ago, you weren't as pretty." "I don't know about that." "Do you remember when we were children and you were the taller one?" "And you were the better-behaved one!" "Oh, Sylvie!" "They used to put us on a donkey, each of us in one side basket." "And we didn't address each other with *vous* . . . Do you remember teaching me to fish for crayfish under the bridges of the Thève and the Nonette?" "And you, do you remember the son of your wet nurse who pulled you out of the water[24] one day?" "Big Curly! He's the one who had told me it was possible to wade across that water!"

I hurriedly changed the subject. That memory had vividly brought to mind the period during which I used to come to the region dressed in a little English-style suit that made the peasants laugh. Only Sylvie thought I was well dressed; but I didn't dare remind her about that opinion of hers so long ago. For some reason or other, my thoughts

avions revêtus chez la vieille tante à Othys. Je demandai ce qu'ils étaient devenus. — Ah! la bonne tante, dit Sylvie, elle m'avait prêté sa robe pour aller danser au carnaval à Dammartin, il y a de cela deux ans. L'année d'après, elle est morte, la pauvre tante!

Elle soupirait et pleurait, si bien que je ne pus lui demander par quelle circonstance elle était allée à un bal masqué; mais, grâce à ses talents d'ouvrière, je comprenais assez que Sylvie n'était plus une paysanne. Ses parents seuls étaient restés dans leur condition, et elle vivait au milieu d'eux comme une fée industrieuse, répandant l'abondance autour d'elle.

XI. — Retour.

La vue se découvrait au sortir du bois. Nous étions arrivés au bord des étangs de Châalis. Les galeries du cloître, la chapelle aux ogives élancées, la tour féodale et le petit château qui abrita les amours de Henri IV et de Gabrielle se teignaient des rougeurs du soir sur le vert sombre de la forêt.

— C'est un paysage de Walter Scott, n'est-ce pas? disait Sylvie. — Et qui vous a parlé de Walter Scott? lui dis-je. Vous avez donc bien lu depuis trois ans! . . . Moi, je tâche d'oublier les livres, et ce qui me charme, c'est de revoir avec vous cette vieille abbaye, où, tout petits enfants, nous nous cachions dans les ruines. Vous souvenez-vous, Sylvie, de la peur que vous aviez quand le gardien nous racontait l'histoire des moines rouges? — Oh! ne m'en parlez pas. — Alors chantez-moi la chanson de la belle fille enlevée au jardin de son père, sous le rosier blanc. — On ne chante plus cela. — Seriez-vous devenue musicienne? — Un peu. — Sylvie, Sylvie, je suis sûr que vous chantez des airs d'opéra! — Pourquoi vous plaindre? — Parce que j'aimais les vieux airs, et que vous ne saurez plus les chanter.

Sylvie modula quelques sons d'un grand air d'opéra moderne . . . Elle *phrasait!*

Nous avions tourné les étangs voisins. Voici la verte pelouse, entourée de tilleuls et d'ormeaux, où nous avons dansé souvent! J'eus l'amour-propre de définir les vieux murs carlovingiens et déchiffrer les armoiries de la maison d'Este. — Et vous! comme vous avez lu plus que moi! dit Sylvie. Vous êtes donc un savant?

J'étais piqué de son ton de reproche. J'avais jusque-là cherché l'endroit convenable pour renouveler le moment d'expansion du matin; mais que lui dire avec l'accompagnement d'un âne et d'un petit garçon très éveillé, qui prenait plaisir à se rapprocher toujours pour

went back to the wedding clothes we had put on at her old aunt's house in Othys. I asked her what had become of them. "Oh, my dear aunt," Sylvie said; "she had lent me her gown to go dancing in Dammartin at carnival time two years ago. The year after that, she died, poor aunt!"

She was sighing and weeping, so that I was unable to ask her what circumstances had led her to attend a masked ball; but I understood well enough that, thanks to her talents as an artisan, Sylvie was no longer a peasant girl. Only her relatives had remained in their walk in life, and she was living in their midst like an industrious fairy, spreading abundance all around her.

XI. Return

As we emerged from the woods, we had a clearer view. We had arrived at the banks of the Chaalis ponds. The galleries of the cloister, the chapel with its slender pointed arches, the feudal tower, and the small château that sheltered the romance of Henri IV and Gabrielle were tinged with the red glow of evening against the dark green of the forest.

"It's a landscape out of Walter Scott, isn't it?" said Sylvie. "And who told you about Walter Scott?" I asked; "so you've read quite a lot in the last three years! As for me, I'm trying to forget books, and what fascinates me is revisiting this old abbey with you; when we were very small children, we used to hide in its ruins. Sylvie, do you remember how frightened you were when the caretaker told us the story of the red monks?" "Oh, don't talk about it!" "Then, sing me the song about the beautiful girl abducted from her father's garden, beneath the white rosebush." "That's not being sung anymore." "Don't tell me you go in for more formal music now!" "A little." "Sylvie, Sylvie, I'm sure that you sing operatic arias!" "Why complain about it?" "Because I used to love the old simple songs, and you won't be able to sing them anymore."

Sylvie sang a short passage from a recent operatic aria . . . She was consciously phrasing!

We had journeyed around the nearer ponds. Here is the green lawn, surrounded by linden trees and young elms, on which we danced so often! I was conceited enough to identify the old Carolingian walls and decipher the coat-of-arms of the house of Este. "And you! You've read so much more than I have!" Sylvie said; "are you a scholar?"

I was hurt by her reproachful tone. Up to then I had been looking for a suitable spot to revive that morning's moment of expansiveness; but what could I say to her, having as escorts a donkey and a very wide-awake little boy who took pleasure in constantly coming near us

entendre parler un Parisien? Alors j'eus le malheur de raconter l'apparition de Châalis, restée dans mes souvenirs. Je menai Sylvie dans la salle même du château où j'avais entendu chanter Adrienne. — Oh! que je vous entende! lui dis-je; que votre voix chérie résonne sous ces voûtes et en chasse l'esprit qui me tourmente, fût-il divin ou bien fatal! — Elle répéta les paroles et le chant après moi:

> Anges, descendez promptement
> Au fond du purgatoire! . . .

— C'est bien triste! me dit-elle.

— C'est sublime . . . Je crois que c'est du Porpora, avec des vers traduits au seizième siècle.

— Je ne sais pas, répondit Sylvie.

Nous sommes revenus par la vallée, en suivant le chemin de Charlepont, que les paysans, peu étymologistes de leur nature, s'obstinent à appeler *Châllepont*. Sylvie, fatiguée de l'âne, s'appuyait sur mon bras. La route était déserte; j'essayai de parler des choses que j'avais dans le cœur, mais, je ne sais pourquoi, je ne trouvais que des expressions vulgaires, ou bien tout à coup quelque phrase pompeuse de roman, — que Sylvie pouvait avoir lue. Je m'arrêtais alors avec un goût tout classique, et elle s'étonnait parfois de ces effusions interrompues. Arrivés aux murs de Saint-S . . . , il fallait prendre garde à notre marche. On traverse des prairies humides où serpentent les ruisseaux. — Qu'est devenue la religieuse? dis-je tout à coup.

— Ah! vous êtes terrible avec votre religieuse . . . Eh bien! . . . eh bien! cela a mal tourné.

Sylvie ne voulut pas m'en dire un mot de plus.

Les femmes sentent-elles vraiment que telle ou telle parole passe sur les lèvres sans sortir du cœur? On ne le croirait pas, à les voir si facilement abusées, à se rendre compte des choix qu'elles font le plus souvent: il y a des hommes qui jouent si bien la comédie de l'amour! Je n'ai jamais pu m'y faire, quoique sachant que certaines acceptent sciemment d'être trompées. D'ailleurs un amour qui remonte à l'enfance est quelque chose de sacré . . . Sylvie, que j'avais vue grandir, était pour moi comme une sœur. Je ne pouvais tenter une séduction . . . Une tout autre idée vint traverser mon esprit. — A cette heure-ci, me dis-je, je serais au théâtre . . . Qu'est-ce qu'Aurélie (c'était le nom de l'actrice) doit donc jouer ce soir? Evidemment le rôle de la princesse dans le drame nouveau. Oh! le troisième acte, qu'elle y est touchante! . . . Et dans la scène d'amour du second! avec ce jeune premier tout ridé . . .

to hear how a Parisian talks? Then I was unlucky enough to tell about the apparition at Chaalis, which had stayed in my mind. I led Sylvie into the very hall of the château where I had heard Adrienne sing. "Oh, let me hear you!" I said; "let your beloved voice ring out beneath these vaults and drive out the spirit that torments me, whether it's divine or deadly!" She repeated the words and music after me:

> "Angels, descend at once
> To the depths of Purgatory!"

"It's very sad," she said.

"It's sublime . . . I think it's by Porpora,[25] with verses translated in the sixteenth century."

"I don't know," Sylvie replied.

We returned by way of the valley, following the road to Charlepont, which the peasants, who are no etymologists by nature, insist on calling Châllepont. Sylvie, tired of riding on the donkey, was leaning on my arm. The road was deserted; I tried to talk about the things that were on my mind, but, somehow or other, I only came up with trivial expressions, or else, all at once, some pompous phrase from a novel—which Sylvie might have read. Then I would stop, in very classical style, and she would be surprised at times by those interrupted effusions. When we reached the walls of Saint-S—, we had to be careful where we were walking. There, one has to cross damp stretches of grass through which brooks meander. "What has become of the nun?" I suddenly asked.

"Oh, you're awful with that nun of yours! . . . Well, . . . well, she didn't end well."

Sylvie refused to say another word about it.

Do women really sense that certain words pass a man's lips without issuing from his heart? You wouldn't think so, seeing them so easily deceived, realizing what choices they make most of the time: there are men who act the part of a lover so skillfully! I've never been able to get used to that, even though I know that some women knowingly agree to be deceived. Besides, a love that goes back to childhood is a sacred thing . . . Sylvie, whom I had seen grow up, was like a sister to me. I couldn't attempt a seduction . . . An altogether different idea flashed across my mind. "At this hour," I said to myself, "I'd normally be in the theater . . . What role is Aurélie (that was the name of the actress) to play tonight? Obviously, the role of the princess in the new drama. Oh, the third act, how touching she is in it! . . . And in the love scene in the second—with that leading man who's all wrinkled . . ."

— Vous êtes dans vos réflexions? dit Sylvie, et elle se mit à chanter:

> A Dammartin l'y a trois belles filles:
> L'y en a z'une plus belle que le jour . . .

— Ah! méchante! m'écriai-je, vous voyez bien que vous en savez encore des vieilles chansons.

— Si vous veniez plus souvent ici, j'en retrouverais, dit-elle, mais il faut songer au solide. Vous avez vos affaires de Paris, j'ai mon travail; ne rentrons pas trop tard: il faut que demain je sois levée avec le soleil.

XII.— Le père Dodu.

J'allais répondre, j'allais tomber à ses pieds, j'allais offrir la maison de mon oncle, qu'il m'était possible encore de racheter, car nous étions plusieurs héritiers, et cette petite propriété était restée indivise; mais en ce moment nous arrivions à Loisy. On nous attendait pour souper. La soupe à l'oignon répandait au loin son parfum patriarcal. Il y avait des voisins invités pour ce lendemain de fête. Je reconnus tout de suite un vieux bûcheron, le père Dodu, qui racontait jadis aux veillées des histoires si comiques ou si terribles. Tour à tour berger, messager, garde-chasse, pêcheur, braconnier même, le père Dodu fabriquait à ses moments perdus des coucous et des tourne-broches. Pendant longtemps il s'était consacré à promener les Anglais dans Ermenonville, en les conduisant aux lieux de méditation de Rousseau et en leur racontant ses derniers moments. C'était lui qui avait été le petit garçon que le philosophe employait à classer ses herbes, et à qui il donna l'ordre de cueillir les ciguës dont il exprima le suc dans sa tasse de café au lait. L'aubergiste de *la Croix d'Or* lui contestait ce détail; de là des haines prolongées. On avait longtemps reproché au père Dodu la possession de quelques secrets bien innocents, comme de guérir les vaches avec un verset dit à rebours et le signe de croix figuré du pied gauche, mais il avait de bonne heure renoncé à ces superstitions, — grâce au souvenir, disait-il, des conversations de Jean-Jacques.

— Te voilà! petit Parisien, me dit le père Dodu. Tu viens pour débaucher nos filles? — Moi, père Dodu? — Tu les emmènes dans les bois pendant que le loup n'y est pas? — Père Dodu, c'est vous qui êtes le loup. — Je l'ai été tant que j'ai trouvé des brebis; à présent je ne rencontre plus que des chèvres, et qu'elles savent bien se défendre! Mais vous autres, vous êtes des malins à Paris. Jean-Jacques avait bien raison

"Lost in thought?" said Sylvie, and she started to sing:

"In Dammartin there are three beautiful girls:
One of them is more beautiful than the day . . ."

"Oh, you mean thing!" I exclaimed. "See! You still know some old songs."

"If you came here more often, I'd remember them," she said, "but I've got to think about the serious things in life. You have your business in Paris, I have my work; let's not get back too late: I have to be up with the sun tomorrow."

XII. Old Dodu

I was going to reply, I was going to fall at her feet, I was going to offer her my uncle's house, which it was still possible for me to buy back, because I was one of several heirs, and that small property had remained undivided; but at that moment we were reaching Loisy. We were awaited at supper. The onion soup was diffusing its patriarchal aroma at a distance. There were neighbors invited for the occasion, the day after a festival. I immediately recognized an old woodcutter, old Dodu,[26] who used to tell such funny or frightening stories during social evenings. In turns a shepherd, messenger, gamekeeper, fisherman, even a poacher, in his spare time old Dodu used to build cuckoo clocks and roasting jacks. For a long time he had worked as a guide for English tourists in Ermenonville, taking them to the places where Rousseau had meditated, and describing his last moments. He had been the little boy whom the philosopher employed to sort his herb collection, and whom he ordered to gather the hemlock whose juice he had squeezed into his cup of café au lait. The innkeeper at the Golden Cross denied that detail, and this gave rise to a long-lasting enmity. For a long time old Dodu had been accused of possessing some very innocent secrets, such as curing cows with a Bible verse recited backwards while his left foot made the sign of the Cross, but he had given up those superstitions early on— thanks, he would say, to his conversations with Jean-Jacques.

"There you are, little Parisian!" said old Dodu. "Have you come here to ruin our girls?" "I, old Dodu?" "You take them into the woods while the wolf is away." "Old Dodu, *you're* the wolf." "I was as long as I found sheep; now I only come across goats, and how well they can defend themselves! But you Parisians, you're sharp customers. Jean-Jacques was very right when he said: 'Man is corrupted in the

de dire: «L'homme se corrompt dans l'air empoisonné des villes.» —
Père Dodu, vous savez trop bien que l'homme se corrompt partout.
Le père Dodu se mit à entonner un air à boire; on voulut en vain
l'arrêter à un certain couplet scabreux que tout le monde savait par
cœur. Sylvie ne voulut pas chanter, malgré nos prières, disant qu'on ne
chantait plus à table. J'avais remarqué déjà que l'amoureux de la veille
était assis à sa gauche. Il y avait je ne sais quoi dans sa figure ronde,
dans ses cheveux ébouriffés, qui ne m'était pas inconnu. Il se leva et
vint derrière ma chaise en disant: «Tu ne me reconnais donc pas,
Parisien?» Une bonne femme, qui venait de rentrer au dessert après
nous avoir servis, me dit à l'oreille: «Vous ne reconnaissez pas votre
frère de lait?» Sans cet avertissement, j'allais être ridicule. «Ah! c'est
toi, *grand frisé!* dis-je, c'est toi, le même qui m'a retiré de *l'ieau!*»
Sylvie riait aux éclats de cette reconnaissance. «Sans compter, disait ce
garçon en m'embrassant, que tu avais une belle montre en argent, et
qu'en revenant tu étais bien plus inquiet de ta montre que de toi-
même, parce qu'elle ne marchait plus; tu disais: "La *bête* est *nayée*, ça
ne fait plus tic-tac; qu'est-ce que mon oncle va dire? . . ."
— Une bête dans une montre! dit le père Dodu, voilà ce qu'on leur
fait croire à Paris, aux enfants!»
Sylvie avait sommeil, je jugeai que j'étais perdu dans son esprit. Elle
remonta à sa chambre, et pendant que je l'embrassais, elle dit: «A demain, venez nous voir!»
Le père Dodu était resté à table avec Sylvain et mon frère de lait;
nous causâmes longtemps autour d'un flacon de *ratafiat* de Louvres.
«Les hommes sont égaux, dit le père Dodu entre deux couplets, je
bois avec un pâtissier comme je ferais avec un prince. — Où est le
pâtissier? dis-je. — Regarde à côté de toi! un jeune homme qui a l'ambition de s'établir.»
Mon frère de lait parut embarrassé. J'avais tout compris. — C'est
une fatalité qui m'était réservée d'avoir un frère de lait dans un pays
illustré par Rousseau, — qui voulait supprimer les nourrices! — Le
père Dodu m'apprit qu'il était fort question du mariage de Sylvie avec
le *grand frisé,* qui voulait aller former un établissement de pâtisserie
à Dammartin. Je n'en demandai pas plus. La voiture de Nanteuil-le-
Haudoin me ramena le lendemain à Paris.

XIII. — Aurélie.

A Paris! — La voiture met cinq heures. Je n'étais pressé que d'arriver
pour le soir. Vers huit heures, j'étais assis dans ma stalle accoutumée;

poisoned air of cities.'" "Old Dodu, you know all too well that man is corrupted everywhere."

Old Dodu started to intone a drinking song; it was impossible to stop him when he got to a certain improper stanza, which everyone knew by heart. Sylvie refused to sing in spite of our entreaties, saying that singing at the table was no longer done. I had already noticed that the suitor of the day before was seated at her left. There was something in his round face and his tousled hair that wasn't unfamiliar to me. He got up and stood behind my chair, saying: "So you don't recognize me, Parisian?" A kind lady, who had just come back for dessert after serving us, said in my ear: "Don't you recognize the son of your wet nurse?" Without that information I would have made a fool of myself. "Oh, it's you, Big Curly!" I said; "it's you, the same fellow who pulled me out of the water." Sylvie laughed out loud at that recognition scene. "Not to mention," that lad said, kissing me, "that you had a beautiful silver watch and on the way home you were much more worried about the watch than about yourself, because it wasn't going any more; you said: 'The little animal is drownded, it doesn't go tick-tock anymore; what is Uncle going to say?'"

"An animal in a watch!" said old Dodu; "that's what they make children believe in Paris!"

Sylvie was sleepy; I felt that I no longer counted for her. She went up to her room, and, while I kissed her, she said: "Come and see us tomorrow!"

Old Dodu had remained at the table with Sylvain and the son of my wet nurse; we had a long conversation over a flagon of ratafia from Louvres. "All men are equal," said old Dodu between two stanzas, "I drink with a pastry cook just as I would do with a prince." "Where's the pastry cook?" I asked. "Look right next to you! A young man with the ambition to set himself up in life."

The son of my wet nurse seemed embarrassed. I had understood the whole thing. It was a fatal blow, stored up for me by destiny, to have a milk brother in a region made famous by Rousseau—who wanted to do away with wet nurses! Old Dodu informed me that there was great likelihood that Sylvie would marry Big Curly, who intended opening up a pastry shop in Dammartin. I asked no more questions. The coach coming from Nanteuil-le-Haudouin brought me back to Paris the next day.

XIII. Aurélie

To Paris! The coach takes five hours. My only concern was to get there by evening. Around eight o'clock I was in my regular seat in the

Aurélie répandit son inspiration et son charme sur des vers faiblement inspirés de Schiller, que l'on devait à un talent de l'époque. Dans la scène du jardin, elle devint sublime. Pendant le quatrième acte, où elle ne paraissait pas, j'allai acheter un bouquet chez madame Prévost. J'y insérai une lettre fort tendre signée: *Un inconnu*. Je me dis: Voilà quelque chose de fixé pour l'avenir, — et le lendemain j'étais sur la route d'Allemagne.

Qu'allais-je y faire? Essayer de remettre de l'ordre dans mes sentiments.—Si j'écrivais un roman, jamais je ne pourrais faire accepter l'histoire d'un cœur épris de deux amours simultanés. Sylvie m'échappait par ma faute; mais la revoir un jour avait suffi pour relever mon âme: je la plaçais désormais comme une statue souriante dans le temple de la Sagesse. Son regard m'avait arrêté au bord de l'abîme. — Je repoussais avec plus de force encore l'idée d'aller me présenter à Aurélie, pour lutter un instant avec tant d'amoureux vulgaires qui brillaient un instant près d'elle et retombaient brisés. — Nous verrons quelque jour, me dis-je, si cette femme a un cœur.

Un matin, je lus dans un journal qu'Aurélie était malade. Je lui écrivis des montagnes de Salzbourg. La lettre était si empreinte de mysticisme germanique, que je n'en devais pas attendre un grand succès, mais aussi je ne demandais pas de réponse. Je comptais un peu sur le hasard et sur — l'*inconnu*.

Des mois se passent. A travers mes courses et mes loisirs, j'avais entrepris de fixer dans une action poétique les amours du peintre Colonna pour la belle Laura, que ses parents firent religieuse, et qu'il aima jusqu'à la mort. Quelque chose dans ce sujet se rapportait à mes préoccupations constantes. Le dernier vers du drame écrit, je ne songeai plus qu'à revenir en France.

Que dire maintenant qui ne soit l'histoire de tant d'autres? J'ai passé par tous les cercles de ces lieux d'épreuves qu'on appelle théâtres. «J'ai mangé du tambour et bu de la cymbale,» comme dit la phrase dénuée de sens apparent des initiés d'Eleusis. — Elle signifie sans doute qu'il faut au besoin passer les bornes du non-sens et de l'absurdité: la raison pour moi, c'était de conquérir et de fixer mon idéal.

Aurélie avait accepté le rôle principal dans le drame que je rapportais d'Allemagne. Je n'oublierai jamais le jour où elle me permit de lui lire la pièce. Les scènes d'amour étaient préparées à son intention. Je crois bien que je les dis avec âme, mais surtout avec enthousiasme. Dans la conversation qui suivit, je me révélai comme l'*inconnu* des

theater; Aurélie was lavishing her inspiration and charm on verses fee-
bly reminiscent of Schiller, written by one of the talents of the era. In
the garden scene she became sublime. During the fourth act, in which
she didn't come on, I went to buy a bouquet from Madame Prévost.[27]
I inserted into it a very loving letter signed: "A stranger." I said to myself: "There's something to look forward to in the future," and the next
day I was on my way to Germany.

What was I going to do there? To try to put my love life in order. If I
were writing a novel, I'd never get people to believe the story of a heart
in love with two women at the same time. Sylvie was slipping away from
me through my own fault; but seeing her again for a day had been
enough to lift up my soul: henceforth I placed her like a smiling statue
in the temple of Wisdom. Her eyes had stopped me at the brink of the
abyss. I rejected even more violently the thought of presenting myself to
Aurélie so that I could briefly contend against all those common lovers
who shone alongside her for a moment and then fell away again, shattered. "Some day," I said to myself, "we'll see if that woman has a heart."

One morning I read in a paper that Aurélie was ill. I wrote to her
from the mountains of Salzburg. My letter was so imbued with
Germanic mysticism that I couldn't expect it to be a great success,
but, then again, I wasn't asking for an answer. I was counting a little
on chance and on—the unknown.

Months went by. During my travels and my leisure time, I had undertaken to set down in a verse drama the love of the painter
Colonna[28] for the beautiful Laura, whom her parents made a nun, and
whom he loved as long as he lived. Something about that subject had
a connection with my constant concerns. When the final line of the
play had been written, I thought of nothing but returning to France.

What can I say now that isn't the same as the story of so many others? I passed through every *bolgia* of those places of punishment
called theaters. "I've eaten of the drum and drunk of the cymbal," according to the outwardly meaningless phrase recited by initiates into
the mysteries of Eleusis. It no doubt means that, if necessary, one
must pass beyond the boundaries of the nonsensical and the absurd:
rationality, for me, meant the conquest and the definition of my ideal.

Aurélie had accepted the main part in the drama I brought back
from Germany. I'll never forget the day when she allowed me to read
her the play. The love scenes had been conceived with her in mind. I
think I recited them with soul, but above all with exaltation. In the
conversation that followed, I revealed myself as the "stranger" of the

deux lettres. Elle me dit: — Vous êtes bien fou; mais revenez me voir
. . . Je n'ai jamais pu trouver quelqu'un qui sût m'aimer.
O femme! tu cherches l'amour . . . Et moi, donc?
Les jours suivants, j'écrivis les lettres les plus tendres, les plus belles
que sans doute elle eût jamais reçues. J'en recevais d'elle qui étaient
pleines de raison. Un instant elle fut touchée, m'appela près d'elle, et
m'avoua qu'il lui était difficile de rompre un attachement plus ancien.
— Si c'est bien *pour moi* que vous m'aimez, dit-elle, vous compren-
drez que je ne puis être qu'à un seul.
Deux mois plus tard, je reçus une lettre pleine d'effusion. Je courus
chez elle. — Quelqu'un me donna dans l'intervalle un détail précieux.
Le beau jeune homme que j'avais rencontré une nuit au cercle venait
de prendre un engagement dans les spahis.
L'été suivant, il y avait des courses à Chantilly. La troupe du théâtre
où jouait Aurélie donnait là une représentation. Une fois dans le pays,
la troupe était pour trois jours aux ordres du régisseur. — Je m'étais
fait l'ami de ce brave homme, ancien Dorante des comédies de
Marivaux, longtemps jeune premier de drame, et dont le dernier succès avait été le rôle d'amoureux dans la pièce imitée de Schiller, où
mon binocle me l'avait montré si ridé. De près, il paraissait plus jeune,
et, resté maigre, il produisait encore de l'effet dans les provinces. Il
avait du feu. J'accompagnais la troupe en qualité de *seigneur poète;* je
persuadai au régisseur d'aller donner des représentations à Senlis et à
Dammartin. Il penchait d'abord pour Compiègne; mais Aurélie fut de
mon avis. Le lendemain, pendant que l'on allait traiter avec les pro-
priétaires des salles et les autorités, je louai des chevaux, et nous
prîmes la route des étangs de Commelle pour aller déjeuner au
château de la reine Blanche. Aurélie, en amazone, avec ses cheveux
blonds flottants, traversait la forêt comme une reine d'autrefois, et les
paysans s'arrêtaient éblouis. — Madame de F . . . était la seule qu'ils
eussent vue si imposante et si gracieuse dans ses saluts. — Après le
déjeuner, nous descendîmes dans des villages rappelant ceux de la
Suisse, où l'eau de la Nonette fait mouvoir des scieries. Ces aspects
chers à mes souvenirs l'intéressaient sans l'arrêter. J'avais projeté de
conduire Aurélie au château, près d'Orry, sur la même place verte où
pour la première fois j'avais vu Adrienne. — Nulle émotion ne parut
en elle. Alors je lui racontai tout; je lui dis la source de cet amour en-
trevu dans les nuits, rêvé plus tard, réalisé en elle. Elle m'écoutait
sérieusement et me dit: — Vous ne m'aimez pas! Vous attendez que
je vous dise: La comédienne est la même que la religieuse; vous

two letters. She said: "You're really crazy, but come see me again . . .
I've never been able to find a man really capable of loving me."
O woman! You're seeking love? Then, what am *I* doing?
During the days that ensued, I wrote the tenderest, no doubt the
most beautiful, letters she had ever received. I received some from
her that were full of practical considerations. For a moment she was
moved, invited me over, and admitted that it was hard for her to break
off an earlier relationship. "If you really love me for myself," she said,
"you'll understand that I can belong to only one man."
Two months later I received an extremely effusive letter. I dashed
over to her place. During the intermission someone had given me a
valuable piece of information. The handsome young man I had seen
one night at the club had just enlisted with the Algerian corps.
The following summer there were races at Chantilly. The theatrical
troupe that Aurélie belonged to was giving a performance there. Once in
the neighborhood, the troupe was under the stage manager's orders for
three days. I had become friends with that worthy man, who used to play
Dorante in Marivaux's comedies and was a leading man in dramas for
some time, and whose last success had been in the lover's role in the play
in Schiller's vein, in which my lorgnette had revealed that he was so wrinkled. At close range he appeared younger and, since he had stayed thin,
he still made a good impression in the provinces. He acted with ardor. I
was accompanying the troupe as their resident playwright; I persuaded
the stage manager to give performances in Senlis and Dammartin. At first
he was leaning toward Compiègne, but Aurélie shared my opinion. The
next day, while negotiations were under way with the theater owners and
the authorities, I hired horses and we headed for the ponds of Commelle,
intending to have luncheon at the château of Queen Blanche.[29] Aurélie,
in a riding habit, with her blond hair floating in the breeze, crossed the
forest like a queen of old, and the peasants stopped in their tracks, dazzled. Madame de F——[30] was the only woman they had seen who was so
imposing and so gracious in her greetings. After luncheon we went down
to the villages which recall those of Switzerland, where the water of the
Nonette powers sawmills. Those sights, dear to my memories, interested
her, but not enough to make her stop. I had planned to take Aurélie to
the château near Orry, on the same green lawn where I had first seen
Adrienne. She showed no emotion. Then I told her the whole story; I told
her the source of that love I had glimpsed during the nights, dreamt of
later on, and found in its reality in her. She listened to me seriously and
said: "You don't love me! You're waiting for me to say to you: 'The actress

cherchez un drame, voilà tout, et le dénouement vous échappe. Allez, je ne vous crois plus!

Cette parole fut en éclair. Ces enthousiasmes bizarres que j'avais ressentis si longtemps, ces rêves, ces pleurs, ces désespoirs et ces tendresses, . . . ce n'était donc pas l'amour? Mais où donc est-il?

Aurélie joua le soir à Senlis. Je crus m'apercevoir qu'elle avait un faible pour le régisseur, — le jeune premier ridé. Cet homme était d'un caractère excellent et lui avait rendu des services.

Aurélie m'a dit un jour: — Celui qui m'aime, le voilà!

XIV. — Dernier feuillet.

Telles sont les chimères qui charment et égarent au matin de la vie. J'ai essayé de les fixer sans beaucoup d'ordre, mais bien des cœurs me comprendront. Les illusions tombent l'une après l'autre, comme les écorces d'un fruit, et le fruit, c'est l'expérience. Sa saveur est amère; elle a pourtant quelque chose d'âcre qui fortifie, — qu'on me pardonne ce style vieilli. Rousseau dit que le spectacle de la nature console de tout. Je cherche parfois à retrouver mes bosquets de Clarens perdus au nord de Paris, dans les brumes. Tout cela est bien changé!

Ermenonville! pays où fleurissait encore l'idylle antique, — traduite une seconde fois d'après Gessner! tu as perdu ta seule étoile, qui chatoyait pour moi d'un double éclat. Tour à tour bleue et rose comme l'astre trompeur d'Aldebaran, c'était Adrienne ou Sylvie, — c'étaient les deux moitiès d'un seul amour. L'une était l'idéal sublime, l'autre la douce réalité. Que me font maintenant tes ombrages et tes lacs, et même ton désert? Othys, Montagny, Loisy, pauvres hameaux voisins, Châalis, — que l'on restaure, — vous n'avez rien gardé de tout ce passé! Quelquefois j'ai besoin de revoir ces lieux de solitude et de rêverie. J'y relève tristement en moi-même les traces fugitives d'une époque où le naturel était affecté; je souris parfois en lisant sur le flanc des granits certains vers de Roucher, qui m'avaient paru sublimes, — ou des maximes de bienfaisance au-dessus d'une fontaine ou d'une grotte consacrée à Pan. Les étangs, creusés à si grands frais, étalent en vain leur eau morte que le cygne dédaigne. Il n'est plus, le temps où les chasses de Condé passaient avec leurs amazones fières, où les cors se répondaient de loin, multipliés par les échos! . . . Pour se rendre à Ermenonville, on ne trouve plus aujourd'hui de route directe.

is the same woman as the nun.' You're looking for a drama, that's all, and the ending escapes you. Go on, I don't believe you anymore!"

Those words were like a lightning flash. Those bizarre fits of exaltation I had experienced for so long, those dreams, those tears, those feelings of despair and of tenderness . . . were they really not love, after all? But, if so, where is love to be found?

That evening Aurélie acted in Senlis. I thought I discerned that she was in love with the stage manager—the leading man with wrinkles. That man was very good-natured and had done favors for her.

Aurélie told me one day: "There's the man who loves me!"

XIV. Final Leaf

Such are the fancies that charm us and lead us astray in the morning of life. I have tried to set them down without sticking to a rigid sequence, but many hearts will understand me. Illusions drop away one after another, like the rind of a fruit, and the fruit is experience. It has a bitter taste, but it has a tart element that braces you—forgive me for this old-fashioned terminology. Rousseau says that the spectacle of nature consoles us for everything. Sometimes I attempt to rediscover my own lost "groves of Clarens"[31] to the north of Paris, in the mists. All of that has really changed!

Ermenonville, land where the idyll of the ancients was still flourishing—translated a second time from Gessner![32]—you have lost your only star, which used to change color for me with a double gleam. In turns blue and pink like the deceptive star Aldebaran, it was now Adrienne, now Sylvie—they were the two halves of a single love. One was the sublime ideal, the other was sweet reality. What are your shade trees and lakes to me now, and even your desert? Othys, Montagny, Loisy, poor nearby hamlets, Chaalis—which is being restored—you have preserved nothing from all that past! Sometimes I feel the need to revisit those places of solitude and daydreams. There I sadly find within myself the fleeting traces of an era when there was a predilection for natural things. I sometimes smile when I read on a granite rock certain verses by Roucher[33] that had once struck me as being sublime—or benevolent maxims over a fountain or a grotto dedicated to Pan. The ponds, excavated at such great expense, display in vain their stagnant water, which the swan disdains. The time is no more when the Condé hunts passed by with their haughty horsewomen, the horns answering one another from a distance, their calls multiplied by the echoes! . . . To go to Ermenonville, you can no

Quelquefois j'y vais par Creil et Senlis, d'autres fois par Dammartin.

A Dammartin, l'on n'arrive jamais que le soir. Je vais coucher alors à l'*Image Saint-Jean*. On me donne d'ordinaire une chambre assez propre tendue en vieille tapisserie avec un trumeau au-dessus de la glace. Cette chambre est un dernier retour vers le bric-à-brac, auquel j'ai depuis longtemps renoncé. On y dort chaudement sous l'édredon, qui est d'usage dans ce pays. Le matin, quand j'ouvre la fenêtre, encadrée de vigne et de roses, je découvre avec ravissement un horizon vert de dix lieues, où les peupliers s'alignent comme des armées. Quelques villages s'abritent çà et là sous leurs clochers aigus, construits, comme on dit là, en pointes d'ossements. On distingue d'abord Othys, — puis Eve, puis Ver; on distinguerait Ermenonville à travers le bois, s'il avait un clocher, — mais dans ce lieu philosophique on a bien négligé l'église. Après avoir rempli mes poumons de l'air si pur qu'on respire sur ces plateaux, je descends gaiement et je vais faire un tour chez le pâtissier. «Te voilà, grand frisé! — Te voilà, petit Parisien!» Nous nous donnons les coups de poings amicaux de l'enfance, puis je gravis un certain escalier où les joyeux cris de deux enfants accueillent ma venue. Le sourire athénien de Sylvie illumine ses traits charmés. Je me dis: «Là était le bonheur peut-être; cependant . . .»

Je l'appelle quelquefois Lolotte, et elle me trouve un peu de ressemblance avec Werther, moins les pistolets, qui ne sont plus de mode. Pendant que le *grand frisé* s'occupe du déjeuner, nous allons promener les enfants dans les allées de tilleuls qui ceignent les débris des vieilles tours de brique du château. Tandis que ces petits s'exercent, au tir des compagnons de l'arc, à ficher dans la paille les flèches paternelles, nous lisons quelques poésies ou quelques pages de ces livres si courts qu'on ne fait plus guère.

J'oubliais de dire que le jour où la troupe dont faisait partie Aurélie a donné une représentation à Dammartin; j'ai conduit Sylvie au spectacle, et je lui ai demandé si elle ne trouvait pas que l'actrice ressemblait à une personne qu'elle avait connue déjà. — A qui donc? — Vous souvenez-vous d'Adrienne?

Elle partit d'un grand éclat de rire en disant: «Quelle idée!» Puis, comme se le reprochant, elle reprit en soupirant: «Pauvre Adrienne! elle est morte au couvent de Saint-S . . . , vers 1832.»

longer find a direct route nowadays. Sometimes I go there by way of Creil and Senlis, other times by way of Dammartin.

You never get to Dammartin before evening. Then I spend the night in the Image of Saint John inn. I'm usually given a fairly clean room hung with old wallpaper with a pier over the mirror. This room is a last return to bric-a-brac, which I've given up for a long time now. It's warm sleeping there under the eiderdown quilt, which they use in that region. In the morning, when I open the window, which is framed by grapevines and roses, I discover with delight a green horizon ten leagues wide, with poplars lining up like armies. A few villages are nestled here and there beneath their pointed belfries, constructed, as the saying goes there, "with dry bones as tips." First you make out Othys, then Eve, then Ver; you could make out Ermenonville across the forest if it had a belfry—but in that realm of philosophy the Church has of course been neglected. After filling my lungs with the very fresh air that one breathes on those plateaus, I go downstairs merrily and take a walk to the pastry shop. "There you are, Big Curly!" "There you are, little Parisian!" We exchange the friendly punches of our childhood, then I climb a certain staircase on which the joyful shouts of two children greet my arrival. Sylvie's Athenian smile lights up her charmed features. I say to myself: "There your happiness lay, perhaps; and yet . . ."

I sometimes call her Lolotte,[34] and she finds that I somewhat resemble Werther, minus the pistols, which are no longer fashionable. While Big Curly is attending to luncheon, we take the children for a walk in the avenues of linden trees surrounding the remains of the château's old brick towers. While the little ones are busy practicing to plant their father's arrows in the straw target on the archery club's shooting range, we read a few poems or a few pages of those very short books that are scarcely published any longer.

I almost forgot to say that, on the day when the troupe that Aurélie belonged to gave a performance in Dammartin, I took Sylvie to the show and asked her whether she didn't think the actress looked like someone she had once known. "Who do you mean?" "Do you remember Adrienne?"

She burst out laughing and said: "What an idea!" Then, as if blaming herself for laughing, she continued, sighing: "Poor Adrienne! She died at the convent of Saint-S—, around 1832."

ALPHONSE DAUDET

La mule du Pape

De tous les jolis dictons, proverbes ou adages, dont nos paysans de Provence passementent leurs discours, je n'en sais pas un plus pittoresque ni plus singulier que celui-ci. A quinze lieues autour de mon moulin, quand on parle d'un homme rancunier, vindicatif, on dit: «Cet homme là! méfiez-vous! . . . il est comme la mule du Pape, qui garde sept ans son coup de pied.»

J'ai cherché bien longtemps d'où ce proverbe pouvait venir, ce que c'était que cette mule papale et ce coup de pied gardé pendant sept ans. Personne ici n'a pu me renseigner à ce sujet, pas même Francet Mamaï, mon joueur de fifre, qui connaît pourtant son légendaire provençal sur le bout du doigt. Francet pense comme moi qu'il y a là-dessous quelque ancienne chronique du pays d'Avignon: mais il n'en a jamais entendu parler autrement que par le proverbe.

«Vous ne trouverez cela qu'à la bibliothèque des Cigales», m'a dit le vieux fifre en riant.

L'idée m'a paru bonne et comme la bibliothèque des Cigales est à ma porte, je suis allé m'y enfermer pendant huit jours.

C'est une bibliothèque merveilleuse, admirablement montée, ouverte aux poètes jour et nuit, et desservie par de petits bibliothécaires à cymbales qui vous font de la musique tout le temps. J'ai passé là quelques journées délicieuses, et, après une semaine de recherches, — sur le dos, — j'ai fini par découvrir ce que je voulais, c'est-à-dire l'histoire de ma mule et de ce fameux coup de pied gardé pendant sept ans. Le conte en est joli quoique un peu naïf, et je vais essayer de vous le dire tel que je l'ai lu hier matin dans un manuscrit couleur du temps, qui sentait bon la lavande sèche et avait de grands fils de la Vierge pour signets.

*

Qui n'a pas vu Avignon du temps des Papes, n'a rien vu. Pour la gaieté, la vie, l'animation, le train des fêtes, jamais une ville pareille.

ALPHONSE DAUDET

The Pope's Mule

Of all the pretty sayings, proverbs, and adages with which our peasants in Provence lace their speech, I don't know any that are more picturesque or more unusual than this one. In a radius of fifteen leagues around my windmill, whenever they talk about a grudge-bearing, vindictive man, they say: "That man! Watch out! . . . He's like the Pope's she-mule, and holds back his kick for seven years."

I searched for a long time to see where that proverb might come from, and the story of that papal mule and that kick held in reserve for seven years. No one here has been able to give me information on that subject, not even Francet Mamaï, my fife player, even though he has his Provençal legends at his fingertips. Francet agrees with me that, at the bottom of it, there's some old chronicle of the Avignon region; but he's never heard talk of it except by way of the proverb.

"You'll only find that in the cicadas' library," the old fifer said to me, laughing.

That sounded like a good idea, and, seeing that the cicadas' library is right outside my door, I went and shut myself up in it for a week.

It's a wonderful library, admirably fitted out, open to poets day and night, and staffed by little librarians with cymbals who make music for you the whole time. I spent a few delightful days there, and after a week of research—on my back—I finally found what I wanted; that is, the history of my mule and that notorious kick held in reserve for seven years. The tale is a pretty one, though somewhat naïve, and I'll try to tell it to you just as I read it yesterday morning in a sky-blue manuscript that had a good smell of dry lavender, with big threads of gossamer for bookmarks.

*

If you didn't see Avignon when the Popes were there, you've never seen a thing. For merriment, liveliness, animation, the busy series of festivals,

C'étaient, du matin au soir, des processions, des pèlerinages, les rues jonchées de fleurs, tapissées de hautes lices, des arrivages de cardinaux par le Rhône, bannières au vent, galères pavoisées, les soldats du Pape qui chantaient du latin sur les places, les crécelles des frères quêteurs; puis, du haut en bas des maisons qui se pressaient en bourdonnant autour du grand palais papal comme des abeilles autour de leur ruche, c'était encore le tic-tac des métiers à dentelles, le va-et-vient des navettes tissant l'or des chasubles, les petits marteaux des ciseleurs de burettes, les tables d'harmonie qu'on ajustait chez les luthiers, les cantiques des ourdisseuses; par là-dessus le bruit des cloches, et toujours quelques tambourins qu'on entendait ronfler, là-bas, du côté du pont. Car chez nous, quand le peuple est content, il faut qu'il danse, il faut qu'il danse; et comme en ce temps-là les rues de la ville étaient trop étroites pour la farandole, fifres et tambourins se postaient sur le pont d'Avignon, au vent frais du Rhône, et jour et nuit l'on y dansait, l'on y dansait . . . Ah! l'heureux temps! l'heureuse ville! Des hallebardes qui ne coupaient pas; des prisons d'État où l'on mettait le vin à rafraîchir. Jamais de disette; jamais de guerre . . . Voilà comment les Papes du Comtat savaient gouverner leur peuple; voilà pourquoi leur peuple les a tant regrettés! . . .

Il y en a un surtout, un bon vieux, qu'on appelait Boniface . . . Oh! celui-là que de larmes on a versées en Avignon, quand il est mort! C'était un prince si aimable, si avenant! Il vous riait si bien du haut de sa mule! Et quand vous passiez près de lui, — fussiez-vous un pauvre petit tireur de garance ou le grand viguier de la ville, — il vous donnait sa bénédiction si poliment! Un vrai pape d'Yvetot, mais d'un Yvetot de Provence, avec quelque chose de fin dans le rire, un brin de marjolaine à sa barrette, et pas la moindre Jeanneton . . . La seule Jeanneton qu'on lui ait jamais connue, à ce bon père, c'était sa vigne, — une petite vigne qu'il avait plantée lui-même, à trois lieues d'Avignon, dans les myrtes de Château-Neuf.

Tous les dimanches, en sortant de vêpres, le digne homme allait lui faire sa cour, et quand il était là-haut, assis au bon soleil, sa mule près de lui, ses cardinaux tout autour étendus aux pieds des souches, alors il faisait déboucher un flacon de vin du cru, — ce beau vin, couleur de rubis, qui s'est appelé depuis le Château-Neuf des Papes, — et il le dégustait par petits coups, en regardant sa vigne d'un air attendri. Puis, le flacon vidé, le jour tombant, il rentrait joyeusement à la ville, suivi de tout son chapitre; et, lorsqu'il passait sur le pont d'Avignon, au milieu des tambours et des farandoles, sa mule, mise en train par

there's never been a city like it. From morning to evening there were processions, pilgrimages, the streets strewn with flowers and overhung by
high-warp tapestries, arrivals of cardinals on the Rhône, banners in the
wind, galleys decked with flags, the Pope's soldiers chanting in Latin on the
squares, the rattles of the monks collecting alms. And then, from top to
bottom of the houses that huddled around the great Palace of the Popes,
buzzing like bees around the hive, there was, besides, the click-clack of the
lace frames, the to-and-fro of shuttles weaving the gold for chasubles, the
little hammers of the engravers of altar cruets, the soundboards being finished in the lute makers' shops, the hymns sung by the women setting up
the warp on looms; and, above all the rest, the sound of the bells, and always a few Provençal drums that could be heard rumbling there, toward
the bridge. Because, where we live, when the populace is happy, it must
dance, it must dance; and, since in those days the city streets were too narrow for the farandole, fife and drum players took up their station on the
bridge of Avignon, in the cool breeze from the Rhône, and day and night
"people danced there, people danced there" . . . Oh, the happy time! The
happy city! Halberds that did not strike; prisons of the state in which wine
was placed to cool. Never a food shortage; never a war . . . That's how the
Popes of the County of Avignon knew how to govern their people; that's
why their people missed them so when they left! . . .

There's one especially, a good old man, who was called Boniface . . .
Oh, how many tears were shed in Avignon for *him* when he died! He
was such an amiable and pleasing ruler! How kindly he smiled at you
while seated on his mule! And whenever you passed by him—whether
you were a poor little extractor of madder dye or the chief justice of
the city—he gave you a blessing so politely! A true Pope of Yvetot,[1]
but of an Yvetot in Provence, with something delicate in his laughter,
a sprig of marjoram in his biretta, and not the slightest Jeanneton . . .
The only "sweetheart Jeanneton" that that kindly father ever had was
his vineyard—a little vineyard he had planted himself, three leagues
from Avignon, among the myrtles of Châteauneuf.

Every Sunday, on leaving vespers, the worthy man went to pay his
court to it, and when he was up there, sitting in the beneficent sunshine,
his mule nearby, his cardinals all around stretched out at the feet of the
vinestocks, then he had a flagon of the local wine uncorked—that beautiful, ruby-colored wine which, ever since, has been called Château-
neuf-du-Pape—and he would taste it in little sips, looking at his
vineyard tenderly. Then, the flagon emptied, the sun setting, he would
return joyously to his city, followed by his entire chapter of canons; and,
when he crossed the bridge of Avignon,[2] in the midst of the drums and

la musique, prenait une petit amble sautillant, tandis que lui-même il marquait le pas de la danse avec sa barrette, ce qui scandalisait fort ses cardinaux, mais faisait dire à tout le peuple: «Ah! le bon prince! Ah! le brave pape!»

✿

Après sa vigne de Château-Neuf, ce que le pape aimait le plus au monde, c'était sa mule. Le bonhomme en raffolait de cette bête-là. Tous les soirs avant de se coucher, il allait voir si son écurie était bien fermée, si rien ne manquait dans sa mangeoire, et jamais il ne se serait levé de table sans faire préparer sous ses yeux un grand bol de vin à la française, avec beaucoup de sucre et d'aromates, qu'il allait lui porter lui-même, malgré les observations de ses cardinaux . . . Il faut dire aussi que la bête en valait la peine. C'était une belle mule noire, mouchetée de rouge, le pied sûr, le poil luisant, la croupe large et pleine, portant fièrement sa petite tête sèche toute harnachée de pompons, de nœuds, de grelots d'argent, de bouffettes; avec cela douce comme un ange, l'œil naïf, et deux longues oreilles, toujours en branle, qui lui donnaient l'air bon enfant. Tout Avignon la respectait, et, quand elle errait dans les rues, il n'y avait pas de bonnes manières qu'on ne lui fît; car chacun savait que c'était le meilleur moyen d'être bien en cour, et qu'avec son air innocent, la mule du Pape en avait mené plus d'un à la fortune, à preuve Tistet Védène et sa prodigieuse aventure.

Ce Tistet Védène était, dans le principe, un effronté galopin, que son père, Guy Védène, le sculpteur d'or, avait été obligé de chasser de chez lui, parce qu'il ne voulait rien faire et débauchait les apprentis. Pendant six mois, on le vit traîner sa jaquette dans tous les ruisseaux d'Avignon, mais principalement du côté de la maison papale; car le drôle avait depuis longtemps son idée sur la mule du Pape, et vous allez voir que c'était quelque chose de malin . . . Un jour que Sa Sainteté se promenait toute seule sous les remparts avec sa bête, voilà mon Tistet qui l'aborde, et lui dit en joignant les mains d'un air d'admiration:

«Ah! mon Dieu! grand Saint-Père, quelle brave mule vous avez là! . . . Laissez un peu que je la regarde . . . Ah! mon Pape, la belle mule! . . . L'empereur d'Allemagne n'en a pas une pareille.»

Et il la caressait, et il lui parlait doucement comme à une demoiselle.

«Venez çà, mon bijou, mon trésor, ma perle fine . . .»

the farandoles, his mule, enlivened by the music, would go into a little hopping amble, while the Pope himself beat time to the dance music with his biretta, which greatly shocked his cardinals but caused all the plain people to say: "Oh, what a good ruler! Oh, what a fine Pope!"

❖

After his vineyard at Châteauneuf, what the Pope loved most in the world was his she-mule. The dear old man was crazy about that animal. Every night before going to bed, he went to see whether her stable was properly closed, whether there was nothing lacking in her feeding trough; and he would never have risen from his table without seeing prepared before his eyes a large bowl of French-style wine,[3] with plenty of sugar and spices, which he himself brought to the mule, despite his cardinals' remarks. . . . It must also be said that the animal was worth all of this. She was a beautiful black mule with red spots, surefooted, with a gleaming coat and wide, full hindquarters; she carried with pride her small, lean head that was lavishly accoutred with pompoms, bows, silver jingle bells, and tassels. In addition, she was as gentle as an angel, with candid eyes and two long ears that were always in motion, giving her a good-natured appearance. All Avignon esteemed her and, when she wandered through the streets, everyone treated her as courteously as possible; because everyone knew that that was the best way to be in good standing at the papal court, and that, with her innocent appearance, the Pope's mule had led more than one person to good fortune— as a proof, Tistet Védène and his prodigious adventure.

This Tistet Védène was basically a brazen-faced young rascal whom his father, Guy Védène, a goldsmith, had been forced to throw out of his house because he refused to do any work and was keeping the apprentices from doing theirs. For six months he was to be seen dragging his coat through every gutter in Avignon, but especially in the vicinity of the papal palace; because for some time the rogue had had a plan concerning the Pope's mule, and you're about to see that it was pretty shrewd. . . . One day, when His Holiness was on an outing, all alone with his mount, alongside the city walls, there was our Tistet, greeting him and saying, with his hands joined together in admiration:

"Oh, my heavens! Great Holy Father, what a fine mule you have there! . . . Let me look at her for a while. . . . Oh, Pope, such a beautiful mule! . . . The Emperor of Germany doesn't have one like her."

And he patted her, and spoke gently to her as if addressing a well-born young lady.

"Come here, my jewel, my treasure, my precious pearl . . ."

Et le bon Pape, tout ému, se disait dans lui-même:
«Quel bon petit garçonnet! . . . Comme il est gentil avec ma mule!»
Et puis le lendemain savez-vous ce qui arriva? Tistet Védène troqua
sa vieille jaquette jaune contre une belle aube en dentelles, un camail
de soie violette, des souliers à boucles, et il entra dans la maîtrise du
Pape, où jamais avant lui on n'avait reçu que des fils de nobles et des
neveux de cardinaux. Voilà ce que c'est que l'intrigue! . . . Mais Tistet
ne s'en tint pas là.

Une fois au service du Pape, le drôle continua le jeu qui lui avait si
bien réussi. Insolent avec tout le monde, il n'avait d'attentions ni de
prévenances que pour la mule, et toujours on le rencontrait par les
cours du palais avec une poignée d'avoine ou une bottelée de sainfoin,
dont il secouait gentiment les grappes roses en regardant le balcon du
Saint-Père, d'un air de dire: «Hein! . . . pour qui ça? . . .» Tant et tant
qu'à la fin le bon Pape qui se sentait devenir vieux, en arriva à lui
laisser le soin de veiller sur l'écurie et de porter à la mule son bol de
vin à la française; ce qui ne faisait pas rire les cardinaux.

*

Ni la mule non plus, cela ne la faisait pas rire . . . Maintenant, à
l'heure de son vin, elle voyait toujours arriver chez elle cinq ou six
petits clercs de maîtrise qui se fourraient vite dans la paille avec leur
camail et leurs dentelles: puis, au bout d'un moment, une bonne
odeur chaude de caramel et d'aromates emplissait l'écurie, et Tistet
Védène apparaissait portant avec précaution le bol de vin à la
française. Alors le martyre de la pauvre bête commençait.

Ce vin parfumé qu'elle aimait tant, qui lui tenait chaud, qui lui mettait des ailes, on avait la cruauté de le lui apporter, là, dans sa mangeoire, de le lui faire respirer; puis, quand elle en avait les narines
pleines, passe, je t'ai vu! la belle liqueur de flamme rose s'en allait
toute dans le gosier de ces garnements . . . Et encore, s'ils n'avaient
fait que lui voler son vin; mais c'étaient comme des diables, tous ces
petits clercs, quand ils avaient bu! . . . L'un lui tirait les oreilles, l'autre
la queue; Quiquet lui montait sur le dos, Béluguet lui essayait sa barrette, et pas un de ces galopins ne songeait que d'un coup de reins ou
d'une ruade la brave bête aurait pu les envoyer tous dans l'étoile po-
laire, et même plus loin . . . Mais non! On n'est pas pour rien la mule
du Pape, la mule des bénédictions et des indulgences . . . Les enfants
avaient beau faire, elle ne se fâchait pas; et ce n'était qu'à Tistet
Védène qu'elle en voulait . . . Celui-là, par exemple, quand elle le sentait derrière elle, son sabot lui démangeait, et vraiment il y avait bien

And the good Pope, sincerely touched, said to himself:

"What a good little boy! . . . How nice he is to my mule!"

And then, the next day, do you know what happened? Tistet Védène swapped his old yellow coat for a beautiful lace alb, a violet silk short cape such as priests wear, and buckled shoes, and he joined the Pope's choir school, where never before that time had anyone been received but noblemen's sons and cardinals' nephews. Just see what intrigue will do! . . . But Tistet didn't stop there.

Once in the Pope's service, the rogue continued the game that had stood him in such good stead. Insolent with everybody, he lavished his cares and kindness only on the mule, and was always to be found in the palace courtyards with a handful of oats or a little bunch of sainfoin, amiably shaking its clusters of pink flowers while looking at the Holy Father's balcony, as if to say: "Well? . . . Who is this for? . . ." So much so, that the good Pope, who felt he was growing old, finally assigned him the task of taking care of the stable and bringing the mule her bowl of French-style wine; this did not make the cardinals happy.

✻

Nor was the mule happy about it, either. . . . Now, when the time for her wine arrived, she always saw arriving in her stable five or six young clerics from the choir school, who quickly nestled in the straw with their short capes and their laces; a moment later, a pleasant, warm aroma of burnt sugar and spices filled the stable, and Tistet Védène appeared, carefully carrying the bowl of French-style wine. Then the martyrdom of the poor animal would begin.

That flavored wine she loved so much, which kept her warm, which lent her wings—they were so cruel as to bring it over to her, there in her feeding trough, to let her inhale it; then, when her nostrils were filled with it—presto, vanished! The beautiful, fiery-pink beverage would completely disappear into the gullets of those little brats. . . . And, as if stealing her wine wasn't enough, all those little clerics were like devils when they were drunk! . . . One of them pulled her ears, another, her tail; Quiquet climbed on her back, Béluguet tried out his biretta on her, and not one of those rascals imagined that, with a flick of her crupper or a kick, the good animal could have sent them all to the pole star, or even farther . . . But no! It's not for nothing that you're the Pope's mule, the mule of benedictions and indulgences. . . . No matter how the youngsters irritated her, she didn't get angry; and her rancor was directed only at Tistet Védène. . . . Now, when she sensed that *he* was behind her, her hooves itched her, and truly she had good

de quoi. Ce vaurien de Tistet lui jouait de si vilains tours! Il avait de si cruelles inventions après boire! . . .

Est-ce qu'un jour il ne s'avisa pas de la faire monter avec lui au clocheton de la maîtrise, là-haut, tout là-haut, à la pointe du palais! . . . Et ce que je vous dis là n'est pas un conte, deux cent mille Provençaux l'ont vu. Vous figurez-vous la terreur de cette malheureuse mule, lorsque, après avoir tourné pendant une heure à l'aveuglette dans un escalier en colimaçon et grimpé je ne sais combien de marches elle se trouva tout à coup sur une plate-forme éblouissante de lumière, et qu'à mille pieds au-dessous d'elle elle aperçut tout un Avignon fantastique, les baraques du marché pas plus grosses que des noisettes, les soldats du Pape devant leur caserne comme des fourmis rouges, et là-bas, sur un fil d'argent, un petit pont microscopique où l'on dansait, où l'on dansait . . . Ah! pauvre bête! quelle panique! Du cri qu'elle en poussa, toutes les vitres du palais tremblèrent.

«Qu'est-ce qu'il y a? qu'est-ce qu'on lui fait?» s'écria le bon Pape en se précipitant sur son balcon.

Tistet Védène était déjà dans la cour, faisant mine de pleurer et de s'arracher les cheveux:

«Ah! grand Saint-Père, ce qu'il y a! Il y a que votre mule est montée dans le clocheton . . .

— Toute seule???

— Oui, grand Saint-Père, toute seule . . . Tenez! regardez-la, là-haut . . . Voyez-vous le bout de ses oreilles qui passe? . . . On dirait deux hirondelles . . .

— Miséricorde! fit le pauvre Pape en levant les yeux . . . Mais elle est donc devenue folle! Mais elle va se tuer . . . Veux-tu bien descendre, malheureuse! . . .»

Pécaïre! elle n'aurait pas mieux demandé, elle, que de descendre . . . mais par où? L'escalier, il n'y fallait pas songer: ça se monte encore ces choses-là; mais, à la descente, il y aurait de quoi se rompre cent fois les jambes . . . Et la pauvre mule se désolait et tout en rôdant sur la plate-forme avec ses gros yeux pleins de vertige, elle pensait à Tistet Védène:

«Ah! bandit, si j'en réchappe . . . quel coup de sabot demain matin!»

Cette idée de coup de sabot lui redonnait un peu de cœur au ventre; sans cela elle n'aurait pas pu se tenir . . . Enfin on parvint à la tirer de là-haut; mais ce fut toute une affaire. Il fallut la descendre avec un cric, des cordes, une civière. Et vous pensez quelle humiliation pour la mule d'un pape de se voir pendue à cette hauteur, nageant les

reasons. That good-for-nothing Tistet played such nasty tricks on her! He thought up such cruel things to do when he got drunk! . . .

Didn't he get the idea one day to make her climb up with him to the bell tower of the choir school, up there, way up there, at the pinnacle of the palace? . . . And what I'm now telling you isn't a fairy tale; two hundred thousand inhabitants of Provence saw it happen. Picture the terror of that unhappy mule when, after twisting her way up a spiral staircase blindly for an hour, and after climbing heaven knows how many steps, she suddenly found herself on a platform inundated with dazzling light, and caught sight, at a thousand feet below her, of an entire fantastic Avignon, the market stalls no bigger than hazelnuts, the Pope's soldiers in front of their barracks like red ants, and, over yonder, on a silver thread, a little, microscopic bridge on which "people were dancing, people were dancing". . . . Oh, the poor animal! What panic she felt! The cry she uttered made all the windows in the palace shake.

"What's wrong? What are they doing to her?" exclaimed the good Pope, dashing out onto his balcony.

Tistet Védène was already in the courtyard, pretending to weep and pull out his hair:

"Oh, great Holy Father, you ask what's wrong? Your mule has climbed the bell tower."

"All by herself?"

"Yes, great Holy Father, all by herself. . . . See! Look at her up there. . . . Do you see the tips of her ears sticking out? . . . They look like a pair of swallows . . ."

"Mercy!" cried the poor Pope, raising his eyes. "But she must have gone crazy! But she's going to get killed. . . . Will you come down from there, you wretched thing?! . . ."

Alas![4] As for her, she would have liked nothing better than to go down . . . but which way? The staircase wasn't even to be thought of; those contraptions can be climbed up, at best; but going down them, you could break your legs a hundred times. . . . And the poor mule was in misery; while walking around the platform, her large eyes glazed over with dizziness, she kept thinking about Tistet Védène.

"Oh, you villain, if I get out of this . . . what a kick you'll get tomorrow morning!"

That thought of the kick put a little heart back into her; otherwise, she wouldn't have been able to stick it out. . . . Finally they managed to get her down from there, but it was quite a job. She had to be let down with a winch, ropes, and a litter. Just imagine how humiliating it was for a Pope's mule to see herself hanging up so high, swimming

pattes dans le vide comme un hanneton au bout d'un fil. Et tout Avignon qui la regardait!

La malheureuse bête n'en dormit pas de la nuit. Il lui semblait toujours qu'elle tournait sur cette maudite plate-forme, avec les rires de la ville au-dessous, puis elle pensait à cet infâme Tistet Védène et au joli coup de sabot qu'elle allait lui détacher le lendemain matin. Ah! mes amis, quel coup de sabot! De Pampérigouste on en verrait la fumée . . . Or, pendant qu'on lui préparait cette belle réception à l'écurie, savez-vous ce que faisait Tistet Védène? Il descendait le Rhône en chantant sur une galère papale et s'en allait à la cour de Naples avec la troupe de jeunes nobles que la ville envoyait tous les ans près de la reine Jeanne pour s'exercer à la diplomatie et aux belles manières. Tistet n'était pas noble; mais le Pape tenait à le récompenser des soins qu'il avait donnés à sa bête, et principalement de l'activité qu'il venait de déployer pendant la journée du sauvetage.

C'est la mule qui fut désappointée le lendemain!

«Ah! le bandit! il s'est douté de quelque chose! . . . pensait-elle en secouant ses grelots avec fureur . . . Mais c'est égal, va, mauvais! tu le retrouveras au retour, ton coup de sabot . . . Je te le garde!»

Et elle le lui garda.

Après le départ de Tistet, la mule du Pape retrouva son train de vie tranquille et ses allures d'autrefois. Plus de Quiquet, plus de Béluguet à l'écurie. Les beaux jours du vin à la française étaient revenus, et avec eux la bonne humeur, les longues siestes, et le petit pas de gavotte quand elle passait sur le pont d'Avignon. Pourtant, depuis son aventure, on lui marquait toujours un peu de froideur dans la ville. Il y avait des chuchotements sur sa route; les vieilles gens hochaient la tête, les enfants riaient en se montrant le clocheton. Le bon Pape lui-même n'avait plus autant de confiance en son amie, et, lorsqu'il se laissait aller à faire un petit somme sur son dos, le dimanche, en revenant de la vigne, il gardait toujours cette arrière-pensée: «Si j'allais me réveiller là-haut, sur la plate-forme!» La mule voyait cela et elle en souffrait, sans rien dire; seulement quand on prononçait le nom de Tistet Védène devant elle, ses longues oreilles frémissaient, et elle aiguisait avec un petit rire le fer de ses sabots sur le pavé.

Sept ans se passèrent ainsi; puis, au bout de ces sept années, Tistet Védène revint de la cour de Naples. Son temps n'était pas encore fini là-bas; mais il avait appris que le premier moutardier du Pape venait de mourir subitement en Avignon, et, comme la place lui semblait bonne, il était arrivé en grande hâte pour se mettre sur les rangs.

with her feet in the air like a June bug at the end of a string! And with everyone in Avignon watching her!

The unhappy animal didn't sleep all night. She kept thinking she was still turning to and fro on that accursed platform, with the laughter of the city below her; then she thought about that vile Tistet Védène and the neat kick she was going to treat him to on the following morning. Oh, my friends, what a kick! They'd see the smoke from it all the way to Pampérigouste.[5] . . . Now, while this lovely reception was being planned for him in the stable, do you know what Tistet Védène was doing? He was going down the Rhône, singing, on a papal galley, on his way to the court of Naples as one of the company of young noblemen that the city used to send annually to Queen Jeanne[6] to perfect themselves in diplomacy and fine manners. Tistet wasn't a nobleman, but the Pope desired to reward him for the attentions he had shown his animal, particularly for his active participation on the day when she was rescued.

Wasn't the mule disappointed the next day!

"Oh, the villain! He suspected something!" she thought, shaking her jingle bells in a rage. "But it's all the same; go on, you rat! You'll find your kick when you get back. . . . I'll save it for you!"

And she saved it for him.

After Tistet's departure, the Pope's mule regained her calm life style and her former ways. No more Quiquet, no more Béluguet in the stable. The good old days of the French-style wine had returned and, with them, her good humor, her long siestas, and her little gavotte step whenever she crossed the bridge of Avignon. And yet, ever since her adventure, people in town always showed a little coolness toward her. There were whispers when she passed by; old folks shook their heads, children laughed and pointed to the bell tower. The good Pope himself no longer had as much confidence in his friend as formerly, and when he allowed himself to take a little nap on her back on Sundays on his way back from the vineyard, he always had this thought in the back of his mind: "What if I were to wake up up there, on the platform?" The mule noticed all this, and suffered from it, but said nothing; it was only when Tistet Védène's name was pronounced in her presence that her long ears quivered, and she sharpened the iron of her shoes on the pavement with a little laugh.

Seven years went by in that way; then, at the end of those seven years, Tistet Védène returned from the court of Naples. His appointed time there was not yet over, but he had learned that the chief purveyor of mustard to the Pope had just died suddenly in Avignon, and, since the office seemed like a good one to him, he had arrived in great haste to apply for it.

Quand cet intrigant de Védène entra dans la salle du palais, le Saint-Père eut peine à le reconnaître, tant il avait grandi et pris du corps. Il faut dire aussi que le bon Pape s'était fait vieux de son côté, et qu'il n'y voyait pas bien sans besicles.

Tistet ne s'intimida pas.

«Comment! grand Saint-Père, vous ne me reconnaissez plus? . . . C'est moi, Tistet Védène! . . .

— Védène? . . .

— Mais oui, vous savez bien . . . celui qui portait le vin français à votre mule.

— Ah! oui . . . oui . . . je me rappelle . . . Un bon petit garçonnet, ce Tistet Védène! . . . Et maintenant, qu'est-ce qu'il veut de nous?

— Oh! peu de chose, grand Saint-Père . . . Je venais vous demander . . . A propos, est-ce que vous l'avez toujours, votre mule? Et elle va bien? . . . Ah! tant mieux! . . . Je venais vous demander la place du premier moutardier qui vient de mourir.

— Premier moutardier, toi! . . . Mais tu es trop jeune. Quel âge as-tu donc?

— Vingt ans deux mois, illustre pontife, juste cinq ans de plus que votre mule . . . Ah! palme de Dieu, la brave bête! . . . Si vous saviez comme je l'aimais cette mule-là! . . . comme je me suis langui d'elle en Italie! . . . Est-ce que vous ne me la laisserez pas voir?

— Si, mon enfant, tu la verras, fit le bon Pape tout ému . . . Et puisque tu l'aimes tant, cette brave bête, je ne veux plus que tu vives loin d'elle. Dès ce jour, je t'attache à ma personne en qualité de premier moutardier . . . Mes cardinaux crieront, mais tant pis! j'y suis habitué . . . Viens nous trouver demain à la sortie des vêpres, nous te remettrons les insignes de ton grade en présence de notre chapitre, et puis . . . je te mènerai voir la mule, et tu viendras à la vigne avec nous deux . . . hé! hé! Allons va . . .»

Si Tistet Védène était content en sortant de la grande salle, avec quelle impatience il attendit la cérémonie du lendemain, je n'ai pas besoin de vous le dire. Pourtant il y avait dans le palais quelqu'un de plus heureux encore, et de plus impatient que lui: c'était la mule. Depuis le retour de Védène jusqu'aux vêpres du jour suivant, la terrible bête ne cessa de se bourrer d'avoine et de tirer au mur avec ses sabots de derrière. Elle aussi se préparait pour la cérémonie . . .

Et donc, le lendemain, lorsque vêpres furent dites, Tistet Védène fit son entrée dans la cour du palais papal. Tout le haut clergé était là, les cardinaux en robes rouges, l'avocat du diable en velours noir, les abbés du couvent avec leurs petites mitres, les marguilliers de

When that intriguer Védène entered the great hall of the palace, the Holy Father had trouble recognizing him, he was so much taller and had filled out so much. It must also be said that, on his part, the good Pope had grown old and didn't see well without his spectacles.

Tistet wasn't intimidated.

"What! Great Holy Father, you no longer recognize me? It's I, Tistet Védène! . . ."

"Védène? . . ."

"Yes, yes, you know . . . the one who used to bring the French-style wine to your mule."

"Oh, yes . . . yes . . . I remember. . . . A good little boy, that Tistet Védène! . . . And now, what does he ask of us?"

"Oh, not much, great Holy Father. . . . I've come to request of you . . . By the way, do you still have her, your mule? And is she in good health? . . . Oh, good! . . . I've come to request of you the office of the chief purveyor of mustard, who has just died."

"Chief purveyor of mustard—you! But you're too young. How old are you, anyway?"

"Twenty years and two months old, illustrious Pontiff, exactly five years older than your mule. . . . Ah, by heaven, that fine animal! . . . If you only knew how I loved that mule! . . . How I missed her when I was in Italy! . . . Won't you let me see her?"

"Yes, my child, you'll see her," said the good Pope, deeply touched. "And since you love that fine animal so much, I don't want you to be separated from her any longer. From this day forward, I attach you to my person as chief purveyor of mustard. . . . My cardinals will raise the roof, but I don't care! I'm used to it. . . . Come see us tomorrow when vespers are over, and we'll hand over to you the insignia of your office in the presence of our chapter of canons; and then . . . I'll take you to see the mule, and you'll come to the vineyard with both of us. . . . Ho, ho! Go now . . ."

I have no need to tell you how happy Tistet Védène was on leaving the great hall, or how impatiently he awaited the ceremony on the following day. And yet there was someone in the palace who was even happier and more impatient than he: it was the mule. From the moment of Védène's return until vespers on the following day, the awesome beast didn't stop stuffing herself with oats and kicking out at the wall with her hind hooves. She, too, was getting ready for the ceremony.

And thus, the next day, after vespers had been recited, Tistet Védène made his entry into the courtyard of the papal palace. All of the high clergymen were there, the cardinals in red robes, the devil's advocate[7] in black velvet, the abbots of the monastery with their little miters, the

Saint-Agrico, les camails violets de la maîtrise, le bas clergé aussi, les soldats du Pape en grand uniforme, les trois confréries de pénitents, les ermites du mont Ventoux avec leurs mines farouches et le petit clerc qui va derrière en portant la clochette, les frères flagellants nus jusqu'à la ceinture, les sacristains fleuris en robes de juges, tous, tous, jusqu'aux donneurs d'eau bénite, et celui qui allume, et celui qui éteint . . . il n'y en avait pas un qui manquât . . . Ah! c'était une belle ordination! Des cloches, des pétards, du soleil, de la musique, et toujours ces enragés de tambourins qui menaient la danse, là-bas, sur le pont d'Avignon.

Quand Védène parut au milieu de l'assemblée, sa prestance et sa belle mine y firent courir un murmure d'admiration. C'était un magnifique Provençal, mais des blonds, avec de grands cheveux frisés au bout et une petite barbe follette qui semblait prise aux copeaux de fin métal tombé du burin de son père, le sculpteur d'or. Le bruit courait que dans cette barbe blonde les doigts de la reine Jeanne avaient quelquefois joué; et le sire de Védène avait bien, en effet, l'air glorieux et le regard distrait des hommes que les reines ont aimés . . . Ce jour-là, pour faire honneur à sa nation, il avait remplacé ses vêtements napolitains par une jaquette bordée de rose à la Provençale et sur son chaperon tremblait une grande plume d'ibis de Camargue.

Sitôt entré, le premier moutardier salua d'un air galant et se dirigea vers le haut perron, où le Pape l'attendait pour lui remettre les insignes de son grade: la cuiller de buis jaune et l'habit de safran. La mule était au bas de l'escalier, toute harnachée et prête à partir pour la vigne . . . Quand il passa près d'elle, Tistet Védène eut un bon sourire et s'arrêta pour lui donner deux ou trois petites tapes amicales sur le dos, en regardant du coin de l'œil si le Pape le voyait. La position était bonne . . . La mule prit son élan:

«Tiens! attrape, bandit! Voilà sept ans que je te le garde!»

Et elle vous lui détacha un coup de sabot si terrible, si terrible, que de Pampérigouste même on en vit la fumée, un tourbillon de fumée blonde où voltigeait une plume d'ibis; tout ce qui restait de l'infortuné Tistet Védène! . . .

Les coups de pied de mule ne sont pas aussi foudroyants d'ordinaire; mais celle-ci était une mule papale; et puis, pensez donc! elle le lui gardait depuis sept ans . . . Il n'y a pas de plus bel exemple de rancune ecclésiastique.

church wardens of Saint-Agrico, the violet short capes of the choir school, as well as the minor clergymen, the Pope's soldiers in dress uniform, the three brotherhoods of penitents, the hermits from Mont Ventoux[8] with their fierce expressions, the young cleric walking behind them carrying the handbell, the flagellant monks stripped to the waist, the florid sacristans in judges' robes, everyone, everyone, down to the people who hand out holy water, who light candles and put them out . . . there wasn't a single one missing. . . . Oh, what a beautiful ordination it was! Bells, firecrackers, sunshine, music, and constantly those rabid drummers leading the dance over yonder on the bridge of Avignon.

When Védène made his appearance in the midst of the assembly, his noble bearing and good looks touched off a murmur of admiration. He was a magnificent Provençal, but one of the blond type, with plentiful hair curling at the tips and a little wisp of beard, which seemed to be made of the filings of fine metal that had fallen from the graving tool of his father, the goldsmith. A rumor was afloat that the fingers of Queen Jeanne had sometimes toyed with that blond beard; and, indeed "Lord" Védène had the boastful air and absentminded gaze of men whom queens have loved. . . . On that day, to honor his native land, he had exchanged his Neapolitan garments for a Provençal-style coat edged with pink, and on his headgear there waved a large ibis plume from the Camargue.[9]

As soon as he came in, the chief purveyor of mustard greeted the assembly gallantly and made his way to the high flight of steps where the Pope was waiting to hand over the insignia of his office: the yellow boxwood spoon and the saffron outfit. The mule was at the foot of the steps, completely harnessed and ready to leave for the vineyard. . . . When he came near her, Tistet Védène had a kind smile for her, and stopped to give her two or three little friendly taps on the back, looking out of the corner of his eye to see whether the Pope was watching. The position was a good one. . . . The mule started into motion:

"Here you are! Take this, villain! I've been saving it for you for seven years now!"

And she launched an awesome kick at him, so awesome that, even as far off as Pampérigouste, they could see the smoke from it, a whirlwind of blond smoke in which an ibis feather was whirling: all that was left of the unfortunate Tistet Védène! . . .

Kicks from mules aren't usually that overwhelming; but this mule belonged to a Pope, and besides, just imagine: she had been saving it for him for seven years. . . . There's no finer example of an ecclesiastical grudge.

GUSTAVE FLAUBERT

Hérodias

I

La citadelle de Machærous se dressait à l'orient de la mer Morte, sur un pic de basalte ayant la forme d'un cône. Quatre vallées profondes l'entouraient, deux vers les flancs, une en face, la quatrième au-delà. Des maisons se tassaient contre sa base, dans le cercle d'un mur qui ondulait suivant les inégalités du terrain; et, par un chemin en zigzag tailladant le rocher, la ville se reliait à la forteresse, dont les murailles étaient hautes de cent vingt coudées, avec des angles nombreux, des créneaux sur le bord, et, çà et là, des tours qui faisaient comme des fleurons à cette couronne de pierres, suspendue au-dessus de l'abîme.

Il y avait dans l'intérieur un palais orné de portiques, et couvert d'une terrasse que fermait une balustrade en bois de sycomore, où des mâts étaient disposés pour tendre un vélarium.

Un matin, avant le jour, le Tétrarque Hérode Antipas vint s'y accouder, et regarda.

Les montagnes, immédiatement sous lui, commençaient à découvrir leurs crêtes, pendant que leur masse, jusqu'au fond des abîmes, était encore dans l'ombre. Un brouillard flottait, il se déchira, et les contours de la mer Morte apparurent. L'aube, qui se levait derrière Machærous, épandait une rougeur. Elle illumina bientôt les sables de la grève, les collines, le désert, et, plus loin, tous les monts de la Judée, inclinant leurs surfaces raboteuses et grises. Engaddi, au milieu, traçait une barre noire; Hébron, dans l'enfoncement, s'arrondissait en dôme; Esquol avait des grenadiers, Sorek des vignes, Karmel des champs de sésame; et la tour Antonia, de son cube monstrueux, dominait Jérusalem. Le Tétrarque en détourna la vue pour contempler, à droite, les palmiers de Jéricho; et il songea aux autres villes de sa Galilée: Capharnaüm, Endor, Nazareth, Tibérias où peut-être il ne

GUSTAVE FLAUBERT

Herodias

I

The citadel of Machaerus stood to the east of the Dead Sea, on a cone-shaped basalt peak. Four deep valleys surrounded it, two at the sides, one facing it, and the fourth behind it. Houses were huddled against its base, within the circle of a wall that wove in and out in conformity with the varied features of the terrain; and, by a zigzagging road slashing through the rock, the town was connected to the fortress, the walls of which were a hundred twenty cubits high, with numerous angles, battlements on their rim, and, here and there, towers that formed finials, as it were, to that crown of stones suspended above the abyss.

Within, there was a palace adorned with porticos, and roofed with a terrace enclosed by a balustrade of sycamore wood, on which there was an arrangement of staffs for supporting a velarium.[1]

One morning, before daybreak, the Tetrarch Herod Antipas came and leaned his elbows on that balustrade, and beheld the scene before him.

The mountains immediately below him were beginning to reveal their crests, while their bulk, down to the very bottom of the chasms, still lay in shadow. A fog was floating, it broke up, and the contours of the Dead Sea became visible. The dawn, which was rising behind Machaerus, diffused a red glow. It soon illuminated the sands of the lake shore, the hills, the desert, and, farther off, all the mountains of Judaea, which inclined their rugged gray surfaces. En-gedi, in the center, showed up as a black bar; Hebron, in the hollow, rounded into a dome. Eshcol had pomegranate trees; Sorek, grapevines; Carmel, fields of sesame; and the Tower of Antonia,[2] with its monstrous cube, dominated Jerusalem. The Tetrarch turned away his eyes from it to contemplate, to the right, the palm trees of Jericho; and he thought about those other cities in his province of Galilee: Capernaum, Endor,

99

reviendrait plus. Cependant le Jourdain coulait sur la plaine aride. Toute blanche, elle éblouissait comme une nappe de neige. Le lac, maintenant, semblait en lapis-lazuli; et à sa pointe méridionale, du côté de l'Yémen, Antipas reconnut ce qu'il craignait d'apercevoir. Des tentes brunes étaient dispersées; des hommes avec des lances circulaient entre les chevaux, et des feux s'éteignant brillaient comme des étincelles à ras du sol.

C'étaient les troupes du roi des Arabes, dont il avait répudié la fille pour prendre Hérodias, mariée à l'un de ses frères qui vivait en Italie, sans prétentions au pouvoir.

Antipas attendait les secours des Romains; et Vitellius, gouverneur de la Syrie, tardant à paraître, il se rongeait d'inquiétudes.

Agrippa, sans doute, l'avait ruiné chez l'Empereur? Philippe, son troisième frère, souverain de la Batanée, s'armait clandestinement. Les Juifs ne voulaient plus de ses mœurs idolâtres, tous les autres de sa domination; si bien qu'il hésitait entre deux projets: adoucir les Arabes ou conclure une alliance avec les Parthes; et, sous le prétexte de fêter son anniversaire, il avait convié, pour ce jour même, à un grand festin, les chefs de ses troupes, les régisseurs de ses campagnes et les principaux de la Galilée.

Il fouilla d'un regard aigu toutes les routes. Elles étaient vides. Des aigles volaient au-dessus de sa tête; les soldats, le long du rempart, dormaient contre les murs; rien ne bougeait dans le château.

Tout à coup, une voix lointaine, comme échappée des profondeurs de la terre, fit pâlir le Tétrarque. Il se pencha pour écouter; elle avait disparu. Elle reprit; et en claquant dans ses mains, il cria: — «Mannaeï! Mannaeï!»

Un homme se présenta, nu jusqu'à la ceinture, comme les masseurs des bains. Il était très grand, vieux, décharné, et portait sur la cuisse un coutelas dans une gaine de bronze. Sa chevelure, relevée par un peigne, exagérait la longueur de son front. Une somnolence décolorait ses yeux, mais ses dents brillaient, et ses orteils posaient légèrement sur les dalles, tout son corps ayant la souplesse d'un singe, et sa figure l'impassibilité d'une momie.

— «Où est-il?» demanda le Tétrarque.

Mannaeï répondit, en indiquant avec son pouce un objet derrière eux:

— «Là! toujours!»

— «J'avais cru l'entendre!»

Et Antipas, quand il eut respiré largement, s'informa de Iaokanann, le même que les Latins appellent saint Jean-Baptiste. Avait-on revu

Nazareth, and Tiberias, to which he might never return. Meanwhile the Jordan was flowing on the arid plain. All white, the plain was as dazzling as a sheet of snow. Now the lake seemed made of lapis lazuli; and at its southern tip, in the direction of Yemen, Antipas recognized that which he had been fearing to discern. Brown tents were scattered there; men with lances were circulating among their horses, and fires going out shone like sparks at ground level.

Those were the troops of the king of the Arabs, whose daughter he had repudiated in order to take Herodias, who was married to a brother of his living in Italy and making no claims to power.

Antipas was awaiting the aid of the Romans; and Vitellius, governor of Syria, being late in appearing, he was gnawed by anxiety.

No doubt, Agrippa had destroyed his good standing with the Emperor. Philip, his third brother, ruler of Batanaea,[3] was secretly arming. The Jews were fed up with his idolatrous ways; all the rest, with his domination; so that he was wavering between two plans: to pacify the Arabs or make an alliance with the Parthians; and, with the pretext of celebrating his birthday, he had invited to a great feast, for that very day, the leaders of his troops, the stewards of his rural holdings, and the chief men of Galilee.

He searched all the roads with an acute gaze. They were empty. Eagles were flying over his head; his soldiers, along the rampart, were sleeping against the walls; nothing was stirring in the castle.

Suddenly a distant voice, as if escaping from the depths of the earth, made the Tetrarch turn pale. He bent over to listen; it had vanished. It resumed; and, clapping his hands together, he called: "Mannaei, Mannaei!"

A man appeared, bare to the waist like masseurs in a bathhouse. He was very tall, old, emaciated, and wore at his thigh a cutlass in a bronze sheath. His hair, held back by a comb, exaggerated the height of his brow. His eyes were glazed over with a sleepy look, but his teeth gleamed, and his toes touched the flagstones lightly, his whole body having the nimbleness of a monkey, and his face the impassiveness of a mummy.

"Where is he?" the Tetrarch asked.

Mannaei replied, indicating an object in back of them with his thumb:

"There! Just as usual!"

"I thought I heard him!"

And Antipas, after taking a deep breath, inquired about Johanan, the same man that the Latins call Saint John the Baptist. Had anyone

ces deux hommes, admis par indulgence, l'autre mois, dans son cachot, et savait-on, depuis lors, ce qu'ils étaient venus faire?

Mannaeï répliqua:

— «Ils ont échangé avec lui des paroles mystérieuses, comme les voleurs, le soir, aux carrefours des routes. Ensuite ils sont partis vers la Haute-Galilée, en annonçant qu'ils apporteraient une grande nouvelle.»

Antipas baissa la tête, puis d'un air d'épouvante:

— «Garde-le! garde-le! Et ne laisse entrer personne! Ferme bien la porte! Couvre la fosse! On ne doit pas même soupçonner qu'il vit!»

Sans avoir reçu ces ordres, Mannaeï les accomplissait; car Iaokanann était Juif, et il exécrait les Juifs comme tous les Samaritains.

Leur temple de Garizim, désigné par Moïse pour être le centre d'Israël, n'existait plus depuis le roi Hyrcan; et celui de Jérusalem les mettait dans la fureur d'un outrage, et d'une injustice permanente. Mannaeï s'y était introduit, afin d'en souiller l'autel avec des os de morts. Ses compagnons, moins rapides, avaient été décapités.

Il l'aperçut dans l'écartement de deux collines. Le soleil faisait resplendir ses murailles de marbre blanc et les lames d'or de sa toiture. C'était comme une montagne lumineuse, quelque chose de surhumain, écrasant tout de son opulence et de son orgueil.

Alors il étendit les bras du côté de Sion; et, la taille droite, le visage en arrière, les poings fermés, lui jeta un anathème, croyant que les mots avaient un pouvoir effectif.

Antipas écoutait, sans paraître scandalisé.

Le Samaritain dit encore:

— «Par moments il s'agite, il voudrait fuir, il espère une délivrance. D'autres fois, il a l'air tranquille d'une bête malade; ou bien je le vois qui marche dans les ténèbres, en répétant: «Qu'importe? Pour qu'il grandisse, il faut que je diminue!»

Antipas et Mannaeï se regardèrent. Mais le Tétrarque était las de réfléchir.

Tous ces monts autour de lui, comme des étages de grands flots pétrifiés, les gouffres noirs sur le flanc des falaises, l'immensité du ciel bleu, l'éclat violent du jour, la profondeur des abîmes le troublaient; et une désolation l'envahissait au spectacle du désert, qui figure, dans le bouleversement de ses terrains, des amphithéâtres et des palais abattus. Le vent chaud apportait, avec l'odeur du soufre, comme l'exhalaison des villes maudites, ensevelies plus bas que le rivage sous les eaux pesantes. Ces marques d'une colère immortelle effrayaient sa

seen again those two men who, out of leniency, had been admitted to his dungeon a month earlier, and had anyone learned since then for what purpose they had come?

Mannaei answered:

"They exchanged mysterious words with him, like thieves at a crossroads at night. Then they left for Upper Galilee, declaring that they would bring back important news."

Antipas lowered his head, then said, with a frightened look:

"Hold onto him! Hold onto him! And don't let anyone in! Lock the door securely! Cover the pit! No one must even suspect he's alive!"

Without having received those orders, Mannaei was already carrying them out; for Johanan was a Jew, and he loathed the Jews just as all Samaritans do.

Their temple at Garizim, designated by Moses as the center of Israel, no longer existed since King Hyrcanus;[4] and the one in Jerusalem infuriated them, since they considered it an outrage and a permanent injustice. Mannaei had made his way into it in order to defile its altar with bones of dead men. His companions, less quick to escape, had been decapitated.

He could make it out in the separation between two hills. The sun made its white marble walls and the gold plates of its roofing shine. It was like a mountain of light, something superhuman, crushing everything with its opulence and its pride.

Then he stretched out his arms toward Zion; and, fully erect, his face drawn back, his fists clenched, he hurled an anathema at it, in the belief that words had a physical power.

Antipas was listening without seeming shocked.

The Samaritan added:

"At times he stirs about, he'd like to run away, he hopes for some deliverance. Other times he has the calm look of a sick animal; or else, I see him walking in the darkness, repeating: 'What does it matter? If He is to increase, I must diminish!'"

Antipas and Mannaei looked at each other. But the Tetrarch was tired of pondering.

All those mountains around him, like levels of great petrified flood waters, the black pits on the cliffsides, the immensity of the blue sky, the violent brightness of the sunlight, the depth of the chasms, troubled him; and an affliction came over him at the sight of the desert, which in the upheaval of its terrain, forms images of amphitheaters and overthrown palaces. The hot wind, along with its odor of sulphur, seemed to carry the effluvia of the accursed cities[5] buried below shore level beneath the heavy waters. Those signs of an immortal wrath alarmed him

pensée; et il restait les deux coudes sur la balustrade, les yeux fixes et les tempes dans les mains. Quelqu'un l'avait touché. Il se retourna. Hérodias était devant lui.

Une simarre de pourpre légère l'enveloppait jusqu'aux sandales. Sortie précipitamment de sa chambre, elle n'avait ni colliers ni pendants d'oreilles; une tresse de ses cheveux noirs lui tombait sur un bras, et s'enfonçait, par le bout, dans l'intervalle de ses deux seins. Ses narines, trop remontées, palpitaient; la joie d'un triomphe éclairait sa figure; et, d'une voix forte, secouant le Tétrarque:

— «César nous aime! Agrippa est en prison!»

— «Qui te l'a dit?»

— «Je le sais!»

Elle ajouta:

— «C'est pour avoir souhaité l'empire à Caïus!»

Tout en vivant de leurs aumônes, il avait brigué le titre de roi, qu'ils ambitionnaient comme lui. Mais dans l'avenir plus de craintes! — «Les cachots de Tibère s'ouvrent difficilement, et quelquefois l'existence n'y est pas sûre!»

Antipas la comprit; et, bien qu'elle fût la sœur d'Agrippa, son intention atroce lui sembla justifiée. Ces meurtres étaient une conséquence des choses, une fatalité des maisons royales. Dans celle d'Hérode, on ne les comptait plus.

Puis elle étala son entreprise: les clients achetés, les lettres découvertes, des espions à toutes les portes, et comment elle était parvenue à séduire Eutychès le dénonciateur. — «Rien ne me coûtait! Pour toi, n'ai-je pas fait plus? . . . J'ai abandonné ma fille!»

Après son divorce, elle avait laissé dans Rome cette enfant, espérant bien en avoir d'autres du Tétrarque. Jamais elle n'en parlait. Il se demanda pourquoi son accès de tendresse.

On avait déplié le vélarium et apporté vivement de larges coussins auprès d'eux. Hérodias s'y affaissa, et pleurait, en tournant le dos. Puis elle se passa la main sur les paupières, dit qu'elle n'y voulait plus songer, qu'elle se trouvait heureuse; et elle lui rappela leurs causeries là-bas, dans l'atrium, les rencontres aux étuves, leurs promenades le long de la voie Sacrée, et les soirs, dans les grandes villas, au murmure des jets d'eau, sous des arcs de fleurs, devant la campagne romaine. Elle le regardait comme autrefois, en se frôlant contre sa poitrine, avec des gestes câlins. — Il la repoussa. L'amour qu'elle tâchait de ranimer était si loin, maintenant! Et tous ses malheurs en découlaient; car, depuis douze ans bientôt, la guerre continuait. Elle avait vieilli le Tétrarque. Ses épaules se voûtaient dans une toge sombre, à bordure

as he thought of them; and he remained with both elbows on the
balustrade, his eyes staring, and his temples in his hands. Someone had
touched him. He turned around. Herodias was before him.

A lightweight purple simar enveloped her down to her sandals.
Having left her bedroom hastily, she was wearing neither necklaces
nor earrings; one lock of her black hair tumbled onto one arm, and its
end was lost in the space between her two breasts. Her nostrils, too
turned-up, were palpitating; a triumphant joy lit up her face; and in a
loud voice, shaking the Tetrarch, she said:

"Caesar loves us! Agrippa is in prison!"

"Who told you?"

"I know!"

She added:

"It's because he wished that Gaius would become emperor!"

Although he lived on their charity, he had canvassed for the title of
king, which they were as ambitious for as he. But no more fears from
now on! "Tiberius's dungeons don't open so easily, and sometimes life
there is uncertain!"

Antipas understood her; and even though she was Agrippa's sister,
her terrible purpose seemed justified to him. Those murders were a
consequence of events, an inevitable malady of royal houses. In
Herod's house they were already beyond counting.

Then she revealed what she had undertaken: dependents suborned,
letters disclosed, spies at every door; and how she had managed to
corrupt Eutyches, the informer. "I spared no effort! For you, haven't
I done more? . . . I've given up my daughter!"

After her divorce she had left that child in Rome, in high hopes of
having others with the Tetrarch. She never spoke about her. He wondered why she had had that sudden fit of affectionateness.

The velarium had been unfurled and large cushions had rapidly
been brought to the couple. Herodias sank into them and wept with
her back turned. Then she drew her hand over her lashes, and said that
she didn't wish to think about that any longer; that she was happy; and
she reminded him of their talks back in Rome in the atrium, their
meetings at the baths, their walks along the Via Sacra, and the evenings
in the great villas, with the murmur of the fountains, under arches of
flowers, facing the Roman countryside. She looked at him as she had
in the past, brushing up against his chest, with wheedling gestures.—
He pushed her away. The love she was trying to revive was now so
far away! And all his troubles were a result of it; for the war had
been going on for close to twelve years. It had aged the Tetrarch. His

violette; ses cheveux blancs se mêlaient à sa barbe, et le soleil, qui traversait le voile, baignait de lumière son front chagrin. Celui d'Hérodias également avait des plis; et, l'un en face de l'autre, ils se considéraient d'une manière farouche.

Les chemins dans la montagne commencèrent à se peupler. Des pasteurs piquaient des bœufs, des enfants tiraient des ânes, des palefreniers conduisaient des chevaux. Ceux qui descendaient les hauteurs au-delà de Machærous disparaissaient derrière le château; d'autres montaient le ravin en face, et, parvenus à la ville, déchargeaient leurs bagages dans les cours. C'étaient les pourvoyeurs du Tétrarque, et des valets, précédant ses convives.

Mais au fond de la terrasse, à gauche, un Essénien parut, en robe blanche, nu-pieds, l'air stoïque. Mannaeï, du côté droit, se précipitait en levant son coutelas.

Hérodias lui cria: — «Tue-le!»

— «Arrête!» dit le Tétrarque.

Il devint immobile; l'autre aussi.

Puis ils se retirèrent, chacun par un escalier différent, à reculons, sans se perdre des yeux.

— «Je le connais!» dit Hérodias, «il se nomme Phanuel, et cherche à voir Iaokanann, puisque tu as l'aveuglement de le conserver!»

Antipas objecta qu'il pouvait un jour servir. Ses attaques contre Jérusalem gagnaient à eux le reste des Juifs.

— «Non!» reprit-elle, «ils acceptent tous les maîtres, et ne sont pas capables de faire une patrie!» Quant à celui qui remuait le peuple avec des espérances conservées depuis Néhémias, la meilleure politique était de le supprimer.

Rien ne pressait, selon le Tétrarque. Iaokanann dangereux! Allons donc! Il affectait d'en rire.

— «Tais-toi!» Et elle redit son humiliation, un jour qu'elle allait vers Galaad, pour la récolte du baume. « — Des gens, au bord du fleuve, remettaient leurs habits sur un monticule, à côté, un homme parlait. Il avait une peau de chameau autour des reins, et sa tête ressemblait à celle d'un lion. Dès qu'il m'aperçut, il cracha sur moi toutes les malédictions des prophètes. Ses prunelles flamboyaient; sa voix rugissait; il levait les bras, comme pour arracher le tonnerre. Impossible de fuir! les roues de mon char avaient du sable jusqu'aux essieux; et je m'éloignais lentement, m'abritant sous mon manteau, glacée par ces injures qui tombaient comme une pluie d'orage.»

Iaokanann l'empêchait de vivre. Quand on l'avait pris et lié avec des

shoulders were stooped in his dark toga with purple edging; his white hair was entangled in his beard, and the sun, penetrating the canvas, bathed his troubled brow in light. Herodias's brow was also wrinkled; and, facing each other, they considered each other in a fierce way.

The mountain roads started to fill with people. Herdsmen were goading oxen, children were pulling donkeys, grooms were leading horses. Those who were descending the heights beyond Machaerus disappeared behind the castle; others were climbing the ravine that faced them, and, having arrived in the town, were unloading their packs in the courtyards. They were the Tetrarch's purveyors, and servants, preceding his guests.

But at the far end of the terrace, to the left, there appeared an Essene, in a white robe, barefoot, with a stoical expression. Mannaei, on the right side, dashed toward him, lifting his cutlass.

Herodias called to him: "Kill him!"

"Stop!" said the Tetrarch.

Mannaei stopped in his tracks; so did the other.

Then they withdrew, each by a different staircase, walking backwards, without taking their eyes off each other.

"I know him!" said Herodias. "He's called Phanuel and he's trying to see Johanan, since you're so blind that you keep him alive!"

Antipas objected that Johanan might be useful some day. His attacks against Jerusalem won over the rest of the Jews for their cause.

"No," she continued, "they accept any master, and they're incapable of forming a nation!" As for the man who was stirring up the people with hopes preserved ever since Nehemiah,[6] the wisest political measure was to do away with him.

There was no hurry, according to the Tetrarch. Johanan dangerous! Come, now! He pretended to laugh at the idea.

"Be still!" And she told him again of her humiliation, one day when she was heading for Gilead for the harvesting of the balsam. "People on the riverbank were putting their clothes back on on a little mound; alongside them, a man was speaking. He had a camel skin around his waist, and his head looked like a lion's. As soon as he caught sight of me, he spat out at me all the curses of the Prophets. His eyes were blazing; his voice was roaring; he was raising his arms as if to tear down a thunderbolt. Impossible to escape! The wheels of my chariot were clogged with sand up to the axles; and I was moving away slowly, hiding myself under my cloak, chilled by those insults, which were falling like a rainstorm."

Johanan prevented her from enjoying life. When he had been captured

cordes, les soldats devaient le poignarder s'il résistait; il s'était montré doux. On avait mis des serpents dans sa prison; ils étaient morts. L'inanité de ces embûches exaspérait Hérodias. D'ailleurs, pourquoi sa guerre contre elle? Quel intérêt le poussait? Ses discours, criés à des foules, s'étaient répandus, circulaient; elle les entendait partout, ils emplissaient l'air. Contre des légions elle aurait eu de la bravoure. Mais cette force plus pernicieuse que les glaives, et qu'on ne pouvait saisir, était stupéfiante; et elle parcourait la terrasse, blêmie par sa colère, manquant de mots pour exprimer ce qui l'étouffait.

Elle songeait aussi que le Tétrarque, cédant à l'opinion, s'aviserait peut-être de la répudier. Alors tout serait perdu! Depuis son enfance, elle nourrissait le rêve d'un grand empire. C'était pour y atteindre que, délaissant son premier époux, elle s'était jointe à celui-là, qui l'avait dupée, pensait-elle.

— «J'ai pris un bon soutien, en entrant dans ta famille!»

— «Elle vaut la tienne!» dit simplement le Tétrarque.

Hérodias sentit bouillonner dans ses veines le sang des prêtres et des rois ses aïeux.

— «Mais ton grand-père balayait le temple d'Ascalon! Les autres étaient bergers, bandits, conducteurs de caravanes, une horde, tributaire de Juda depuis le roi David! Tous mes ancêtres ont battu les tiens! Le premier des Makkabi vous a chassés d'Hébron, Hyrcan forcés à vous circoncire!» Et, exhalant le mépris de la patricienne pour le plébéien, la haine de Jacob contre Édom, elle lui reprocha son indifférence aux outrages, sa mollesse envers les Pharisiens qui le trahissaient, sa lâcheté pour le peuple qui la détestait. «Tu es comme lui, avoue-le! et tu regrettes la fille arabe qui danse autour des pierres. Reprends-la! Va-t'en vivre avec elle, dans sa maison de toile! dévore son pain cuit sous la cendre! avale le lait caillé de ses brebis! baise ses joues bleues! et oublie-moi!»

Le Tétrarque n'écoutait plus. Il regardait la plate-forme d'une maison, où il y avait une jeune fille, et une vieille femme tenant un parasol à manche de roseau, long comme la ligne d'un pêcheur. Au milieu du tapis, un grand panier de voyage restait ouvert. Des ceintures, des voiles, des pendeloques d'orfèvrerie en débordaient confusément. La jeune fille, par intervalles, se penchait vers ces choses, et les secouait à l'air. Elle était vêtue comme les Romaines, d'une tunique calamistrée avec un péplum à glands d'émeraude; et des lanières bleues enfermaient sa chevelure, trop lourde, sans doute, car, de temps à autre, elle y portait la main. L'ombre du parasol se promenait

and tied with ropes, the soldiers were ordered to stab him if he resisted; he had acted gently. Snakes had been placed in his prison; they had died.

The futility of those snares exasperated Herodias. Besides, what was the reason for his war against her? What interests drove him to it? His words, shouted to crowds, had spread abroad and were making the rounds; she heard them all over, they filled the air. If combating legions, she would have been brave. But this force, which was more pernicious than swords, which one couldn't take hold of, was stupefying; and she ran to and fro on the terrace, pale with anger, finding no words to express the feelings that choked her.

She also thought that the Tetrarch might yield to public opinion and decide to repudiate her. Then all would be lost! Since her childhood she had been nurturing the dream of a great empire. It was in order to attain it that she had deserted her first husband and married this one, who had hoodwinked her, as she thought.

"I took hold of a firm prop when I married into your family!"

"It's as good as yours!" the Tetrarch said, simply.

Herodias felt the blood of the priests and kings, her forefathers, boiling in her veins.

"But your grandfather used to sweep the temple at Ashkelon! The rest were shepherds, highway robbers, caravan drivers, a horde of nomads, subject to Judah ever since King David! All of my ancestors conquered yours! The first Maccabee drove you out of Hebron, Hyrcanus compelled you to get circumcised!" And, venting the scorn of the patrician for the plebeian, the hatred of Jacob for Edom,[7] she reproached him for his indifference to insults, his weakness toward the Pharisees who were betraying him, his cowardice toward the populace who detested her. "You're like him, admit it! And you miss that Arab girl who dances around stones. Take her back! Go off and live with her in her canvas home! Eat her bread baked in the ashes! Swallow the curdled milk from her sheep! Kiss her blue cheeks! And forget me!"

The Tetrarch was no longer listening. He was watching the flat roof of a house on which there were a girl and an old woman holding a parasol with a reed handle as long as a fisherman's rod. In the center of the carpet, a large traveling basket was open. Belts, veils, and pendants of precious metal spilled out of it in confusion. From time to time the girl stooped over those things and shook them in the air. She was dressed like Roman women, in a goffered tunic and a peplum with emerald tassels; blue thongs contained her hair, which was no doubt too heavy, because she occasionally lifted her hand to it. The shade of the parasol moved around above her, half-concealing her.

au-dessus d'elle, en la cachant à demi. Antipas aperçut deux ou trois fois son col délicat, l'angle d'un œil, le coin d'une petite bouche. Mais il voyait, des hanches à la nuque, toute sa taille qui s'inclinait pour se redresser d'une manière élastique. Il épiait le retour de ce mouvement, et sa respiration devenait plus forte; des flammes s'allumaient dans ses yeux. Hérodias l'observait.

Il demanda: — «Qui est-ce?»

Elle répondit n'en rien savoir, et s'en alla soudainement apaisée.

Le Tétrarque était attendu sous les portiques par des Galiléens, le maître des écritures, le chef des pâturages, l'administrateur des salines et un Juif de Babylone, commandant ses cavaliers. Tous le saluèrent d'une acclamation. Puis, il disparut vers les chambres intérieures.

Phanuel surgit à l'angle d'un couloir.

— «Ah! encore? Tu viens pour Iaokanann, sans doute?»

— «Et pour toi! j'ai à t'apprendre une chose considérable.»

Et, sans quitter Antipas, il pénétra, derrière lui, dans un appartement obscur.

Le jour tombait par un grillage, se développant tout du long sous la corniche. Les murailles étaient peintes d'une couleur grenat, presque noir. Dans le fond s'étalait un lit d'ébène, avec des sangles en peau de bœuf. Un bouclier d'or, au-dessus, luisait comme un soleil.

Antipas traversa toute la salle, se coucha sur le lit.

Phanuel était debout. Il leva son bras, et dans une attitude inspirée:

— «Le Très-Haut envoie par moments un de ses fils. Iaokanann en est un. Si tu l'opprimes, tu seras châtié.»

— «C'est lui qui me persécute!» s'écria Antipas. «Il a voulu de moi une action impossible. Depuis ce temps-là il me déchire. Et je n'étais pas dur, au commencement! Il a même dépêché de Machærous des hommes qui bouleversent mes provinces. Malheur à sa vie! Puisqu'il m'attaque, je me défends!»

— «Ses colères ont trop de violence», répliqua Phanuel. «N'importe! Il faut le délivrer.»

— «On ne relâche pas les bêtes furieuses!» dit le Tétrarque.

L'Essénien répondit:

— «Ne t'inquiète plus! Il ira chez les Arabes, les Gaulois, les Scythes. Son œuvre doit s'étendre jusqu'au bout de la terre!»

Antipas semblait perdu dans une vision.

— «Sa puissance est forte! . . . Malgré moi, je l'aime!»

— «Alors, qu'il soit libre?»

Two or three times Antipas caught sight of her delicate neck, the corner of an eye, one corner of her small mouth. But, from the hips to the nape of the neck, he saw her whole torso stooping down and straightening up again in a supple manner. He waited for her to make that movement again, and his breathing grew heavier; flames lit up in his eyes. Herodias was observing him.

He asked: "Who is that?"

She replied that she had no idea, and she left, suddenly calmed.

The Tetrarch was awaited beneath the porticos by Galileans, his chief accountant, the supervisor of his pasture land, the administrator of his saltworks, and a Jew from Babylon, who commanded his cavalry. They all greeted him with an acclamation. Then he disappeared, headed for the inner rooms.

Phanuel loomed up at the corner of a corridor.

"Oh, still here? No doubt you've come on account of Johanan."

"And on your account! I have something important to tell you."

And, without leaving Antipas, he entered a dark apartment after him.

Daylight entered through a grille, which extended the length of the room below the ceiling molding. The walls were painted garnet-red, almost black. At the end of the room was an ebony bed supported by an oxhide frame. A round golden shield above it was gleaming like a sun.

Antipas crossed the whole room and lay down on the bed.

Phanuel was standing. He raised his arm, and said, like a man divinely inspired:

"At times the Most High sends down one of His sons. Johanan is one of them. If you oppress him, you will be chastised."

"It's *he* that persecutes *me!*" exclaimed Antipas. "He asked me to do something impossible. Ever since then, he's been tearing me apart. And I wasn't a hard man at the beginning! He even sent men out from Machaerus to subvert my provinces. Ill luck to his life! Since he attacks me, I defend myself!"

"His fits of anger are too violent," Phanuel replied. "But what of it? He must be set free."

"People don't release raging animals!" said the Tetrarch.

The Essene responded:

"Don't worry any more! He'll visit the Arabs, the Gauls, the Scythians. His work must spread to the ends of the earth."

Antipas seemed lost in a vision.

"His power is great! . . . In spite of myself, I love him!"

"Then, can he go free?"

Le Tétrarque hocha la tête. Il craignait Hérodias, Mannaeï et l'inconnu.

Phanuel tâcha de le persuader, en alléguant, pour garantie de ses projets, la soumission des Esséniens aux rois. On respectait ces hommes pauvres, indomptables par les supplices, vêtus de lin, et qui lisaient l'avenir dans les étoiles.

Antipas se rappela un mot de lui, tout à l'heure.

— «Quelle est cette chose, que tu m'annonçais comme importante?»

Un nègre survint. Son corps était blanc de poussière. Il râlait et ne put que dire:

— «Vitellius!»

— «Comment? Il arrive?»

— «Je l'ai vu. Avant trois heures, il est ici!»

Les portières des corridors furent agitées comme par le vent. Une rumeur emplit le château, un vacarme de gens qui couraient, de meubles qu'on traînait, d'argenteries s'écroulant; et, du haut des tours, des buccins sonnaient, pour avertir les esclaves dispersés.

II

Les remparts étaient couverts de monde quand Vitellius entra dans la cour. Il s'appuyait sur le bras de son interprète, suivi d'une grande litière rouge ornée de panaches et de miroirs, ayant la toge, le laticlave, les brodequins d'un consul et des licteurs autour de sa personne.

Ils plantèrent contre la porte leurs douze faisceaux, des baguettes reliées par une courroie avec une hache dans le milieu. Alors, tous frémirent devant la majesté du peuple romain.

La litière, que huit hommes manœuvraient, s'arrêta. Il en sortit un adolescent, le ventre gros, la face bourgeonnée, des perles le long des doigts. On lui offrit une coupe pleine de vin et d'aromates. Il la but, et en réclama une seconde.

Le Tétrarque était tombé aux genoux du Proconsul, chagrin, disait-il, de n'avoir pas connu plus tôt la faveur de sa présence. Autrement, il eût ordonné sur les routes tout ce qu'il fallait pour les Vitellius. Ils descendaient de la déesse Vitellia. Une voie, menant du Janicule à la mer, portait encore leur nom. Les questures, les consulats étaient innombrables dans la famille; et quant à Lucius, maintenant son hôte, on devait le remercier comme vainqueur des Clites et père de ce jeune Aulus, qui semblait revenir dans son domaine, puisque l'Orient

The Tetrarch shook his head. He feared Herodias, Mannaei, and the unknown.

Phanuel tried to persuade him, promising, as a guarantee of his plans, the submission of the Essenes to the rulers. People respected these indigent men, unshakable by torture, clad in linen, and able to read the future in the stars.

Antipas remembered a remark that Phanuel had made a little earlier.

"What is this thing you wanted to tell me that was important?"

A black man arrived. His body was white with dust. He was at his last gasp, and all he could say was:

"Vitellius!"

"What! He's arriving?"

"I've seen him. In less than three hours, he'll be here!"

The door curtains in the corridors were shaken as if by the wind. A buzzing filled the castle, a racket of people running, furniture being dragged, silver plates toppling; and, from the top of the towers, buccinae[8] were sounding to notify the scattered slaves.

II

The ramparts were covered with people when Vitellius entered the courtyard. He was leaning on his interpreter's arm, and was followed by a large red litter adorned with plumes and mirrors; he wore the toga, laticlave,[9] and ankle boots of a consul, and had lictors around him.

They stacked their twelve fasces against the door; these were bundles of sticks tied by a strap with an axe in the midst of them. Then, everyone trembled before the majesty of the Roman nation.

The litter, which was being handled by eight men, came to a halt. Out of it stepped an adolescent with a big belly and a pimply face, with pearls up and down his fingers. He was offered a goblet filled with wine and spices. He emptied it and asked for another.

The Tetrarch had fallen at the knees of the Proconsul, vexed, as he said, not to have learned of the honor of his presence sooner. Otherwise, he would have seen to it that everything the Vitellii might need was in readiness on the roads. They were descended from the goddess Vitellia, he went on. A highway, which led from the Janiculum to the sea, still bore their name.[10] Questorships and consulships had been held numberless times by family members; and, as for Lucius, now his guest, he was to be thanked as conqueror of the Clitae[11] and

était la patrie des dieux. Ces hyperboles furent exprimées en latin. Vitellius les accepta impassiblement.

Il répondit que le grand Hérode suffisait à la gloire d'une nation. Les Athéniens lui avaient donné la surintendance des jeux Olympiques. Il avait bâti des temples en l'honneur d'Auguste, été patient, ingénieux, terrible, et fidèle toujours aux Césars.

Entre les colonnes à chapiteaux d'airain, on aperçut Hérodias qui s'avançait d'un air d'impératrice, au milieu de femmes et d'eunuques tenant sur des plateaux de vermeil des parfums allumés.

Le Proconsul fit trois pas à sa rencontre; et, l'ayant saluée d'une inclinaison de tête:

— «Quel bonheur!» s'écria-t-elle, «que désormais Agrippa, l'ennemi de Tibère, fût dans l'impossibilité de nuire!»

Il ignorait l'événement, elle lui parut dangereuse; et comme Antipas jurait qu'il ferait tout pour l'Empereur, Vitellius ajouta: «Même au détriment des autres?»

Il avait tiré des otages du roi des Parthes, et l'Empereur n'y songeait plus; car Antipas, présent à la conférence, pour se faire valoir, en avait tout de suite expédié la nouvelle. De là, une haine profonde, et les retards à fournir des secours.

Le Tétrarque balbutia. Mais Aulus dit en riant:

— «Calme-toi, je te protège!»

Le Proconsul feignit de n'avoir pas entendu. La fortune du père dépendait de la souillure du fils; et cette fleur des fanges de Caprée lui procurait des bénéfices tellement considérables, qu'il l'entourait d'égards, tout en se méfiant, parce qu'elle était vénéneuse.

Un tumulte s'éleva sous la porte. On introduisait une file de mules blanches, montées par des personnages en costume de prêtres. C'étaient des Sadducéens et des Pharisiens, que la même ambition poussait à Machærous, les premiers voulant obtenir la sacrificature, et les autres la conserver. Leurs visages étaient sombres, ceux des Pharisiens surtout, ennemis de Rome et du Tétrarque. Les pans de leur tunique les embarrassaient dans la cohue; et leur tiare chancelait à leur front par-dessus des bandelettes de parchemin, où des écritures étaient tracées.

Presque en même temps, arrivèrent des soldats de l'avant-garde. Ils avaient mis leurs boucliers dans des sacs, par précaution contre la poussière; et derrière eux était Marcellus, lieutenant du Proconsul, avec des publicains, serrant sous leurs aisselles des tablettes de bois.

as father of this young Aulus, who seemed to be returning to his own domain, since the Orient was the homeland of the gods. These hyperboles were expressed in Latin. Vitellius received them impassively.

He replied that Herod the Great by himself sufficed for the glory of a nation. The Athenians had bestowed on him the superintendence of the Olympic Games. He had built temples in honor of Augustus; he had been patient, ingenious, fear-inspiring, and constantly loyal to the Caesars.

Among the columns with bronze capitals, they caught sight of Herodias, who was advancing with an imperial air, amid women and eunuchs carrying burning incense on silver-gilt trays.

The Proconsul took three steps forward to meet her; and, when he had greeted her with a nod, she exclaimed:

"What good fortune that, from now on, Agrippa, the enemy of Tiberius, is no longer capable of doing harm!"

He was unaware of the event, and she struck him as being dangerous; and when Antipas swore that he would do anything for the Emperor, Vitellius added: "Even if it injures others?"

He had taken hostages from the king of the Parthians, but the Emperor no longer cared, because Antipas, who had been present at the peace conference, had immediately sent the news to Rome to boost his own standing. Hence, a deep-seated hatred, and the delays in supplying aid.

The Tetrarch stammered. But Aulus said, laughing:

"Calm down, I'm your protector!"

The Proconsul pretended not to have heard. The father's fortunes depended on the son's depravity; and that blossom of the filth of Capri[12] procured such important profits for him that he lavished all kinds of attentions on him, distrusting him all the while, because this "blossom" was poisonous.

A tumult arose at the gate. A line of white mules was being led in, on which men dressed as priests were riding. These were Sadducees and Pharisees, drawn to Machaerus by the same ambition, the former wishing to obtain the chief priesthood in the Jerusalem Temple, the latter wishing to retain it. Their faces were somber, especially those of the Pharisees, enemies of Rome and of the Tetrarch. The skirts of their tunics hindered them in the press of people; and their tiaras were bouncing on their foreheads above the narrow parchment bands on which religious formulas were written.

Almost at the same time, soldiers of the advanced guard arrived. They had put their round shields in sacks as a precaution against the dust; and behind them was Marcellus, the Proconsul's lieutenant, with publicans[13] who clutched wooden tablets beneath their armpits.

Antipas nomma les principaux de son entourage: Tolmaï, Kanthera, Séhon, Ammonius d'Alexandrie, qui lui achetait de l'asphalte, Naâmann, capitaine de ses vélites, Iaçim le Babylonien.

Vitellius avait remarqué Mannaeï.

— «Celui-là, qu'est-ce donc?»

Le Tétrarque fit comprendre, d'un geste, que c'était le bourreau. Puis, il présenta les Sadducéens.

Jonathas, un petit homme libre d'allures et parlant grec, supplia le maître de les honorer d'une visite à Jérusalem. Il s'y rendrait probablement.

Éléazar, le nez crochu et la barbe longue, réclama pour les Pharisiens le manteau du grand prêtre détenu dans la tour Antonia par l'autorité civile.

Ensuite, les Galiléens dénoncèrent Ponce Pilate. A l'occasion d'un fou qui cherchait les vases d'or de David dans une caverne, près de Samarie, il avait tué des habitants; et tous parlaient à la fois, Mannaeï plus violemment que les autres. Vitellius affirma que les criminels seraient punis.

Des vociférations éclatèrent en face d'un portique, où les soldats avaient suspendu leurs boucliers. Les housses étant défaites, on voyait sur les *umbo* la figure de César. C'était pour les Juifs une idolâtrie. Antipas les harangua, pendant que Vitellius, dans la colonnade, sur un siège élevé, s'étonnait de leur fureur. Tibère avait eu raison d'en exiler quatre cents en Sardaigne. Mais chez eux ils étaient forts; et il commanda de retirer les boucliers.

Alors, ils entourèrent le Proconsul, en implorant des réparations d'injustice, des privilèges, des aumônes. Les vêtements étaient déchirés, on s'écrasait; et, pour faire de la place, des esclaves avec des bâtons frappaient de droite et de gauche. Les plus voisins de la porte descendirent sur le sentier, d'autres le montaient; ils refluèrent; deux courants se croisaient dans cette masse d'hommes qui oscillait, comprimée par l'enceinte des murs.

Vitellius demanda pourquoi tant de monde. Antipas en dit la cause: le festin de son anniversaire; et il montra plusieurs de ses gens, qui, penchés sur les créneaux, halaient d'immenses corbeilles de viandes, de fruits, de légumes, des antilopes et des cigognes, de larges poissons couleur d'azur, des raisins, des pastèques, des grenades élevées en pyramides. Aulus n'y tint pas. Il se précipita vers les cuisines, emporté par cette goinfrerie qui devait surprendre l'univers.

En passant près d'un caveau, il aperçut des marmites pareilles à des

Antipas named the chief men in his entourage: Tolmai, Kanthera, Sehon; Ammonius of Alexandria, who bought asphalt for him; Naaman, the captain of his velites;[14] Iacim the Babylonian.

Vitellius had noticed Mannaei.

"What does that fellow do?"

With a gesture the Tetrarch gave him to understand that he was the executioner.

Then he introduced the Sadducees.

Jonathas, a short man of easy manners who spoke Greek, asked his host to honor them with a visit to Jerusalem. He would probably go there, he said.

Eleazar, with a hooked nose and a long beard, requested for the Pharisees the mantle of the high priest being kept in the Tower of Antonia by the civil authorities.

Next, the Galileans denounced Pontius Pilate. When a madman was seeking David's gold vessels in a cave near Samaria, Pilate had killed some local people; and everyone was speaking at the same time, Mannaei with more violence than the rest. Vitellius assured them that the criminals would be punished.

Shouts erupted opposite a portico where the soldiers had hung their shields. The cloth coverings having been removed, Caesar's face was to be seen on the *umbos*.[15] For the Jews this was idolatry. Antipas harangued them, while Vitellius, in the colonnade, on a raised seat, marveled at their rage. Tiberius had been right to exile four hundred of them to Sardinia. But in their own country they were powerful; and he ordered the shields taken away.

Then they surrounded the Proconsul, begging him to redress various wrongs, to grant privileges and benefactions. Their clothing was torn, they were crushed together; and, to make room, slaves armed with sticks were striking to the right and to the left. Those closest to the gate went down onto the path; others were ascending it; they fell back; two currents were crossing in that wavering mass of men contained by the girdle of walls.

Vitellius asked why there was such a crowd. Antipas told him the reason: his birthday feast; and he pointed out several of his servants who were leaning over the battlements and hauling up immense baskets of meat, fruit, and vegetables, antelopes and storks, large sky-blue fish, grapes, watermelons, pyramids of pomegranates. Aulus couldn't resist. He made a dash for the kitchens, carried away by that gluttony which was later to amaze the universe.

Passing by a vaulted cellar, he caught sight of cooking pots that

cuirasses. Vitellius vint les regarder; et exigea qu'on lui ouvrît les chambres souterraines de la forteresse.

Elles étaient taillées dans le roc en hautes voûtes, avec des piliers de distance en distance. La première contenait de vieilles armures; mais la seconde regorgeait de piques, et qui allongeaient toutes leurs pointes, émergeant d'un bouquet de plumes. La troisième semblait tapissée en nattes de roseaux, tant les flèches minces étaient perpendiculairement les unes à côté des autres. Des lames de cimeterres couvraient les parois de la quatrième. Au milieu de la cinquième, des rangs de casques faisaient, avec leurs crêtes, comme un bataillon de serpents rouges. On ne voyait dans la sixième que des carquois; dans la septième, que des cnémides; dans la huitième, que des brassards; dans les suivantes, des fourches, des grappins, des échelles, des cordages, jusqu'à des mâts pour les catapultes, jusqu'à des grelots pour le poitrail des dromadaires! et comme la montagne allait en s'élargissant vers sa base, évidée à l'intérieur telle qu'une ruche d'abeilles, au-dessous de ces chambres il y en avait de plus nombreuses, et d'encore plus profondes.

Vitellius, Phinées son interprète, et Sisenna le chef des publicains, les parcouraient à la lumière des flambeaux, que portaient trois eunuques.

On distinguait dans l'ombre des choses hideuses inventées par les barbares: casse-tête garnis de clous, javelots empoisonnant les blessures, tenailles qui ressemblaient à des mâchoires de crocodile; enfin le Tétrarque possédait dans Machærous des munitions de guerre pour quarante mille hommes.

Il les avait rassemblées en prévision d'une alliance de ses ennemis. Mais le Proconsul pouvait croire, ou dire, que c'était pour combattre les Romains, et il cherchait des explications.

Elles n'étaient pas à lui; beaucoup servaient à se défendre des brigands; d'ailleurs il en fallait contre les Arabes; ou bien, tout cela avait appartenu à son père. Et, au lieu de marcher derrière le Proconsul, il allait devant, à pas rapides. Puis il se rangea le long du mur, qu'il masquait de sa toge, avec ses deux coudes écartés; mais le haut d'une porte dépassait sa tête. Vitellius la remarqua, et voulut savoir ce qu'elle enfermait.

Le Babylonien pouvait seul l'ouvrir.

— «Appelle le Babylonien!»

On l'attendit.

Son père était venu des bords de l'Euphrate s'offrir au grand Hérode, avec cinq cents cavaliers, pour défendre les frontières orien-

looked like breastplates. Vitellius went over to look at them, and demanded that the underground rooms of the fortress be opened for him.

They were carved into the rock, with lofty vaulted ceilings, supported here and there by pillars. The first one contained old armor, but the second was chock-full of pikes, all presenting their points as they emerged from a bouquet of feathers. The third room seemed to be carpeted with reed mats, so numerous were the thin arrows laid perpendicularly to one another in groups. Scimitar blades covered the walls of the fourth room. In the middle of the fifth, rows of helmets, with their crests, seemed to constitute a battalion of red serpents. Nothing was to be seen in the sixth except quivers; in the seventh, nothing but shin greaves; in the eighth, nothing but arm guards; in the following rooms, large forks, grappling hooks, ladders, ropes, even spars for catapults, even jingle bells for the breast straps of dromedaries! And since the mountain got wider toward its base, and was hollowed out inside, like a beehive, below those rooms there were more numerous ones and even deeper ones.

Vitellius, his interpreter Phineas, and Sisenna, the chief of the publicans, roamed through them by the light of torches carried by three eunuchs.

They could make out in the shadow hideous things invented by the barbarians: maces studded with nails, javelins that poisoned the wounds they made, pincers that looked like crocodiles' jaws; in short, in Machaerus the Tetrarch possessed armaments for forty thousand men.

He had assembled them foreseeing an alliance among his enemies. But the Proconsul could well believe, or say, that they were for fighting the Romans, and he asked for explanations.

They didn't belong to him, he said; many of them were used for defending himself against bandits; moreover, he needed some against the Arabs; or else, it had all belonged to his father. And, instead of walking behind the Proconsul, he went on ahead, at a rapid pace. Then he placed himself against the wall, which he cloaked with his toga, his two elbows jutting out; but the top of a door showed above his head. Vitellius noticed it, and wanted to know what was behind it.

Only the Babylonian was able to open it, he said.

"Call the Babylonian!"

They waited for him.

His father had come from the banks of the Euphrates to offer his services to Herod the Great with five hundred cavalrymen, to defend

tales. Après le partage du royaume, Iaçum était demeuré chez Philippe, et maintenant servait Antipas.

Il se présenta, un arc sur l'épaule, un fouet à la main. Des cordons multicolores serraient étroitement ses jambes torses. Ses gros bras sortaient d'une tunique sans manches, et un bonnet de fourrure ombrageait sa mine, dont la barbe était frisée en anneaux.

D'abord, il eut l'air de ne pas comprendre l'interprète. Mais Vitellius lança un coup d'œil à Antipas, qui répéta tout de suite son commandement. Alors Iaçim appliqua ses deux mains contre la porte. Elle glissa dans le mur.

Un souffle d'air chaud s'exhala des ténèbres. Une allée descendait en tournant; ils la prirent et arrivèrent au seuil d'une grotte, plus étendue que les autres souterrains.

Une arcade s'ouvrait au fond sur le précipice, qui de ce côté-là défendait la citadelle. Un chèvrefeuille, se cramponnant à la voûte, laissait retomber ses fleurs en pleine lumière. A ras du sol, un filet d'eau murmurait.

Des chevaux blancs étaient là, une centaine peut-être, et qui mangeaient de l'orge sur une planche au niveau de leur bouche. Ils avaient tous la crinière peinte en bleu, les sabots dans des mitaines de sparterie, et les poils d'entre les oreilles bouffant sur le frontal, comme une perruque. Avec leur queue très longue, ils se battaient mollement les jarrets. Le Proconsul en resta muet d'admiration.

C'étaient de merveilleuses bêtes, souples comme des serpents, légères comme des oiseaux. Elles partaient avec la flèche du cavalier, renversaient les hommes en les mordant au ventre, se tiraient de l'embarras des rochers, sautaient par-dessus des abîmes, et pendant tout un jour continuaient dans les plaines leur galop frénétique; un mot les arrêtait. Dès que Iaçim entra, elles vinrent à lui, comme des moutons quand paraît le berger; et, avançant leur encolure, elles le regardaient inquiètes avec leurs yeux d'enfant. Par habitude, il lança du fond de sa gorge un cri rauque qui les mit en gaieté; et elles se cabraient, affamées d'espace, demandant à courir.

Antipas, de peur que Vitellius ne les enlevât, les avait emprisonnées dans cet endroit, spécial pour les animaux, en cas de siège.

— «L'écurie est mauvaise», dit le Proconsul, «et tu risques de les perdre! Fais l'inventaire, Sisenna!»

Le publicain retira une tablette de sa ceinture, compta les chevaux et les inscrivit.

Les agents des compagnies fiscales corrompaient les gouverneurs,

the eastern borders. After the partition of the kingdom, Iacim had stayed with Philip, and was now serving Antipas.

He arrived with a bow on his shoulder and a whip in his hand. Multicolored cords were tightly twined around his crooked legs. His heavy arms emerged from a sleeveless tunic, and a fur cap cast a shadow on his face, with its beard curled into ringlets.

At first he seemed not to understand the interpreter. But Vitellius darted a glance at Antipas, who immediately repeated his order. Then Iacim placed his two hands against the door. It slid into the wall.

A puff of hot air blew out of the darkness. A passageway led downward, turning as it went; they followed it and arrived at the threshold to a grotto, more extensive than the other underground rooms.

At the far end, an arcade opened onto the precipice that defended the citadel in that direction. A woodbine, clinging to the vaulted ceiling, let its blossoms droop in full daylight. At floor level, a rivulet of water was murmuring.

There were white horses there, about a hundred perhaps, eating barley placed on a board at the level of their muzzles. They all had their manes painted blue, their hooves encased in esparto-grass basketwork mittens; and the hair between their ears was combed out over their browbands like wigs. With their very long tails they were gently lashing their hocks. The Proconsul stood there mute with admiration.

They were wonderful animals, supple as serpents, light as birds. They could spurt ahead at the speed of their horseman's arrow, they could knock men over and bite their bellies, they could work their way through impeding rocks, jump across chasms, and keep up their frenetic gallop in the plains for a full day; they would halt at a single word. The moment that Iacim entered, they came up to him like sheep when their shepherd appears, and, stretching out their necks, they looked at him anxiously with eyes like those of children. Out of habit, he emitted from deep within his throat a raucous cry that cheered them up, and they reared and bucked, thirsty for space, begging to be allowed to run at large.

Antipas, fearing that Vitellius might confiscate them, had imprisoned them in that place, which was set aside for animals in case of siege.

"This is a bad stable," said the Proconsul, "and you risk losing them. Draw up an inventory, Sisenna!"

The publican drew a tablet out of his belt, counted the horses, and set down the number.

The agents of financial companies were corrupting the governors so

pour piller les provinces. Celui-là flairait partout, avec sa mâchoire de fouine et ses paupières clignotantes.

Enfin, on remonta dans la cour.

Des rondelles de bronze au milieu des pavés, çà et là, couvraient les citernes. Il en observa une, plus grande que les autres, et qui n'avait pas sous les talons leur sonorité. Il les frappa toutes alternativement, puis hurla, en piétinant:

— «Je l'ai! je l'ai! C'est ici le trésor d'Hérode!»

La recherche de ses trésors était une folie des Romains.

Ils n'existaient pas, jura le Tétrarque.

Cependant, qu'y avait-il là-dessous?

— «Rien! un homme, un prisonnier.»

— «Montre-le!» dit Vitellius.

Le Tétrarque n'obéit pas; les Juifs auraient connu son secret. Sa répugnance à ouvrir la rondelle impatientait Vitellius.

— «Enfoncez-la!» cria-t-il aux licteurs.

Mannaeï avait deviné ce qui les occupait. Il crut, en voyant une hache, qu'on allait décapiter Iaokanann; et il arrêta le licteur au premier coup sur la plaque, insinua entre elle et les pavés une manière de crochet, puis, roidissant ses longs bras maigres, la souleva doucement, elle s'abattit; tous admirèrent la force de ce vieillard. Sous le couvercle doublé de bois, s'étendait une trappe de même dimension. D'un coup de poing, elle se replia en deux panneaux; on vit alors un trou, une fosse énorme que contournait un escalier sans rampe; et ceux qui se penchèrent sur le bord aperçurent au fond quelque chose de vague et d'effrayant.

Un être humain était couché par terre sous de longs cheveux se confondant avec les poils de bête qui garnissaient son dos. Il se leva. Son front touchait à une grille horizontalement scellée; et, de temps à autre, il disparaissait dans les profondeurs de son antre.

Le soleil faisait briller la pointe des tiares, le pommeau des glaives, chauffait à outrance les dalles; et des colombes, s'envolant des frises, tournoyaient au-dessus de la cour. C'était l'heure où Mannaeï, ordinairement, leur jetait du grain. Il se tenait accroupi devant le Tétrarque, qui était debout près de Vitellius. Les Galiléens, les prêtres, les soldats, formaient un cercle par-derrière; tous se taisaient, dans l'angoisse de ce qui allait arriver.

Ce fut d'abord un grand soupir, poussé d'une voix caverneuse.

Hérodias l'entendit à l'autre bout du palais. Vaincue par une fascination, elle traversa la foule; et elle écoutait, une main sur l'épaule de Mannaeï, le corps incliné.

they could plunder the provinces. This one sniffed about everywhere, with his ferret's jaw and blinking eyelashes.

Finally they went back up to the courtyard.

Bronze roundels amid the paving blocks covered cisterns here and there. He noticed one that was bigger than the others and didn't sound as hollow beneath their heels. He struck them all in turn; then, stamping, he howled:

"I have it! I have it! Herod's treasure is here!"

The search for his treasures was an obsession with the Romans.

They didn't exist, the Tetrarch swore.

So, what was down there?

"Nothing! A man, a prisoner."

"Show him!" said Vitellius.

The Tetrarch didn't obey; the Jews would have learned his secret. His reluctance to open the roundel made Vitellius impatient.

"Break it in!" he shouted to the lictors.

Mannaei had guessed what was on their mind. Seeing an axe, he thought they were going to behead Johanan; and he stopped the lictor at the first blow on the cover; he inserted a sort of hook between it and the pavement; then, stiffening his long, thin arms, he raised it gently and it fell over; everyone marveled at that old man's strength. Below the cover, which was lined with wood, there lay a trapdoor of the same size. At a blow of the fist, it folded into two panels; then they could see a hole, an enormous pit containing a circular staircase without a banister; and those who were leaning over the edge saw at the bottom something vague and frightening.

A human being was lying on the ground, covered by his long hair, which mingled with the furry animal skins he wore on his back. He stood up. His forehead touched a grille that was inserted horizontally; and, from time to time, he disappeared into the depths of his lair.

The sun made the tips of the tiaras and the pommels of the swords shine; it heated the flagstones beyond endurance; and doves, flying out of the friezes, were wheeling over the courtyard. It was the hour when Mannaei usually threw them grain. He remained squatting in front of the Tetrarch, who was standing near Vitellius. The Galileans, the priests, and the soldiers formed a circle behind them; everyone was silent, anxiously awaiting what was to come.

At first there was a great sigh, uttered by a cavernous voice.

Herodias heard it at the other end of the palace. Spellbound, she made her way through the crowd, and stood listening, one hand on Mannaei's shoulder, her body leaning forward.

La voix s'éleva:

«Malheur à vous, Pharisiens et Sadducéens, race de vipères, outres gonflées, cymbales retentissantes!»

On avait reconnu Iaokanann. Son nom circulait. D'autres accoururent.

— «Malheur à toi, ô peuple! et aux traîtres de Juda, aux ivrognes d'Ephraïm, à ceux qui habitent la vallée grasse, et que les vapeurs du vin font chanceler!

«Qu'ils se dissipent comme l'eau qui s'écoule, comme la limace qui se fond en marchant, comme l'avorton d'une femme qui ne voit pas le soleil.

«Il faudra, Moab, te réfugier dans les cyprès comme les passereaux, dans les cavernes comme les gerboises. Les portes des forteresses seront plus vite brisées que des écailles de noix, les murs crouleront, les villes brûleront; et le fléau de l'Éternel ne s'arrêtera pas. Il retournera vos membres dans votre sang, comme de la laine dans la cuve d'un teinturier. Il vous déchirera comme une herse neuve; il répandra sur les montagnes tous les morceaux de votre chair!»

De quel conquérant parlait-il? Était-ce de Vitellius? Les Romains seuls pouvaient produire cette extermination. Des plaintes s'échappaient: — «Assez! assez! qu'il finisse!»

Il continua, plus haut:

— «Auprès du cadavre de leurs mères, les petits enfants se traîneront sur les cendres. On ira, la nuit, chercher son pain à travers les décombres, au hasard des épées. Les chacals s'arracheront des ossements sur les places publiques, où le soir les vieillards causaient. Tes vierges, en avalant leurs pleurs, joueront de la cithare dans les festins de l'étranger, et tes fils les plus braves baisseront leur échine, écorchée par des fardeaux trop lourds!»

Le peuple revoyait les jours de son exil, toutes les catastrophes de son histoire. C'étaient les paroles des anciens prophètes. Iaokanann les envoyait, comme de grands coups, l'une après l'autre.

Mais la voix se fit douce, harmonieuse, chantante. Il annonçait un affranchissement, des splendeurs au ciel, le nouveau-né un bras dans la caverne du dragon, l'or à la place de l'argile, le désert s'épanouissant comme une rose: — «Ce qui maintenant vaut soixante kiccars ne coûtera pas une obole. Des fontaines de lait jailliront des rochers; on s'endormira dans les pressoirs le ventre plein! Quand viendras-tu, toi que j'espère? D'avance, tous les peuples s'agenouillent, et ta domination sera éternelle, Fils de David!»

The voice was raised:

"Misfortune befall you, Pharisees and Sadducees, generation of vipers, swollen wineskins, sounding brass!"

They had recognized Johanan. His name made the rounds. More people ran over.

"Misfortune befall you, O nation, and the traitors of Judah, the drunkards of Ephraim, those who inhabit the fat valley and whom the fumes of wine make to stagger!

"May they be dispersed like water that runs off, like the slug that melts as it walks, like a woman's miscarried child that never sees the sun.

"Moab, you shall have to take refuge in the cypresses like the sparrows, in caves like the jerboas. The gates of the fortresses will be broken more quickly than nutshells, the walls will collapse, the cities will burn; and the scourge of the Everlasting Lord shall not rest. He will roll your limbs in your blood, like wool in a dyer's vat. He will tear you like a new harrow; He will scatter all the pieces of your flesh on the mountains!"

Of what conqueror was he speaking? Was it of Vitellius? Only the Romans could bring about that degree of extermination. Complaints were heard: "Enough! Enough! Make him stop!"

He went on, even louder:

"Next to their mothers' corpses, the little children shall drag themselves through the ashes. At night, people will go seeking their bread among the ruins, facing the chance of swordplay. The jackals will tear the bones away from one another on the public squares, where the old men used to talk in the evening. Your virgins, swallowing their tears, will play the cithara at the feasts of the foreigner, and your bravest sons will bend their backs, which will be flayed by burdens that are too heavy!"

The people recalled the days of their exile, all the catastrophes of their history. These were the words of the old Prophets. Johanan flung them out like mighty blows, one after the other.

But now his voice became gentle, harmonious, as if chanting. He was announcing a liberation, splendors in the sky, the newborn child with one arm in the dragon's cave, gold in place of clay, the desert opening like a rose: "That which now is worth sixty kikkars will not cost an obol.[16] Fountains of milk will gush from the rocks; men will fall asleep in the wine presses with their stomachs full! When will You come, You whom I await? Even before then, all nations will kneel down, and Your reign will be everlasting, Son of David!"

Le Tétrarque se rejeta en arrière, l'existence d'un Fils de David l'outrageant comme une menace.

Iaokanann l'invectiva pour sa royauté. — «Il n'y a pas d'autre roi que l'Éternel! et pour ses jardins, pour ses statues, pour ses meubles d'ivoire, comme l'impie Achab!»

Antipas brisa la cordelette du cachet suspendu à sa poitrine, et le lança dans la fosse, en lui commandant de se taire.

La voix répondit:

— «Je crierai comme un ours, comme un âne sauvage, comme une femme qui enfante!

«Le châtiment est déjà dans ton inceste. Dieu t'afflige de la stérilité du mulet!»

Et des rires s'élevèrent, pareils au clapotement des flots.

Vitellius s'obstinait à rester. L'interprète, d'un ton impassible, redisait, dans la langue des Romains, toutes les injures que Iaokanann rugissait dans la sienne. Le Tétrarque et Hérodias étaient forcés de les subir deux fois. Il haletait, pendant qu'elle observait béante le fond du puits.

L'homme effroyable se renversa la tête; et, empoignant les barreaux, y colla son visage, qui avait l'air d'une broussaille, où étincelaient deux charbons:

— «Ah! c'est toi, Iézabel!

«Tu as pris son cœur avec le craquement de ta chaussure. Tu hennissais comme une cavale. Tu as dressé ta couche sur les monts, pour accomplir tes sacrifices!

«Le Seigneur arrachera tes pendants d'oreilles, tes robes de pourpre, tes voiles de lin, les anneaux de tes bras, les bagues de tes pieds, et les petits croissants d'or qui tremblent sur ton front, tes miroirs d'argent, tes éventails en plumes d'autruche, les patins de nacre qui haussent ta taille, l'orgueil de tes diamants, les senteurs de tes cheveux, la peinture de tes ongles, tous les artifices de ta mollesse; et les cailloux manqueront pour lapider l'adultère!»

Elle chercha du regard une défense autour d'elle. Les Pharisiens baissaient hypocritement leurs yeux. Les Sadducéens tournaient la tête, craignant d'offenser le Proconsul. Antipas paraissait mourir.

La voix grossissait, se développait, roulait avec des déchirements de tonnerre, et, l'écho dans la montagne la répétant, elle foudroyait Machærous d'éclats multipliés.

— «Étale-toi dans la poussière, fille de Babylone! Fais moudre de la farine! Ote ta ceinture, détache ton soulier, trousse-toi, passe les fleuves! ta honte sera découverte, ton opprobre sera vu! tes sanglots

The Tetrarch reeled backwards, the existence of a Son of David upsetting him like a threat.

Johanan railed against him with regard to his royalty—"There is no king other than the Everlasting Lord!"—and on account of his gardens, his statues, and his ivory furniture, like those of the impious Ahab.

Antipas broke the string of the seal that hung on his chest, and hurled it into the pit, ordering him to be silent.

The voice replied:

"I shall cry out like a bear, like a wild ass, like a woman in labor!

"The punishment is already present, in your incest. God is afflicting you with the sterility of a mule!"

And laughter arose, similar to the lapping of waves.

Vitellius insisted on remaining. His interpreter, in an unemotional voice, translated into the tongue of the Romans all the insults that Johanan was roaring out in his own. The Tetrarch and Herodias were compelled to undergo them twice. He was panting, while she was gaping and studying the bottom of the well.

The terrifying man bent back his head; and, clutching the bars, he glued his face to them, that face resembling a thicket, in which two live coals sparkled.

"Ah, it's you, Jezebel!

"You have captured his heart with the creaking of your shoes. You were neighing like a mare. You have set up your bed on the mountains to perform your sacrifices!

"The Lord will tear off your earrings, your purple gowns, your linen veils, the circlets on your arms, the rings on your toes, and the little gold crescents that tremble on your brow, your silver mirrors, your ostrich-plume fans, the mother-of-pearl pattens that make you taller, the pride of your diamonds, the perfumes in your hair, the paint on your nails, every artifice of your indolence; and there won't be enough stones to throw at the adulteress!"

She looked around for someone to defend her. The Pharisees hypocritically lowered their eyes. The Sadducees turned away their heads, fearing to offend the Proconsul. Antipas looked as if he were dying.

The voice grew louder and more powerful, rolling and slashing like thunder and lightning; the mountain echoes repeated its words, so that it lashed at Machaerus with multiplied force.

"Stretch out in the dust, daughter of Babylon! Have flour ground! Remove your belt, undo your shoe, tuck up your clothes, and cross the rivers! Your shame will be revealed, your infamy will be seen! Your

te briseront les dents! L'Éternel exècre la puanteur de tes crimes!
Maudite! maudite! Crève comme une chienne!»
    La trappe se ferma, le couvercle se rabattit. Mannaeï voulait étran-
gler Iaokanann.
    Hérodias disparut. Les Pharisiens étaient scandalisés. Antipas, au
milieu d'eux, se justifiait.
    — «Sans doute», reprit Éléazar, «il faut épouser la femme de son
frère, mais Hérodias n'était pas veuve, et de plus elle avait un enfant,
ce qui constituait l'abomination.»
    — «Erreur! erreur!» objecta le Sadducéen Jonathas. «La Loi con-
damne ces mariages, sans les proscrire absolument.»
    — «N'importe! On est pour moi bien injuste!» disait Antipas, «car,
enfin, Absalon a couché avec les femmes de son père, Juda avec sa
bru, Amnon avec sa sœur, Loth avec ses filles.»
    Aulus, qui venait de dormir, reparut à ce moment-là. Quand il fut
instruit de l'affaire, il approuva le Tétrarque. On ne devait point se
gêner pour de pareilles sottises; et il riait beaucoup du blâme des
prêtres, et de la fureur de Iaokanann.
    Hérodias, au milieu du perron, se retourna vers lui.
    — «Tu as tort, mon maître! Il ordonne au peuple de refuser l'impôt.»
    — «Est-ce vrai?» demanda tout de suite le Publicain.
    Les réponses furent généralement affirmatives. Le Tétrarque les
renforçait.
    Vitellius songea que le prisonnier pouvait s'enfuir; et comme la con-
duite d'Antipas lui semblait douteuse, il établit des sentinelles aux
portes, le long des murs et dans la cour.
    Ensuite, il alla vers son appartement. Les députations des prêtres
l'accompagnèrent.
    Sans aborder la question de la sacrificature, chacune émettait ses
griefs.
    Tous l'obsédaient. Il les congédia.
    Jonathas le quittait, quand il aperçut, dans un créneau, Antipas cau-
sant avec un homme à longs cheveux et en robe blanche, un Essénien;
et il regretta de l'avoir soutenu.
    Une réflexion avait consolé le Tétrarque. Iaokanann ne dépendait
plus de lui; les Romains s'en chargeaient. Quel soulagement! Phanuel
se promenait alors sur le chemin de ronde.
    Il l'appela et, désignant les soldats:
    — «Ils sont les plus forts! je ne peux le délivrer! ce n'est pas ma
faute!»
    La cour était vide. Les esclaves se reposaient. Sur la rougeur du

sobs will split your teeth! The Everlasting Lord loathes the stench of your crimes! You are accursed! Accursed! Die like a bitch!"

The trapdoor closed, the cover fell back into place. Mannaei wanted to throttle Johanan.

Herodias vanished. The Pharisees were shocked. Antipas, standing in their midst, tried to justify himself.

"No doubt," Eleazar went on, "a man is obliged to marry his brother's wife, but Herodias wasn't a widow, and, besides, she had a child, and that's what made it an abomination."

"Wrong! Wrong!" the Sadducee Jonathas objected. "The Law condemns such marriages, but doesn't absolutely forbid them."

"No matter! People are being very unfair to me," Antipas was saying, "because, after all, Absalom slept with his father's wives, Judah with his daughter-in-law, Amnon with his sister, Lot with his daughters."

Aulus, who had just been napping, showed up again at that moment. When he was informed of the matter, he sided with the Tetrarch. People shouldn't be bothered over such foolishness; and he had a good laugh at the reproaches of the priests and Johanan's frenzy.

Herodias, on the middle of the staircase, turned toward him.

"You're wrong, master! He orders the people not to pay their taxes."

"Is that right?" the publican immediately asked.

The replies were generally in the affirmative. The Tetrarch backed them up.

It occurred to Vitellius that the prisoner could escape; and, since Antipas's behavior seemed suspect to him, he posted sentinels at the gates, along the walls, and in the courtyard.

Then he went to his apartment. The deputations of priests accompanied him.

Without broaching the question of the office of high priest, each deputation was stating its grievances.

They were all besieging him. He dismissed them.

Jonathas was leaving him when he noticed, at a battlement, Antipas talking with a man who had long hair and a white robe, an Essene; and he was sorry he had spoken in his favor.

One reflection had consoled the Tetrarch. Johanan was no longer his responsibility; the Romans were taking charge of him. What a relief! Phanuel was then strolling on the military walkway behind the battlements.

He summoned him, and, indicating the soldiers, said:

"They're stronger than I am! I can't release him! It isn't my fault!"

The courtyard was empty. The slaves were resting. Against the

ciel, qui enflammait l'horizon, les moindres objets perpendiculaires se détachaient en noir. Antipas distingua les salines à l'autre bout de la mer Morte, et ne voyait plus les tentes des Arabes. Sans doute ils étaient partis? La lune se levait; un apaisement descendait dans son cœur.

Phanuel, accablé, restait le menton sur la poitrine. Enfin, il révéla ce qu'il avait à dire.

Depuis le commencement du mois, il étudiait le ciel avant l'aube, la constellation de Persée se trouvant au zénith. Agalah se montrait à peine, Algol brillait moins, Mira-Cœti avait disparu; d'où il augurait la mort d'un homme considérable, cette nuit même, dans Machærous. Lequel? Vitellius était trop bien entouré. On n'exécuterait pas Iaokanann. «C'est donc moi!» pensa le Tétrarque.

Peut-être que les Arabes allaient revenir? Le Proconsul découvrirait ses relations avec les Parthes! Des sicaires de Jérusalem escortaient les prêtres; ils avaient sous leurs vêtements des poignards; et le Tétrarque ne doutait pas de la science de Phanuel.

Il eut l'idée de recourir à Hérodias. Il la haïssait pourtant. Mais elle lui donnerait du courage; et tous les liens n'étaient pas rompus de l'ensorcellement qu'il avait autrefois subi.

Quand il entra dans sa chambre, du cinnamome fumait sur une vasque de porphyre; et des poudres, des onguents, des étoffes pareilles à des nuages, des broderies plus légères que des plumes, étaient dispersés.

Il ne dit pas la prédiction de Phanuel, ni sa peur des Juifs et des Arabes; elle l'eût accusé d'être lâche. Il parla seulement des Romains; Vitellius ne lui avait rien confié de ses projets militaires. Il le supposait ami de Caïus, que fréquentait Agrippa; et il serait envoyé en exil, ou peut-être on l'égorgerait.

Hérodias, avec une indulgence dédaigneuse, tâcha de le rassurer. Enfin, elle tira d'un petit coffre une médaille bizarre, ornée du profil de Tibère. Cela suffisait à faire pâlir les licteurs et fondre les accusations.

Antipas, ému de reconnaissance, lui demanda comment elle l'avait.

— «On me l'a donnée», reprit-elle.

Sous une portière en face, un bras nu s'avança, un bras jeune, charmant et comme tourné dans l'ivoire par Polyclète. D'une façon un peu gauche, et cependant gracieuse, il ramait dans l'air pour saisir une tunique oubliée sur une escabelle près de la muraille.

Une vieille femme la passa doucement, en écartant le rideau.

Le Tétrarque eut un souvenir, qu'il ne pouvait préciser.

redness of the sky, which set the horizon ablaze, the slightest vertical objects stood out in black. Antipas could make out the saltworks at the other end of the Dead Sea, and he no longer saw the tents of the Arabs. They had no doubt departed. The moon was rising; a feeling of calm settled over his heart.

Phanuel, bitterly disappointed, stood there with his chin on his chest. Finally he revealed what he had to say.

Since the beginning of the month, he had been studying the sky before dawn, the constellation Perseus being at the zenith. Agalah was barely visible, Algol was shining less brightly, Mira Ceti had vanished;[17] from that, he foresaw the death of an important man, that very night, at Machaerus.

Who? Vitellius was too well guarded. They wouldn't execute Johanan. "Then it's I!" the Tetrarch thought.

Maybe the Arabs were going to return. The Proconsul would discover his dealings with the Parthians! Assassins from Jerusalem were escorting the priests; they had daggers under their clothes; and the Tetrarch believed fully in Phanuel's science.

The thought occurred to him to go to Herodias for aid. And yet he hated her. But she would give him courage; and the bonds formed between them by the witchcraft he had undergone in the past were not all broken.

When he entered her room, cinnamon was smoking on a porphyry basin; and powders, ointments, fabrics that resembled clouds, embroideries lighter than feathers, were scattered around.

He didn't report Phanuel's prediction, or his fear of the Jews and the Arabs; she would have accused him of cowardice. He spoke of the Romans only; Vitellius hadn't trusted him with any of his military plans. He imagined that he was a friend of Gaius, whom Agrippa used to frequent; and he would be sent into exile, or perhaps murdered.

Herodias, with scornful indulgence, tried to reassure him. Finally, she took from a small jewel box a bizarre medallion adorned with the profile of Tiberius. That would be enough to make the lictors turn pale and the accusations melt away.

Antipas, touched and grateful, asked her how she had come by it.

"It was given to me," she replied.

Beneath a door curtain opposite them, a bare arm came forward, a young, charming arm, as if sculpted in ivory by Polycletus. In a slightly awkward, and yet graceful, manner it was groping in the air to take hold of a tunic that had been forgotten on a stool near the wall.

An old woman passed it through gently, moving aside the curtain.

The Tetrarch remembered something, but couldn't say precisely what it was.

— «Cette esclave est-elle à toi?»
— «Que t'importe?» répondit Hérodias.

III

Les convives emplissaient la salle du festin.

Elle avait trois nefs, comme une basilique, et que séparaient des colonnes en bois d'algumim, avec des chapiteaux de bronze couverts de sculptures. Deux galeries à claire-voie s'appuyaient dessus; et une troisième en filigrane d'or se bombait au fond, vis-à-vis d'un cintre énorme, qui s'ouvrait à l'autre bout.

Des candélabres, brûlant sur les tables alignées dans toute la longueur du vaisseau, faisaient des buissons de feux, entre les coupes de terre peinte et les plats de cuivre, les cubes de neige, les monceaux de raisin; mais ces clartés rouges se perdaient progressivement, à cause de la hauteur du plafond, et des points lumineux brillaient, comme des étoiles, la nuit, à travers des branches. Par l'ouverture de la grande baie, on apercevait des flambeaux sur les terrasses des maisons; car Antipas fêtait ses amis, son peuple, et tous ceux qui s'étaient présentés.

Des esclaves, alertes comme des chiens et les orteils dans des sandales de feutre, circulaient, en portant des plateaux.

La table proconsulaire occupait, sous la tribune dorée, une estrade en planches de sycomore. Des tapis de Babylone l'enfermaient dans une espèce de pavillon.

Trois lits d'ivoire, un en face et deux sur les flancs, contenaient Vitellius, son fils et Antipas; le Proconsul étant près de la porte, à gauche, Aulus à droite, le Tétrarque au milieu.

Il avait un lourd manteau noir, dont la trame disparaissait sous des applications de couleur, du fard aux pommettes, la barbe en éventail, et de la poudre d'azur dans ses cheveux, serrés par un diadème de pierreries. Vitellius gardait son baudrier de pourpre, qui descendait en diagonale sur une toge de lin. Aulus s'était fait nouer dans le dos les manches de sa robe en soie violette, lamée d'argent. Les boudins de sa chevelure formaient des étages, et un collier de saphirs étincelait à sa poitrine, grasse et blanche comme celle d'une femme. Près de lui, sur une natte et jambes croisées, se tenait un enfant très beau, qui souriait toujours. Il l'avait vu dans les cuisines, ne pouvait plus s'en passer, et, ayant peine à retenir son nom chaldéen, l'appelait simplement: «l'Asiatique». De temps à autre, il s'étalait sur le triclinium. Alors, ses pieds nus dominaient l'assemblée.

"Is that slave girl yours?"

"What do you care?" Herodias replied.

III

The guests filled the banqueting hall.

It had three naves, like a basilica, which were separated by columns of *algum*[18] wood, with bronze capitals covered with sculptures. Two clerestory galleries rested on them; and a third convex gallery of gold filigree was located at the back, opposite an enormous archway opening at the other end.

Candelabra, burning on the tables that were lined up along the full length of the central space, created bushes of flame among the painted earthenware goblets and the copper plates, the blocks of snow, the piles of grapes; but these bright red areas became progressively lost to view because of the height of the ceiling, and points of light were shining like stars seen through branches at night. Through the opening of the great arched bay could be seen torches on the terrace roofs of the houses; for Antipas was entertaining his friends, his people, and all those who had come.

Slaves, as alert as dogs, their toes thrust into felt sandals, were circulating, carrying trays.

The Proconsul's table, beneath the gilded gallery, occupied a dais of sycamore planks. Babylonian carpets enclosed it in a sort of pavilion.

Three ivory couches, one facing the table and two at the sides, held Vitellius, his son, and Antipas. The Proconsul was near the door, to the left; Aulus, to the right; the Tetrarch, in the center.

He was wearing a heavy black mantle, the weave of which was hidden by laid-on paints; there was rouge on his cheeks, his beard was cut fan-shape, and there was azure powder in his hair, which was contained by a jeweled diadem. Vitellius had kept on his purple shoulder belt, which descended diagonally over his linen toga. Aulus had had the sleeves of his violet silk robe with silver spangles tied behind him. His corkscrew curls rose in stages, and a sapphire necklace sparkled on his bosom, which was as plump and white as a woman's. Near him, his legs crossed on a mat, was a very good-looking boy who was constantly smiling. He had seen him in the kitchens and could no longer get on without him; having trouble remembering his Chaldaean name, he simply called him "the Asiatic." From time to time he stretched out on the triclinium.[19] At such times, his bare feet dominated the entire gathering.

De ce côté-là, il y avait les prêtres et les officiers d'Antipas, des habitants de Jérusalem, les principaux des villes grecques; et, sous le Proconsul: Marcellus avec les Publicains, des amis du Tétrarque, les personnages de Kana, Ptolémaïde, Jéricho; puis, pêle-mêle, des montagnards du Liban, et les vieux soldats d'Hérode: douze Thraces, un Gaulois, deux Germains, des chasseurs de gazelles, des pâtres de l'Idumée, le sultan de Palmyre, des marins d'Éziongaber. Chacun avait devant soi une galette de pâte molle, pour s'essuyer les doigts; et les bras, s'allongeant comme des cous de vautour, prenaient des olives, des pistaches, des amandes. Toutes les figures étaient joyeuses, sous des couronnes de fleurs.

Les Pharisiens les avaient repoussées comme indécence romaine. Ils frisonnèrent quand on les aspergea de galbanum et d'encens, composition réservée aux usages du Temple.

Aulus en frotta son aisselle; et Antipas lui en promit tout un chargement, avec trois couffes de ce véritable baume, qui avait fait convoiter la Palestine à Cléopâtre.

Un capitaine de sa garnison de Tibériade, survenu tout à l'heure, s'était placé derrière lui, pour l'entretenir d'événements extraordinaires. Mais son attention était partagée entre le Proconsul et ce qu'on disait aux tables voisines.

On y causait de Iaokanann et des gens de son espèce; Simon de Gittoï lavait les péchés avec du feu. Un certain Jésus . . .

— «Le pire de tous», s'écria Éléazar. «Quel infâme bateleur!»

Derrière le Tétrarque, un homme se leva, pâle comme la bordure de sa chlamyde. Il descendit l'estrade, et, interpellant les Pharisiens:

— «Mensonge! Jésus fait des miracles!»

Antipas désirait en voir.

— «Tu aurais dû l'amener! Renseigne-nous!»

Alors il conta que lui, Jacob, ayant une fille malade, s'était rendu à Capharnaüm, pour supplier le Maître de vouloir la guérir. Le Maître avait répondu: «Retourne chez toi, elle est guérie!» Et il l'avait trouvée sur le seuil, étant sortie de sa couche quand le gnomon du palais marquait la troisième heure, l'instant même où il abordait Jésus.

Certainement, objectèrent les Pharisiens, il existait des pratiques, des herbes puissantes! Ici même, à Machærous, quelquefois on trouvait le baaras qui rend invulnérable; mais guérir sans voir ni toucher était une chose impossible, à moins que Jésus n'employât les démons.

Et les amis d'Antipas, les principaux de la Galilée, reprirent, en hochant la tête:

On that side were located the priests and Antipas' officers, some inhabitants of Jerusalem, the leaders of the Greek cities. Below the Proconsul were Marcellus and the publicans, friends of the Tetrarch, important people from Cana, Ptolemais, and Jericho; then, intermingled, Lebanese mountaineers and old soldiers of Herod the Great—twelve Thracians, a Gaul, two Germans—gazelle hunters, shepherds from Idumaea,[20] the sultan of Palmyra, sailors from Ezion-geber. Each man had in front of him a cake of soft dough on which to wipe his fingers; arms, stretching out like vultures' necks, were taking olives, pistachios, almonds. All faces were merry, beneath garlands of flowers.

The Pharisees had rejected the garlands as being an example of Roman indecency. They shuddered when they were sprinkled with galbanum and frankincense, since that mixture was reserved for Temple ceremonies.

Aulus rubbed his armpits with it; and Antipas promised him a whole shipment of it, along with three baskets of that genuine balsam which had made Cleopatra covet after Palestine.

A captain from his garrison at Tiberias, who had arrived shortly before, had taken a place behind him in order to inform him of extraordinary events. But his attention was divided between the Proconsul and what was being said at the neighboring tables.

The talk there was of Johanan and people of his type; Simon of Gitta was cleansing people of sin with fire. A certain Jesus . . .

"The worst of them all!" exclaimed Eleazar. "What an unspeakable charlatan!"

Behind the Tetrarch a man stood up, pale as the edging of his chlamys.[21] He stepped down from the dais and, challenging the Pharisees, cried:

"That's a lie! Jesus performs miracles!"

Antipas said he wanted to see some.

"You should have brought him with you! Tell us about him!"

Then the man related that he, Jacob, having a sick daughter, had gone to Capernaum to beseech the Master to deign to cure her. The Master had replied: "Go back home, she is cured!" And he had found her on the threshold; she had arisen from her bed when the palace sundial indicated the third hour, the very moment when he had approached Jesus.

Of course, the Pharisees objected, there were professional methods, powerful herbs! Right here in Machaerus there was sometimes to be found the herb *baaras*, which makes men invulnerable; but to cure someone without seeing or touching him was an impossibility, unless Jesus was making use of demons.

And Antipas's friends, the chief men of Galilee, replied, shaking their heads:

— «Les démons, évidemment.»

Jacob, debout entre leur table et celle des prêtres, se taisait d'une manière hautaine et douce.

Ils le sommaient de parler: — «Justifie son pouvoir!»

Il courba les épaules, et à voix basse, lentement, comme effrayé de lui-même:

— «Vous ne savez donc pas que c'est le Messie?»

Tous les prêtres se regardèrent; et Vitellius demanda l'explication du mot. Son interprète fut une minute avant de répondre.

Ils appelaient ainsi un libérateur qui leur apporterait la jouissance de tous les biens et la domination de tous les peuples. Quelques-uns même soutenaient qu'il fallait compter sur deux. Le premier serait vaincu par Gog et Magog, des démons du Nord; mais l'autre exterminerait le Prince du Mal; et, depuis des siècles, ils l'attendaient à chaque minute.

Les prêtres s'étant concertés, Éléazar prit la parole.

D'abord le Messie serait enfant de David, et non d'un charpentier; il confirmerait la Loi. Ce Nazaréen l'attaquait; et, argument plus fort, il devait être précédé par la venue d'Élie.

Jacob répliqua:

— «Mais il est venu, Élie!»

— «Élie! Élie!» répéta la foule, jusqu'à l'autre bout de la salle.

Tous, par l'imagination, apercevaient un vieillard sous un vol de corbeaux, la foudre allumant un autel, des pontifes idolâtres jetés aux torrents; et les femmes, dans les tribunes, songeaient à la veuve de Sarepta.

Jacob s'épuisait à redire qu'il le connaissait! Il l'avait vu! et le peuple aussi!

— «Son nom?»

Alors, il cria de toutes ses forces:

— «Iaokanann!»

Antipas se renversa comme frappé en pleine poitrine. Les Sadducéens avaient bondi sur Jacob. Éléazar pérorait, pour se faire écouter.

Quand le silence fut établi, il drapa son manteau, et comme un juge posa des questions.

— «Puisque le prophète est mort . . .»

Des murmures l'interrompirent. On croyait Élie disparu seulement.

"Demons, obviously."

Jacob, standing between their table and that of the priests, kept his silence in a proud but gentle manner.

They called upon him to speak: "Explain his power!"

He bent his shoulders, and in a low voice, slowly, as if frightened of himself, he said:

"Don't you know, then, that He is the Messiah?"

The priests all looked at one another, and Vitellius asked what the word meant. His interpreter waited a minute before replying.

That was their name for a liberator who would bring them the possession of all good things and sovereignty over all nations. Some even asserted that two such men were to be expected. The first of them would be conquered by Gog and Magog, demons of the North, but the second one would exterminate the Prince of Evil; and for centuries they had been awaiting him momentarily.

The priests had parleyed with one another, and Eleazar was now their spokesman.

First of all, the Messiah would be a child of David, not the child of a carpenter. He would confirm the Law, whereas this Nazarene was attacking it. And—a stronger argument—the Messiah had to be preceded by the coming of Elijah.

Jacob retorted:

"But Elijah *has* come!"

"Elijah! Elijah!" repeated the crowd, all the way to the other end of the hall.

Everyone, in his imagination, pictured an old man with ravens flying over him, lightning setting fire to an altar, idol-worshipping pontiffs thrown into torrents; and the women, in the galleries, were thinking about the widow of Zarephath.

Jacob wore himself out repeating that he knew him! He had seen him! And so had all the people!

"His name?"

Then he shouted with all his might:

"Johanan!"

Antipas fell backwards as if he had been struck full in the chest. The Sadducees had leapt upon Jacob. Eleazar was orating loudly to get everyone to listen to him.

When silence had been restored, he draped his mantle around himself, and asked questions like a judge.

"Seeing that the prophet is dead . . ."

He was interrupted by murmurs. Most thought Elijah had merely disappeared.

Il s'emporta contre la foule, et, continuant son enquête:

— «Tu penses qu'il est ressuscité?»

— «Pourquoi pas?» dit Jacob.

Les Sadducéens haussèrent les épaules; Jonathas, écarquillant ses petits yeux, s'efforçait de rire comme un bouffon. Rien de plus sot que la prétention du corps à la vie éternelle; et il déclama, pour le Proconsul, ce vers d'un poète contemporain:

Nec crescit, nec post mortem durare videtur.

Mais Aulus était penché au bord du triclinium, le front en sueur, le visage vert, les poings sur l'estomac.

Les Sadducéens feignirent un grand émoi; — le lendemain, la sacrificature leur fut rendue; — Antipas étalait du désespoir; Vitellius demeurait impassible. Ses angoisses étaient pourtant violentes; avec son fils il perdait sa fortune.

Aulus n'avait pas fini de se faire vomir, qu'il voulut remanger.

— «Qu'on me donne de la râpure de marbre, du schiste de Naxos, de l'eau de mer, n'importe quoi! Si je prenais un bain?»

Il croqua de la neige, puis, ayant balancé entre une terrine de Commagène et des merles roses, se décida pour des courges au miel. L'Asiatique le contemplait, cette faculté d'engloutissement dénotant un être prodigieux et d'une race supérieure.

On servit des rognons de taureau, des loirs, des rossignols, des hachis dans les feuilles de pampre; et les prêtres discutaient sur la résurrection. Ammonius, élève de Philon le Platonicien, les jugeait stupides, et le disait à des Grecs qui se moquaient des oracles. Marcellus et Jacob s'étaient joints. Le premier narrait au second le bonheur qu'il avait ressenti sous le baptême de Mithra, et Jacob l'engageait à suivre Jésus. Les vins de palme et de tamaris, ceux de Safet et de Byblos, coulaient des amphores dans les cratères, des cratères dans les coupes, des coupes dans les gosiers; on bavardait, les cœurs s'épanchaient. Iaçim, bien que Juif, ne cachait plus son adoration des planètes. Un marchand d'Aphaka ébahissait des nomades, en détaillant les merveilles du temple d'Hiérapolis; et ils demandaient combien coûterait le pèlerinage. D'autres tenaient à leur religion natale. Un Germain presque aveugle chantait un hymne célébrant ce promontoire de la Scandinavie, où les dieux apparaissent avec les rayons de leurs figures; et des gens de Sichem ne mangèrent pas de tourterelles, par déférence pour la colombe Azima.

Plusieurs causaient debout, au milieu de la salle; et la vapeur des

Eleazar lost his temper with the crowd and continued his inquiry: "Do you think he has come back to life?"

"Why not?" said Jacob.

The Sadducees shrugged their shoulders; Jonathas, opening his little eyes wide, tried to laugh like a jester. There was nothing more foolish than the claims of the body to eternal life; and, for the benefit of the Proconsul, he recited this verse by a poet of the day:

"Nec crescit, nec post mortem durare videtur."[22]

But Aulus was bent over the edge of his triclinium, his forehead covered in sweat, his face green, his fists pressed to his stomach.

The Sadducees pretended to be greatly alarmed—the next day they were given back the office of high priest—Antipas displayed conspicuous despair; Vitellius remained impassive. And yet his anguish was extreme; if he lost his son, he would lose his fortune.

Aulus had not yet completed the process of vomiting when he wanted to go on eating.

"Let me have some marble filings, some schist from Naxos, some seawater, it doesn't matter what! Maybe I should take a bath."

He munched on some snow; then, after hesitating between a terrine from Commagene and pink thrushes, he decided on honeyed squash. "The Asiatic" was observing him, since that ability to stow away food was the sign of a remarkable being, one of a higher race.

They served bull's kidneys, dormice, nightingales, mincemeat wrapped in vine leaves; and the priests discussed resurrection. Ammonius, a disciple of Philo the Platonist, thought they were stupid, and said so to some Greeks who derided oracles. Marcellus and Jacob were now seated together. The former was telling the latter about the happiness he had felt when baptized in the name of Mithra, and Jacob was urging him to follow Jesus. The palm and tamarisk wines, and those from Safed and Byblos, flowed from the amphoras into the kraters,[23] from the kraters into the goblets, from the goblets into the gullets; people were chatting and unbosoming themselves. Iacim, though a Jew, no longer concealed his worship of the heavenly bodies. A merchant from Aphek was astounding some nomads with details of the wonders of the temple at Hierapolis, and they were asking how much a pilgrimage there would cost. Others were loyal to their native religions. A nearly blind German was singing a hymn celebrating that promontory in Scandinavia where the gods appear with their faces radiating light, and some people from Schechem refused to eat turtle-doves out of respect for the dove Azima.

Several were talking standing up, in the middle of the hall, and the

haleines avec les fumées des candélabres faisaient un brouillard
dans l'air. Phanuel passa le long des murs. Il venait encore
d'étudier le firmament, mais n'avançait pas jusqu'au Tétrarque,
redoutant les taches d'huile qui, pour les Esséniens, étaient une
grande souillure.

Des coups retentirent contre la porte du château.

On savait maintenant que Iaokanann s'y trouvait détenu. Des
hommes avec des torches grimpaient le sentier; une masse noire four-
millait dans le ravin; et ils hurlaient de temps à autre: — «Iaokanann!
Iaokanann!»

— «Il dérange tout!» dit Jonathas.

— «On n'aura plus d'argent, s'il continue!» ajoutèrent les
Pharisiens.

Et des récriminations partaient:

— «Protège-nous!»

— «Qu'on en finisse!»

— «Tu abandonnes la religion!»

— «Impie comme les Hérode!»

— «Moins que vous!» répliqua Antipas. «C'est mon père qui a
édifié votre temple!»

Alors, les Pharisiens, les fils des proscrits, les partisans des
Matathias, accusèrent le Tétrarque des crimes de sa famille.

Ils avaient des crânes pointus, la barbe hérissée, des mains faibles
et méchantes, ou la face camuse, de gros yeux ronds, l'air de boule-
dogues. Une douzaine, scribes et valets des prêtres, nourris par le
rebut des holocaustes, s'élancèrent jusqu'au bas de l'estrade; et avec
des couteaux ils menaçaient Antipas, qui les haranguait, pendant que
les Sadducéens le défendaient mollement. Il aperçut Mannaeï, et lui
fit signe de s'en aller, Vitellius indiquant par sa contenance que ces
choses ne le regardaient pas.

Les Pharisiens, restés sur leur triclinium, se mirent dans une
fureur démoniaque. Ils brisèrent les plats devant eux. On leur avait
servi le ragoût chéri de Mécène, de l'âne sauvage, une viande im-
monde.

Aulus les railla à propos de la tête d'âne, qu'ils honoraient, disait-
on, et débita d'autres sarcasmes sur leur antipathie du pourceau.
C'était sans doute parce que cette grosse bête avait tué leur Bacchus;
et ils aimaient trop le vin, puisqu'on avait découvert dans le Temple
une vigne d'or.

Les prêtres ne comprenaient pas ses paroles. Phinées, Galiléen
d'origine, refusa de les traduire. Alors sa colère fut démesurée,

vapor of human breath, mingling with the smoke from the candelabra, created a mist in the air. Phanuel moved along the walls. He had just been studying the firmament again, but he didn't proceed all the way to the Tetrarch, since he dreaded oil stains, which for Essenes were a great defilement.

Blows were heard being struck at the castle gate.

Now it was known that Johanan was being held prisoner there. Men with torches were climbing the path; a dark crowd was swarming in the ravine, and from time to time they howled: "Johanan! Johanan!"

"He's upsetting everything," said Jonathas.

"We won't have any more money if he goes on this way!" added the Pharisees.

And recriminations flew:

"Protect us!"

"Put an end to this!"

"You're abandoning your religion!"

"As impious as all the Herods!"

"Not as much as you!" Antipas retorted. "It was my father who built your Temple!"

Then the Pharisees, the sons of the exiles, the partisans of the Mattathias clan,[24] accused the Tetrarch of his family's crimes.

They had pointed heads, bristling beards, weak, malicious hands, or were snub-nosed with big round eyes, resembling bulldogs. A dozen of them, scribes and priests' servants, nourished on the waste from the burnt offerings, dashed to the foot of the dais; and with knives they threatened Antipas, who was haranguing them, while the Sadducees were defending him ineffectually. He caught sight of Mannaei and beckoned to him to leave, while Vitellius's demeanor showed that those things were of no concern to him.

The Pharisees, who had remained on their triclinium, went into a demonic rage. They broke the dishes that were in front of them. They had been served that stew which Maecenas[25] had been so fond of, wild ass, an unclean meat.

Aulus chaffed them on the subject of the donkey's head that they were said to honor, and came out with other sarcastic remarks about their hatred of pork. No doubt it was because that fat animal had killed their Bacchus;[26] and they liked wine all too well, because a golden grapevine had been discovered in the Temple.

The priests failed to understand his words. Phineas, a Galilean by birth, refused to translate them. Then Aulus's anger broke all bounds,

d'autant plus que l'Asiatique, pris de peur, avait disparu; et le repas lui déplaisait, les mets étaient vulgaires, point déguisés suffisamment! Il se calma, en voyant des queues de brebis syriennes, qui sont des paquets de graisse. Le caractère des Juifs semblait hideux à Vitellius. Leur Dieu pouvait bien être Moloch, dont il avait rencontré des autels sur la route; et les sacrifices d'enfants lui revinrent à l'esprit, avec l'histoire de l'homme qu'ils engraissaient mystérieusement. Son cœur de Latin était soulevé de dégoût par leur intolérance, leur rage iconoclaste, leur achoppement de brute. Le Proconsul voulait partir. Aulus s'y refusa.

La robe abaissée jusqu'aux hanches, il gisait derrière un monceau de victuailles, trop repu pour en prendre, mais s'obstinant à ne point les quitter.

L'exaltation du peuple grandit. Ils s'abandonnèrent à des projets d'indépendance. On rappelait la gloire d'Israël. Tous les conquérants avaient été châtiés: Antigone, Crassus, Varus . . .

— «Misérables!» dit le Proconsul; car il entendait le syriaque; son interprète ne servait qu'à lui donner du loisir pour répondre.

Antipas, bien vite, tira la médaille de l'Empereur, et, l'observant avec tremblement, il la présentait du côté de l'image.

Les panneaux de la tribune d'or se déployèrent tout à coup; et à la splendeur des cierges, entre ses esclaves et des festons d'anémone, Hérodias apparut, — coiffée d'une mitre assyrienne qu'une mentonnière attachait à son front; ses cheveux en spirales s'épandaient sur un péplos d'écarlate, fendu dans la longueur des manches. Deux monstres en pierre, pareils à ceux du trésor des Atrides, se dressant contre la porte, elle ressemblait à Cybèle accotée de ses lions; et du haut de la balustrade qui dominait Antipas, avec une patère à la main, elle cria:

— «Longue vie à César!»

Cet hommage fut répété par Vitellius, Antipas et les prêtres.

Mais il arriva du fond de la salle un bourdonnement de surprise et d'admiration. Une jeune fille venait d'entrer.

Sous un voile bleuâtre lui cachant la poitrine et la tête, on distinguait les arcs de ses yeux, les calcédoines de ses oreilles, la blancheur de sa peau. Un carré de soie gorge-pigeon, en couvrant les épaules, tenait aux reins par une ceinture d'orfèvrerie. Ses caleçons noirs étaient semés de mandragores, et d'une manière indolente elle faisait claquer de petites pantoufles en duvet de colibri.

Sur le haut de l'estrade, elle retira son voile. C'était Hérodias, comme autrefois dans sa jeunesse. Puis, elle se mit à danser.

Ses pieds passaient l'un devant l'autre, au rythme de la flûte et

all the more so because "the Asiatic," who had become frightened, had vanished; besides, he didn't like the meal: the dishes were commonplace, not elaborately enough prepared! He calmed down when he saw Syrian sheep tails, which are pure bundles of fat.

The character of the Jews seemed detestable to Vitellius. Their God might very well be Moloch,[27] whose altars he had come across on his journey; and he recalled the child sacrifices and the story of the man who mysteriously grew fat on them. His Roman heart was disgusted by their intolerance, their iconoclastic fury, their brutish obstinacy. The Proconsul wanted to leave. Aulus wouldn't hear of it.

His robe lowered to his hips, he was lying behind a mound of food, too stuffed to take any, but persisting in not letting it go.

The people's excitement increased. They were indulging in plans for independence. They were recalling the glory of Israel. All their conquerors had been chastised: Antigonus, Crassus, Varus . . .

"Miserable creatures!" said the Proconsul, for he understood Aramaic; his interpreter was only there to afford him plenty of time to reply.

Very quickly Antipas pulled out the Emperor's medallion and, looking at it with trembling, he showed it, image side up.

The panels of the golden gallery suddenly opened, and in the glow of wax tapers, among her slaves and festoons of anemone, Herodias appeared—on her head an Assyrian miter attached to her brow with a chin strap. Her hair, in spirals, spread out over a scarlet peplos,[28] its sleeves slashed down their length. Since two stone monsters like those on the Treasury of the Atrides[29] stood against the door, she resembled Cybele flanked by her lions; and from the balustrade that loomed high above Antipas, a patera[30] in her hand, she cried:

"Long life to Caesar!"

That homage was repeated by Vitellius, Antipas, and the priests.

But, from the far end of the hall, a buzzing of surprise and wonderment was heard. A girl had just entered.

Beneath a bluish veil that concealed her bosom and her head, they could make out the arches of her eyebrows, the chalcedonies in her ears, the whiteness of her skin. A square piece of dove-colored shot silk covered her shoulders and was held behind her waist by a belt of goldsmith's work. Her black trousers had a powdered pattern of mandrakes, and in an indolent manner she was making her little hummingbird-down slippers clip-clop.

After ascending the dais, she removed her veil. She resembled Herodias as she had been long ago, when young. Then she started to dance.

Her feet moved one in front of the other, to the rhythm of the

d'une paire de crotales. Ses bras arrondis appelaient quelqu'un, qui s'enfuyait toujours. Elle le poursuivait, plus légère qu'un papillon, comme une Psyché curieuse, comme une âme vagabonde, et semblait prête à s'envoler.

Les sons funèbres de la gingras remplacèrent les crotales. L'accablement avait suivi l'espoir. Ses attitudes exprimaient des soupirs, et toute sa personne une telle langueur qu'on ne savait pas si elle pleurait un dieu, ou se mourait dans sa caresse. Les paupières entre-closes, elle se tordait la taille, balançait son ventre avec des ondulations de houle, faisait trembler ses deux seins, et son visage demeurait immobile, et ses pieds n'arrêtaient pas.

Vitellius la compara à Mnester, le pantomime. Aulus vomissait encore. Le Tétrarque se perdait dans un rêve, et ne songeait plus à Hérodias. Il crut la voir près des Sadducéens. La vision s'éloigna.

Ce n'était pas une vision. Elle avait fait instruire, loin de Machærous, Salomé sa fille, que le Tétrarque aimerait; et l'idée était bonne. Elle en était sûre, maintenant!

Puis, ce fut l'emportement de l'amour qui veut être assouvi. Elle dansa comme les prêtresses des Indes, comme les Nubiennes des cataractes, comme les bacchantes de Lydie. Elle se renversait de tous les côtés, pareille à une fleur que la tempête agite. Les brillants de ses oreilles sautaient, l'étoffe de son dos chatoyait; de ses bras, de ses pieds, de ses vêtements jaillissaient d'invisibles étincelles qui enflammaient les hommes. Une harpe chanta; la multitude y répondit par des acclamations. Sans fléchir ses genoux en écartant les jambes, elle se courba si bien que son menton frôlait le plancher; et les nomades habitués à l'abstinence, les soldats de Rome experts en débauches, les avares publicains, les vieux prêtres aigris par les disputes, tous, dilatant leurs narines, palpitaient de convoitise.

Ensuite elle tourna autour de la table d'Antipas, frénétiquement, comme le rhombe des sorcières; et d'une voix que des sanglots de volupté entrecoupaient, il lui disait: — «Viens! viens!» Elle tournait toujours; les tympanons sonnaient à éclater, la foule hurlait. Mais le Tétrarque criait plus fort: «Viens! viens! Tu auras Capharnaüm! la plaine de Tibérias! mes citadelles! la moitié de mon royaume!»

Elle se jeta sur les mains, les talons en l'air, parcourut ainsi l'estrade comme un grand scarabée; et s'arrêta, brusquement.

Sa nuque et ses vertèbres faisaient un angle droit. Les fourreaux de couleur qui enveloppaient ses jambes, lui passant par-dessus l'épaule, comme des arcs-en-ciel, accompagnaient sa figure, à une coudée du

flute and a pair of castanets. Her rounded arms were reaching out to someone who kept fleeing. She pursued him, lighter than a butterfly, like an inquisitive Psyche,[31] like a wandering soul, and she seemed ready to fly away.

The funereal sounds of the *gingras*[32] replaced the castanets. Despair had followed hope. Her attitudes expressed sighs, and her whole body spoke of such languor that one couldn't tell whether she was lamenting the death of a god or dying of bliss in his embrace. Her eyelids half-closed, she twisted her waist, rocked her stomach in waves like those of the surf, made her two breasts quiver; her features remained motionless while her feet never stopped.

Vitellius compared her to the pantomime artist Mnester. Aulus was vomiting again. The Tetrarch was getting lost in a dream and was no longer thinking of Herodias. He thought he saw her near the Sadducees. The vision departed.

It was no vision. She had had Salome, her daughter, trained far away from Machaerus, so that the Tetrarch would love the girl; and it was a good idea. Now she was sure of it!

Then came the transport of love that wishes to be satisfied. She danced like the priestesses of India, like the Nubian women of the Nile cataracts, like the bacchantes of Lydia. She flung herself from side to side, like a flower tossed by the storm. The jewels in her ears leaped; the fabric on her back kept changing color; her arms, her feet, her clothing emitted invisible sparks that set men on fire. A harp sang; the crowd responded with applause. Spreading her legs without bending her knees, she bent over so low that her chin grazed the floor; and the nomads accustomed to abstinence, the Roman soldiers well versed in debauchery, the greedy publicans, the old priests soured by disputes, all of them, their nostrils flaring, were palpitating with lust.

Then she spun around Antipas's table, frenetically, like a witch's rhomb;[33] and with a voice broken by sighs of desire, he was saying to her: "Come! Come!" She was still spinning; the tympanons[34] were beating to the point of bursting, the crowd was howling. But the Tetrarch was shouting even louder: "Come! Come! You shall have Capernaum, the plain of Tiberias, my citadels, half of my kingdom!"

She stood on her hands, her heels in the air, and in that posture she proceeded around the entire dais, like a giant scarab beetle. Then, all of a sudden, she stopped.

The nape of her neck and her vertebrae formed a right angle. The colored sheaths that enveloped her legs, passing over her shoulders like rainbows, hung beside her face, a cubit from the

sol. Ses lèvres étaient peintes, ses sourcils très noirs, ses yeux presque terribles, et des gouttelettes à son front semblaient une vapeur sur du marbre blanc.

Elle ne parlait pas. Ils se regardaient.

Un claquement de doigts se fit dans la tribune. Elle y monta, reparut; et, en zézayant un peu, prononça ces mots, d'un air enfantin:

— «Je veux que tu me donnes dans un plat, la tête . . .» Elle avait oublié le nom, mais reprit en souriant: «La tête de Iaokanann!»

Le Tétrarque s'affaissa sur lui-même, écrasé.

Il était contraint par sa parole, et le peuple attendait. Mais la mort qu'on lui avait prédite, en s'appliquant à un autre, peut-être détournerait la sienne? Si Iaokanann était véritablement Élie, il pourrait s'y soustraire; s'il ne l'était pas, le meurtre n'avait plus d'importance.

Mannaeï était à ses côtés, et comprit son intention.

Vitellius le rappela pour lui confier le mot d'ordre, des sentinelles gardant la fosse.

Ce fut un soulagement. Dans une minute, tout serait fini!

Cependant Mannaeï n'était guère prompt en besogne.

Il rentra, mais bouleversé.

Depuis quarante ans il exerçait la fonction de bourreau. C'était lui qui avait noyé Aristobule, étranglé Alexandre, brûlé vif Matathias, décapité Zosime, Pappus, Joseph et Antipater; et il n'osait tuer Iaokanann! Ses dents claquaient, tout son corps tremblait.

Il avait aperçu devant la fosse le Grand Ange des Samaritains, tout couvert d'yeux et brandissant un immense glaive, rouge, et dentelé comme une flamme. Deux soldats amenés en témoignage pouvaient le dire.

Ils n'avaient rien vu, sauf un capitaine juif, qui s'était précipité sur eux, et qui n'existait plus.

La fureur d'Hérodias dégorgea en un torrent d'injures populacières et sanglantes. Elle se cassa les ongles au grillage de la tribune, et les deux lions sculptés semblaient mordre ses épaules et rugir comme elle.

Antipas l'imita, les prêtres, les soldats, les Pharisiens, tous réclamant une vengeance, et les autres, indignés qu'on retardât leur plaisir.

Mannaeï sortit, en se cachant la face.

Les convives trouvèrent le temps encore plus long que la première fois. On s'ennuyait.

Tout à coup, un bruit de pas se répercuta dans les couloirs. Le malaise devenait intolérable.

ground. Her lips were painted, her eyebrows very black, her eyes almost frightening, and little drops on her brow were like a vapor on white marble.

She didn't speak. They looked at each other.

A snapping of fingers was heard in the gallery. She went up there, reappeared; and, lisping a little, pronounced these words, in a child-like manner:

"I want you to give me, on a platter, the head . . ." She had forgotten the name, but then continued, with a smile: "The head of Johanan!"

The Tetrarch slumped down, crushed.

He was bound by his word, and the people were waiting. But perhaps if the death that had been predicted to him referred to someone else, his own death might be avoided. If Johanan was truly Elijah, he would be able to save himself; if he wasn't, the murder had no further importance.

Mannaei was at his side and understood his intention.

Vitellius called him back to tell him the password, since sentinels were guarding the pit.

This was a relief. In a minute everything would be over!

Meanwhile Mannaei was hardly quick to act.

He returned, but quite upset.

For forty years he had been fulfilling the duties of an executioner. It was he who had drowned Aristobulus, strangled Alexander, burned Matthathias alive, beheaded Zosimus, Pappus, Joseph, and Antipater;[35] and he didn't dare kill Johanan! His teeth were chattering, his whole body was trembling.

In front of the pit he had seen the Great Angel of the Samaritans, all covered with eyes and brandishing an immense sword, red and spiky as a flame. Two soldiers, brought along as witnesses, could testify to it.

They had seen nothing but a Jewish captain, who had thrown himself upon them and who was no longer alive.

Herodias's fury vented itself in a torrent of plebeian and bloody invective. She broke her fingernails on the grillwork of the gallery, and the two sculptured lions seemed to be biting her shoulders and roaring like her.

Antipas imitated her; the priests, the soldiers, the Pharisees were all calling for vengeance, and the others were indignant because their pleasure was being delayed.

Mannaei left, hiding his face.

The guests were even more impatient than the first time. They were getting bored.

Suddenly, the sound of footsteps echoed through the corridors. The unease was becoming unbearable.

La tête entra; — et Mannaeï la tenait par les cheveux, au bout de son bras, fier des applaudissements.

Quand il l'eut mise sur un plat, il l'offrit à Salomé.

Elle monta lestement dans la tribune; plusieurs minutes après, la tête fut rapportée par cette vieille femme que le Tétrarque avait distinguée le matin sur la plate-forme d'une maison, et tantôt dans la chambre d'Hérodias.

Il se reculait pour ne pas la voir. Vitellius y jeta un regard indifférent.

Mannaeï descendit l'estrade, et l'exhiba aux capitaines romains, puis à tous ceux qui mangeaient de ce côté.

Ils l'examinèrent.

La lame aiguë de l'instrument, glissant du haut en bas, avait entamé la mâchoire. Une convulsion tirait les coins de la bouche. Du sang, caillé déjà, parsemait la barbe. Les paupières closes étaient blêmes comme des coquilles; et les candélabres à l'entour envoyaient des rayons.

Elle arriva à la table des prêtres. Un Pharisien la retourna curieusement; et Mannaeï, l'ayant remise d'aplomb, la posa devant Aulus, qui en fut réveillé. Par l'ouverture de leurs cils, les prunelles mortes et les prunelles éteintes semblaient se dire quelque chose.

Ensuite Mannaeï la présenta à Antipas. Des pleurs coulèrent sur les joues du Tétrarque.

Les flambeaux s'éteignaient. Les convives partirent; et il ne resta plus dans la salle qu'Antipas, les mains contre ses tempes, et regardant toujours la tête coupée, tandis que Phanuel, debout au milieu de la grande nef, murmurait des prières, les bras étendus.

A l'instant où se levait le soleil, deux hommes, expédiés autrefois par Iaokanann, survinrent, avec la réponse si longtemps espérée.

Ils la confièrent à Phanuel, qui en eut un ravissement.

Puis il leur montra l'objet lugubre, sur le plateau, entre les débris du festin. Un des hommes dit:

— «Console-toi! Il est descendu chez les morts annoncer le Christ!»

L'Essénien comprenait maintenant ces paroles:

«Pour qu'il croisse, il faut que je diminue.»

Et tous les trois, ayant pris la tête de Iaokanann, s'en allèrent du côté de la Galilée.

Comme elle était très lourde, ils la portaient alternativement.

The head appeared—Mannaei was holding it by the hair, at arm's length, proud of the applause.

When he had placed it on a platter, he presented it to Salome.

She nimbly walked up into the gallery; several minutes later, the head was brought back by that old woman the Tetrarch had espied that morning on the flat roof of a house and a while later in Herodias's room.

He recoiled so as not to see it. Vitellius cast an indifferent glance at it.

Mannaei stepped down from the dais, and exhibited it to the Roman captains, then to all those who were eating on that side.

They examined it.

The sharp blade of the sword, gliding downward, had cut into the jaw. A convulsion distorted the corners of the mouth. Blood, already clotted, was sprinkled over the beard. The closed eyelids were as pallid as eggshells; and the candelabra all around shed rays of light on the head.

It arrived at the priests' table. A Pharisee turned it over inquisitively; and Mannaei, having set it upright again, placed it in front of Aulus, who was awakened by this. Through the opening of their lashes, the dead pupils and the somnolent ones seemed to tell each other something.

Next, Mannaei presented it to Antipas. Tears were flowing down the Tetrarch's cheeks.

The torches were going out. The guests departed, and there was no one left in the hall but Antipas, his hands against his temples as he kept looking at the severed head, while Phanuel, standing in the center of the principal nave, was muttering prayers with his arms outstretched.

At the moment the sun rose, two men, sent out previously by Johanan, arrived with the response that had been awaited for so long.

They gave it to Phanuel, who went into ecstasies over it.

Then he showed them the lugubrious object, on the tray, amid the leftovers from the feast. One of the men said:

"Be consoled! He has descended to the dead to announce the Christ!"

Now the Essene understood those words:

"If He is to increase, I must diminish."

And all three of them, taking up the head of Johanan, departed in the direction of Galilee.

Since it was very heavy, they took turns carrying it.

EMILE ZOLA

L'attaque du moulin

I

Le moulin du père Merlier, par cette belle soirée d'été, était en grande fête. Dans la cour, on avait mis trois tables, placées bout à bout, et qui attendaient les convives. Tout le pays savait qu'on devait fiancer, ce jour-là, la fille Merlier, Françoise, avec Dominique, un garçon qu'on accusait de fainéantise, mais que les femmes, à trois lieues à la ronde, regardaient avec des yeux luisants, tant il avait bon air.

Ce moulin du père Merlier était une vraie gaieté. Il se trouvait juste au milieu de Rocreuse, à l'endroit où la grand-route fait un coude. Le village n'a qu'une rue, deux files de masures, une file à chaque bord de la route; mais là, au coude, des prés s'élargissent, de grands arbres, qui suivent le cours de la Morelle, couvrent le fond de la vallée d'ombrages magnifiques. Il n'y a pas, dans toute la Lorraine, un coin de nature plus adorable. A droite et à gauche, des bois épais, des futaies séculaires montent des pentes douces, emplissent l'horizon d'une mer de verdure; tandis que, vers le midi, la plaine s'étend, d'une fertilité merveilleuse, déroulant à l'infini des pièces de terre coupées de haies vives. Mais ce qui fait surtout le charme de Rocreuse, c'est la fraîcheur de ce trou de verdure, aux journées les plus chaudes de juillet et d'août. La Morelle descend des feuillages sous lesquels elle coule pendant des lieues; elle apporte les bruits murmurants, l'ombre glacée et recueillie des forêts. Et elle n'est point la seule fraîcheur: toutes sortes d'eaux courantes chantent sous les bois; à chaque pas, des sources jaillissent; on sent, lorsqu'on suit les étroits sentiers, comme des lacs souterrains qui percent sous la mousse et profitent des moindres fentes, au pied des arbres, entre les roches, pour s'épancher en fontaines cristallines. Les voix chuchotantes de ces

EMILE ZOLA

The Attack on the Mill

I

Old Merlier's mill, that fine summer evening, was extremely festive. In the courtyard three tables had been laid, placed end to end, and were awaiting the guests. Everyone in the vicinity knew that on that day Merlier's daughter Françoise was to be betrothed to Dominique, a young man who was reproached for laziness, but whom the women for three leagues around looked upon with a gleam in their eyes, he was so handsome.

This mill of old Merlier's was a real treat. It was located right in the center of Rocreuse, in the spot where the highway makes a bend. The village has only one street, two rows of cottages, one row on each side of the road; but there, at the bend, meadows open out, and tall trees, following the course of the Morelle, cover the bottom of the valley with magnificent shade. In all of Lorraine, there isn't a more charming corner of nature. To the right and to the left, dense forests and centuries-old woods climb gentle slopes, filling the horizon with an ocean of greenery; while, toward the south, the plain stretches, wonderfully fertile, unfurling to infinity plots of ground divided by quickset hedges. But the charm of Rocreuse is chiefly due to the coolness of this pocket of greenery on the hottest days of July and August. The Morelle comes down from the forests, beneath which it flows for leagues; it brings along the murmuring sounds, the chilly and meditative shade of the woods. And that stream isn't the only source of coolness; all sorts of running streams sing beneath the trees; at each step, springs gush forth; when you follow the narrow paths, you feel as if underground lakes are penetrating the moss and taking advantage of the slightest cracks, at the foot of the trees, between the rocks, to pour out in crystal fountains. The whispering voices of these brooks are

ruisseaux s'élèvent si nombreuses et si hautes, qu'elles couvrent le chant des bouvreuils. On se croirait dans quelque parc enchanté, avec des cascades tombant de toutes parts. En bas, les prairies sont trempées. Des marronniers gigantesques font des ombres noires. Au bord des prés, de longs rideaux de peupliers alignent leurs tentures bruissantes. Il y a deux avenues d'énormes platanes qui montent, à travers champs, vers l'ancien château de Gagny, aujourd'hui en ruine. Dans cette terre continuellement arrosée, les herbes grandissent démesurément. C'est comme un fond de parterre entre les deux coteaux boisés, mais de parterre naturel, dont les prairies sont les pelouses, et dont les arbres géants dessinent les colossales corbeilles. Quand le soleil, à midi, tombe d'aplomb, les ombres bleuissent, les herbes allumées dorment dans la chaleur, tandis qu'un frisson glacé passe sous les feuillages.

Et c'était là que le moulin du père Merlier égayait de son tic-tac un coin de verdures folles. La bâtisse, faite de plâtre et de planches, semblait vieille comme le monde. Elle trempait à moitié dans la Morelle, qui arrondit à cet endroit un clair bassin. Une écluse était ménagée, la chute tombait de quelques mètres sur la roue du moulin, qui craquait en tournant, avec la toux asthmatique d'une fidèle servante vieillie dans la maison. Quand on conseillait au père Merlier de la changer, il hochait la tête en disant qu'une jeune roue serait plus paresseuse et ne connaîtrait pas si bien le travail; et il raccommodait l'ancienne avec tout ce qui lui tombait sous la main, des douves de tonneau, des ferrures rouillées, du zinc, du plomb. La roue en paraissait plus gaie, avec son profil devenu étrange, tout empanachée d'herbes et de mousses. Lorsque l'eau la battait de son flot d'argent, elle se couvrait de perles, on voyait passer son étrange carcasse sous une parure éclatante de colliers de nacre.

La partie du moulin qui trempait ainsi dans la Morelle, avait l'air d'une arche barbare, échouée là. Une bonne moitié du logis était bâtie sur des pieux. L'eau entrait sous le plancher, il y avait des trous, bien connus dans le pays pour les anguilles et les écrevisses énormes qu'on y prenait. En dessous de la chute, le bassin était limpide comme un miroir, et lorsque la roue ne le troublait pas de son écume, on apercevait des bandes de gros poissons qui nageaient avec des lenteurs d'escadre. Un escalier rompu descendait à la rivière, près d'un pieu où était amarrée une barque. Une galerie de bois passait au-dessus de la rue. Des fenêtres s'ouvraient, percées irrégulièrement. C'était un pêle-mêle d'encoignures, de petites murailles, de constructions ajoutées après coup, de poutres et de toitures qui donnaient au

raised so loud and in such numbers that they drown out the song of the bullfinches. You'd think you were in some enchanted park, with cascades falling everywhere.

Farther down, the grasslands are soaked. Gigantic chestnut trees cast black shadows. Along the edges of the meadows, long curtains of poplars align their rustling tapestries. There are two avenues of enormous plane trees that cross the fields as they ascend to the old Château de Gagny, today in ruins. In this continually watered land, the grass grows luxuriantly. It forms a sort of garden plot between the two wooded hills, but a natural garden, with the meadows for lawns and the giant trees constituting the colossal flower beds. When the noonday sun beams down vertically, the shadows grow blue and the illuminated grass sleeps in the heat, while a chilly shudder runs through the foliage.

And it was there that old Merlier's mill brightened a corner of that wild greenery with its click-clack. The building, made of plaster and boards, seemed as old as the world. Half of it dipped into the Morelle, which at that spot rounds out into a clear pool. A sluice had been installed, with the water dropping several meters onto the mill wheel, which creaked as it turned with the asthmatic cough of a loyal servant who had grown old in the household. When people advised old Merlier to replace it, he shook his head, saying that a young wheel would be lazier and wouldn't know its job so well; and he used to patch up the old one with anything that came to hand, barrel staves, rusty scraps of iron, zinc, lead. The wheel seemed all the merrier for it, with its profile that had become strange, with its tufts of grass and moss all over. When the water struck it with its silvery current, it was covered with pearls, and its strange framework seemed to be adorned with a shining set of mother-of-pearl necklaces.

The part of the mill that dipped into the Morelle that way looked like a barbarian ark that had washed up there. A good half of the dwelling was built on piles. The water came in under the floor, there were deep places well known in the vicinity for the eels and enormous crayfish that were caught there. Downstream from the water drop, the pool was as limpid as a mirror, and when the wheel wasn't disturbing it with its foam, you could see schools of large fish swimming as slowly as a naval squadron. A broken staircase led down to the stream, near a piling to which a boat was tied up. A wooden gallery passed over the street. The mill had irregularly spaced windows. It was a hodgepodge of angles, small walls, belatedly added constructions, beams, and roof levels, which made it look like an old citadel

moulin un aspect d'ancienne citadelle démantelée. Mais des lierres avaient poussé, toutes sortes de plantes grimpantes bouchaient les crevasses trop grandes et mettaient un manteau vert à la vieille demeure. Les demoiselles qui passaient dessinaient sur leurs albums le moulin du père Merlier.

Du côté de la route, la maison était plus solide. Un portail en pierre s'ouvrait sur la grande cour, que bordaient à droite et à gauche des hangars et des écuries. Près d'un puits, un orme immense couvrait de son ombre la moitié de la cour. Au fond, la maison alignait les quatre fenêtres de son premier étage, surmonté d'un colombier. La seule coquetterie du père Merlier était de faire badigeonner cette façade tous les dix ans. Elle venait justement d'être blanchie, et elle éblouissait le village, lorsque le soleil l'allumait, au milieu du jour.

Depuis vingt ans, le père Merlier était maire de Rocreuse. On l'estimait pour la fortune qu'il avait su faire. On lui donnait quelque chose comme quatre-vingt mille francs, amassés sou à sou. Quand il avait épousé Madeleine Guillard, qui lui apportait en dot le moulin, il ne possédait guère que ses deux bras. Mais Madeleine ne s'était jamais repentie de son choix, tant il avait su mener gaillardement les affaires du ménage. Aujourd'hui, la femme était défunte, il restait veuf avec sa fille Françoise. Sans doute, il aurait pu se reposer, laisser la roue du moulin dormir dans la mousse; mais il se serait trop ennuyé, et la maison lui aurait semblé morte. Il travaillait toujours, pour le plaisir. Le père Merlier était alors un grand vieillard, à longue figure silencieuse, qui ne riait jamais, mais qui était tout de même très gai en dedans. On l'avait choisi pour maire, à cause de son argent, et aussi pour le bel air qu'il savait prendre lorsqu'il faisait un mariage.

Françoise Merlier venait d'avoir dix-huit ans. Elle ne passait pas pour une des belles filles du pays, parce qu'elle était chétive. Jusqu'à quinze ans, elle avait même été laide. On ne pouvait pas comprendre, à Rocreuse, comment la fille du père et de la mère Merlier, tous deux si bien plantés, poussait mal et d'un air de regret. Mais à quinze ans, tout en restant délicate, elle prit une petite figure, la plus jolie du monde. Elle avait des cheveux noirs, des yeux noirs, et elle était toute rose avec ça; une bouche qui riait toujours, des trous dans les joues, un front clair où il y avait comme une couronne de soleil. Quoique chétive pour le pays, elle n'était pas maigre, loin de là; on voulait dire simplement qu'elle n'aurait pas pu lever un sac de blé; mais elle devenait toute potelée avec l'âge, elle devait finir par être ronde et friande comme une caille. Seulement, les longs silences de son père

that had been dismantled. But ivy had grown on it, and all sorts of climbing plants stopped up the cracks that were too big and threw a green mantle over the old dwelling. The well-born young ladies who passed that way used to draw old Merlier's mill in their sketchbooks.

On the side facing the road, the house was more solid. A stone gate led into the large courtyard, which was bordered on the right and left with sheds and stables. Near a well, an immense elm covered half the courtyard with its shade. At the far end of the yard, the house aligned the four windows of its second story, surmounted by a dovecote. Old Merlier's only concession to finery was to have that house front white-washed every ten years. It had just been repainted, and it dazzled the village when the sun lit it up at midday.

For twenty years, old Merlier had been mayor of Rocreuse. He was esteemed for the fortune he had been able to earn. People thought he was worth about eighty thousand francs, accumulated one sou at a time. When he married Madeleine Guillard, who brought him the mill as dowry, he barely owned more than his two arms. But Madeleine had never regretted her choice, because he had carried on the business of the couple so vigorously. Now his wife was dead and he remained a widower with his daughter Françoise. No doubt, he could have retired and let his mill wheel sleep in the moss; but he would have been too bored, and the house would have seemed dead to him. He kept on working for the pleasure of it. At the time, old Merlier was a tall old man, with a long, taciturn face; he never laughed, but all the same he was very jolly inside. He had been elected mayor on account of his money, and also for the fine appearance he made when officiating at a wedding.

Françoise Merlier had just turned eighteen. She wasn't considered one of the real beauties of the vicinity, because she was puny. Up to the age of fifteen she had even been homely. People in Rocreuse couldn't understand why the daughter of Mr. and Mrs. Merlier, both so sturdy, grew up so unsatisfactorily, as if regretfully. But at fifteen, though she remained frail, she developed a little face that was the prettiest in the world. She had black hair and dark eyes, and yet was very pink; her lips were always laughing, her cheeks were dimpled, and there seemed to be a wreath of sunlight on her clear brow. Although underdeveloped for local tastes, she wasn't scrawny, far from it; what they really meant to say was that she wouldn't have been able to lift a sack of wheat; but, as she grew older, she was becoming quite chubby, and in time she would be as round and luscious as a quail. Only, her father's long periods of silence had made her sensible

l'avaient rendue raisonnable très jeune. Si elle riait toujours, c'était pour faire plaisir aux autres. Au fond, elle était sérieuse.

Naturellement, tout le pays la courtisait, plus encore pour ses écus que pour sa gentillesse. Et elle avait fini par faire un choix, qui venait de scandaliser la contrée. De l'autre côté de la Morelle, vivait un grand garçon, que l'on nommait Dominique Penquer. Il n'était pas de Rocreuse. Dix ans auparavant, il était arrivé de Belgique, pour hériter d'un oncle, qui possédait un petit bien, sur la lisière même de la forêt de Gagny, juste en face du moulin, à quelques portées de fusil. Il venait pour vendre ce bien, disait-il, et retourner chez lui. Mais le pays le charma, paraît-il, car il n'en bougea plus. On le vit cultiver son bout de champ, récolter quelques légumes dont il vivait. Il pêchait, il chassait; plusieurs fois, les gardes faillirent le prendre et lui dresser des procès-verbaux. Cette existence libre, dont les paysans ne s'expliquaient pas bien les ressources, avait fini par lui donner un mauvais renom. On le traitait vaguement de braconnier. En tout cas, il était paresseux, car on le trouvait souvent endormi dans l'herbe, à des heures où il aurait dû travailler. La masure qu'il habitait, sous les derniers arbres de la forêt, ne semblait pas non plus la demeure d'un honnête garçon. Il aurait eu un commerce avec les loups des ruines de Gagny, que cela n'aurait point surpris les vieilles femmes. Pourtant, les jeunes filles, parfois, se hasardaient à le défendre, car il était superbe, cet homme louche, souple et grand comme un peuplier, très blanc de peau, avec une barbe et des cheveux blonds qui semblaient de l'or au soleil. Or, un beau matin, Françoise avait déclaré au père Merlier qu'elle aimait Dominique et que jamais elle ne consentirait à épouser un autre garçon.

On pense quel coup de massue le père Merlier reçut, ce jour-là! Il ne dit rien, selon son habitude. Il avait son visage réfléchi; seulement sa gaieté intérieure ne luisait plus dans ses yeux. On se bouda pendant une semaine. Françoise, elle aussi, était toute grave. Ce qui tourmentait le père Merlier, c'était de savoir comment ce gredin de braconnier avait bien pu ensorceler sa fille. Jamais Dominique n'était venu au moulin. Le meunier guetta et il aperçut le galant, de l'autre côté de la Morelle, couché dans l'herbe et feignant de dormir. Françoise, de sa chambre, pouvait le voir. La chose était claire, ils avaient dû s'aimer, en se faisant les doux yeux par-dessus la roue du moulin.

Cependant, huit autres jours s'écoulèrent. Françoise devenait de plus en plus grave. Le père Merlier ne disait toujours rien. Puis, un soir, silencieusement, il amena lui-même Dominique. Françoise, justement, mettait la table. Elle ne parut pas étonnée, elle se contenta

while still quite young. If she was constantly laughing, that was to give pleasure to others. Deep down, she was serious.

Naturally, every local lad wooed her, even more for her money than for her pleasant personality. And she had finally made a choice that had just shocked the countryside. Across the Morelle lived a tall young fellow called Dominique Penquer. He wasn't from Rocreuse. Ten years earlier, he had come from Belgium to take over an inheritance from an uncle; this small property was located at the very edge of the Forest of Gagny, just opposite the mill, at a few rifle shots' distance. He said he had come merely to sell that property and go back home, but it seems that the area delighted him, because he never moved away. He was seen cultivating his little field and harvesting a few vegetables, which he lived on. He used to fish and hunt; several times the gamekeepers almost caught him and reported him to the police. This free-wheeling existence, which the peasants couldn't rightly see how he could afford, had finally given him a bad reputation. They vaguely called him a poacher. At any rate, he was lazy, because he was often found asleep on the grass at hours when he should have been working. The cottage he lived in, underneath the outermost trees in the forest, didn't resemble an honest fellow's home, either. If he had had dealings with the wolves in the ruins of Gagny, that wouldn't have surprised the old women one bit. And yet at times the girls ventured to defend him, because he was splendid-looking, that suspicious character, supple and tall as a poplar, with a very white skin and blond beard and hair that looked like gold in the sunlight. Now, one fine morning Françoise had announced to old Merlier that she loved Dominique and would never consent to marry any other man.

Just imagine what a cudgel blow old Merlier received that day! As was his custom, he said nothing. He was wearing his meditative expression, but his inner jollity was no longer gleaming from his eyes. They both sulked for a week. Françoise, too, was quite solemn. What was tormenting old Merlier was his failure to understand how that rascally poacher had been able to bewitch his daughter. Dominique had never come to the mill. The miller kept a lookout, and observed the wooer on the other side of the Morelle lying on the grass and pretending to be asleep. From her room Françoise could see him. The matter was clear; they must have fallen in love making eyes at each other over the mill wheel.

Meanwhile, another week went by. Françoise was becoming more and more solemn. Old Merlier still wasn't saying anything. Then, one evening, silently, he himself brought in Dominique. Françoise was just laying the table. She didn't appear surprised; all she did was add

d'ajouter un couvert; seulement, les petits trous de ses joues venaient de se creuser de nouveau, et son rire avait reparu. Le matin, le père Merlier était allé trouver Dominique dans la masure, sur la lisière du bois. Là, les deux hommes avaient causé pendant trois heures, les portes et les fenêtres fermées. Jamais personne n'a su ce qu'ils avaient pu se dire. Ce qu'il y a de certain, c'est que le père Merlier en sortant traitait déjà Dominique comme son fils. Sans doute, le vieillard avait trouvé le garçon qu'il était allé chercher, un brave garçon, dans ce paresseux qui se couchait sur l'herbe pour se faire aimer des filles.

Tout Rocreuse clabauda. Les femmes, sur les portes, ne tarissaient pas au sujet de la folie du père Merlier, qui introduisait ainsi chez lui un garnement. Il laissa dire. Peut-être, s'était-il souvenu de son propre mariage. Lui non plus ne possédait pas un sou vaillant, lorsqu'il avait épousé Madeleine et son moulin; cela pourtant ne l'avait point empêché de faire un bon mari. D'ailleurs, Dominique coupa court aux cancans, en se mettant si rudement à la besogne, que le pays en fut émerveillé. Justement le garçon du moulin était tombé au sort, et jamais Dominique ne voulut qu'on en engageât un autre. Il porta les sacs, conduisit la charrette, se battit avec la vieille roue, quand elle se faisait prier pour tourner, tout cela d'un tel cœur, qu'on venait le voir par plaisir. Le père Merlier avait son rire silencieux. Il était très fier d'avoir deviné ce garçon. Il n'y a rien comme l'amour pour donner du courage aux jeunes gens.

Au milieu de toute cette grosse besogne, Françoise et Dominique s'adoraient. Ils ne se parlaient guère, mais ils se regardaient avec une douceur souriante. Jusque-là, le père Merlier n'avait pas dit un seul mot au sujet du mariage; et tous deux respectaient ce silence, attendant la volonté du vieillard. Enfin, un jour, vers le milieu de juillet, il avait fait mettre trois tables dans la cour, sous le grand orme, en invitant ses amis de Rocreuse à venir le soir boire un coup avec lui. Quand la cour fut pleine et que tout le monde eut le verre en main, le père Merlier leva le sien très haut, en disant:

— C'est pour avoir le plaisir de vous annoncer que Françoise épousera ce gaillard-là dans un mois, le jour de la Saint-Louis.

Alors on trinqua bruyamment. Tout le monde riait. Mais le père Merlier, haussant la voix, dit encore:

— Dominique, embrasse ta promise. Ça se doit.

Et ils s'embrassèrent, très rouges pendant que l'assistance riait plus fort. Ce fut une vraie fête. On vida un petit tonneau. Puis, quand il n'y eut là que les amis intimes, on causa d'une façon calme. La nuit était tombée, une nuit étoilée et très claire. Dominique et Françoise, assis

another setting; but the little dimples in her cheeks had just appeared again, and her laughter had returned. That morning, old Merlier had gone to see Dominique in his cottage on the edge of the woods. There the two men had talked for three hours, with doors and windows shut. No one ever found out what it was they said to each other. What is certain is that, when he came out, old Merlier was already treating Dominique like his son. No doubt the old man had found the lad he had gone looking for, an upstanding lad, in that lazybones who stretched out on the grass to get the girls to love him.

All Rocreuse talked. The women, in their doorways, couldn't say enough about the folly of old Merlier, who was taking a scoundrel into his house that way. He let them talk. Perhaps he had recalled his own wedding. He hadn't owned a red cent, either, when he had married Madeleine and her mill, but that hadn't prevented him from being a good husband. Besides, Dominique put an end to the gossip by beginning to work so hard that the locals were amazed. The mill hand had just been drafted into the army,[1] and Dominique wouldn't hear of their hiring anyone else. He carried the sacks, drove the cart, and struggled with the ancient wheel when it needed to be coaxed to turn—all this so cheerfully that people came to watch him for their pleasure. Old Merlier wore his taciturn smile. He was very proud of having realized what that lad had in him. There's nothing like love to put heart into young men.

Amid all this heavy labor, Françoise and Dominique adored each other. They rarely spoke to each other, but they looked at each other with a smiling tenderness. Up to then old Merlier hadn't said a word about the wedding; and both of them respected that silence, awaiting the old man's pleasure. Finally, one day toward the middle of July, he had had three tables laid in the courtyard, under the big elm, inviting his friends from Rocreuse to come that evening for a drink with him. When the courtyard was full and everyone had his glass in his hand, old Merlier raised his very high and said:

"It's to have the pleasure of announcing to you that Françoise will marry that strapping fellow there in a month, on Saint Louis's Day."[2]

Then they clinked glasses noisily. Everyone was laughing. But old Merlier, raising his voice, went on to say:

"Dominique, kiss your betrothed. It's the thing to do."

And they kissed, their faces red, while the guests laughed even louder. It was a real celebration. They emptied a small cask. Then, when only close friends were left, they chatted tranquilly. Night had fallen, a starry, very bright night. Dominique and Françoise, seated on

sur un banc, l'un près de l'autre, ne disaient rien. Un vieux paysan parlait de la guerre que l'empereur avait déclarée à la Prusse. Tous les gars du village étaient déjà partis. La veille, des troupes avaient encore passé. On allait se cogner dur.

— Bah! dit le père Merlier avec l'égoïsme d'un homme heureux, Dominique est étranger, il ne partira pas . . . Et si les Prussiens venaient, il serait là pour défendre sa femme.

Cette idée que les Prussiens pouvaient venir parut une bonne plaisanterie. On allait leur franquer une raclée soignée, et ce serait vite fini.

— Je les ai déjà vus, je les ai déjà vus, répéta d'une voix sourde le vieux paysan.

Il y eut un silence. Puis, on trinqua une fois encore. Françoise et Dominique n'avaient rien entendu; ils s'étaient pris doucement la main, derrière le banc, sans qu'on pût les voir, et cela leur semblait si bon, qu'ils restaient là, les yeux perdus au fond des ténèbres.

Quelle nuit tiède et superbe! Le village s'endormait aux deux bords de la route blanche, dans une tranquillité d'enfant. On n'entendait plus, de loin en loin, que le chant de quelque coq éveillé trop tôt. Des grands bois voisins, descendaient de longues haleines qui passaient sur les toitures comme des caresses. Les prairies, avec leurs ombrages noirs, prenaient une majesté mystérieuse et recueillie, tandis que toutes les sources, toutes les eaux courantes qui jaillisaient dans l'ombre, semblaient être la respiration fraîche et rythmée de la campagne endormie. Par instants, la vieille roue du moulin, ensommeillée, paraissait rêver comme ces vieux chiens de garde qui aboient en ronflant; elle avait des craquements, elle causait toute seule, bercée par la chute de la Morelle, dont la nappe rendait le son musical et continu d'un tuyau d'orgues. Jamais une paix plus large n'était descendue sur un coin plus heureux de nature.

II

Un mois plus tard, jour pour jour, juste la veille de la Saint-Louis, Rocreuse était dans l'épouvante. Les Prussiens avaient battu l'empereur et s'avançaient à marches forcées vers le village. Depuis une semaine, des gens qui passaient sur la route annonçaient les Prussiens: «Ils sont à Lormières, ils sont à Novelles»; et, à entendre dire qu'ils se rapprochaient si vite, Rocreuse, chaque matin, croyait les voir descendre par les bois de Gagny. Ils ne venaient point cependant, cela effrayait davantage. Bien sûr qu'ils

a bench one next to the other, said nothing. An old peasant was talking about the war that the Emperor had declared on Prussia.[3] All the village boys had already left. The day before, troops had gone by again. The fight was going to be a tough one.

"Bah!" said old Merlier, with the egotism of a happy man. "Dominique is a foreigner, he won't have to go . . ." And if the Prussians came, he'd be there to defend his wife.

The idea that the Prussians might come seemed like a good joke. They were going to get a real drubbing, and all would soon be over.

"I've already seen them, I've already seen them," the old peasant repeated in a hollow voice.

There was a silence. Then they clinked glasses again. Françoise and Dominique hadn't heard any of this; they had taken each other's hand gently, behind the bench so that they couldn't be seen doing it, and they felt so good that way that they just sat there, their eyes lost in the depths of the darkness.

What a warm, splendid night! The village was falling asleep on the two sides of the white highway, as untroubled as a child. All that was still heard, at long intervals, was the crowing of some rooster that had awakened too early. From the great forests nearby, long exhalations descended and passed over the rooftops like caresses. The meadows, with their dark shade trees, took on a mysterious, reflective majesty, while all the springs, all the running waters that gushed forth in the dark, seemed to be the cool, rhythmic breathing of the sleeping countryside. At moments, the old mill wheel, in slumber, seemed to be having dreams, like those old watchdogs that bark as they snore; it creaked, it spoke to itself, rocked by the water drop in the Morelle; that sheet of water emitted a steady musical sound like an organ pipe. Never had such extensive peace been spread over a more fortunate corner of nature.

II

One month later to the day, precisely on the eve of Saint Louis's Day, Rocreuse was living in terror. The Prussians had beaten the Emperor, and were advancing toward the village in forced marches. For a week, people passing along the road had been announcing the Prussians: "They're at Lormières, they're at Novelles"; and, hearing these reports that they were drawing near so quickly, every morning the people of Rocreuse thought they saw them coming down through the Forest of Gagny. But they didn't come, and that frightened people

tomberaient sur le village pendant la nuit et qu'ils égorgeraient tout le monde.

La nuit précédente, un peu avant le jour, il y avait eu une alerte. Les habitants s'étaient réveillés, en entendant un grand bruit d'hommes sur la route. Les femmes déjà se jetaient à genoux et faisaient des signes de croix, lorsqu'on avait reconnu des pantalons rouges, en entrouvrant prudemment les fenêtres. C'était un détachement français. Le capitaine avait tout de suite demandé le maire du pays, et il était resté au moulin, après avoir causé avec le père Merlier.

Le soleil se levait gaiement, ce jour-là. Il ferait chaud, à midi. Sur les bois, une clarté blonde flottait, tandis que dans les fonds, au-dessus des prairies, montaient des vapeurs blanches. Le village, propre et joli, s'éveillait dans la fraîcheur, et la campagne, avec sa rivière et ses fontaines, avait des grâces mouillées de bouquet. Mais cette belle journée ne faisait rire personne. On venait de voir le capitaine tourner autour du moulin, regarder les maisons voisines, passer de l'autre côté de la Morelle, et de là, étudier le pays avec une lorgnette; le père Merlier, qui l'accompagnait, semblait donner des explications. Puis, le capitaine avait posté des soldats derrière des murs, derrière des arbres, dans les trous. Le gros du détachement campait dans la cour du moulin. On allait donc se battre? Et quand le père Merlier revint, on l'interrogea. Il fit un long signe de tête, sans parler. Oui, on allait se battre.

Françoise et Dominique étaient là, dans la cour, qui le regardaient. Il finit par ôter sa pipe de la bouche, et dit cette simple phrase:

— Ah! mes pauvres petits, ce n'est pas demain que je vous marierai!

Dominique, les lèvres serrées, avec un pli de colère au front, se haussait parfois, restait les yeux fixés sur les bois de Gagny, comme s'il eût voulu voir arriver les Prussiens. Françoise, très pâle, sérieuse, allait et venait, fournissant aux soldats ce dont ils avaient besoin. Ils faisaient la soupe dans un coin de la cour, et plaisantaient, en attendant de manger.

Cependant, le capitaine paraissait ravi. Il avait visité les chambres et la grande salle du moulin donnant sur la rivière. Maintenant, assis près du puits, il causait avec le père Merlier.

— Vous avez là une vraie forteresse, disait-il. Nous tiendrons bien jusqu'à ce soir . . . Les bandits sont en retard. Ils devraient être ici.

Le meunier restait grave. Il voyait son moulin flamber comme une torche. Mais il ne se plaignait pas, jugeant cela inutile. Il ouvrit seulement la bouche pour dire:

even more. They would surely fall upon the village at night and slaughter everyone.

On the night before, a little before daybreak, there had been an alarm. The inhabitants had awakened, hearing a loud noise of men on the road. The women were already falling on their knees and crossing themselves, when some people recognized red trousers through their cautiously half-opened windows. It was a French detachment. Their captain had immediately asked for the local mayor, and he had remained at the mill after talking with old Merlier.

The sun was rising cheerfully that day. It would be hot at noon. A golden brightness hovered over the woods, while down below, above the meadows, white mists were rising. The village, clean and pretty, was waking up in the cool air, and the countryside, with its stream and fountains, had the moist charms of a bunch of flowers. But that beautiful day didn't make anyone smile. They had just seen the captain walking to and fro around the mill, looking at the neighboring houses, crossing the Morelle, and, from there, studying the region with binoculars. Old Merlier, who accompanied him, seemed to be giving him explanations. Next, the captain had stationed soldiers behind walls, behind trees, in hollows. The bulk of the detachment was camping in the courtyard of the mill. Was there going to be a battle, then? And when old Merlier got back, he was questioned. He gave a long nod but didn't speak. Yes, there was going to be a battle.

Françoise and Dominique were there in the courtyard looking at him. Finally he took his pipe out of his mouth, and spoke this simple sentence:

"Ah, my poor children, it's not tomorrow that I'll marry you!"

Dominique, his lips taut, with an angry wrinkle on his brow, raised himself up at times, keeping his eyes fixed on the Forest of Gagny, as if he wanted to see the Prussians arrive. Françoise, very pale and solemn, was coming and going, supplying the soldiers' needs. They were cooking soup in a corner of the courtyard and were joking while awaiting their food.

Meanwhile, the captain seemed delighted. He had inspected the bedrooms and main parlor of the mill that faced the stream. Now, seated near the well, he was talking with old Merlier.

"It's a real fortress you've got there," he was saying. "We'll hold out until this evening . . . The bandits are late. They should have been here by now."

The miller remained solemn. He pictured his mill blazing like a torch. But he wasn't lamenting, since he considered that futile. He only opened his mouth to say:

— Vous devriez faire cacher la barque derrière la roue. Il y a là un trou où elle tient . . . Peut-être qu'elle pourra servir.

Le capitaine donna un ordre. Ce capitaine était un bel homme d'une quarantaine d'années, grand et de figure aimable. La vue de Françoise et de Dominique semblait le réjouir. Il s'occupait d'eux, comme s'il avait oublié la lutte prochaine. Il suivait Françoise des yeux, et son air disait clairement qu'il la trouvait charmante. Puis, se tournant vers Dominique:

— Vous n'êtes donc pas à l'armée, mon garçon? lui demanda-t-il brusquement.

— Je suis étranger, répondit le jeune homme.

Le capitaine parut goûter médiocrement cette raison. Il cligna les yeux et sourit. Françoise était plus agréable à fréquenter que le canon. Alors, en le voyant sourire, Dominique ajouta:

— Je suis étranger; mais je loge une balle dans une pomme, à cinq cents mètres . . . Tenez, mon fusil de chasse est là, derrière vous.

— Il pourra vous servir, répliqua simplement le capitaine.

Françoise s'était approchée, un peu tremblante. Et, sans se soucier du monde qui était là, Dominique prit et serra dans les siennes les deux mains qu'elle lui tendait, comme pour se mettre sous sa protection. Le capitaine avait souri de nouveau, mais il n'ajouta pas une parole. Il demeurait assis, son épée entre les jambes, les yeux perdus, paraissant rêver.

Il était déjà dix heures. La chaleur devenait très forte. Un lourd silence se faisait. Dans la cour, à l'ombre des hangars, les soldats s'étaient mis à manger la soupe. Aucun bruit ne venait du village, dont les habitants avaient tous barricadé leurs maisons, portes et fenêtres. Un chien, resté seul sur la route, hurlait. Des bois et des prairies voisines, pâmés par la chaleur, sortait une voix lointaine, prolongée, faite de tous les souffles épars. Un coucou chanta. Puis, le silence s'élargit encore.

Et, dans cet air endormi, brusquement, un coup de feu éclata. Le capitaine se leva vivement, les soldats lâchèrent leurs assiettes de soupe, encore à moitié pleines. En quelques secondes, tous furent à leur poste de combat; de bas en haut, le moulin se trouvait occupé. Cependant, le capitaine, qui s'était porté sur la route, n'avait rien vu; à droite, à gauche, la route s'étendait, vide et toute blanche. Un deuxième coup de feu se fit entendre, et toujours rien, pas une ombre. Mais, en se retournant, il aperçut du côté de Gagny entre deux arbres, un léger flocon de fumée qui s'envolait, pareil à un fil de la Vierge. Le bois restait profond et doux.

"You ought to have the boat hidden behind the wheel. There's a space there where it fits . . . It might come in handy."

The captain issued an order. This captain was a fine-looking man of about forty, tall, with a pleasant face. The sight of Françoise and Dominique seemed to gladden him. He was paying attention to them as if he had forgotten about the coming fight. His eyes followed Françoise's movements, and his expression made it clear that he found her charming. Then, turning toward Dominique, he asked him, point-blank:

"You aren't in the army, son?"

"I'm a foreigner," the young man replied.

The captain seemed to find this reason less than satisfactory. He blinked his eyes and smiled. Françoise was more pleasant to be around than cannons. Then, seeing him smile, Dominique added:

"I'm a foreigner; but I can put a bullet in an apple at five hundred meters . . . Look, my hunting rifle is there behind you."

"You may find use for it," was the captain's simple reply.

Françoise had come up to them, trembling slightly. And without caring about the people around, Dominique took the two hands she reached out to him, as if putting herself under his protection, and held them tightly in his own. The captain had smiled again, but didn't add a word. He remained seated, his sword between his legs, his eyes far away as if he were dreaming.

It was already ten o'clock. It was beginning to get very hot. A heavy silence ensued. In the courtyard, in the shade of the sheds, the soldiers had begun eating their soup. No sound was coming from the village; the inhabitants had all barricaded their houses, doors, and windows. A dog, left alone on the road, was howling. From the woods and the nearby meadows, which were fainting under the heat, came a distant, prolonged sound, comprised of all their scattered exhalations. A cuckoo called. Then the silence spread even further.

And in this sleeping air, all of a sudden, a shot rang out. The captain rose briskly, and the soldiers abandoned their plates of soup, which were still half-full. In a few seconds, they were all at their battle stations; the mill was occupied from top to bottom. Meanwhile, the captain, who had gone out to the road, couldn't see a thing; to his right, to his left, the road stretched into the distance, empty and all white. A second shot was heard, and still nothing, not even a shadow. But, turning around, between two trees in the direction of Gagny, he espied a light wisp of smoke floating away like a thread of gossamer. The forest remained deep and gentle.

— Les gredins se sont jetés dans la forêt, murmura-t-il. Ils nous savent ici.

Alors, la fusillade continua, de plus en plus nourrie, entre les soldats français, postés autour du moulin, et les Prussiens, cachés derrière les arbres. Les balles sifflaient au-dessus de la Morelle, sans causer de pertes, ni d'un côté ni de l'autre. Les coups étaient irréguliers, partaient de chaque buisson; et l'on n'apercevait toujours que les petites fumées, balancées mollement par le vent. Cela dura près de deux heures. L'officier chantonnait d'un air indifférent. Françoise et Dominique, qui étaient restés dans la cour, se haussaient et regardaient par-dessus une muraille basse. Ils s'intéressaient surtout à un petit soldat, posté au bord de la Morelle, derrière la carcasse d'un vieux bateau; il était à plat ventre, guettait, lâchait son coup de feu, puis se laissait glisser dans un fossé, un peu en arrière, pour recharger son fusil; et ses mouvements étaient si drôles, si rusés, si souples, qu'on se laissait aller à sourire en le voyant. Il dut apercevoir quelque tête de Prussien, car il se leva vivement et épaula; mais, avant qu'il eût tiré, il jeta un cri, tourna sur lui-même et roula dans le fossé, où ses jambes eurent un instant le roidissement convulsif des pattes d'un poulet qu'on égorge. Le petit soldat venait de recevoir une balle en pleine poitrine. C'était le premier mort. Instinctivement, Françoise avait saisi la main de Dominique et la lui serrait, dans une crispation nerveuse.

— Ne restez pas là, dit le capitaine. Les balles viennent jusqu'ici.

En effet, un petit coup sec s'était fait entendre dans le vieil orme, et un bout de branche tombait en se balançant. Mais les deux jeunes gens ne bougèrent pas, cloués par l'anxiété du spectacle. A la lisière du bois, un Prussien était brusquement sorti de derrière un arbre comme d'une coulisse, battant l'air de ses bras et tombant à la renverse. Et rien ne bougea plus, les deux morts semblaient dormir au grand soleil, on ne voyait toujours personne dans la campagne alourdie. Le pétillement de la fusillade lui-même cessa. Seule, la Morelle chuchotait avec son bruit clair.

Le père Merlier regarda le capitaine d'un air de surprise, comme pour lui demander si c'était fini.

— Voilà le grand coup, murmura celui-ci. Méfiez-vous. Ne restez pas là.

Il n'avait pas achevé qu'une décharge effroyable eut lieu. Le grand orme fut comme fauché, une volée de feuilles tournoya. Les Prussiens avaient heureusement tiré trop haut. Dominique entraîna,

"The scoundrels have hidden in the forest," he muttered. "They know we're here."

Then the fusillade continued, getting heavier all the while, between the French soldiers stationed around the mill and the Prussians concealed behind the trees. The bullets were whistling across the Morelle, without resulting in casualties on either side. The shots were irregularly spaced, coming from every bush; and all that could be seen so far was little puffs of smoke gently shaking on the breeze. That lasted nearly two hours. The officer was humming nonchalantly. Françoise and Dominique, who had remained in the courtyard, were raising their heads and looking over a low wall. They were especially interested in a little soldier stationed on the bank of the Morelle behind the skeleton of an old boat; lying on his stomach, he would observe, fire, then lower himself into a ditch a little behind him to reload his rifle; and his movements were so comical, so sly, so nimble, that they allowed themselves a smile as they watched him. He must have caught sight of some Prussian's head, because he stood up briskly and took aim; but before he could fire, he uttered a cry, spun around, and rolled into the ditch, where for a moment his legs underwent a convulsive stiffening like the feet of a chicken being slaughtered. The little soldier had just received a bullet full in the chest. He was the first fatality. Instinctively Françoise had gripped Dominique's hand and was seizing it in a nervous reaction.

"Don't stay here," said the captain. "The bullets are reaching this area."

Indeed, a little dry thud had been heard in the old elm, and the tip of a branch was rocking as it fell. But the two young people didn't budge; they were riveted there by their anguish at what they saw. At the edge of the woods, a Prussian had suddenly emerged from behind a tree as if from behind a stage flat, beating the air with his arms and falling over backwards. And nothing else stirred; the two dead men seemed to be sleeping in the broad daylight; even now no one was to be seen in the dull countryside. Even the crackling of the fusillade ceased. The only sound was the bright whispering of the Morelle.

Old Merlier looked at the captain with an air of surprise, as if to ask him whether it was all over.

"Here comes the main attack," the captain muttered. "Watch out! Don't stay here."

Before he had finished speaking, a terrifying volley was fired. The big elm had its foliage virtually mowed; a bunch of leaves were whirling in the air. Luckily the Prussians had fired too high.

emporta presque Françoise, tandis que le père Merlier les suivait en criant:

— Mettez-vous dans le petit caveau, les murs sont solides.

Mais ils ne l'écoutèrent pas, ils entrèrent dans la grande salle, où une dizaine de soldats attendaient en silence, les volets fermés, guettant par des fentes. Le capitaine était resté seul dans la cour, accroupi derrière la petite muraille, pendant que des décharges furieuses continuaient. Au-dehors, les soldats qu'il avait postés, ne cédaient le terrain que pied à pied. Pourtant, ils rentraient un à un en rampant, quand l'ennemi les avait délogés de leurs cachettes. Leur consigne était de gagner du temps, de ne point se montrer, pour que les Prussiens ne pussent savoir quelles forces ils avaient devant eux. Une heure encore s'écoula. Et, comme un sergent arrivait, disant qu'il n'y avait plus dehors que deux ou trois hommes, l'officier tira sa montre, en murmurant:

— Deux heures et demie . . . Allons, il faut tenir quatre heures.

Il fit fermer le grand portail de la cour, et tout fut préparé pour une résistance énergique. Comme les Prussiens se trouvaient de l'autre côté de la Morelle, un assaut immédiat n'était pas à craindre. Il y avait bien un pont à deux kilomètres, mais ils ignoraient sans doute son existence, et il était peu croyable qu'ils tenteraient de passer à gué la rivière. L'officier fit donc simplement surveiller la route. Tout l'effort allait porter du côté de la campagne.

La fusillade, de nouveau, avait cessé. Le moulin semblait mort sous le grand soleil. Pas un volet n'était ouvert, aucun bruit ne sortait de l'intérieur. Peu à peu, cependant, des Prussiens se montraient à la lisière du bois de Gagny. Ils allongeaient la tête, s'enhardissaient. Dans le moulin, plusieurs soldats épaulaient déjà; mais le capitaine cria:

— Non, non, attendez . . . Laissez-les s'approcher.

Ils y mirent beaucoup de prudence, regardant le moulin d'un air méfiant. Cette vieille demeure, silencieuse et morne, avec ses rideaux de lierre, les inquiétait. Pourtant, ils avançaient. Quand ils furent une cinquantaine dans la prairie, en face, l'officier dit un seul mot:

— Allez!

Un déchirement se fit entendre, des coups isolés suivirent. Françoise, agitée d'un tremblement, avait porté malgré elle les mains à ses oreilles. Dominique, derrière les soldats, regardait; et, quand la fumée se fut un peu dissipée, il aperçut trois Prussiens étendus sur le dos, au milieu du pré. Les autres s'étaient jetés derrière les saules et les peupliers. Et le siège commença.

Dominique dragged away Françoise—nearly carried her away—while old Merlier was following them, shouting:

"Go into the little cellar; the walls are solid."

But they didn't listen to him; they went into the main parlor, where some ten soldiers were waiting silently, the shutters closed, looking out through cracks. The captain had remained alone in the courtyard, crouching behind the little wall, while furious volleys continued. Beyond the wall the soldiers he had stationed were only yielding ground a foot at a time. And yet they would creep back to cover one by one when the enemy had dislodged them from their hiding places. Their orders were to gain time and not to show themselves, so that the Prussians couldn't learn the strength of the unit that was facing them. Another hour went by. And when a sergeant came to report that there were only two or three men left outside, the officer pulled out his watch, muttering:

"Two-thirty . . . Look, we've got to hold out for four hours."

He had the big gate to the courtyard closed, and everything was put in readiness for an energetic resistance. Since the Prussians were on the other side of the Morelle, an immediate attack wasn't to be feared. True, there was a bridge two kilometers away, but they were no doubt unaware of its existence, and it was very hard to believe that they would try to ford the stream. And so the officer merely had the road watched. Their entire effort would be centered on the side facing the open country.

The fusillade had ceased again. The mill seemed dead in the strong sunlight. Not one shutter was open, no sound came from inside. Meanwhile, the Prussians were gradually showing themselves at the edge of the Forest of Gagny. They were sticking out their heads, they were growing bolder. In the mill several soldiers were already taking aim, but the captain shouted.

"No, no, wait! . . . Let them come closer."

They were very cautious doing so, looking at the mill distrustfully. That old dwelling, silent and gloomy, with its curtains of ivy, worried them. Still, they were moving forward. When there were about fifty of them in the meadow opposite, the officer said a single word:

"Go!"

A lacerating volley was to be heard; isolated shots followed. Françoise, shaking all over, had put her hands to her ears in spite of herself. Dominique, standing behind the soldiers, was watching; and when the smoke had cleared away a bit, he saw three Prussians lying on their back in the middle of the meadow. The others had taken cover behind the willows and the poplars. And the siege began.

Pendant plus d'une heure, le moulin fut criblé de balles. Elles en fouettaient les vieux murs comme une grêle. Lorsqu'elles frappaient sur de la pierre, on les entendait s'écraser et retomber à l'eau. Dans le bois, elles s'enfonçaient avec un bruit sourd. Parfois, un craquement annonçait que la roue venait d'être touchée. Les soldats, à l'intérieur, ménageaient leurs coups, ne tiraient que lorsqu'ils pouvaient viser. De temps à autre, le capitaine consultait sa montre. Et, comme une balle fendait un volet et allait se loger dans le plafond:

— Quatre heures, murmura-t-il. Nous ne tiendrons jamais.

Peu à peu, en effet, cette fusillade terrible ébranlait le vieux moulin. Un volet tomba à l'eau, troué comme une dentelle, et il fallut le remplacer par un matelas. Le père Merlier, à chaque instant, s'exposait pour constater les avaries de sa pauvre roue, dont les craquements lui allaient au cœur. Elle était bien finie, cette fois; jamais il ne pourrait la raccommoder. Dominique avait supplié Françoise de se retirer, mais elle voulait rester avec lui; elle s'était assise derrière une grande armoire de chêne, qui la protégeait. Une balle pourtant arriva dans l'armoire, dont les flancs rendirent un son grave. Alors, Dominique se plaça devant Françoise. Il n'avait pas encore tiré, il tenait son fusil à la main, ne pouvant approcher des fenêtres dont les soldats tenaient toute la largeur. A chaque décharge, le plancher tressaillait.

— Attention! attention! cria tout d'un coup le capitaine.

Il venait de voir sortir du bois toute une masse sombre. Aussitôt s'ouvrit un formidable feu de peloton. Ce fut comme une trombe qui passa sur le moulin. Un autre volet partit et, par l'ouverture béante de la fenêtre, les balles entrèrent. Deux soldats roulèrent sur le carreau. L'un ne remua plus; on le poussa contre le mur, parce qu'il encombrait. L'autre se tordit en demandant qu'on l'achevât; mais on ne l'écoutait point, les balles entraient toujours, chacun se garait et tâchait de trouver une meurtrière pour riposter. Un troisième soldat fut blessé; celui-là ne dit pas une parole, il laissa couler au bord d'une table, avec des yeux fixes et hagards. En face de ces morts, Françoise, prise d'horreur, avait repoussé machinalement sa chaise, pour s'asseoir à terre, contre le mur; elle se croyait là plus petite et moins en danger. Cependant, on était allé prendre tous les matelas de la maison, on avait rebouché à moitié la fenêtre. La salle s'emplissait de débris, d'armes rompues, de meubles éventrés.

— Cinq heures, dit le capitaine. Tenez bon . . . Ils vont chercher à passer l'eau.

For over an hour the mill was riddled with bullets. They whipped its old walls like hail. When they struck stone, they could be heard squashing and bouncing off into the water. They penetrated wood with a muffled sound. At times a creaking indicated that the wheel had just been hit. The soldiers inside economized their shots, firing only when they could take proper aim. From time to time the captain consulted his watch. And, when a bullet split a shutter and lodged in the ceiling, he muttered:

"Four o'clock. We'll never make it."

In fact, that terrible fusillade was gradually shaking the old mill to pieces. A shutter fell into the water, riddled like a piece of lace, and had to be replaced by a mattress. Every minute old Merlier was leaving cover to check on the damage to his poor wheel, whose creaking made his heart ache. This time it was really finished off; he'd never be able to patch it up. Dominique had implored Françoise to go to her room, but she insisted on staying with him; she had taken a seat behind a big oak armoire that protected her. And yet a bullet struck the armoire, whose sides emitted a deep sound. Then Dominique took a stand in front of Françoise. He had not yet fired; he was holding his rifle in his hand, being unable to get near the windows, the full breadth of which was occupied by the soldiers. At each volley the floor shook.

"Watch out! Watch out!" the captain suddenly cried.

He had just seen a large dark mass emerging from the woods. Immediately a formidable volley firing began. It was like a whirlwind passing over the mill. Another shutter was blown away and bullets came in through the gaping window opening. Two soldiers rolled on the floor tiles. One stopped moving; they shoved him against the wall because he was in the way. The other writhed, asking to be finished off; but he wasn't listened to; the bullets were still coming in; everyone was getting out of their way and trying to find a loophole in order to return the fire. A third soldier was wounded; this one didn't say a word, but sank down beside a table with wildly staring eyes. Seeing these dead men, Françoise, horror-stricken, had automatically pushed away her chair; she sat down on the floor against the wall, believing she'd be a smaller target there, and in less danger. Meanwhile, all the mattresses in the house had been collected, and the gap in the window had been half-filled again. The room was filling up with debris, shattered weapons, and ripped-open furniture.

"Five o'clock," said the captain. "Hold tight . . . they're going to try to cross the stream."

A ce moment, Françoise poussa un cri. Une balle, qui avait ricoché, venait de lui effleurer le front. Quelques gouttes de sang parurent. Dominique la regarda; puis, s'approchant de la fenêtre, il lâcha son premier coup de feu, et il ne s'arrêta plus. Il chargeait, tirait, sans s'occuper de ce qui se passait près de lui; de temps à autre seulement, il jetait un coup d'œil sur Françoise. D'ailleurs, il ne se pressait pas, visait avec soin. Les Prussiens, longeant les peupliers, tentaient le passage de la Morelle, comme le capitaine l'avait prévu; mais, dès qu'un d'entre eux se hasardait, il tombait frappé à la tête par une balle de Dominique. Le capitaine, qui suivait ce jeu, était émerveillé. Il complimenta le jeune homme, en lui disant qu'il serait heureux d'avoir beaucoup de tireurs de sa force. Dominique ne l'entendait pas. Une balle lui entama l'épaule, une autre lui contusionna le bras. Et il tirait toujours.

Il y eut deux nouveaux morts. Les matelas, déchiquetés, ne bouchaient plus les fenêtres. Une dernière décharge semblait devoir emporter le moulin. La position n'était plus tenable. Cependant, l'officier répétait:

— Tenez bon . . . Encore une demi-heure.

Maintenant, il comptait les minutes. Il avait promis à ses chefs d'arrêter l'ennemi là jusqu'au soir, et il n'aurait pas reculé d'une semelle avant l'heure qu'il avait fixée pour la retraite. Il gardait son air aimable, souriait à Françoise, afin de la rassurer. Lui-même venait de ramasser le fusil d'un soldat mort et faisait le coup de feu.

Il n'y avait plus que quatre soldats dans la salle.

Les Prussiens se montraient en masse sur l'autre bord de la Morelle, et il était évident qu'ils allaient passer la rivière d'un moment à l'autre. Quelques minutes s'écoulèrent encore. Le capitaine s'entêtait, ne voulait pas donner l'ordre de la retraite, lorsqu'un sergent accourut, en disant:

— Ils sont sur la route, ils vont nous prendre par-derrière.

Les Prussiens devaient avoir trouvé le pont. Le capitaine tira sa montre.

— Encore cinq minutes, dit-il. Ils ne seront pas ici avant cinq minutes.

Puis, à six heures précises, il consentit enfin à faire sortir ses hommes par une petite porte qui donnait sur une ruelle. De là, ils se jetèrent dans un fossé, ils gagnèrent la forêt de Sauval. Le capitaine avait, avant de partir, salué très poliment le père Merlier, en s'excusant. Et il avait même ajouté:

— Amusez-les . . . Nous reviendrons.

At that moment Françoise uttered a cry. A bullet that had ricocheted had just grazed her forehead. A few drops of blood appeared. Dominique looked at her; then, going up to the window, he fired his first shot and didn't stop after that. He would load and fire, unconcerned with what was going on around him; only, from time to time, he would glance at Françoise. Moreover, he wasn't in a hurry, he took careful aim. The Prussians, moving along the poplars, were trying to cross the Morelle, as the captain had foreseen; but as soon as one of them ventured to do so, he fell, with one of Dominique's bullets in his head. The captain, who was observing this course of events, was amazed. He complimented the young man, saying that he'd be glad to have many marksmen of that quality. Dominique wasn't paying attention to him. A bullet cut into his shoulder, another bruised his arm. And he was still firing.

There were two more dead men. The mattresses, cut to ribbons, were no longing filling up the window spaces. A final volley seemed as if it would carry off the mill. Their position could no longer be held. And yet, the officer kept repeating:

"Hold tight . . . Another half-hour."

By now he was counting the minutes. He had promised his superiors to pin the enemy down there until evening, and he hadn't taken a step backward before the hour he had determined on for his retreat. He maintained his likable attitude, smiling at Françoise to reassure her. He himself had just picked up a dead soldier's rifle and was firing.

Only four soldiers were now left in the room.

The Prussians appeared en masse on the far bank of the Morelle, and they were obviously going to cross the stream at any moment. A few more minutes went by. The captain was still stubbornly refusing to give the order to retreat when a sergeant ran up and said:

"They're on the road, they're going to take us from behind."

The Prussians must have found the bridge. The captain pulled out his watch.

"Five more minutes," he said. "They won't be here for five minutes."

Then, at six o'clock precisely, he finally consented to have his men leave through a little door that opened onto an alleyway. From there they took cover in a ditch and reached the Forest of Sauval. Before going, the captain had taken very polite leave of old Merlier, apologizing for what had happened. And he had even added:

"Keep them entertained . . . We'll be back."

Cependant, Dominique était resté seul dans la salle. Il tirait toujours, n'entendant rien, ne comprenant rien. Il n'éprouvait que le besoin de défendre Françoise. Les soldats étaient partis, sans qu'il s'en doutât le moins du monde. Il visait et tuait son homme à chaque coup. Brusquement, il y eut un grand bruit. Les Prussiens, par-derrière, venaient d'envahir la cour. Il lâcha un dernier coup, et ils tombèrent sur lui, comme son fusil fumait encore.

Quatre hommes le tenaient. D'autres vociféraient autour de lui, dans une langue effroyable. Ils faillirent l'égorger tout de suite. Françoise s'était jetée en avant, suppliante. Mais un officier entra et se fit remettre le prisonnier. Après quelques phrases qu'il échangea en allemand avec les soldats, il se tourna vers Dominique et lui dit rudement, en très bon français:

— Vous serez fusillé dans deux heures.

III

C'était une règle posée par l'état-major allemand: tout Français n'appartenant pas à l'armée régulière et pris les armes à la main, devait être fusillé. Les compagnies franches elles-mêmes n'étaient pas reconnues comme belligérantes. En faisant ainsi de terribles exemples sur les paysans qui défendaient leurs foyers, les Allemands voulaient empêcher la levée en masse, qu'ils redoutaient.

L'officier, un homme grand et sec, d'une cinquantaine d'années, fit subir à Dominique un bref interrogatoire. Bien qu'il parlât le français très purement, il avait une raideur toute prussienne.

— Vous êtes de ce pays?

— Non, je suis Belge.

— Pourquoi avez-vous pris les armes?... Tout ceci ne doit pas vous regarder.

Dominique ne répondit pas. A ce moment, l'officier aperçut François debout et très pâle, qui écoutait; sur son front blanc, sa légère blessure mettait une barre rouge. Il regarda les jeunes gens l'un après l'autre, parut comprendre, et se contenta d'ajouter:

— Vous ne niez pas avoir tiré?

— J'ai tiré tant que j'ai pu, répondit tranquillement Dominique.

Cet aveu était inutile, car il était noir de poudre, couvert de sueur, taché de quelques gouttes de sang qui avaient coulé de l'éraflure de son épaule.

— C'est bien, répéta l'officier. Vous serez fusillé dans deux heures.

Françoise ne cria pas. Elle joignit les mains et les éleva dans un

Meanwhile Dominique had remained alone in the parlor. He was still firing, paying attention to nothing, comprehending nothing. All he felt was the need to defend Françoise. The soldiers had left without his being aware of it in the least. He kept on aiming and killing a man with each shot. Suddenly there was a loud noise. From behind, the Prussians had just invaded the courtyard. He fired one last shot before they fell upon him, while his rifle was still smoking.

Four men held him fast. Others were shouting all around him in a terrifying language. They almost slaughtered him on the spot. Françoise had thrown herself in front of him imploringly. But an officer entered and had the prisoner handed over to himself. After exchanging a few sentences with the soldiers in German, he turned to Dominique and said to him roughly, in very good French:

"You'll be shot in two hours."

III

It was a regulation issued by the German general staff: any Frenchman, not belonging to the regular army, captured with weapon in hand, was to be shot. Even the companies of partisans weren't recognized as belligerents. By thus making terrible examples of the peasants who were defending their homes, the Germans were trying to prevent a universal call to arms, which they dreaded.

The officer, a tall, lean man about fifty, subjected Dominique to a brief interrogation. Even though he spoke French very correctly, he had a thoroughly Prussian severity.

"You're from this area?"

"No, I'm Belgian."

"Why did you take up arms? . . . All this should be no concern of yours."

Dominique didn't reply. At that moment the officer caught sight of Françoise standing, very pale, and listening; on her white forehead her light wound made a red streak. He looked at the young couple one at a time, seemed to understand the situation, and merely added:

"You don't deny that you fired?"

"I fired as much as I could," Dominique calmly replied.

That confession was needless, because he was black with powder, drenched in sweat, and stained with a few drops of blood that had flowed from the scratch on his shoulder.

"Very well," the officer repeated. "You'll be shot in two hours."

Françoise didn't cry out. She joined her hands and raised them in a

geste de muet désespoir. L'officier remarqua ce geste. Deux soldats avaient emmené Dominique dans une pièce voisine, où ils devaient le garder à vue. La jeune fille était tombée sur une chaise, les jambes brisées; elle ne pouvait pleurer, elle étouffait. Cependant, l'officier l'examinait toujours. Il finit par lui adresser la parole:

— Ce garçon est votre frère? demanda-t-il.

Elle dit non de la tête. Il resta raide, sans un sourire. Puis, au bout d'un silence:

— Il habite le pays depuis longtemps?

Elle dit oui, d'un nouveau signe.

— Alors, il doit très bien connaître les bois voisins?

Cette fois, elle parla.

— Oui, monsieur, dit-elle en le regardant avec quelque surprise.

Il n'ajouta rien et tourna sur ses talons, en demandant qu'on lui amenât le maire du village. Mais Françoise s'était levée, une légère rougeur au visage, croyant avoir saisi le but de ses questions et reprise d'espoir. Ce fut elle-même qui courut pour trouver son père.

Le père Merlier, dès que les coups de feu avaient cessé, était vivement descendu par la galerie de bois, pour visiter sa roue. Il adorait sa fille, il avait une solide amitié pour Dominique, son futur gendre; mais sa roue tenait aussi une large place dans son cœur. Puisque les deux petits, comme il les appelait, étaient sortis sains et saufs de la bagarre, il songeait à son autre tendresse, qui avait singulièrement souffert, celle-là. Et, penché sur la grande carcasse de bois, il en étudiait les blessures d'un air navré. Cinq palettes étaient en miettes, la charpente centrale était criblée. Il fourrait les doigts dans les trous des balles, pour en mesurer la profondeur; il réfléchissait à la façon dont il pourrait réparer toutes ces avaries. Françoise le trouva qui bouchait déjà des fentes avec des débris et de la mousse.

— Père, dit-elle, ils vous demandent.

Et elle pleura enfin, en lui contant ce qu'elle venait d'entendre. Le père Merlier hocha la tête. On ne fusillait pas les gens comme ça. Il fallait voir. Et il rentra dans le moulin, de son air silencieux et paisible. Quand l'officier lui eut demandé des vivres pour ses hommes, il répondit que les gens de Rocreuse n'étaient pas habitués à être brutalisés, et qu'on n'obtiendrait rien d'eux si l'on employait la violence. Il se chargeait de tout, mais à la condition qu'on le laissât agir seul. L'officier parut se fâcher d'abord de ce ton tranquille; puis, il céda, devant les paroles brèves et nettes du vieillard. Même il le rappela, pour lui demander:

— Ces bois-là, en face, comment les nommez-vous?

gesture of wordless despair. The officer noticed that gesture. Two soldiers had taken Dominique into an adjoining room, where they were
to keep watch over him. The girl had dropped onto a chair, her legs
giving way under her; she was unable to cry, she was stifling.
Meanwhile the officer kept observing her. Finally he spoke to her:

"Is that boy your brother?" he asked.

She shook her head "no." He remained stiff and unsmiling. Then,
after a silence:

"Has he lived in the area very long?"

She said "yes" with a nod.

"So he must be very familiar with the forests around here?"

This time she spoke.

"Yes, sir," she said, looking at him in some surprise.

He said nothing further, but turned on his heels, asking that the village mayor be brought to him. But Françoise had stood up, her face
slightly red, believing she had grasped the intention of his questions,
and feeling some hope again. She herself ran to find her father.

Old Merlier, the moment the firing had ceased, had briskly gone
down by way of the wooden gallery to inspect his wheel. He adored
his daughter, and had a staunch friendly feeling toward Dominique,
his future son-in-law; but his wheel also had a big place in his heart.
Since the two children, as he called them, had come out of the scrape
safe and sound, he was thinking about his other love—and that one
had really suffered. Leaning over the big wooden framework, he was
studying its wounds brokenheartedly. Five paddles were in
smithereens, and the central timberwork was riddled. He thrust his
fingers into the bullet holes to measure their depth; he was wonder-
ing how he could repair all that damage. Françoise found him already
plugging up cracks with debris and moss.

"Father," she said, "they're asking for you."

And finally she was able to cry, telling him what she had just heard.
Old Merlier shook his head. People weren't shot like that. They had
to wait and see. And he went back inside the mill in his taciturn,
peaceful way. When the officer asked him for provisions for his men,
he replied that the inhabitants of Rocreuse weren't accustomed to be
bullied, and that he'd get nothing out of them if he used force. He
would take care of everything, but only if he was allowed to act inde-
pendently. At first the officer seemed angry at that calm tone; then he
gave in to the old man's short, clear terms. He even called him back,
to ask him:

"What do you call those woods opposite?"

— Les bois de Sauval.

— Et quelle est leur étendue?

Le meunier le regarda fixement.

— Je ne sais pas, répondit-il.

Et il s'éloigna. Une heure plus tard, la contribution de guerre en vivres et en argent, réclamée par l'officier, était dans la cour du moulin. La nuit venait, Françoise suivait avec anxiété les mouvements des soldats. Elle ne s'éloignait pas de la pièce dans laquelle était enfermé Dominique. Vers sept heures, elle eut une émotion poignante; elle vit l'officier entrer chez le prisonnier, et, pendant un quart d'heure, elle entendit leurs voix qui s'élevaient. Un instant, l'officier reparut sur le seuil, pour donner un ordre en allemand, qu'elle ne comprit pas; mais, lorsque douze hommes furent venus se ranger dans la cour, le fusil au bras, un tremblement la saisit, elle se sentit mourir. C'en était donc fait; l'exécution allait avoir lieu. Les douze hommes restèrent là dix minutes, la voix de Dominique continuait à s'élever sur un ton de refus violent. Enfin, l'officier sortit, en fermant brutalement la porte et en disant:

— C'est bien, réfléchissez . . . Je vous donne jusqu'à demain matin.

Et, d'un geste, il fit rompre les rangs aux douze hommes. Françoise restait hébétée. Le père Merlier, qui avait continué de fumer sa pipe, en regardant le peloton d'un air simplement curieux, vint la prendre par le bras, avec une douceur paternelle. Il l'emmena dans sa chambre.

— Tiens-toi tranquille, lui dit-il, tâche de dormir . . . Demain, il fera jour, et nous verrons.

En se retirant, il l'enferma par prudence. Il avait pour principe que les femmes ne sont bonnes à rien, et qu'elles gâtent tout, lorsqu'elles s'occupent d'une affaire sérieuse. Cependant, Françoise ne se coucha pas. Elle demeura longtemps assise sur son lit, écoutant les rumeurs de la maison. Les soldats allemands, campés dans la cour, chantaient et riaient; ils durent manger et boire jusqu'à onze heures, car le tapage ne cessa pas un instant. Dans le moulin même, des pas lourds résonnaient de temps à autre, sans doute des sentinelles qu'on relevait. Mais, ce qui l'intéressait surtout, c'étaient les bruits qu'elle pouvait saisir dans la pièce qui se trouvait sous sa chambre. Plusieurs fois, elle se coucha par terre, elle appliqua son oreille contre le plancher. Cette pièce était justement celle où l'on avait enfermé Dominique. Il devait marcher du mur à la fenêtre, car elle entendit longtemps la cadence régulière de sa promenade; puis, il se fit un grand silence, il s'était sans doute assis. D'ailleurs, les rumeurs cessaient, tout s'endormait.

"The Forest of Sauval."

"And how far do they extend?"

The miller stared at him.

"I don't know," he answered.

And he left. An hour later, the forced contribution of provisions and money that the officer had requested was in the courtyard of the mill. Night was approaching; Françoise observed the movements of the soldiers in anguish. She didn't go far from the room in which Dominique was locked up. About seven o'clock, she had a strong emotional shock; she saw the officer enter the prisoner's room, and for fifteen minutes she heard their voices raised. For a moment the officer reappeared on the threshold to give an order in German that she didn't understand; but when twelve men had taken up positions in the courtyard carrying rifles, a tremor seized her and she thought she would die. And so it was a sure thing; the execution was going to take place. The twelve men stayed there ten minutes; Dominique's voice was constantly raised in a tone of decided refusal. Finally the officer came out, slamming the door violently and saying:

"Very well, think it over . . . , I give you till tomorrow morning."

And with a gesture he had the twelve men fall out. Françoise remained numb. Old Merlier, who had continued to smoke his pipe, looking at the platoon with a merely curious expression, came and took her by the arm with a father's gentleness. He took her to her room.

"Stay calm," he said, "try to sleep . . . Tomorrow it will be daylight, and we'll see."

As he went out, he locked her in out of caution. He believed firmly that women are totally incapable and spoil everything when they meddle in a serious matter. But Françoise didn't go to sleep. For a long time she remained seated on her bed, listening to the noises in the house. The German soldiers, who were camping in the courtyard, were singing and laughing; they must have been eating and drinking until eleven, because the racket didn't stop for a minute. Even inside the mill, heavy steps resounded from time to time, no doubt sentries being relieved. But what were especially interesting to her were the sounds she could make out in the room below her bedroom. Several times she stretched out on the floor, putting her ear down to it. That room was the very one in which Dominique had been locked up. He must be walking from the wall to the window, because for some time she heard the regular cadence of his footsteps; then came a long silence; he had probably sat down. In addition, all the noises ceased,

Quand la maison lui parut s'assoupir, elle ouvrit sa fenêtre le plus doucement possible, elle s'accouda.

Au-dehors, la nuit avait une sérénité tiède. Le mince croissant de la lune, qui se couchait derrière les bois de Sauval, éclairait la campagne d'une lueur de veilleuse. L'ombre allongée des grands arbres barrait de noir les prairies, tandis que l'herbe, aux endroits découverts, prenait une douceur de velours verdâtre. Mais Françoise ne s'arrêtait guère au charme mystérieux de la nuit. Elle étudiait la campagne, cherchant les sentinelles que les Allemands avaient dû poster de ce côté. Elle voyait parfaitement leurs ombres s'échelonner le long de la Morelle. Une seule se trouvait devant le moulin, de l'autre côté de la rivière, près d'un saule dont les branches trempaient dans l'eau. Françoise la distinguait parfaitement. C'était un grand garçon qui se tenait immobile, la face tournée vers le ciel, de l'air rêveur d'un berger.

Alors, quand elle eut ainsi inspecté les lieux avec soin, elle revint s'asseoir sur son lit. Elle y resta une heure, profondément absorbée. Puis elle écouta de nouveau: la maison n'avait plus un souffle. Elle retourna à la fenêtre, jeta un coup d'œil; mais sans doute une des cornes de la lune qui apparaissait encore derrière les arbres, lui parut gênante, car elle se remit à attendre. Enfin, l'heure lui sembla venue. La nuit était toute noire, elle n'apercevait plus la sentinelle en face, la campagne s'étalait comme une mare d'encre. Elle tendit l'oreille un instant et se décida. Il y avait là, passant près de la fenêtre, une échelle de fer, des barres scellées dans le mur, qui montait de la roue au grenier, et qui servait autrefois aux meuniers pour visiter certains rouages; puis le mécanisme avait été modifié, depuis longtemps l'échelle disparaissait sous les lierres épais qui couvraient ce côté du moulin.

Françoise, bravement, enjamba la balustrade de sa fenêtre, saisit une des barres de fer et se trouva dans le vide. Elle commença à descendre. Ses jupons l'embarrassaient beaucoup. Brusquement, une pierre se détacha de la muraille et tomba dans la Morelle avec un rejaillissement sonore. Elle s'était arrêtée, glacée d'un frisson. Mais elle comprit que la chute d'eau, de son ronflement continu, couvrait à distance tous les bruits qu'elle pouvait faire, et elle descendit alors plus hardiment, tâtant le lierre du pied, s'assurant des échelons. Lorsqu'elle fut à la hauteur de la chambre qui servait de prison à Dominique, elle s'arrêta. Une difficulté imprévue faillit lui faire perdre tout son courage: la fenêtre de la pièce du bas n'était pas régulièrement percée au-dessous de la fenêtre de sa chambre, elle

everything was falling asleep. When she thought that the house was at rest, she opened her window as quietly as possible and leaned out.

Outside, the night was warm and clear. The narrow crescent of the moon, setting behind the Forest of Sauval, was illuminating the countryside as if with a night light. The long shadows of the tall trees made black lines across the meadows, while the grass in the open places took on the softness of greenish velvet. But Françoise was scarcely detained by the mysterious charm of the night. She was observing the countryside, looking for the sentries that the Germans must have stationed in that direction. She clearly saw their shadows spaced out along the Morelle. A single one was located in front of the mill, across the stream, near a willow whose branches dipped into the water. Françoise could make him out clearly. He was a tall lad who was standing still, his face turned skyward with the dreamy expression of a shepherd.

Then, after carefully inspecting the terrain in this manner, she returned to her bed and sat down again. She stayed there for an hour, deeply absorbed. Then she listened again: there was no longer a breath in the house. She returned to the window and glanced outside; but one tip of the moon that was still visible behind the trees must have seemed like an impediment to her, because she started waiting again. Finally, she thought the right time had come. The night was completely black; she could no longer see the sentry opposite her; the countryside stretched out like a sea of ink. She listened hard for a moment and made up her mind. Extending past the window, and near it, there was an iron ladder, bars sealed into the wall, running from the wheel to the attic. It had formerly been used by the millers to inspect certain gears; later on, the wheel works had been altered, and for a long time the ladder had been hidden beneath the dense ivy which covered that side of the mill.

Françoise bravely straddled the railing of her window, seized one of the iron bars, and found herself completely out in the open. She started to climb down. Her petticoats were a great nuisance to her. Suddenly a stone was dislodged from the wall and fell into the Morelle with a loud splash. She had stopped in her tracks, shivering with fright. But she realized that the water drop, with its unceasing drone, drowned out for distant ears any noise she could make, and then she descended more boldly, feeling the ivy with her foot and making sure of each rung. When she was level with the bedroom that was serving as Dominique's prison, she stopped. An unforeseen difficulty almost made her lose all her courage; the window of the lower room didn't open directly below her own bedroom window; it was at some

s'écartait de l'échelle, et lorsqu'elle allongea la main, elle ne rencontra que la muraille. Lui faudrait-il donc remonter, sans pousser son projet jusqu'au bout? Ses bras se lassaient, le murmure de la Morelle, au-dessous d'elle, commençait à lui donner des vertiges. Alors, elle arracha du mur de petits fragments de plâtre et les lança dans la fenêtre de Dominique. Il n'entendait pas, peut-être dormait-il. Elle émietta encore la muraille, elle s'écorchait les doigts. Et elle était à bout de force, elle se sentait tomber à la renverse, lorsque Dominique ouvrit enfin doucement.

— C'est moi, murmura-t-elle. Prends-moi vite, je tombe.

C'était la première fois qu'elle le tutoyait. Il la saisit, en se penchant, et l'apporta dans la chambre. Là, elle eut une crise de larmes, étouffant ses sanglots, pour qu'on ne l'entendît pas. Puis, par un effort suprême, elle se calma.

— Vous êtes gardé? demanda-t-elle à voix basse.

Dominique, encore stupéfait de la voir ainsi, fit un simple signe, en montrant sa porte. De l'autre côté, on entendait un ronflement; la sentinelle, cédant au sommeil, avait dû se coucher par terre, contre la porte, en se disant que, de cette façon le prisonnier ne pouvait bouger.

— Il faut fuir, reprit-elle vivement. Je suis venue pour vous supplier de fuir et pour vous dire adieu.

Mais lui ne paraissait pas l'entendre. Il répétait:

— Comment, c'est vous, c'est vous . . . Oh! que vous m'avez fait peur! Vous pouviez vous tuer.

Il lui prit les mains, il les baisa.

— Que je vous aime, Françoise! . . . Vous êtes aussi courageuse que bonne. Je n'avais qu'une crainte, c'était de mourir sans vous avoir revue . . . Mais vous êtes là, et maintenant ils peuvent me fusiller. Quand j'aurai passé un quart d'heure avec vous, je serai prêt.

Peu à peu, il l'avait attirée à lui, et elle appuyait sa tête sur son épaule. Le danger les rapprochait. Ils oubliaient tout dans cette étreinte.

— Ah! Françoise, reprit Dominique d'une voix caressante, c'est aujourd'hui la Saint-Louis, le jour si longtemps attendu de notre mariage. Rien n'a pu nous séparer, puisque nous voilà tous les deux seuls, fidèles au rendez-vous . . . N'est-ce pas? c'est à cette heure le matin des noces.

— Oui, oui, répéta-t-elle, le matin des noces.

Ils échangèrent un baiser en frissonnant. Mais, tout d'un coup, elle se dégagea, la terrible réalité se dressait devant elle.

distance from the ladder, and when she reached out her hand she felt only the wall. Would she have to climb back up, then, without carrying out her plan? Her arms were getting tired; the murmuring of the Morelle, below her, was beginning to make her dizzy. Then she detached little bits of plaster from the wall and threw them into Dominique's window. He didn't hear them; perhaps he was asleep. She crumbled more of the wall, skinning her fingers. And her strength was deserting her, she felt herself falling backward, when Dominique finally opened his window quietly.

"It's me," she murmured. "Catch me fast, I'm falling."

It was the first time she had ever used a familiar verb form in addressing him. He grabbed her, leaning out, and brought her into the room. Once inside, she had a crying fit, stifling her sobs so that she wouldn't be heard. Then, making a supreme effort, she calmed down.

"Are you being guarded?" she asked in a low voice.

Dominique, still amazed at seeing her arrive that way, merely nodded, pointing to his door. On the other side of it they could hear snoring; the sentry, succumbing to his weariness, must have lain down on the floor, up against the door, certain that, in that way, the prisoner would be unable to get out.

"You must run away," she continued briskly. "I've come to beg you to run away and to say good-bye to you."

But he didn't seem to hear her. He kept repeating:

"What! It's you, it's you . . . Oh, how you scared me! You could have been killed."

He took her hands and kissed them.

"How I love you, Françoise! . . . You're as brave as you're beautiful. I had only one fear: dying without seeing you again . . . But here you are, and now they can shoot me. After spending a quarter of an hour with you, I'll be ready."

Gradually he had drawn her close to him, and she was resting her head on his shoulder. Their danger brought them closer together. They forgot everything else while embracing that way.

"Oh, Françoise," Dominique went on in a caressing voice, "today is Saint Louis's Day, our wedding day that we waited for so long. Nothing has been able to separate us, since here we are alone together, faithful to the appointed date . . . Isn't that so? Right now it's our wedding morning."

"Yes, yes," she repeated, "our wedding morning."

They exchanged a kiss tremblingly. But all at once she pulled away from him; the awful reality loomed up before her.

— Il faut fuir, il faut fuir, bégaya-t-elle. Ne perdons pas une minute.

Et comme il tendait les bras dans l'ombre pour la reprendre, elle le tutoya de nouveau:

— Oh! je t'en prie, écoute-moi . . . Si tu meurs, je mourrai. Dans une heure, il fera jour. Je veux que tu partes tout de suite.

Alors, rapidement, elle expliqua son plan. L'échelle de fer descendait jusqu'à la roue; là, il pourrait s'aider des palettes et entrer dans la barque qui se trouvait dans un enfoncement. Il lui serait facile ensuite de gagner l'autre bord de la rivière et de s'échapper.

— Mais il doit y avoir des sentinelles? dit-il.

— Une seule, en face, au pied du premier saule.

— Et si elle m'aperçoit, si elle veut crier?

Françoise frissonna. Elle lui mit dans la main un couteau qu'elle avait descendu. Il y eut un silence.

— Et votre père, et vous? reprit Dominique. Mais non, je ne puis fuir . . . Quand je ne serai plus là, ces soldats vous massacreront peut-être . . . Vous ne les connaissez pas. Ils m'ont proposé de me faire grâce, si je consentais à les guider dans la forêt de Sauval. Lorsqu'ils ne me trouveront plus, ils sont capables de tout.

La jeune fille ne s'arrêta pas à discuter. Elle répondait simplement à toutes les raisons qu'il donnait:

— Par amour pour moi, fuyez . . . Si vous m'aimez, Dominique, ne restez pas ici une minute de plus.

Puis, elle promit de remonter dans sa chambre. On ne saurait pas qu'elle l'avait aidé. Elle finit par le prendre dans ses bras, par l'embrasser, pour le convaincre, avec un élan de passion extraordinaire. Lui, était vaincu. Il ne posa plus qu'une question.

— Jurez-moi que votre père connaît votre démarche et qu'il me conseille la fuite?

— C'est mon père qui m'a envoyée, répondit hardiment Françoise.

Elle mentait. Dans ce moment, elle n'avait qu'un besoin immense, le savoir en sûreté, échapper à cette abominable pensée que le soleil allait être le signal de sa mort. Quand il serait loin, tous les malheurs pouvaient fondre sur elle; cela lui paraîtrait doux, du moment où il vivrait. L'égoïsme de sa tendresse le voulait vivant, avant toutes choses.

— C'est bien, dit Dominique, je ferai comme il vous plaira.

Alors, ils ne parlèrent plus. Dominique alla rouvrir la fenêtre. Mais, brusquement, un bruit les glaça. La porte fut ébranlée, et ils crurent qu'on l'ouvrait. Évidemment, une ronde avait entendu leurs voix. Et tous deux debout, serrés l'un contre l'autre, attendaient dans une

"You must flee, you must flee," she stammered. "Don't waste a minute."

And as he reached out his arms in the darkness to take hold of her again, she addressed him as *tu* once more:

"Oh, please, listen to me . . . If *you* die, *I'll* die. In an hour it will be daylight. I want you to leave at once."

Then, rapidly, she detailed her plan. The iron ladder went all the way down to the wheel; there, he could use the wheel paddles and get into the boat that was located in a recess. Then he could easily reach the far bank of the stream and get away.

"But there must be sentries there," he said.

"Just one, directly opposite, at the foot of the nearest willow."

"And what if he notices me, what if he calls out?"

Françoise shuddered. She placed in his hands a knife she had brought down with her. There was a silence.

"And your father? And you?" Dominique went on. "No, no, I can't run away . . . After I'm gone, these soldiers might murder you . . . You don't know them. They offered to spare me if I agreed to guide them through the Forest of Sauval. When they find that I'm gone, they're capable of anything."

The girl wasted no time arguing. To every reason he gave she merely replied:

"Out of love for me, run away . . . If you love me, Dominique, don't stay here a minute longer."

Then she promised she would go back up to her room. No one would know she had helped him. Finally she took him in her arms, to kiss him, to persuade him, in an unusual burst of passion. He was vanquished. He didn't ask another question.

"Swear to me that your father knows what you're doing and that he advises me to run away."

"It was my father who sent me," Françoise boldly replied.

She was lying. At that moment she felt only one overpowering need, to know he was safe, to rid herself of the abominable thought that sunrise would be the signal for his death. Once he was far away, any misfortune could befall her; it would seem sweet to her, provided he was alive. The egotism of her affection wanted him alive, above all else.

"All right," said Dominique, "I'll do as you wish."

After that, they spoke no more. Dominique went and opened the window again. But suddenly a sound chilled them with fright. The door was shaken, and they thought it was being opened. Obviously, soldiers making their rounds had heard their voices. And the two of them,

angoisse indicible. La porte fut de nouveau secouée; mais elle ne s'ouvrit pas. Ils eurent chacun un soupir étouffé; ils venaient de comprendre, ce devait être le soldat couché en travers du seuil, qui s'était retourné. En effet, le silence se fit, les ronflements recommencèrent. Dominique voulut absolument que Françoise remontât d'abord chez elle. Il la prit dans ses bras, il lui dit un muet adieu. Puis, il l'aida à saisir l'échelle et se cramponna à son tour. Mais il refusa de descendre un seul échelon avant de la savoir dans sa chambre. Quand Françoise fut rentrée, elle laissa tomber d'une voix légère comme un souffle:

— Au revoir, je t'aime!

Elle resta accoudée, elle tâcha de suivre Dominique. La nuit était toujours très noire. Elle chercha la sentinelle et ne l'aperçut pas; seul, le saule faisait une tache pâle, au milieu des ténèbres. Pendant un instant, elle entendit le frôlement du corps de Dominique le long du lierre. Ensuite la roue craqua, et il y eut un léger clapotement qui lui annonça que le jeune homme venait de trouver la barque. Une minute plus tard, en effet, elle distingua la silhouette sombre de la barque sur la nappe grise de la Morelle. Alors, une angoisse terrible la reprit à la gorge. A chaque instant, elle croyait entendre le cri d'alarme de la sentinelle; les moindres bruits, épars dans l'ombre, lui semblaient des pas précipités de soldats, des froissements d'armes, des bruits de fusils qu'on armait. Pourtant, les secondes s'écoulaient, la campagne gardait sa paix souveraine. Dominique devait aborder à l'autre rive. Françoise ne voyait plus rien. Le silence était majestueux. Et elle entendit un piétinement, un cri rauque, la chute d'un corps. Puis, le silence se fit plus profond. Alors, comme si elle eût senti la mort passer, elle resta toute froide, en face de l'épaisse nuit.

IV

Dès le petit jour, des éclats de voix ébranlèrent le moulin. Le père Merlier était venu ouvrir la porte de Françoise. Elle descendit dans la cour, pâle et très calme. Mais là, elle ne put réprimer un frisson, en face du cadavre d'un soldat prussien, qui était allongé près du puits, sur un manteau étalé.

Autour du corps, des soldats gesticulaient, criaient sur un ton de fureur. Plusieurs d'entre eux montraient les poings au village. Cependant, l'officier venait de faire appeler le père Merlier, comme maire de la commune.

— Voici, lui dit-il d'une voix étranglée par la colère, un de nos

standing there close together, waited in unspeakable anguish. The door was rattled again, but it didn't open. Both of them stifled a sigh; they had just realized it must be the soldier sleeping on the threshold, who had turned over. In fact, silence ensued and the snoring resumed.

Dominique absolutely insisted that Françoise must first climb back up to her room. He took her in his arms, and took leave of her wordlessly. Then he helped her take hold of the ladder and clung to it himself. But he wouldn't go down a single rung before he was sure she was in her room. When Françoise was back in, she called down in a voice as light as a breath:

"Good-bye, I love you!"

She remained leaning out, trying to follow Dominique's movements. The night was still very dark. She looked for the sentry but couldn't see him; only the willow created a pale spot amid the darkness. For a moment she heard Dominique's body brushing against the ivy. Then the wheel creaked and there was a light lapping of water that indicated that the young man had just found the boat. In fact, a minute later, she made out the dark silhouette of the boat on the gray surface of the Morelle. Then a terrible anguish seized her by the throat again. Any moment she expected to hear the sentry's shout of alarm; the slightest sounds, scattered in the darkness, seemed to her like the hurried steps of soldiers, the clatter of weapons, the sound of rifles being cocked. And yet the seconds were passing, and the countryside retained its prevailing peace. Dominique must be reaching the far bank. Françoise could no longer see a thing. The silence was majestic. And she heard a stamping of feet, a hoarse cry, the fall of a body. Next, the silence became deeper. Then, as if she felt death passing by, she remained there, completely chilled, looking out onto the dense night.

IV

As soon as day broke, shouts rocked the mill. Old Merlier had come to unlock Françoise's door. She went down into the courtyard, pale and very calm. But, once there, she was unable to repress a shudder at the sight of the corpse of a Prussian soldier stretched out near the well on an outspread cloak.

Around the body soldiers were gesticulating and shouting in rage. Several of them were shaking their fists at the village. Meanwhile, the captain had just had old Merlier summoned, as mayor of the parish.

"Here," he said to him in a voice choked with anger, "is one of our

hommes que l'on a trouvé assassiné sur le bord de la rivière . . . Il nous faut un exemple éclatant, et je compte que vous allez nous aider à découvrir le meurtrier.

— Tout ce que vous voudrez, répondit le meunier avec son flegme. Seulement, ce ne sera pas commode.

L'officier s'était baissé pour écarter un pan du manteau, qui cachait la figure du mort. Alors apparut une horrible blessure. La sentinelle avait été frappée à la gorge, et l'arme était restée dans la plaie. C'était un couteau de cuisine à manche noir.

— Regardez ce couteau, dit l'officier au père Merlier, peut-être nous aidera-t-il dans nos recherches.

Le vieillard avait eu un tressaillement. Mais il se remit aussitôt, il répondit, sans qu'un muscle de sa face bougeât:

— Tout le monde a des couteaux pareils dans nos campagnes . . . Peut-être que votre homme s'ennuyait de se battre et qu'il se sera fait son affaire lui-même. Ça se voit.

— Taisez-vous! cria furieusement l'officier. Je ne sais ce qui me retient de mettre le feu aux quatre coins du village.

La colère heureusement l'empêchait de remarquer la profonde altération du visage de Françoise. Elle avait dû s'asseoir sur le banc de pierre, près du puits. Malgré elle, ses regards ne quittaient plus ce cadavre, étendu à terre, presque à ses pieds. C'était un grand et beau garçon, qui ressemblait à Dominique, avec des cheveux blonds et des yeux bleus. Cette ressemblance lui retournait le cœur. Elle pensait que le mort avait peut-être laissé là-bas, en Allemagne, quelque amoureuse qui allait pleurer. Et elle reconnaissait son couteau dans la gorge du mort. Elle l'avait tué.

Cependant l'officier parlait de frapper Rocreuse de mesures terribles, lorsque des soldats accoururent. On venait de s'apercevoir seulement de l'évasion de Dominique. Cela causa une agitation extrême. L'officier se rendit sur les lieux, regarda par la fenêtre laissée ouverte, comprit tout, et revint exaspéré.

Le père Merlier parut très contrarié de la fuite de Dominique.

— L'imbécile! murmura-t-il, il gâte tout.

Françoise qui l'entendit, fut prise d'angoisse. Son père, d'ailleurs, ne soupçonnait pas sa complicité. Il hocha la tête, en lui disant à demivoix:

— A présent, nous voilà propres!

— C'est ce gredin! c'est ce gredin! criait l'officier. Il aura gagné les bois . . . Mais il faut qu'on nous le retrouve, ou le village payera pour lui.

men who has been found murdered on the bank of the stream . . . We must make a conspicuous example, and I'm counting on you to help us locate the killer."

"I'll do anything you want," the miller replied with his customary nonchalance. "But it won't be easy."

The officer had stooped down to remove a corner of the cloak that was concealing the dead man's face. A terrible wound was thus revealed. The sentry had been struck in the throat, and the weapon had remained in the wound. It was a kitchen knife with a black handle.

"Look at this knife," the officer said to old Merlier. "Maybe it will help us in our investigation."

The old man had given a start. But he controlled himself at once; he replied, without moving a muscle in his face:

"Everyone in our area has knives like this . . . Maybe your man was tired of fighting and polished himself off. Things like that happen."

"Be still!" the officer shouted furiously. "I don't know what's keeping me from setting fire to the entire village."

Fortunately his anger prevented him from noticing the strong emotions in Françoise's face. She had felt it necessary to sit down on the stone bench near the well. In spite of herself, she couldn't take her eyes off that corpse stretched out on the ground almost at her feet. He was a tall, good-looking young fellow, who resembled Dominique, with blond hair and blue eyes. That resemblance made her heartsick. She was thinking that the dead man might have left behind, there in Germany, some sweetheart who was going to mourn for him. And she recognized her knife in the dead man's throat. She had killed him.

Meanwhile, the officer was speaking of taking awful measures against Rocreuse, when some soldiers ran up to him. Only now had they noticed that Dominique had escaped. That caused an enormous row. The officer went to the scene of the deed, looked out of the window, which had been left open, understood the whole thing, and returned, exasperated.

Old Merlier seemed quite annoyed at Dominique's flight.

"The fool!" he muttered. "He's ruining everything."

Françoise, who heard him, was anguish-stricken. But her father didn't suspect her complicity. He shook his head, saying to her quietly:

"Now we're in for it!"

"It's that scoundrel! It's that scoundrel!" the officer was shouting. "He probably made it into the woods . . . But we've got to find him again, or else the village will pay for what he did."

Et, s'adressant au meunier:

— Voyons, vous devez savoir où il se cache?

Le père Merlier eut son rire silencieux, en montrant la large étendue des coteaux boisés.

— Comment voulez-vous trouver un homme là-dedans? dit-il.

— Oh! il doit y avoir des trous que vous connaissez. Je vais vous
donner dix hommes. Vous les guiderez.

— Je veux bien. Seulement, il nous faudra huit jours pour battre
tous les bois des environs.

La tranquillité du vieillard enrageait l'officier. Il comprenait en
effet le ridicule de cette battue. Ce fut alors qu'il aperçut sur le banc
Françoise pâle et tremblante. L'attitude anxieuse de la jeune fille le
frappa. Il se tut un instant, examinant tour à tour le meunier et
Françoise.

— Est-ce que cet homme, finit-il par demander brutalement au
vieillard, n'est pas l'amant de votre fille?

Le père Merlier devint livide, et l'on put croire qu'il allait se jeter
sur l'officier pour l'étrangler. Il se raidit, il ne répondit pas. Françoise
avait mis son visage entre ses mains.

— Oui, c'est cela, continua le Prussien, vous ou votre fille l'avez
aidé à fuir. Vous êtes son complice . . . Une dernière fois, voulez-vous
nous le livrer?

Le meunier ne répondit pas. Il s'était détourné, regardant au loin
d'un air indifférent, comme si l'officier ne s'adressait pas à lui. Cela
mit le comble à la colère de ce dernier.

— Eh bien! déclara-t-il, vous allez être fusillé à sa place.

Et il commanda une fois encore le peloton d'exécution. Le père
Merlier garda son flegme. Il eut à peine un léger haussement d'é-
paules, tout ce drame lui semblait d'un goût médiocre. Sans doute il
ne croyait pas qu'on fusillât un homme si aisément. Puis, quand le
peloton fut là, il dit avec gravité:

— Alors, c'est sérieux? . . . Je veux bien. S'il vous en faut un absolument, moi autant qu'un autre.

Mais Françoise s'était levée, affolée, bégayant:

— Grâce, monsieur, ne faites pas du mal à mon père. Tuez-moi à sa
place . . . C'est moi qui ai aidé Dominique à fuir. Moi seule suis coupable.

— Tais-toi, fillette, s'écria le père Merlier. Pourquoi mens-tu? . . .
Elle a passé la nuit enfermée dans sa chambre, monsieur. Elle ment,
je vous assure.

— Non, je ne mens pas, reprit ardemment la jeune fille. Je suis

And, addressing the miller:

"Come on now, you must know where he's hiding."

Old Merlier gave one of his silent laughs, pointing to the wide extent of the wooded hills.

"How do you expect to find a man in there?" he said.

"Oh, there must be hiding places there that you know. I'll give you ten men. You'll guide them."

"I'm perfectly willing. But it'll take us a week to comb through all the woods in the vicinity."

The old man's calmness infuriated the officer. Of course he understood how ridiculous such a search would be. It was then that he noticed Françoise, pale and trembling on the bench. He was struck by the anxiety in the girl's appearance. He kept silent for a moment, examining now the miller, now Françoise.

Finally he asked the old man harshly, "Isn't that man your daughter's lover?"

Old Merlier turned livid, and looked as if he was going to pounce on the officer and choke him. He stiffened up and didn't reply. Françoise had put her hands to her face.

"Yes, that's it," the Prussian continued; "you or your daughter helped him get away. You're his accomplice . . . For the last time, will you turn him over to us?"

The miller didn't reply. He had turned aside and was looking into the distance with an unconcerned expression, as if the officer weren't taking to *him*. That raised the captain's anger to the highest pitch.

"Very well," he announced, "you'll be shot in his place."

And once again he called out a firing squad. Old Merlier kept calm. He merely shrugged his shoulders slightly; all this drama struck him as being in poor taste. Most likely, he didn't believe that they would shoot a man so readily. Then, when the firing squad was there, he said earnestly:

"So you're serious? . . . I'm willing. If you must absolutely have somebody, it may as well be me as anyone else."

But Françoise had risen, mad with fright, stammering:

"Mercy, sir, don't hurt my father! Kill me instead . . . I'm the one who helped Dominique get away. I'm the only guilty party."

"Quiet, daughter!" old Merlier exclaimed. "Why are you lying? . . . She spent the night locked up in her room, sir. She's lying, I assure you."

"No, I'm not lying," the girl went on ardently. "I climbed down

descendue par la fenêtre, j'ai poussé Dominique à s'enfuir . . . C'est la vérité, la seule vérité . . .

Le vieillard était devenu très pâle. Il voyait bien dans ses yeux qu'elle ne mentait pas, et cette histoire d'épouvantait. Ah! ces enfants, avec leurs cœurs, comme ils gâtaient tout! Alors, il se fâcha.

— Elle est folle, ne l'écoutez pas. Elle vous raconte des histoires stupides . . . Allons, finissons-en.

Elle voulut protester encore. Elle s'agenouilla, elle joignit les mains. L'officier, tranquillement, assistait à cette lutte douloureuse.

— Mon Dieu! finit-il par dire, je prends votre père, parce que je ne tiens plus l'autre . . . Tâchez de retrouver l'autre, et votre père sera libre.

Un moment, elle le regarda, les yeux agrandis par l'atrocité de cette proposition.

— C'est horrible, murmura-t-elle. Où voulez-vous que je retrouve Dominique, à cette heure? Il est parti, je ne sais plus.

— Enfin, choisissez. Lui ou votre père.

— Oh! mon Dieu! est-ce que je puis choisir? Mais je saurais où est Dominique, que je ne pourrais pas choisir! . . . C'est mon cœur que vous coupez . . . J'aimerais mieux mourir tout de suite. Oui, ce serait plus tôt fait. Tuez-moi, je vous en prie, tuez-moi . . .

Cette scène de désespoir et de larmes finissait par impatienter l'officier. Il s'écria:

— En voilà assez! Je veux être bon, je consens à vous donner deux heures . . . Si, dans deux heures, votre amoureux n'est pas là, votre père payera pour lui.

Et il fit conduire le père Merlier dans la chambre qui avait servi de prison à Dominique. Le vieux demanda du tabac et se mit à fumer. Sur son visage impassible on ne lisait aucune émotion. Seulement, quand il fut seul, tout en fumant, il pleura deux grosses larmes qui coulèrent lentement sur ses joues. Sa pauvre et chère enfant, comme elle souffrait!

Françoise était restée au milieu de la cour. Des soldats prussiens passaient en riant. Certains lui jetaient des mots, des plaisanteries qu'elle ne comprenait pas. Elle regardait la porte par laquelle son père venait de disparaître. Et, d'un geste lent, elle portait la main à son front, comme pour l'empêcher d'éclater.

L'officier tourna sur ses talons, en répétant:

— Vous avez deux heures. Tâchez de les utiliser.

Elle avait deux heures. Cette phrase bourdonnait dans sa tête. Alors, machinalement, elle sortit de la cour, elle marcha devant

through the window, I urged Dominique to run away . . . It's the truth, that and nothing else . . ."

The old man had become very pale. He could see from her eyes that she wasn't lying, and the whole affair frightened him. Oh, these children, with their emotions, how they ruined everything! Then he got angry.

"She's crazy, don't listen to her. She's telling you stupid stories . . . Come, let's get it over with."

She tried to protest again. She knelt down, she joined her hands. The officer was a calm spectator of that painful struggle.

"By God!" he finally said. "I'm taking your father because I no longer have the other man . . . Try to locate the other one, and your father will be free."

For a moment she looked at him, her eyes wide open at the atrociousness of that proposition.

"It's awful," she muttered. "Where do you expect me to find Dominique by this time? He's gone, I don't know where."

"Well, choose. He or your father."

"Oh, God, am I able to choose? Even if I knew where Dominique is, I couldn't choose! . . . You're breaking my heart . . . I'd rather die on the spot. Yes, that would be an end of it. Kill me, I beg you, kill me . . ."

This scene of tearful despair finally made the officer impatient. He exclaimed:

"Enough of this! I want to be kind; I consent to give you two hours . . . If your sweetheart isn't here in two hours, your father will pay the price for him."

And he had old Merlier led to the room that had served as Dominique's prison. The old man asked for tobacco and started smoking. No emotion could be read on his impassive face. But when he was alone, smoking, he shed two fat tears that slowly trickled down his cheeks. How his poor, dear child was suffering!

Françoise had remained in the middle of the courtyard. Prussian soldiers passed by laughing. Some of them flung remarks at her, jokes she didn't understand. She was looking at the door through which her father had just disappeared. And, in a slow gesture, she raised her hand to her forehead, as if to keep it from bursting.

The officer turned on his heels, repeating:

"You have two hours. Try to make good use of them."

She had two hours. That sentence kept buzzing in her head. Then, like an automaton, she left the courtyard and walked straight ahead.

elle. Où aller? que faire? Elle n'essayait même pas de prendre un parti, parce qu'elle sentait bien l'inutilité de ses efforts. Pourtant, elle aurait voulu voir Dominique. Ils se seraient entendus tous les deux, ils auraient peut-être trouvé un expédient. Et, au milieu de la confusion de ses pensées, elle descendit au bord de la Morelle, qu'elle traversa en dessous de l'écluse, à un endroit où il y avait de grosses pierres. Ses pieds la conduisirent sous le premier saule, au coin de la prairie. Comme elle se baissait, elle aperçut une mare de sang qui la fit pâlir. C'était bien là. Et elle suivit les traces de Dominique dans l'herbe foulée; il avait dû courir, on voyait une ligne de grands pas coupant la prairie de biais. Puis, au-delà, elle perdit ces traces. Mais, dans un pré voisin, elle crut les retrouver. Cela la conduisit à la lisière de la forêt, où toute indication s'effaçait.

Françoise s'enfonça quand même sous les arbres. Cela la soulageait d'être seule. Elle s'assit un instant. Puis, en songeant que l'heure s'écoulait, elle se remit debout. Depuis combien de temps avait-elle quitté le moulin? Cinq minutes? une demi-heure? Elle n'avait plus conscience du temps. Peut-être Dominique était-il allé se cacher dans un taillis qu'elle connaissait, et où ils avaient, une après-midi, mangé des noisettes ensemble. Elle se rendit au taillis, le visita. Un merle seul s'envola, en sifflant sa phrase douce et triste. Alors, elle pensa qu'il s'était réfugié dans un creux de roches, où il se mettait parfois à l'affût; mais le creux de roches était vide. A quoi bon le chercher? Elle ne le trouverait pas; et peu à peu le désir de le découvrir la passionnait, elle marchait plus vite. L'idée qu'il avait dû monter dans un arbre lui vint brusquement. Elle avança dès lors, les yeux levés, et pour qu'il la sût près de lui, elle l'appelait tous les quinze à vingt pas. Des coucous répondaient, un souffle qui passait dans les branches lui faisait croire qu'il était là et qu'il descendait. Une fois même, elle s'imagina le voir; elle s'arrêta, étranglée, avec l'envie de fuir. Qu'allait-elle lui dire? Venait-elle donc pour l'emmener et le faire fusiller? Oh! non, elle ne parlerait point de ces choses. Elle lui crierait de se sauver, de ne pas rester dans les environs. Puis, la pensée de son père qui l'attendait, lui causa une douleur aiguë. Elle tomba sur le gazon, en pleurant, en répétant tout haut:

— Mon Dieu! mon Dieu! pourquoi suis-je là!

Elle était folle d'être venue. Et, comme prise de peur, elle courut, elle chercha à sortir de la forêt. Trois fois, elle se trompa, et elle croyait qu'elle ne retrouverait plus le moulin, lorsqu'elle déboucha dans

Where to go? What to do? She wasn't even attempting to make a decision, because she was well aware how futile her efforts would be. And yet, she would have liked to see Dominique. They would have reached an understanding together, they might have found a way out of their difficulties. And, amid the confusion of her thoughts, she went down to the bank of the Morelle, which she crossed downstream from the sluice in a spot where there were big stepping stones. Her feet led her to the nearest willow, at the corner of the meadow. As she bent down, she saw a pool of blood that made her turn pale. That must have been the spot. And she followed Dominique's trail in the trodden grass; he must have run; you could see a line of widely spaced steps cutting across the meadow obliquely. Then, beyond that, she lost the trail. But in a nearby meadow she thought she picked it up again. That led her to the edge of the forest, where all signs were obliterated.

All the same, Françoise plunged in beneath the trees. It was a relief to her to be alone. She sat down for a while. Then, recalling that time was slipping away, she stood up again. How long was it since she had left the mill? Five minutes? A half-hour? She was no longer aware of the time. Maybe Dominique had gone to hide in a thicket she knew, where they had eaten hazelnuts together one afternoon. She went to the thicket and inspected it. A single blackbird flew out, whistling its sweet, sad phrase. Then it occurred to her that he might have hidden out in a rocky hollow where he sometimes lay in ambush for game; but the rocky hollow was empty. What was the good of looking for him? She wouldn't find him. And gradually the desire to discover him excited her, and she walked more quickly. Suddenly she got the idea that he must have climbed a tree. From then on she walked with her eyes raised, and, so that he would know she was near him, she called him every fifteen or twenty paces. Cuckoos answered her; a breeze blowing through the branches made her think he was there and climbing down. Once she even imagined she saw him; she stopped, choking and feeling an urge to run away. What would she tell him? Had she really come to take him back and get him shot? Oh, no, she wouldn't talk about those things at all. She would call to him to escape, not to remain in the vicinity. Then, the thought of her father, who was awaiting her, caused her a burning grief. She fell onto the grass, weeping, and repeating out loud:

"My God! My God! Why am I here?"

It was mad of her to have come. And, as if terror-stricken, she ran, trying to get out of the forest. Three times she took a wrong turn, and she was thinking that she'd never find the mill again, when she

une prairie, juste en face de Rocreuse. Dès qu'elle aperçut le village, elle s'arrêta. Est-ce qu'elle allait rentrer seule?

Elle restait debout, quand une voix l'appela doucement:

— Françoise! Françoise!

Et elle vit Dominique qui levait la tête, au bord d'un fossé. Juste Dieu! elle l'avait trouvé! Le ciel voulait donc sa mort? Elle retint un cri, elle se laissa glisser dans le fossé.

— Tu me cherchais? demanda-t-il.

— Oui, répondit-elle, la tête bourdonnante, ne sachant ce qu'elle disait.

— Ah! que se passe-t-il?

— Mais rien, j'étais inquiète, je désirais te voir.

Alors, tranquillisé, il lui expliqua qu'il n'avait pas voulu s'éloigner. Il craignait pour eux. Ces gredins de Prussiens étaient très capables de se venger sur les femmes et sur les vieillards. Enfin, tout allait bien, et il ajouta en riant:

— La noce sera pour dans huit jours, voilà tout.

Puis, comme elle restait bouleversée, il redevint grave.

— Mais, qu'as-tu? tu me caches quelque chose.

— Non, je te jure. J'ai couru pour venir.

Il l'embrassa, en disant que c'était imprudent pour elle et pour lui de causer davantage; et il voulut remonter le fossé, afin de rentrer dans la forêt. Elle le retint. Elle tremblait.

— Ecoute, tu ferais peut-être bien tout de même de rester là . . . Personne ne te cherche, tu ne crains rien.

— Françoise, tu me caches quelque chose, répéta-t-il.

De nouveau, elle jura qu'elle ne lui cachait rien. Seulement, elle aimait mieux le savoir près d'elle. Et elle bégaya encore d'autres raisons. Elle lui parut si singulière, que maintenant lui-même aurait refusé de s'éloigner. D'ailleurs, il croyait au retour des Français. On avait vu des troupes du côté de Sauval.

— Ah! qu'ils se pressent, qu'ils soient ici le plus tôt possible! murmura-t-elle avec ferveur.

A ce moment, onze heures sonnèrent au clocher de Rocreuse. Les coups arrivaient, clairs et distincts. Elle se leva, effarée; il y avait deux heures qu'elle avait quitté le moulin.

— Écoute, dit-elle rapidement, si nous avions besoin de toi, je monterai dans ma chambre et j'agiterai mon mouchoir.

Et elle partit en courant, pendant que Dominique, très inquiet, s'allongeait au bord du fossé, pour surveiller le moulin. Comme elle allait rentrer dans Rocreuse, Françoise rencontra un vieux mendiant, le père Bontemps, qui connaissait tout le pays. Il la salua,

emerged onto a meadow directly opposite Rocreuse. As soon as she saw the village, she halted. Was she going to go back alone?

She was still standing there when a voice softly called her: "Françoise! Françoise!"

And she saw Dominique raising his head over the rim of a ditch. Good God! She had found him! Did heaven, then, want him to die? She held back a cry, and slid into the ditch.

"You were looking for me?" he asked.

"Yes," she answered, her head buzzing, not knowing what she was saying.

"Ah! What's been going on?"

"Nothing, I was worried, I wanted to see you."

Then, feeling calmer, he explained to her that he hadn't wanted to go far away. He was afraid for them. Those scoundrelly Prussians were quite capable of taking revenge on women and old men. But after all, everything was going well; and he added, laughing:

"Our wedding will be postponed for a week, that's all."

Then, since she was still obviously upset, he became serious again. "But what's the matter? You're hiding something from me."

"No, I swear I'm not. I had to run to get here."

He kissed her, saying that it would be imprudent for her and for him to talk any longer; and he made a move to climb out of the ditch so as to reenter the forest. She held him back. She was trembling.

"Listen, maybe it would be better all the same if you stayed here . . . No one is looking for you, you have nothing to fear."

"Françoise, you're hiding something from me," he repeated.

Again she swore that she wasn't hiding anything from him. It was just that she preferred knowing he wasn't far away from her. And she stammered out other excuses. She seemed to him to be acting so oddly that now he himself would have refused to go far away. Besides, he firmly believed that the French would return. Troops had been sighted in the direction of Sauval.

"Oh, make them hurry, let them be here as soon as possible!" she murmured fervently.

At that moment the church bell of Rocreuse struck eleven. The ringing reached them clearly and distinctly. She stood up, frightened; it was two hours since she had left the mill.

"Listen," she said swiftly, "if we should have need of you, I'll go up to my room and wave my handkerchief."

And she left at a run, while Dominique, very worried, stretched out on the rim of the ditch to survey the mill. As she was about to enter Rocreuse, Françoise met an elderly beggar, old Bontemps, who was

il venait de voir le meunier au milieu des Prussiens; puis, en faisant des signes de croix et en marmottant des mots entrecoupés, il continua sa route.

— Les deux heures sont passées, dit l'officier quand Françoise parut. Le père Merlier était là, assis sur le banc, près du puits, il fumait toujours. La jeune fille, de nouveau, supplia, pleura, s'agenouilla. Elle voulait gagner du temps. L'espoir de voir revenir les Français avait grandi en elle, et tandis qu'elle se lamentait, elle croyait entendre au loin les pas cadencés d'une armée. Oh! s'ils avaient paru, s'ils les avaient tous délivrés!

— Écoutez, monsieur, une heure, encore une heure . . . Vous pouvez bien nous accorder une heure!

Mais l'officier restait inflexible. Il ordonna même à deux hommes de s'emparer d'elle et de l'emmener, pour qu'on procédât à l'exécution du vieux tranquillement. Alors, un combat affreux se passa dans le cœur de Françoise. Elle ne pouvait laisser ainsi assassiner son père. Non, non, elle mourrait plutôt avec Dominique; et elle s'élançait vers sa chambre, lorsque Dominique lui-même entra dans la cour.

L'officier et les soldats poussèrent un cri de triomphe. Mais lui, comme s'il n'y avait eu là que Françoise, s'avança vers elle, tranquille, un peu sévère.

— C'est mal, dit-il. Pourquoi ne m'avez-vous pas ramené? Il a fallu que le père Bontemps me contât les choses . . . Enfin, me voilà.

V

Il était trois heures. De grands nuages noirs avaient lentement empli le ciel, la queue de quelque orage voisin. Ce ciel jaune, ces haillons cuivrés changeaient la vallée de Rocreuse, si gaie au soleil, en un coupe-gorge plein d'une ombre louche. L'officier prussien s'était contenté de faire enfermer Dominique, sans se prononcer sur le sort qu'il lui réservait. Depuis midi, Françoise agonisait dans une angoisse abominable. Elle ne voulait pas quitter la cour, malgré les instances de son père. Elle attendait les Français. Mais les heures s'écoulaient, la nuit allait venir, et elle souffrait d'autant plus, que tout ce temps gagné ne paraissait pas devoir changer l'affreux dénouement.

Cependant, vers trois heures, les Prussiens firent leurs préparatifs de départ. Depuis un instant, l'officier s'était, comme la veille, enfermé avec Dominique. Françoise avait compris que la vie du jeune homme se décidait. Alors, elle joignit les mains, elle pria. Le père

familiar with the whole region. He greeted her; he had just seen the miller in the midst of the Prussians; then, crossing himself repeatedly and muttering broken phrases, he continued on his way.

"The two hours have passed," said the officer when Françoise appeared.

Old Merlier was there, sitting on the bench near the well, and still smoking. Once again the girl begged, wept, knelt. She wanted to gain time. The hope of seeing the French return had grown stronger in her mind, and while she was lamenting she thought she could hear far off the regular steps of an army on the march. Oh, if they would only appear, if they would only set them all free!

"Listen, sir, an hour, just one more hour . . . You surely can grant us an hour!"

But the officer remained unbending. He even ordered two men to seize her and take her away, so they could proceed calmly with the execution of the old man. Then, a fearful combat took place in Françoise's heart. She couldn't let her father be murdered that way. No, no, rather than that, she would die along with Dominique; and she was dashing toward her room when Dominique himself entered the courtyard.

The officer and the soldiers uttered a cry of triumph. But as for him, as if no one were around but Françoise, he walked over to her calmly and a little sternly.

"This is bad," he said. "Why didn't you bring me back with you? I had to hear about everything from old Bontemps . . . Anyway, here I am."

V

It was three o'clock. Big black clouds had slowly filled the sky, the tip of some nearby storm. That yellow sky, those coppery shreds, changed the valley of Rocreuse, so cheerful in the sunlight, into a lair of assassins filled with suspicious shadows. The Prussian officer had simply had Dominique locked up, without making a declaration about the fate he had in store for him. Since noon, Françoise had felt the agonies of an unspeakable anguish. She didn't want to leave the courtyard in spite of her father's urging. She was waiting for the French to come. But the hours went by, night was on the way, and she was suffering all the more because it didn't seem as if all that time gained could change the awful ending.

Meanwhile, about three, the Prussians made their preparations to withdraw. For a while, as on the day before, the officer had closeted himself with Dominique. Françoise had understood that the young man's future was being decided. Then she joined her hands in prayer.

Merlier, à côté d'elle, gardait son attitude muette et rigide de vieux paysan, qui ne lutte pas contre la fatalité des faits.

— Oh! mon Dieu! oh! mon Dieu! balbutiait Françoise, ils vont le tuer . . .

Le meunier l'attira près de lui et la prit sur ses genoux comme un enfant.

A ce moment, l'officier sortait, tandis que, derrière lui, deux hommes amenaient Dominique.

— Jamais, jamais! criait ce dernier. Je suis prêt à mourir.

— Réfléchissez bien, reprit l'officier. Ce service que vous me refusez, un autre nous le rendra. Je vous offre la vie, je suis généreux . . . Il s'agit simplement de nous conduire à Montredon, à travers bois. Il doit y avoir des sentiers.

Dominique ne répondait plus.

— Alors, vous vous entêtez?

— Tuez-moi, et finissons-en, répondit-il.

Françoise, les mains jointes, le suppliait de loin. Elle oubliait tout, elle lui aurait conseillé une lâcheté. Mais le père Merlier lui saisit les mains, pour que les Prussiens ne vissent pas son geste de femme affolée.

— Il a raison, murmura-t-il, il vaut mieux mourir.

Le peloton d'exécution était là. L'officier attendait une faiblesse de Dominique. Il comptait toujours le décider. Il y eut un silence. Au loin, on entendait de violents coups de tonnerre. Une chaleur lourde écrasait la campagne. Et ce fut dans ce silence qu'un cri retentit:

— Les Français! les Français!

C'étaient eux, en effet. Sur la route de Sauval, à la lisière du bois, on distinguait la ligne des pantalons rouges. Ce fut, dans le moulin, une agitation extraordinaire. Les soldats prussiens couraient, avec des exclamations gutturales. D'ailleurs, pas un coup de feu n'avait encore été tiré.

— Les Français! les Français! cria Françoise en battant des mains.

Elle était comme folle. Elle venait de s'échapper de l'étreinte de son père, et elle riait, les bras en l'air. Enfin, ils arrivaient donc, et ils arrivaient à temps, puisque Dominique était encore là, debout!

Un feu de peloton terrible qui éclata comme un coup de foudre à ses oreilles, la fit se retourner. L'officier venait de murmurer:

— Avant tout, réglons cette affaire.

Et, poussant lui-même Dominique contre le mur d'un hangar, avait commandé le feu. Quand Françoise se tourna, Dominique était par terre, la poitrine trouée de douze balles.

Elle ne pleura pas, elle resta stupide. Ses yeux devinrent fixes, et elle alla s'asseoir sous le hangar, à quelques pas du corps. Elle

Old Merlier, beside her, maintained his wordless, rigid bearing, that of an old peasant who doesn't fight against the inevitability of facts.

"Oh, God! Oh, God!" Françoise stammered. "They're going to kill him . . ."

The miller drew her near him and took her on his knees like a child.

At that moment the officer came out, while, behind him, two men were bringing Dominique.

"Never! Never!" the young man was shouting. "I'm ready to die."

"Think it over carefully," the officer replied. "This service you refuse to do for me will be done for us by someone else. I offer you your life, I'm generous . . . All you need to do is guide us to Montredon across the woods. There must be paths there."

Dominique no longer answered.

"So you remain obstinate?"

"Kill me and get it over with," he replied.

Françoise, her hands joined, was beseeching him from a distance. She forgot everything else, she would have advised him to be a coward. But old Merlier took hold of her hands, so that the Prussians wouldn't see her gesture, like that of a maddened woman.

"He's right," he murmured, "it's better to die."

The firing squad was there. The officer was waiting for Dominique to weaken. He still expected to convince him. There was a silence. Far off violent thunderclaps were heard. An oppressive heat crushed the countryside. It was during that silence that a shout resounded:

"The French! The French!"

It was, in fact, they. On the Sauval road, at the edge of the forest, the line of red trousers could be discerned. There was an unusual bustle in the mill. The Prussian soldiers were running, with guttural exclamations. Still, not a shot had yet been fired.

"The French! The French!" cried Françoise, clapping her hands.

She acted like a lunatic. She had wrenched herself from her father's grasp, and she laughed, arms in the air. So they had finally come, and had come in time, because Dominique was still there, standing!

A terrible volley of shots, which exploded in her ears like a thunderclap, made her turn around. The officer had just muttered:

"Before anything else, let's finish off this business."

And, he himself shoving Dominique against the wall of a shed, he had given the order to fire. When Françoise turned, Dominique was on the ground with twelve bullet holes in his chest.

She didn't weep, she stood there in a stupor. Her eyes became fixed, and she went and sat down below the shed, a few steps from the

regardait, elle avait par moments un geste vague et enfantin de la main. Les Prussiens s'étaient emparés du père Merlier comme d'un otage. Ce fut un beau combat. Rapidement, l'officier avait posté ses hommes, comprenant qu'il ne pouvait battre en retraite, sans se faire écraser. Autant valait-il vendre chèrement sa vie. Maintenant, c'étaient les Prussiens qui défendaient le moulin, et les Français qui l'attaquaient. La fusillade commença avec une violence inouïe. Pendant une demi-heure, elle ne cessa pas. Puis, un éclat sourd se fit entendre, et un boulet cassa une maîtresse branche de l'orme séculaire. Les Français avaient du canon. Une batterie, dressée juste au-dessus du fossé, dans lequel s'était caché Dominique, balayait la grande rue de Rocreuse. La lutte, désormais, ne pouvait être longue.

Ah! le pauvre moulin! Des boulets le perçaient de part en part. Une moitié de la toiture fut enlevée. Deux murs s'écroulèrent. Mais c'était surtout du côté de la Morelle que le désastre devint lamentable. Les lierres, arrachés des murailles ébranlées, pendaient comme des guenilles; la rivière emportait des débris de toutes sortes, et l'on voyait, par une brèche, la chambre de Françoise, avec son lit, dont les rideaux blancs étaient soigneusement tirés. Coup sur coup, la vieille roue reçut deux boulets, et elle eut un gémissement suprême: les palettes furent charriées dans le courant, la carcasse s'écrasa. C'était l'âme du gai moulin qui venait de s'exhaler.

Puis, les Français donnèrent l'assaut. Il y eut un furieux combat à l'arme blanche. Sous le ciel couleur de rouille, le coupe-gorge de la vallée s'emplissait de morts. Les larges prairies semblaient farouches, avec leurs grands arbres isolés, leurs rideaux de peupliers qui les tachaient d'ombre. A droite et à gauche, les forêts étaient comme les murailles d'un cirque qui enfermaient les combattants, tandis que les sources, les fontaines et les eaux courantes prenaient des bruits de sanglots, dans la panique de la campagne.

Sous le hangar, Françoise n'avait pas bougé, accroupie en face du corps de Dominique. Le père Merlier venait d'être tué raide par une balle perdue. Alors, comme les Prussiens étaient exterminés et que le moulin brûlait, le capitaine français entra le premier dans la cour. Depuis le commencement de la campagne, c'était l'unique succès qu'il remportait. Aussi, tout enflammé, grandissant sa haute taille, riait-il de son air aimable de beau cavalier. Et, apercevant Françoise imbécile entre les cadavres de son mari et de son père, au milieu des ruines fumantes du moulin, il la salua galamment de son épée, en criant:

— Victoire! victoire!

body. She was watching; at moments she made a vague, childish gesture with her hand. The Prussians had seized old Merlier as a hostage.

It was a fine fight. The officer had rapidly stationed his men, realizing he couldn't beat a retreat without being overpowered. His best bet was to sell his life dearly. Now it was the Prussians who were defending the mill and the French who were attacking it. The fusillade began with unheard-of violence. It didn't stop for a half-hour. Then, a muffled explosion was heard and a cannonball broke one of the biggest boughs of the centuries-old elm. The French had artillery. A battery, located right above the ditch in which Dominique had hidden, was sweeping the main street of Rocreuse. The battle couldn't last long, after that.

Ah, the poor mill! Cannonballs were piercing it through and through. Half the roofing was blown away. Two walls collapsed. But it was especially on the Morelle side that the disaster became lamentable. The ivy, torn away from the shaken walls, was hanging like ragged clothing; the stream was carrying off debris of all sorts, and through a breach in the wall could be seen Françoise's bedroom, with its bed, whose white curtains were carefully drawn. One after another, the old wheel was hit by two cannonballs, and emitted one last moan: the wheel paddles were carried away in the current, and the framework crashed. The soul of the jolly mill had just been breathed away.

Then the French moved in for the attack. There was a furious combat with swords. Beneath the rust-colored sky, the assassins' lair of the valley filled up with dead men. The wide meadows seemed fierce, with their tall, isolated trees and their curtains of poplars casting blotches of darkness. To the right and to the left, the forests were like the walls of an amphitheater that enclosed the combatants; while the springs, fountains, and running waters began to sound like sobbing, in the panic of the countryside.

Below the shed, Françoise hadn't stirred, crouched there opposite Dominique's body. Old Merlier had just been killed outright by a stray bullet. Then, when the Prussians were wiped out and the mill was burning, the French captain was the first to enter the courtyard. Since the beginning of the campaign, this had been his only success. And so, at the height of excitement, straightening up his tall body to the utmost, he was laughing with his affable air of a dashing cavalier. And, catching sight of Françoise insensible between the bodies of her husband and her father, amid the smoking ruins of the mill, he saluted her gallantly with his sword, crying:

"Victory! Victory!"

GUY DE MAUPASSANT

Mademoiselle Perle

I

Quelle singulière idée j'ai eue, vraiment, ce soir-là, de choisir pour reine Mlle Perle.

Je vais tous les ans faire les Rois chez mon vieil ami Chantal. Mon père, dont il était le plus intime camarade, m'y conduisait quand j'étais enfant. J'ai continué, et je continuerai sans doute tant que je vivrai, et tant qu'il y aura un Chantal en ce monde.

Les Chantal, d'ailleurs, ont une existence singulière; ils vivent à Paris comme s'ils habitaient Grasse, Yvetot ou Pont-à-Mousson.

Ils possèdent, auprès de l'Observatoire, une maison dans un petit jardin. Ils sont chez eux, là, comme en province. De Paris, du vrai Paris, ils ne connaissent rien, ils ne soupçonnent rien; ils sont si loin, si loin! Parfois, cependant, ils y font un voyage, un long voyage. Mme Chantal va aux grandes provisions, comme on dit dans la famille. Voici comment on va aux grandes provisions.

Mlle Perle, qui a les clefs des armoires de cuisine (car les armoires au linge sont administrées par la maîtresse elle-même), Mlle Perle prévient que le sucre touche à sa fin, que les conserves sont épuisées, qu'il ne reste plus grand-chose au fond du sac à café.

Ainsi mise en garde contre la famine, Mme Chantal passe l'inspection des restes, en prenant des notes sur un calepin. Puis, quand elle a inscrit beaucoup de chiffres, elle se livre d'abord à de longs calculs et ensuite à de longues discussions avec Mlle Perle. On finit cependant par se mettre d'accord et par fixer les quantités de chaque chose dont on se pourvoira pour trois mois: sucre, riz, pruneaux, café, confitures, boîtes de petits pois, de haricots, de homard, poissons salés ou fumés, etc.

Après quoi, on arrête le jour des achats, et on s'en va, en fiacre,

GUY DE MAUPASSANT

Miss Pearl

I

What an odd notion it was of mine, really, to choose Miss Pearl as queen that evening!

Every year I go to celebrate Twelfth Night at the home of my old friend Chantal. My father, whose closest comrade he was, used to take me there when I was a child. I've kept on going, and no doubt I'll keep on as long as I live and as long as there's a Chantal in this world.

Incidentally, the Chantals's whole existence is an odd one; they live in Paris as if they were inhabitants of Grasse, Yvetot, or Pont-à-Mousson.[1]

They own a house standing in a little garden near the Observatory.[2] There, they live snugly at home like provincials. Of Paris, the true Paris, they know nothing, they suspect nothing; they're so far away, so far away! Sometimes, however, they take a trip to it, a long trip. Mrs. Chantal goes out for serious marketing, as they say in the family. Here's how they go out for serious marketing.

Miss Pearl, who has the keys to the kitchen cupboards (because the linen closets are administered by the lady of the house in person), Miss Pearl announces that the sugar supply is running out, that the preserves are all gone, and that not much is left on the bottom of the coffee sack.

Thus put on her guard against famine, Mrs. Chantal inspects what remains of the provisions, taking notes in a notebook. Then, after writing down a lot of figures, she first devotes herself to lengthy calculations and then to lengthy discussions with Miss Pearl. Anyway, they finally reach an agreement and settle on the quantity of each item that they'll stock up on for three months: sugar, rice, prunes, coffee, jams; tins of peas, beans, and lobster; salted or smoked fish, etc.

After that, they decide on a day for the purchases, and in a hackney

dans un fiacre à galerie, chez un épicier considérable qui habite au-delà des ponts, dans les quartiers neufs.

Mme Chantal et Mlle Perle font ce voyage ensemble, mystérieuse-ment, et reviennent à l'heure du dîner, exténuées, bien qu'émues en-core, et cahotées dans le coupé, dont le toit est couvert de paquets et de sacs, comme une voiture de déménagement.

Pour les Chantal, toute la partie de Paris située de l'autre côté de la Seine constitue les quartiers neufs, quartiers habités par une popula-tion singulière, bruyante, peu honorable, qui passe les jours en dissi-pations, les nuits en fêtes, et qui jette l'argent par les fenêtres. De temps en temps cependant, on mène les jeunes filles au théâtre, à l'Opéra-Comique ou au Français, quand la pièce est recommandée par le journal que lit M. Chantal.

Les jeunes filles ont aujourd'hui dix-neuf et dix-sept ans; ce sont deux belles filles, grandes et fraîches, très bien élevées, trop bien élevées, si bien élevées qu'elles passent inaperçues comme deux jolies poupées. Jamais l'idée ne me viendrait de faire attention ou de faire la cour aux demoiselles Chantal; c'est à peine si on ose leur parler, tant on les sent immaculées; on a presque peur d'être inconvenant en les saluant.

Quant au père, c'est un charmant homme, très instruit, très ouvert, très cordial, mais qui aime avant tout le repos, le calme, la tranquillité, et qui a fortement contribué à momifier ainsi sa famille pour vivre à son gré, dans une stagnante immobilité. Il lit beaucoup, cause volon-tiers, et s'attendrit facilement. L'absence de contacts, de coudoie-ments et de heurts a rendu très sensible et délicat son épiderme, son épiderme moral. La moindre chose l'émeut, l'agite et le fait souffrir.

Les Chantal ont des relations cependant, mais des relations re-streintes, choisies avec soin dans le voisinage. Ils échangent aussi deux ou trois visites par an avec des parents qui habitent au loin.

Quant à moi, je vais dîner chez eux le 15 août et le jour des Rois. Cela fait partie de mes devoirs comme la communion de Pâques pour les catholiques.

Le 15 août, on invite quelques amis, mais aux Rois, je suis le seul convive étranger.

II

Donc, cette année, comme les autres années, j'ai été dîner chez les Chantal pour fêter l'Epiphanie.

carriage, one with a luggage rail, they visit a grocer of good repute who lives beyond the Seine bridges, in the new developments.

Mrs. Chantal and Miss Pearl make that trip together, with an air of mystery, and return home at dinnertime, worn out though still excited, and bumping around in the vehicle, whose top is covered with packages and bags like a moving van.

For the Chantals, the entire portion of Paris located across the Seine comprises the "new developments," neighborhoods inhabited by an odd, noisy, not very respectable population that spends its days in dissipation, its nights in carousals, and tosses its money out the window. Nevertheless, from time to time they take their young daughters to the theater, to the Opéra-Comique or to the Comédie-Française,[3] when the play is recommended by the paper that Mr. Chantal reads.

One of the girls is now nineteen and the other seventeen; they are two beautiful girls, tall and healthy, very well brought up—too well brought up—so well brought up that they go unnoticed like two pretty dolls. It would never occur to me to pay special attention to the Chantal girls or to woo them; a man scarcely has the boldness to speak to them, since he feels they are so immaculate; he's almost afraid of acting improperly if he says hello to them.

As for the father, he's a likable man, very well educated, very open, very cordial; but above all else he prizes repose, calm, tranquillity, and it's largely through his doing that his family has turned into such mummies, so that he can live the way he likes, in a stagnant immobility. He reads a lot, likes to chat, and easily gives way to emotions. The absence of contacts, elbow rubbing, and jolts has made his epidermis, his psychological epidermis, very sensitive and delicate. The least little thing moves him, upsets him, and makes him suffer.

And yet, the Chantals have a circle of acquaintances, but a restricted circle, carefully chosen from among their neighbors. They also exchange two or three visits a year with relatives who live far away.

As for me, I dine with them on the fifteenth of August[4] and on Twelfth Night. That forms a part of my duties, like Communion at Easter for Catholics.

On the fifteenth of August they invite a few friends, but on Twelfth Night I'm the only guest who's not a member of the family.

II

And so, this year, as in other years, I went to dine with the Chantals to celebrate Epiphany.

Selon la coutume, j'embrassai M. Chantal, Mme Chantal et Mlle Perle, et je fis un grand salut à Mlles Louise et Pauline. On m'interrogea sur mille choses, sur les événements du boulevard, sur la politique, sur ce qu'on pensait dans le public des affaires du Tonkin, et sur nos représentants. Mme Chantal, une grosse dame dont toutes les idées me font l'effet d'être carrées à la façon des pierres de taille, avait coutume d'émettre cette phrase comme conclusion à toute discussion politique: «Tout cela est de la mauvaise graine pour plus tard.» Pourquoi me suis-je toujours imaginé que les idées de Mme Chantal sont carrées? Je n'en sais rien; mais tout ce qu'elle dit prend cette forme dans mon esprit; un carré, un gros carré avec quatre angles symétriques. Il y a d'autres personnes dont les idées me semblent toujours rondes et roulantes comme des cerceaux. Dès qu'elles ont commencé une phrase sur quelque chose, ça roule, ça va, ça sort par dix, vingt, cinquante idées rondes, des grandes et des petites que je vois courir l'une derrière l'autre, jusqu'au bout de l'horizon. D'autres personnes aussi ont des idées pointues . . . Enfin, cela importe peu.

On se mit à table comme toujours, et le dîner s'acheva sans qu'on eût rien à retenir.

Au dessert, on apporta le gâteau des Rois. Or, chaque année, M. Chantal était roi. Etait-ce l'effet d'un hasard continu ou d'une convention familiale, je n'en sais rien, mais il trouvait infailliblement la fève dans sa part de pâtisserie, et il proclamait reine Mme Chantal. Aussi, fus-je stupéfait en sentant dans une bouchée de brioche quelque chose de très dur qui faillit me casser une dent. J'ôtai doucement cet objet de ma bouche et j'aperçus une petite poupée de porcelaine, pas plus grosse qu'un haricot. La surprise me fit dire: «Ah!» On me regarda, et Chantal s'écria en battant des mains: «C'est Gaston! C'est Gaston! Vive le roi! Vive le roi!»

Tout le monde reprit en chœur: «Vive le roi!» Et je rougis jusqu'aux oreilles, comme on rougit souvent, sans raison, dans les situations un peu sottes. Je demeurais les yeux baissés, tenant entre deux doigts ce grain de faïence, m'efforçant de rire et ne sachant que faire ni que dire, lorsque Chantal reprit: «Maintenant, il faut choisir une reine.»

Alors je fus atterré. En une seconde, mille pensées, mille suppositions me traversèrent l'esprit. Voulait-on me faire désigner une des demoiselles Chantal? Etait-ce là un moyen de me faire dire celle que je préférais? Etait-ce une douce, légère, insensible poussée des parents vers un mariage possible? L'idée de mariage rôde sans cesse

As usual, I kissed Mr. Chantal, Mrs. Chantal, and Miss Pearl, and made a ceremonious bow to the girls, Louise and Pauline. They questioned me about a thousand things, about what was going on on the boulevards,[5] about politics, about what the public thought of the situation in Tonking,[6] and about our government representatives. Mrs. Chantal, a stout lady, all of whose ideas give me the feeling they've been squared off like construction stones, had the habit of emitting this sentence as the conclusion of every discussion of politics: "All that is bad seeds, which we'll see sprouting in the future." Why have I always pictured Mrs. Chantal's ideas as being square? I haven't any notion; but everything she says takes on that shape in my mind; a square, a big square with four symmetrical angles. There are other people whose ideas strike me as being always round, rolling like children's hoops. Once they've begun a sentence on any topic, things start out on a roll and keep going, coming out as ten, twenty, or fifty round ideas, big ones and little ones, which I see running one after the other to the very edge of the horizon. Likewise, other people have pointed ideas . . . Anyway, it doesn't much matter.

We sat down at the table as always, and the dinner ended without anything memorable for anyone.

For dessert we were served the Twelfth-cake. Now, every year Mr. Chantal was king. I surely don't know whether it was the result of an unbroken string of luck or a family agreement, but he never failed to find the bean in his slice of pastry, and he would proclaim Mrs. Chantal as queen. And so I was dumbfounded when I felt, in a mouthful of brioche, something very hard that I almost broke a tooth on. I gently removed that object from my mouth and saw a little porcelain doll no bigger than a bean. The surprise made me say "Ah!" They looked at me, and Chantal exclaimed, clapping his hands: "It's Gaston! It's Gaston! Long live the King! Long live the King!"

Everybody repeated in chorus: "Long live the King!" And I blushed all the way to my ears, in the way one often does, without a reason, in somewhat foolish situations. I was sitting there with my eyes lowered, holding that grain of porcelain between two fingers, making an effort to laugh and not knowing what to do or say, when Chantal resumed: "Now you must choose a queen."

At that, I was horror stricken. In a second, a thousand thoughts, a thousand suppositions raced through my mind. Did they want to make me designate one of the Chantal girls? Was that a way of making me say which one I preferred? Was it a gentle, light, imperceptible shove on their parents' part toward a possible marriage? The idea

dans toutes les maisons à grandes filles et prend toutes les formes, tous les déguisements, tous les moyens. Une peur atroce de me compromettre m'envahit, et aussi une extrême timidité devant l'attitude si obstinément correcte et fermée de Mlles Louise et Pauline. Elire l'une d'elles au détriment de l'autre me sembla aussi difficile que de choisir entre deux gouttes d'eau; et puis, la crainte de m'aventurer dans une histoire où je serais conduit au mariage malgré moi, tout doucement, par des procédés aussi discrets, aussi inaperçus et aussi calmes que cette royauté insignifiante, me troublait horriblement.

Mais tout à coup, j'eus une inspiration, et je tendis à Mlle Perle la poupée symbolique. Tout le monde fut d'abord surpris, puis on apprécia sans doute ma délicatesse et ma discrétion, car on applaudit avec furie. On criait: «Vive la reine! Vive la reine!»

Quant à elle, la pauvre vieille fille, elle avait perdu toute contenance; elle tremblait, effarée, et balbutiait: «Mais non . . . mais non . . . mais non . . . pas moi . . . je vous en prie . . . pas moi . . . je vous en prie . . .»

Alors, pour la première fois de ma vie, je regardai Mlle Perle, et je me demandai ce qu'elle était.

J'étais habitué à la voir dans cette maison, comme on voit les vieux fauteuils de tapisserie sur lesquels on s'assied depuis son enfance sans y avoir jamais pris garde. Un jour, on ne sait pourquoi, parce qu'un rayon de soleil tombe sur le siège, on se dit tout à coup: «Tiens, mais il est fort curieux, ce meuble»; et on découvre que le bois a été travaillé par un artiste, et que l'étoffe est remarquable. Jamais je n'avais pris garde à Mlle Perle.

Elle faisait partie de la famille Chantal, voilà tout; mais comment? A quel titre? — C'était une grande personne maigre qui s'efforçait de rester inaperçue, mais qui n'était pas insignifiante. On la traitait amicalement, mieux qu'une femme de charge, moins bien qu'une parente. Je saisissais tout à coup, maintenant, une quantité de nuances dont je ne m'étais point soucié jusqu'ici! Mme Chantal disait: «Perle.» Les jeunes filles: «Mlle Perle», et Chantal ne l'appelait que Mademoiselle, d'un air plus révérend peut-être.

Je me mis à la regarder. — Quel âge avait-elle? Quarante ans? Oui, quarante ans. — Elle n'était pas vieille, cette fille, elle se vieillissait. Je fus soudain frappé par cette remarque. Elle se coiffait, s'habillait, se parait ridiculement, et, malgré tout, elle n'était point ridicule, tant elle portait en elle de grâce simple, naturelle, de grâce voilée, cachée avec soin. Quelle drôle de créature, vraiment! Comment ne l'avais-je jamais mieux observée? Elle se coif-

of marriage incessantly prowls around in every household with grown-up daughters, assuming all shapes, disguises, and ploys. An atrocious fear of committing myself took hold of me, and also an extreme shyness in the face of Louise's and Pauline's deportment, which was so stubbornly correct and unresponsive. To pick one of them over the other seemed as hard to me as choosing between two drops of water; besides, the fear of venturing into a situation in which I would be led to the altar against my will, quite smoothly, with procedures as discreet, imperceptible, and calm as that insignificant "kingship," worried me no end.

But suddenly I had an inspiration, and I held out the symbolic doll to Miss Pearl. Everyone was surprised at first, then they must have realized how tactful and discreet I had been, because I was furiously applauded. They were shouting: "Long live the Queen! Long live the Queen!"

As for her, that poor old maid, she had totally lost her composure; she was trembling with alarm and stammering: "Oh, no . . . oh, no . . . oh, no . . . not me . . . please . . . not me . . . please . . ."

Then, for the first time in my life, I took a real look at Miss Pearl and I wondered who she really was.

I was accustomed to seeing her in that house, just as you see the old upholstered armchairs you've been sitting on since childhood without ever having really noticed them. One day, for some unknown reason, because a sunbeam falls on the chair, you suddenly say to yourself, "Well, well, this piece of furniture is very remarkable," and you discover that the wood was carved by an artist and that the fabric is noteworthy. I had never really noticed Miss Pearl.

She was part of the Chantal family, and that's that; but in what way, upon what grounds?—She was a tall, thin person who strove to remain unseen but who wasn't insignificant. She was treated in a friendly way, better than a housekeeper, but not as well as a relative. Now I suddenly recalled a large number of nuances I hadn't been concerned about before! Mrs. Chantal called her "Pearl." The girls addressed her as "Miss Pearl," and Chantal never called her anything but "Miss," perhaps in a more respectful tone.

I started to observe her—How old was she? Forty? Yes, forty.—That spinster wasn't old, she deliberately made herself older. I was suddenly struck by that observation. She did her hair, dressed, and chose her jewelry in a ridiculous manner, but, in spite of everything, she wasn't at all ridiculous, because she had in her so much simple, natural grace, grace that was veiled and concealed with care. What a funny creature, truly! How was it that I had never studied her more closely? She arranged her

fait d'une façon grotesque, avec de petits frisons vieillots tout à
fait farces; et, sous cette chevelure à la Vierge conservée, on voyait un grand front calme, coupé par deux rides profondes, deux
rides de longues tristesses, puis deux yeux bleus, larges et doux, si
timides, si craintifs, si humbles, deux beaux yeux restés si naïfs,
pleins d'étonnements de fillette, de sensations jeunes et aussi de
chagrins qui avaient passé dedans, en les attendrissant sans les
troubler.

Tout le visage était fin et discret, un de ces visages qui se sont
éteints sans avoir été usés, ou fanés par les fatigues ou les grandes
émotions de la vie.

Quelle jolie bouche! et quelles jolies dents! Mais on eût dit qu'elle
n'osait pas sourire!

Et, brusquement, je la comparai à Mme Chantal! Certes! Mlle
Perle était mieux, cent fois mieux, plus fine, plus noble, plus fière.

J'étais stupéfait de mes observations. On versait du champagne. Je
tendis mon verre à la reine, en portant sa santé avec un compliment
bien tourné. Elle eut envie, je m'en aperçus, de se cacher la figure
dans sa serviette; puis, comme elle trempait ses lèvres dans le vin clair,
tout le monde cria: «La reine boit! la reine boit!» Elle devint alors
toute rouge et s'étrangla. On riait; mais je vis bien qu'on l'aimait beaucoup dans la maison.

III

Dès que le dîner fut fini, Chantal me prit par le bras. C'était
l'heure de son cigare, heure sacrée. Quand il était seul, il allait le
fumer dans la rue; quand il avait quelqu'un à dîner, on montait au
billard, et il jouait en fumant. Ce soir-là, on avait même fait du feu
dans le billard, à cause des Rois; et mon vieil ami prit sa queue,
une queue très fine qu'il frotta de blanc avec grand soin, puis il
dit:

— A toi, mon garçon!

Car il me tutoyait, bien que j'eusse vingt-cinq ans, mais il m'avait vu
tout enfant.

Je commençai donc la partie; je fis quelques carambolages; j'en
manquai quelques autres; mais comme la pensée de Mlle Perle me rô-
dait dans la tête, je demandai tout à coup:

— Dites donc, monsieur Chantal, est-ce que Mlle Perle est votre
parente?

Il cessa de jouer, très étonné, et me regarda.

hair in a grotesque fashion, with little old-fashioned curls that were an absolute laugh; and, below that Madonna-braided hairdo she was still faithful to, could be seen a high, calm forehead, marked by two deep lines, lines indicative of long-lasting sorrows; then, two blue eyes, wide and gentle, so shy, so fearful, so humble, two beautiful eyes that had remained so naïve, full of a little girl's surprise, youthful feelings, and also sadness, which had lodged in them, making them tender though unclouded.

Her whole face was delicate and discreet, one of those faces that have been dimmed, but not worn down or withered by life's labors or strong emotions.

What a pretty mouth! And what pretty teeth! But it seemed as if she didn't dare to smile!

And, all of a sudden, I compared her with Mrs. Chantal! Of course! Miss Pearl was finer, a hundred times finer, more delicate, more noble, more proud.

I was dumbfounded by my observations. Champagne was being poured. I held out my glass to the Queen, drinking her health with a cleverly worded compliment. I saw that she wanted to hide her face in her napkin; then, as she was moistening her lips in the light-colored wine, everyone shouted: "The Queen is drinking! The Queen is drinking!" Then she turned bright red and gagged. They laughed, but I could tell she was well liked in the house.

III

As soon as dinner was over, Chantal took me by the arm. It was time for his cigar, a sacrosanct hour. When he was alone, he would go out into the street to smoke it; when he had someone over for dinner, they would go upstairs to the billiard room, and he would have a game while he smoked. That evening, they had even lit a fire in the billiard room on account of Twelfth Night; and my old friend took his cue, a very fine cue, which he rubbed with chalk with great care; and then he said:

"You begin, son!"

He addressed me as *tu* even though I was twenty-five, but of course he had known me ever since I was a small child.

And so I began the game; I made a few caroms, I mussed a few others; but, since the thought of Miss Pearl was stalking through my brain, I suddenly asked:

"Tell me, Mr. Chantal, is Miss Pearl a relative of yours?"

Very surprised, he stopped playing and looked at me.

— Comment, tu ne sais pas? tu ne connais pas l'histoire de Mlle Perle?

— Mais non.

— Ton père ne te l'a jamais racontée?

— Mais non.

— Tiens, tiens, que c'est drôle! ah! par exemple, que c'est drôle! Oh! mais c'est toute une aventure!

Il se tut, puis reprit:

— Et si tu savais comme c'est singulier que tu me demandes ça aujourd'hui, un jour des Rois!

— Pourquoi?

—Ah! pourquoi! Ecoute. Voilà de cela quarante et un ans, quarante et un ans aujourd'hui même, jour de l'Epiphanie. Nous habitions alors Roüy-le-Tors, sur les remparts; mais il faut d'abord t'expliquer la maison pour que tu comprennes bien. Roüy est bâti sur une côte, ou plutôt sur un mamelon qui domine un grand pays de prairies. Nous avions là une maison avec un beau jardin suspendu, soutenu en l'air par les vieux murs de défense. Donc la maison était dans la ville, dans la rue, tandis que le jardin dominait la plaine. Il y avait aussi une porte de sortie de ce jardin sur la campagne, au bout d'un escalier secret qui descendait dans l'épaisseur des murs, comme on en trouve dans les romans. Une route passait devant cette porte qui était munie d'une grosse cloche, car les paysans, pour éviter le grand tour, apportaient par là leurs provisions.

Tu vois bien les lieux, n'est-ce pas? Or, cette année-là, aux Rois, il neigeait depuis une semaine. On eût dit la fin du monde. Quand nous allions aux remparts regarder la plaine, ça nous faisait froid dans l'âme, cet immense pays blanc, tout blanc, glacé, et qui luisait comme du vernis. On eût dit que le bon Dieu avait empaqueté la terre pour l'envoyer au grenier des vieux mondes. Je t'assure que c'était bien triste.

Nous demeurions en famille à ce moment-là, et nombreux, très nombreux: mon père, ma mère, mon oncle et ma tante, mes deux frères et mes quatre cousines; c'étaient de jolies fillettes; j'ai épousé la dernière. De tout ce monde-là, nous ne sommes plus que trois survivants: ma femme, moi et ma belle-sœur qui habite Marseille. Sacristi, comme ça s'égrène, une famille! ça me fait trembler quand j'y pense! Moi, j'avais quinze ans, puisque j'en ai cinquante-six.

Donc, nous allions fêter les Rois, et nous étions très gais, très gais! Tout le monde attendait le dîner dans le salon, quand mon frère aîné, Jacques, se mit à dire: «Il y a un chien qui hurle dans la plaine depuis dix minutes; ça doit être une pauvre bête perdue.»

"What, you don't know? You haven't heard the story of Miss Pearl?"

"Not at all."

"Your father never told it to you?"

"Not at all."

"Well, well, that's funny! My, I'll say that's funny! Oh, it's quite an adventure!"

He fell silent, then resumed:

"And if you only knew how odd it is that you should ask me that today, on Twelfth Night!"

"Why?"

"You ask why! Listen. It's been forty-one years, forty-one years to the very day, Twelfth Night. We were then living at Roüy-le-Tors,[7] on the ramparts; but first I have to explain the house to you so you can understand properly. Roüy is built on a slope, or, rather, on a rounded hill that dominates a vast countryside of grassland. We had a house there with a beautiful hanging garden held up in the air by the old defensive walls. And so the house was in the town, on the street, while the garden overlooked the plain. There was also a door leading out of that garden into the countryside, at the end of a secret staircase built into the thickness of the walls, of the kind found in novels. A road passed in front of that door, which was furnished with a big bell, because the farmers, to avoid the long way around, used to bring us their produce on that side.

"You picture the place clearly now? Well, that year, on Twelfth Night, it had been snowing for a week. We thought it was the end of the world. When we went to the ramparts to look at the plain, we got chilled to the soul at the sight of that immense white landscape, all white, frozen over, and gleaming like shellac. It looked as if God had wrapped up the earth in order to send it to the attic where old worlds are stored. I assure you it was very melancholy.

"At that time our whole family was living together, and there were a lot of us, a whole lot: my father, my mother, my uncle and my aunt, my two brothers and my four female cousins. They were pretty little girls; I married the youngest. Of all that crowd, only three of us are still living: my wife, I, and my sister-in-law, who lives in Marseilles. Damn, how family members drop away! It makes me shiver when I think of it! I was fifteen at the time, since I'm fifty-six now.

"Well, we were about to celebrate Twelfth Night, and we were very merry, very merry! Everyone was waiting for dinner in the parlor when my older brother, Jacques, started saying: 'There's a dog that's been howling in the plain for ten minutes now; it must be a poor lost animal.'

Il n'avait pas fini de parler, que la cloche du jardin tinta. Elle avait un gros son de cloche d'église qui faisait penser aux morts. Tout le monde en frissonna. Mon père appela le domestique et lui dit d'aller voir. On attendit en grand silence; nous pensions à la neige qui couvrait toute la terre. Quand l'homme revint, il affirma qu'il n'avait rien vu. Le chien hurlait toujours, sans cesse, et sa voix ne changeait point de place.

On se mit à table; mais nous étions un peu émus, surtout les jeunes. Ça alla bien jusqu'au rôti, puis voilà que la cloche se remet à sonner trois fois de suite, trois grands coups, longs, qui ont vibré jusqu'au bout de nos doigts et qui nous ont coupé le souffle, tout net. Nous restions à nous regarder, la fourchette en l'air, écoutant toujours, et saisis d'une espèce de peur surnaturelle.

Ma mère enfin parla: «C'est étonnant qu'on ait attendu si longtemps pour revenir; n'allez pas seul, Baptiste; un de ces messieurs va vous accompagner.»

Mon oncle François se leva. C'était une espèce d'hercule, très fier de sa force et qui ne craignait rien au monde. Mon père lui dit: «Prends un fusil. On ne sait pas ce que ça peut être.»

Mais mon oncle ne prit qu'une canne et sortit aussitôt avec le domestique.

Nous autres, nous demeurâmes frémissants de terreur et d'angoisse, sans manger, sans parler. Mon père essaya de nous rassurer. «Vous allez voir, dit-il, que ce sera quelque mendiant ou quelque passant perdu dans la neige. Après avoir sonné une première fois, voyant qu'on n'ouvrait pas tout de suite, il a tenté de retrouver son chemin, puis, n'ayant pu y parvenir, il est revenu à notre porte.»

L'absence de mon oncle nous parut durer une heure. Il revint enfin, furieux, jurant: «Rien, nom de nom, c'est un farceur! Rien que ce maudit chien qui hurle à cent mètres des murs. Si j'avais pris un fusil, je l'aurais tué pour le faire taire.»

On se remit à dîner, mais tout le monde demeurait anxieux; on sentait bien que ce n'était pas fini, qu'il allait se passer quelque chose, que la cloche, tout à l'heure, sonnerait encore.

Et elle sonna, juste au moment où l'on coupait le gâteau des Rois. Tous les hommes se levèrent ensemble. Mon oncle François, qui avait bu du champagne, affirma qu'il allait LE massacrer, avec tant de fureur, que ma mère et ma tante se jetèrent sur lui pour l'empêcher. Mon père, bien que très calme et un peu impotent (il traînait la jambe depuis qu'il se l'était cassée en tombant de cheval), déclara à son tour qu'il voulait savoir ce que c'était, et qu'il irait. Mes frères, âgés de

"Before he had even finished speaking, the garden bell rang. It had a heavy sound, like a church bell, that reminded you of the dead. Everyone shuddered when it rang. My father called the servant and told him to go and see what it was. We waited in total silence; we were thinking about the snow that covered all the ground. When the man returned, he assured us that he hadn't seen a thing. The dog was still howling, without a letup, and its voice was always coming from the same spot.

"We sat down at the table, but we were a little excited, especially we young ones. All went well up to the roast, and then, there was the bell ringing again, three times in a row, three loud, long rings that vibrated to our fingertips and took our breath away altogether. We sat there looking at each other, our forks in the air, constantly listening, and gripped with a sort of supernatural fear.

"Finally my mother spoke up: 'It's surprising that whoever it is waited so long before coming back. Don't go out alone, Baptiste; one of these gentlemen will accompany you.'

"My uncle François got up. He was a sort of Hercules, very proud of his strength and not afraid of anything in the world. My father said to him: 'Take along a gun. You can't tell what it might be.'

"But my uncle took only a walking stick and went out immediately with the servant.

"The rest of us remained trembling with terror and anguish, without eating, without speaking. My father tried to reassure us. 'You'll see,' he said, 'it'll be some beggar or some passer-by lost in the snow. After ringing the first time and seeing that no one was opening up right away, he tried to find his way again; then, when unable to succeed, he came back to our door.'

"My uncle's absence seemed to us to last an hour. Finally he came back, in a rage, swearing: 'Nothing, by God, it's some practical joker! Only that damned dog howling a hundred meters away from the walls. If I had taken a gun, I'd have killed him to make him shut up.'

"We resumed our meal, but everyone was still nervous; we had a firm feeling that all was not yet over, that something was going to happen, that the bell would ring again in a little while.

"And ring it did, just at the moment when the Twelfth-cake was being sliced. All the men got up at the same time. My uncle François, who had drunk champagne, swore he was going to massacre 'him,' and with such rage that my mother and my aunt pounced on him to hold him back. My father, though very calm and a little lame (he limped after breaking a leg in a fall from a horse), declared in turn that he wanted to know what was going on, and he would go along. My

dix-huit et de vingt ans, coururent chercher leurs fusils; et comme on ne faisait guère attention à moi, je m'emparai d'une carabine de jardin et je me disposai aussi à accompagner l'expédition. Elle partit aussitôt. Mon père et mon oncle marchaient devant, avec Baptiste, qui portait une lanterne. Mes frères Jacques et Paul suivaient, et je venais derrière, malgré les supplications de ma mère, qui demeurait avec sa sœur et mes cousines sur le seuil de la maison.

La neige s'était remis à tomber depuis une heure; et les arbres en étaient chargés. Les sapins pliaient sous ce lourd vêtement livide, pareils à des pyramides blanches, à d'énormes pains de sucre; et on apercevait à peine, à travers le rideau gris des flocons menus et pressés, les arbustes plus légers, tout pâles dans l'ombre. Elle tombait si épaisse, la neige, qu'on y voyait tout juste à dix pas. Mais la lanterne jetait une grande clarté devant nous. Quand on commença à descendre par l'escalier tournant creusé dans la muraille, j'eus peur, vraiment. Il me sembla qu'on marchait derrière moi; qu'on allait me saisir par les épaules et m'emporter; et j'eus envie de retourner; mais comme il fallait retraverser tout le jardin, je n'osai pas.

J'entendis qu'on ouvrait la porte sur la plaine; puis mon oncle se remit à jurer: «Nom d'un nom, il est reparti! Si j'aperçois seulement son ombre, je ne le rate pas, ce c . . .-là.»

C'était sinistre de voir la plaine, ou, plutôt, de la sentir devant soi, car on ne la voyait pas; on ne voyait qu'un voile de neige sans fin, en haut, en bas, en face, à droite, à gauche, partout.

Mon oncle reprit: «Tiens, revoilà le chien qui hurle; je vais lui apprendre comment je tire, moi. Ça sera toujours ça de gagné.»

Mais mon père, qui était bon, reprit: «Il vaut mieux l'aller chercher, ce pauvre animal qui crie la faim. Il aboie au secours, ce misérable; il appelle comme un homme en détresse. Allons-y.»

Et on se mit en route à travers ce rideau, à travers cette tombée épaisse, continue, à travers cette mousse qui emplissait la nuit et l'air, qui remuait, flottait, tombait et glaçait la chair en fondant, la glaçait comme elle l'aurait brûlée, par une douleur vive et rapide sur la peau, à chaque toucher des petits flocons blancs.

Nous enfoncions jusqu'aux genoux dans cette pâte molle et froide; et il fallait lever très haut la jambe pour marcher. A mesure que nous avancions, la voix du chien devenait plus claire, plus forte. Mon oncle cria: «Le voici!» On s'arrêta pour l'observer, comme on doit faire en face d'un ennemi qu'on rencontre dans la nuit.

brothers, one eighteen and the other twenty, ran to get their guns; and since hardly anyone was paying attention to me, I took hold of a small-bore rifle and got ready to join the expedition myself.

"It set out at once. My father and my uncle led the way, along with Baptiste, who was carrying a lantern. My brothers Jacques and Paul were next, and I brought up the rear, despite the pleading of my mother, who remained behind with her sister and my cousins on the threshold of the house.

"The snow had started to fall again an hour earlier, and the trees were laden with it. The firs were bending under that heavy, ghastly-pale garment; they looked like white pyramids or gigantic sugar loaves; and through the gray curtain of small, closely spaced snowflakes, we could hardly see the smaller shrubbery, very pale in the shadow. The snow was falling so thickly that we could see just ten paces around us. But the lantern was casting a bright light ahead of us. When we started walking down the circular staircase carved out of the rampart wall, I was really frightened. It sounded as if someone were walking behind me, that I would be grabbed by my shoulders and carried off. I felt like going back, but since it would have been necessary to cross the entire garden again, I didn't dare to.

"I heard the door onto the plain being opened; then my uncle started swearing once more: 'By God, he went away again! If I catch sight of as much as his shadow, I won't miss that a--h--e!'[8]

"It was eerie to see the plain, or, rather, to sense it in front of us, because we couldn't see it; all we saw was an infinite veil of snow, above, below, facing us, to our right, to our left, everywhere.

"My uncle continued: 'Look, there's the howling dog again; I'm going to show him how I can shoot. That will be something gained, anyway.'

"But my father, who was a kind man, said: 'It would be better to go and find that poor animal, which is crying with hunger. The poor thing is barking for help; he's calling like a man in distress. Let's go!'

"And we set out through that curtain, through that dense, continuous snowfall, through that foam which was filling the night and the air, which was whizzing, floating, falling, and chilling our flesh as it melted, chilling it as if burning it, with a quick, sharp pain on the skin at every contact with the little white flakes.

"We were sinking up to the knees in that soft, cold paste, and we had to lift our legs very high in order to walk. As we advanced, the dog's voice became clearer and louder. My uncle yelled: 'Here he is!' We stopped to observe him, as people ought to do in the face of an enemy encountered at night.

Je ne voyais rien, moi; alors, je rejoignis les autres, et je l'aperçus; il était effrayant et fantastique à voir, ce chien, un gros chien noir, un chien de berger à grands poils et à tête de loup, dressé sur ses quatre pattes, tout au bout de la longue traînée de lumière que faisait la lanterne sur la neige. Il ne bougeait pas; il s'était tu; et il nous regardait.

Mon oncle dit: «C'est singulier, il n'avance ni ne recule. J'ai bien envie de lui flanquer un coup de fusil.»

Mon père reprit d'une vois ferme: «Non, il faut le prendre.»

Alors mon frère Jacques ajouta: «Mais il n'est pas seul. Il y a quelque chose à côté de lui.»

Il y avait quelque chose derrière lui, en effet, quelque chose de gris, d'impossible à distinguer. On se remit en marche avec précaution.

En nous voyant approcher, le chien s'assit sur son derrière. Il n'avait pas l'air méchant. Il semblait plutôt content d'avoir réussi à attirer des gens.

Mon père alla droit à lui et le caressa. Le chien lui lécha les mains; et on reconnut qu'il était attaché à la roue d'une petite voiture, d'une sorte de voiture joujou enveloppée tout entière dans trois ou quatre couvertures de laine. On enleva ces linges avec soin, et comme Baptiste approchait sa lanterne de la porte de cette carriole qui ressemblait à une niche roulante, on aperçut dedans un petit enfant qui dormait.

Nous fûmes tellement stupéfaits que nous ne pouvions dire un mot. Mon père se remit le premier, et comme il était de grand cœur et d'âme un peu exaltée, il étendit la main sur le toit de la voiture et il dit: «Pauvre abandonné, tu seras des nôtres!» Et il ordonna à mon frère Jacques de rouler devant nous notre trouvaille.

Mon père reprit, pensant tout haut:

«Quelque enfant d'amour dont la pauvre mère est venue sonner à ma porte en cette nuit de l'Epiphanie, en souvenir de l'Enfant-Dieu.»

Il s'arrêta de nouveau, et, de toute sa force, il cria quatre fois à travers la nuit vers les quatre coins du ciel: «Nous l'avons recueilli!» Puis, posant la main sur l'épaule de son frère, il murmura: «Si tu avais tiré sur le chien, François? . . .»

Mon oncle ne répondit pas, mais il fit dans l'ombre un grand signe de croix, car il était très religieux malgré ses airs fanfarons.

On avait détaché le chien, qui nous suivait.

Ah! par exemple, ce qui fut gentil à voir, c'est la rentrée à la maison. On eut d'abord beaucoup de mal à monter la voiture par l'escalier des

"I myself could see nothing; then I came up with the others, and I caught sight of him; he was frightening and fantastic to see, that dog, a big black dog, a sheep dog with long hair and a wolf's head, standing on all four paws at the very end of the long trail of light cast by the lantern on the snow. He wasn't moving; he had fallen silent; and he was watching us.

"My uncle said: 'It's odd, he isn't coming forward or moving away from us. I have a good mind to take a shot at him.'

"My father said in a firm voice: 'No, we've got to catch him.'

"Then my brother Jacques added: 'But he's not alone. There's something beside him.'

"In fact, there was something behind him, something gray and impossible to make out. We started walking again, cautiously.

"Seeing us approach, the dog sat down on his haunches. He didn't look vicious. Instead, he seemed pleased at his success in attracting people.

"My father went right up to him and petted him. The dog licked his hands, and we realized that he was tied to the wheel of a little carriage, a sort of toy carriage all wrapped up in three or four woolen blankets. We undid those wrappings carefully, and when Baptiste brought his lantern close to the door of that wagon, which looked like a doghouse on wheels, we saw a little child sleeping inside.

"We were so dumbfounded that we couldn't say a word. My father was the first to regain his composure, and, since he had a big heart and a rather enthusiastic nature, he held out his hand over the top of the carriage and said: 'Poor abandoned child, you shall be one of us!' And he ordered my brother Jacques to lead the way back, wheeling our find.

"My father went on, thinking out loud:

"'Some love child whose mother came to ring at my door on this Twelfth Night, in memory of the Holy Infant.'

"He stopped again and, with all his might, he shouted four times into the night to the four corners of the heavens: 'We have taken it in!' Then, laying his hand on his brother's shoulder, he murmured: 'François, what if you had shot at the dog? . . .'

"My uncle made no reply, but in the darkness he crossed himself vigorously, because he was very religious in spite of his swaggering ways.

"The dog had been untied and was following us.

"Oh, I can tell you, our return to the house was something to see! At first we had a lot of trouble getting the carriage up the staircase in

remparts; on y parvint cependant et on la roula jusque dans le vestibule.

Comme maman était drôle, contente et effarée! Et mes quatre petites cousines (la plus jeune avait six ans), elles ressemblaient à quatre poules autour d'un nid. On retira enfin de sa voiture l'enfant qui dormait toujours. C'était une fille, âgée de six semaines environ. Et on trouva dans ses langes dix mille francs en or, oui, dix mille francs! que papa plaça pour lui faire une dot. Ce n'était donc pas un enfant de pauvres . . . mais peut-être l'enfant de quelque noble avec une petite bourgeoise de la ville . . . ou encore . . . nous avons fait mille suppositions et on n'a jamais rien su . . . mais là, jamais rien . . . jamais rien . . . Le chien lui-même ne fut reconnu par personne. Il était étranger au pays. Dans tous les cas, celui ou celle qui était venu sonner trois fois à notre porte connaissait bien mes parents, pour les avoir choisis ainsi.

Voilà donc comment Mlle Perle entra, à l'âge de six semaines, dans la maison Chantal.

On ne la nomma que plus tard Mlle Perle, d'ailleurs. On la fit baptiser d'abord: «Marie, Simonne, Claire.» Claire devant lui servir de nom de famille.

Je vous assure que ce fut une drôle de rentrée dans la salle à manger avec cette mioche réveillée qui regardait autour d'elle ces gens et ces lumières, de ses yeux vagues, bleus et troubles.

On se remit à table et le gâteau fut partagé. J'étais roi; et je pris pour reine Mlle Perle, comme toi tout à l'heure. Elle ne se douta guère, ce jour-là, de l'honneur qu'on lui faisait.

Donc, l'enfant fut adoptée, et élevée dans la famille. Elle grandit; des années passèrent. Elle était gentille, douce, obéissante. Tout le monde l'aimait et on l'aurait abominablement gâtée si ma mère ne l'eût empêché.

Ma mère était une femme d'ordre et de hiérarchie. Elle consentit à traiter la petite Claire comme ses propres fils, mais elle tenait cependant à ce que la distance qui nous séparait fût bien marquée, et la situation bien établie.

Aussi, dès que l'enfant put comprendre, elle lui fit connaître son histoire et fit pénétrer tout doucement, même tendrement dans l'esprit de la petite, qu'elle était pour les Chantal une fille adoptive, recueillie, mais en somme une étrangère.

Claire comprit cette situation avec une singulière intelligence, avec un instinct surprenant; et elle sut prendre et garder la place qui lui

the ramparts; but we managed to do it and we wheeled it all the way into the vestibule.

"How funny Mother was, both pleased and frightened! And my four little cousins (the youngest was six), they looked like four hens around a nest. Finally we took the child, still sleeping, out of its carriage. It was a girl about six weeks old. And in her swaddling clothes we found ten thousand francs in gold—yes, ten thousand francs!—which Father invested to create a dowry for her. So she wasn't a child of poor people . . . but perhaps the child some nobleman had had with a lower middle-class woman in town . . . or else . . . we made a thousand guesses but never found out a thing . . . I tell you, not a thing . . . not a thing . . . Even the dog wasn't recognized by anybody. He was unknown in the vicinity. In any case, the man or woman who had rung the bell at our door three times must have been quite familiar with my parents to have selected them that way.

"So that's how Miss Pearl entered the Chantal household at the age of six weeks.

"By the way, it was only later that she was dubbed 'Miss Pearl.' At first we had her baptized as 'Marie Simonne Claire.' Claire was to be the name we called her.

"I assure you that our return to the dining room was comical, with that little tot, now awake and looking at those people and lights all around her with her vacant, clouded blue eyes.

"We sat down at the table again and distributed the slices of cake. I was king, and I chose Miss Pearl as queen, just as you did a while ago. That day she was hardly aware of the honor being conferred on her.

"And so, the child was adopted and brought up within the family. She grew up; years went by. She was pleasant, gentle, obedient. Everyone loved her, and she would have been terribly spoiled if my mother hadn't prevented it.

"My mother was a woman concerned with order and rank. She agreed to treat little Claire the same as her own sons, but she insisted that the distance that separated us should be clearly indicated, and the situation clearly defined.

"And so, as soon as the child was old enough to understand, she told her her history, and very gently, even tenderly, made the girl fully aware that for the Chantals she was a child they had taken in and adopted, but, when you came right down to it, an outsider.

"Claire understood that situation with unusual intelligence, with a surprising instinct; and she was able to assume and retain the position

était laissée, avec tant de tact, de grâce et de gentillesse, qu'elle
touchait mon père à le faire pleurer.

Ma mère elle-même fut tellement émue par la reconnaissance pas-
sionnée et le dévouement un peu craintif de cette mignonne et tendre
créature, qu'elle se mit à l'appeler «ma fille». Parfois, quand la petite
avait fait quelque chose de bon, de délicat, ma mère relevait ses lunettes
sur son front, ce qui indiquait toujours une émotion chez elle, et elle
répétait: «Mais c'est une perle, une vraie perle, cette enfant!» — Ce nom
en resta à la petite Claire qui devint et demeura pour nous Mlle Perle.

IV

M. Chantal se tut. Il était assis sur le billard, les pieds ballants, et il ma-
niait une boule de la main gauche, tandis que de la droite il tripotait un
linge qui servait à effacer les points sur le tableau d'ardoise et que nous
appelions «le linge à craie». Un peu rouge, la voix sourde, il parlait
pour lui maintenant, parti dans ses souvenirs, allant doucement, à travers les choses anciennes et les vieux événements qui se réveillaient
dans sa pensée, comme on va, en se promenant, dans les vieux jardins
de la famille où l'on fut élevé, et où chaque arbre, chaque chemin,
chaque plante, les houx pointus, les lauriers qui sentent bon, les ifs
dont la graine rouge et grasse s'écrase entre les doigts, font surgir, à
chaque pas, un petit fait de notre vie passée, un de ces faits insignifi-
ants et délicieux qui forment le fond même, la trame de l'existence.

Moi, je restais en face de lui, adossé à la muraille, les mains ap-
puyées sur ma queue de billard inutile.

Il reprit, au bout d'une minute: «Cristi, qu'elle était jolie à dix-huit
ans . . . et gracieuse . . . et parfaite . . . Ah! la jolie . . . jolie . . . jolie et
bonne . . . et brave . . . et charmante fille! . . . Elle avait des yeux . . .
des yeux bleus . . . transparents . . . clairs . . . comme je n'en ai jamais
vu de pareils . . . jamais!

Il se tut encore. Je demandai: «Pourquoi ne s'est-elle pas mariée?»

Il répondit, non pas à moi, mais à ce mot qui passait: «mariée».

— Pourquoi? pourquoi? Elle n'a pas voulu . . . pas voulu. Elle avait
pourtant trente mille francs de dot, et elle fut demandée plusieurs fois
. . . elle n'a pas voulu! Elle semblait triste à cette époque-là. C'est
quand j'épousai ma cousine, la petite Charlotte, ma femme, avec qui
j'étais fiancé depuis six ans.

Je regardais M. Chantal et il me semblait que je pénétrais dans
son esprit, que je pénétrais tout à coup dans un de ces humbles et
cruels drames des cœurs honnêtes, des cœurs droits, des cœurs sans

that was left for her with so much tact, grace, and good nature that she moved my father to the point of tears.

"My mother herself was so touched by the impassioned gratitude and somewhat timid devotion of this sweet, tender creature that she began calling her 'daughter.' At times, when the girl had done something kind and discreet, my mother would push her glasses up to her forehead—a sure sign that she felt some emotion—and would repeat: 'But this child is a pearl, a real pearl!'—That name stuck to little Claire, who became and has remained for us 'Miss Pearl.'"

IV

Mr. Chantal fell silent. He was seated on the billiard table, his legs swinging, and was handling a ball with his left hand, while with his right he was crumpling a cloth that was used to erase the scores on the slate; we called it the "chalk cloth." A little red in the face, his voice muffled, by this time he was talking to himself, lost in his memories. He was gently moving among the past things and old events that were reawakened in his mind, just as we stroll through the old gardens of the home where we grew up, in which every tree, every path, every plant, the sharp-pointed holly, the sweet-smelling laurels, the yew trees whose fatty, red berries squash between your fingers, recall to us, with each step we take, one of those insignificant but delightful occasions that form the very basis and fabric of existence.

As for me, I stood there facing him, my back against the wall, my hands resting on my inactive billiard cue.

After a minute, he went on: "Damn, but she was pretty at eighteen . . . and graceful . . . and perfect . . . Oh, that pretty . . . pretty . . . pretty and kindly . . . and decent . . . and charming girl! Her eyes . . . were blue . . . limpid . . . bright . . . like no others I've ever seen . . . ever!"

He fell silent again. I asked: "Why didn't she marry?"

His reply was not to me, but to that word that had been uttered: "marry."

"Why? Why? she didn't want to . . . didn't want to. And yet she had a dowry of thirty thousand francs, and several men asked for her hand . . . she didn't want to! She seemed sad in those days. It was when I married my cousin, little Charlotte, my wife, to whom I had been engaged for six years."

I was watching Mr. Chantal, and I felt as if I were entering his mind and suddenly discovering one of those humble and cruel dramas of honorable hearts, upright hearts, blameless hearts; discovering one of

reproches, dans un de ces cœurs inavoués, inexplorés, que personne n'a connu, pas même ceux qui en sont les muettes et résignées victimes. Et une curiosité hardie me poussant tout à coup, je prononçai:

— C'est vous qui auriez dû l'épouser, monsieur Chantal!

Il tressaillit, me regarda, et dit:

— Moi? Epouser qui?

— Mlle Perle.

— Pourquoi ça?

— Parce que vous l'aimiez plus que votre cousine.

Il me regarda avec des yeux étranges, ronds, effarés, puis il balbutia:

— Je l'ai aimée . . . moi? . . . comment? qu'est-ce qui t'a dit ça? . . .

— Parbleu, ça se voit . . . et c'est même à cause d'elle que vous avez tardé si longtemps à épouser votre cousine qui vous attendait depuis six ans.

Il lâcha la bille qu'il tenait de la main gauche, saisit à deux mains le linge à craie, et s'en couvrant le visage, se mit à sangloter dedans. Il pleurait d'une façon désolante et ridicule, comme pleure une éponge qu'on presse, par les yeux, le nez et la bouche en même temps. Et il toussait, crachait, se mouchait dans le linge à craie, s'essuyait les yeux, éternuait, recommençait à couler par toutes les fentes de son visage, avec un bruit de gorge qui faisait penser aux gargarismes.

Moi, effaré, honteux, j'avais envie de me sauver et je ne savais plus que dire, que faire, que tenter.

Et soudain, la voix de Mme Chantal résonna dans l'escalier: «Est-ce bientôt fini, votre fumerie?»

J'ouvris la porte et je criai: «Oui, madame, nous descendons.»

Puis, je me précipitai vers son mari, et, le saisissant par les coudes: «Monsieur Chantal, mon ami Chantal, écoutez-moi; votre femme vous appelle, remettez-vous, remettez-vous vite, il faut descendre; remettez-vous.»

Il bégaya: «Oui . . . , oui . . . , je viens . . . , pauvre fille . . . , je viens . . . , dites-lui que j'arrive.»

Et il commença à s'essuyer consciencieusement la figure avec le linge qui, depuis deux ou trois ans, essuyait toutes les marques de l'ardoise, puis il apparut, moitié blanc et moitié rouge, le front, le nez, les joues et le menton barbouillés de craie, et les yeux gonflés, encore pleins de larmes.

Je le pris par les mains et l'entraînai dans sa chambre en murmurant: «Je vous demande pardon, je vous demande bien pardon, mon-

those unconfessed, unexplored hearts that no one has really known, not even those who are their silent, resigned victims.

And, suddenly impelled by a bold curiosity, I declared:

"You're the one who should have married her, Mr. Chantal!"

He gave a start, looked at me, and said:

"I? Marry whom?"

"Miss Pearl."

"Why so?"

"Because you loved her more than you loved your cousin."

He looked at me with strange, rounded, frightened eyes, and then stammered:

"I loved her? . . . I? . . . How so? Who told you that? . . ."

"It's obvious, of course . . . and, in fact, it was on her account that you took so long to marry your cousin, who was waiting for you for six years."

He dropped the ball he had been holding in his left hand; seizing the chalk cloth with both hands, he covered his face with it and started to sob into it. He was crying in a tiresome, ridiculous way, like a sponge being squeezed—from his eyes, nose, and mouth all at the same time. And he was coughing, spitting, blowing his nose into the chalk cloth, wiping his eyes, sneezing, and beginning again to pour out liquid through every crack in his face, with a sound in his throat that reminded you of gargling.

I was frightened and ashamed; I felt like running away, and I no longer knew what to do, say, or attempt.

Then, suddenly, Mrs. Chantal's voice resounded on the stairs: "Will you be through soon with your smoking session?"

I opened the door and called: "Yes, ma'am, we're coming down."

Then I dashed over to her husband and, gripping him by his elbows, I said: "Mr. Chantal, my friend Chantal, listen to me; your wife is calling you, pull yourself together, pull yourself together fast, we've got to go down; pull yourself together."

He stuttered: "Yes . . . , yes . . . , I'm coming . . . , poor girl . . . , I'm coming . . . , tell her I'll be right there."

And he began wiping his face conscientiously with the cloth that for two or three years had wiped off all the notations on the slate. Then his face reappeared, half white and half red, his forehead, nose, cheeks, and chin smeared with chalk, and his eyes swollen and still filled with tears.

I took him by both hands and dragged him into his bedroom, murmuring: "I beg your forgiveness, I sincerely beg your forgiveness, Mr.

sieur Chantal, de vous avoir fait de la peine . . . mais . . . je ne savais pas . . . vous . . . vous comprenez . . .»

Il me serra la main: «Oui . . . oui . . . il y a des moments difficiles . . .»

Puis il se plongea la figure dans sa cuvette. Quand il en sortit, il ne me parut pas encore présentable; mais j'eus l'idée d'une petite ruse. Comme il s'inquiétait, en se regardant dans la glace, je lui dis: «Il suffira de raconter que vous avez un grain de poussière dans l'œil, et vous pourrez pleurer devant tout le monde autant qu'il vous plaira.»

Il descendit, en effet, en se frottant les yeux avec son mouchoir. On s'inquiéta; chacun voulut chercher le grain de poussière qu'on ne trouva point, et on raconta des cas semblables où il était devenu nécessaire d'aller chercher le médecin.

Moi, j'avais rejoint Mlle Perle et je la regardais, tourmenté par une curiosité ardente, une curiosité qui devenait une souffrance. Elle avait dû être bien jolie, en effet, avec ses yeux doux, si grands, si calmes, si larges qu'elle avait l'air de ne les jamais fermer, comme font les autres humains. Sa toilette était un peu ridicule, une vraie toilette de vieille fille, et la déparait sans la rendre gauche.

Il me semblait que je voyais en elle, comme j'avais vu tout à l'heure dans l'âme de M. Chantal, que j'apercevais, d'un bout à l'autre, cette vie humble, simple et dévouée; mais un besoin me venait aux lèvres, un besoin harcelant de l'interroger, de savoir si, elle aussi, l'avait aimé, lui; si elle avait souffert comme lui de cette longue souffrance secrète, aiguë, qu'on ne voit pas, qu'on ne sait pas, qu'on ne devine pas, mais qui s'échappe, la nuit, dans la solitude de la chambre noire. Je la regardais, je voyais battre son cœur sous son corsage à guimpe, et je me demandais si cette douce figure candide avait gémi chaque soir, dans l'épaisseur moite de l'oreiller, et sangloté, le corps secoué de sursauts, dans la fièvre du lit brûlant.

Et je lui dis tout bas, comme font les enfants qui cassent un bijou pour voir dedans: «Si vous aviez vu pleurer M. Chantal tout à l'heure, il vous aurait fait pitié.»

Elle tressaillit: «Comment, il pleurait?

— Oh! oui, il pleurait!

— Et pourquoi ça?

Elle semblait très émue. Je répondis:

— A votre sujet.

— A mon sujet?

Chantal, for distressing you this way . . . but . . . I didn't know . . . you . . . you understand . . ."

He squeezed my hand: "Yes . . . yes . . . there are difficult moments."

Then he plunged his face into his wash basin. When he came out again, he still didn't look presentable, but a little ruse occurred to me. Since he was worried when he looked in the mirror, I said: "You only have to say that you have a speck of dust in your eye, and you'll be able to cry in front of everybody as much as you like."

And, in fact, he went downstairs rubbing his eyes with his handkerchief. They were worried; everyone tried looking for the speck of dust, which wasn't to be found, and they told of similar cases in which it had become necessary to send for the doctor.

As for me, I had rejoined Miss Pearl, and I was looking at her, tormented as I was by a burning curiosity, a curiosity that was becoming a physical pain. She must have been very pretty, in fact, with her gentle eyes, which were so big, calm, and wide that she looked as if she never closed them as other human beings do. Her clothing was a little laughable, a real old maid's outfit, and it gave her a dowdy appearance without making her appear awkward.

I felt as if I saw through her, just as I had looked into Mr. Chantal's soul a little earlier; as if I were viewing in its entirety that humble, simple, and devoted life. But an urge to speak was taking hold of me, a nagging urge to question her, to learn whether she had loved him, as well; whether she had suffered, as he had, with that long, secret, sharp suffering which nobody sees, nobody knows, nobody guesses, but which breaks out at night in the loneliness of your dark bedroom. I was watching her, seeing her heart beat beneath the tucker of her bodice, and I wondered whether that sweet, candid face had moaned every night into her thick, damp pillow, and sobbed in the fever of her burning bed, while her body was shaken with sorrow.

And, like a child breaking a piece of jewelry to see what's inside, I said to her, very quietly: "If you had seen Mr. Chantal crying a while ago, you would have felt sorry for him."

She gave a start: "What, he was crying?"

"Oh, yes, he was crying!"

"But why?"

She seemed quite upset. I replied:

"On your account."

"On my account?"

— Oui. Il me racontait combien il vous avait aimée autrefois; et combien il lui en avait coûté d'épouser sa femme au lieu de vous . . .»

Sa figure pâle me parut s'allonger un peu; ses yeux toujours ouverts, ses yeux calmes se fermèrent tout à coup, si vite qu'ils semblaient s'être clos pour toujours. Elle glissa de sa chaise sur le plancher et s'y affaissa doucement, lentement, comme aurait fait une écharpe tombée.

Je criai: «Au secours! Au secours! Mlle Perle se trouve mal!»

Mme Chantal et ses filles se précipitèrent, et comme on cherchait de l'eau, une serviette et du vinaigre, je pris mon chapeau et me sauvai.

Je m'en allai à grands pas, le cœur secoué, l'esprit plein de remords et de regrets. Et parfois aussi j'étais content; il me semblait que j'avais fait une chose louable et nécessaire.

Je me demandais: «Ai-je eu tort? Ai-je eu raison?» Ils avaient cela dans l'âme comme on garde du plomb dans une plaie fermée. Maintenant ne seront-ils pas plus heureux? Il était trop tard pour que recommençât leur torture et assez tôt pour qu'ils s'en souvinssent avec attendrissement.

Et peut-être qu'un soir du prochain printemps, émus par un rayon de lune tombé sur l'herbe, à leurs pieds, à travers les branches, ils se prendront et se serreront la main en souvenir de toute cette souffrance étouffée et cruelle; et peut-être aussi que cette courte étreinte fera passer dans leurs veines un peu de ce frisson qu'ils n'auront point connu, et leur jettera, à ces morts ressuscités en une seconde, la rapide et divine sensation de cette ivresse, de cette folie qui donne aux amoureux plus de bonheur en un tressaillement, que n'en peuvent cueillir, en toute leur vie, les autres hommes!

"Yes. He was telling me how much he loved you in the past, and how much it had cost him to marry his wife instead of you . . ."

Her pale face seemed to grow a little longer; her eternally open eyes, those calm eyes, suddenly closed, so swiftly that they seemed to have closed forever. She slipped off her chair onto the floor, where she collapsed gently, slowly, like a dropped scarf.

I shouted: "Help! Help! Miss Pearl has fainted!"

Mrs. Chantal and her daughters rushed over, and while they were going for water, a towel, and vinegar, I grabbed my hat and made my escape.

I left the house taking big strides, my heart shaken up, my mind filled with remorse and regrets. And, at moments, I was pleased, too; I felt as if I had done something praiseworthy and necessary.

I asked myself: "Was I wrong? Was I right?" They were retaining all that in their soul the way the lead is still contained in a closed-over gunshot wound. Wouldn't they be happier now? It was too late for their torture to start all over again, and too soon for them to look back on it with tender feelings.

And perhaps, one evening of the coming spring, stirred by a moonbeam shining through the boughs and falling on the grass at their feet, they will take hold of each other and squeeze each other's hands in memory of all that cruelly repressed suffering. And perhaps, too, that brief embrace will send coursing through their veins a little of that thrill they had never known, and will inject these dead people, restored to life in a second, with the rapid, divine sensation of that rapture, that madness, which gives lovers more happiness in one moment's spasm of joy than other people can accumulate in their entire lives!

NOTES

Mérimée, "Mateo Falcone"

On Corsica and the place names, see the Introduction.
1. Traditionally, top boots had bands of light-colored leather.
2. In all likelihood, this phrase is to be completed (in standard Italian—the *me* indicates that the original is in dialect) as *Perchè mi coglioni?* Mérimée omitted the verb out of humorous modesty, since it is derived from the word for testicles.
3. Are Gianetto's hands completely untied at this moment?
4. An error? "My uncle the *caporale*"? "My cousin the sergeant"?

Nerval, "Sylvie"

On the Valois region and its towns and natural features, see the Introduction.
1. A town buried by the eruption of Vesuvius in A.D. 79, along with Pompeii.
2. Elis was a city in the Peloponnese (Greece); Trebizond was a city in Asia Minor, seat of an independent state during parts of the Middle Ages.
3. That is, before the revolution of 1789.
4. The basic framework of the story takes place about twenty years before the time of writing; that is, during the 1830s. The revolution of 1830 drove out the last of the Bourbon kings (Charles X) and ushered in the constitutional monarchy of Louis-Philippe. The gross materialism of this new era, in which the middle class grew wealthy and powerful, alienated many creative spirits.
5. The Fronde (late 1640s to early 1650s) was a revolt of part of the

232

nobility against the very young Louis XIV; the Regency (1715–1723) was the period when Louis XV was still a minor; the Directoire (1795–1799) was the last revolutionary government before Napoleon's takeover.

6. Both lived in the second century A.D. Peregrinus was a philosopher of the Cynic school. Apuleius was an author (writing in Latin) whose chief work, *The Golden Ass* (*Metamorphoses*), was a favorite of Nerval's, with its tales of witchcraft and its description of an initiation into the mystery rites of the Egyptian goddess Isis.

7. Reigned 1589–1610; the first Bourbon king of France, succeeding Henri III, the last Valois king.

8. This probably refers to Diane de Poitiers (1499–1566), famous mistress of King Henri II.

9. The Catholic confederacy (1576–1594) in the French wars of religion. For the Fronde, see Note 5.

10. Urania: the Muse of astronomy. The two poets named are Stanislas-Jean de Boufflers (1738–1815) and Guillaume Amfrye de Chaulieu (1639–1720), both pale imitators of the great Roman poet Horace (Quintus Horatius Flaccus, 65–8 B.C.).

11. In ancient Greece, a deputation marching in a religious procession.

12. Saint-Sulpice-du-Désert.

13. Probably a legendary Celtic chieftain (or a deity?). The translator could find no references, even in dictionaries of Celtic lore.

14. *La nouvelle Héloïse* is Jean-Jacques Rousseau's great novel. The Lafontaine in question was a German writer (1758–1831) of sentimental novels, very popular at the time.

15. A popular Parisian theater in which visually imaginative entertainments were offered; made famous in more recent times by the film *Les enfants du paradis*.

16. Colonna was the author of one of the world's great illustrated books, the 1499 *Hypnerotomachia Poliphili* (Strife of Love in a Dream), a favorite of Nerval's.

17. The famous girls' school for which Racine wrote his last two plays, *Esther* (1689) and *Athalie* (1691).

18. Catherine de Médicis, queen mother, was largely responsible for the massacre of Protestants in Paris on Saint Bartholomew's Eve of 1572.

19. The Ermenonville area is full of eighteenth-century imitations of Greco-Roman monuments. Rousseau, author of the pedagogical novel *Emile*, was buried there. Nearby is a real small "desert" with

sand dunes. "*Anacharsis*" is short for *Le voyage du jeune Anacharsis en Grèce* by the abbé Jean-Jacques Barthélemy (1788).

20. Well-known French folk song: "Nous n'irons plus au bois, les lauriers sont coupés."

21. "To learn the reasons for things' existence": a quotation from Vergil's *Georgics*.

22. His remains were transferred to the Panthéon in Paris in 1794, six years after his death.

23. Refers to Gabrielle d'Estrées, famous mistress of King Henri IV.

24. In the French, the word for "water" is in the local dialect, as it is whenever this incident is recalled later in the story. There is also a meaningful alternation between *tu* and *vous* throughout this passage.

25. Nicola Porpora (1686–1768), eminent Neapolitan composer.

26. As an ordinary adjective, *dodu* means "plump, chubby."

27. The real name of the flower seller at the Théâtre des Variétés.

28. See Note 16.

29. A legendary character.

30. Sophie de Feuchères (née Dawes) was an English adventuress who had grown wealthy as the mistress of a great French nobleman, and had owned property in the Valois during Nerval's childhood; physically, she resembled the Aurélie of the story.

31. Clarens, on the Lake of Geneva near Montreux, is said to be the locale of Rousseau's novel *La nouvelle Héloïse*.

32. The original idyllic poetry of Greece and Rome had been imitated in the eighteenth century by the Swiss-German poet Salomon Gessner (1730–1788), whose works were translated into French by Diderot and others.

33. The French poet Jean-Antoine Roucher (1745–1794).

34. A French pet name for Lotte (Charlotte), the woman loved in vain by the hero of Goethe's novel *The Sorrows of Young Werther* (1774); Werther shoots himself.

Daudet, "La mule du Pape"

On Avignon and the historical background, see the Introduction.

1. A word play with reference to a humorous song text by Pierre-Jean de Béranger (1780–1857), "Le roi d'Yvetot," about a very plain-living, jolly king with a sweetheart named Jeanneton. (Yvetot is a small town in Normandy.)

2. Every French commentator gleefully points out that Château-

neuf and Avignon are on the same side of the Rhône, so that this crossing of the bridge is an error (or a fantasy?).

3. Warmed-up red wine with sugar, cinnamon, and other flavorings.

4. The French word here, *"pécaïre!,"* is a typically Provençal exclamation.

5. A fictitious village mentioned in several of the *Letters from My Windmill* stories.

6. Jeanne I of Anjou, ruler of the Kingdom of Naples from 1343 to 1382.

7. The theologian appointed to plead against a candidate for canonization; the entire ceremony here is wildly exaggerated in a spirit of burlesque.

8. A mountain in the same modern *département* as Avignon (Vaucluse).

9. Wetlands in the delta of the Rhône.

Flaubert, "Hérodias"

On the historical background, characters, and topography, see the Introduction.

1. In ancient Roman architecture, a roll-up awning that could be stretched over theater or amphitheater seats in sunny weather; here, intended for a flat palace roof.

2. On the temple mount.

3. The Bashan of the Old Testament, well to the east of the Sea of Galilee, today in southern Syria. This formed only part of Philip's tetrarchy, which was generally referred to as Ituraea.

4. John Hyrcanus, king of Judaea from 135 to 105 B.C.

5. Sodom and Gomorrah.

6. The leader who rebuilt Jerusalem in the fifth century B.C. after the Babylonian conquest.

7. Herod was said to have been descended from the Edomites, who lived southeast of the Dead Sea and had been enemies of the Hebrews under the latter's early kings. "Edom" also sometimes stands for Esau, Jacob's hostile brother.

8. Roman curved military trumpets.

9. Broad purple stripes on his tunic, a badge of high rank; the fasces and the lictors who carry them are particular emblems of the office of consul.

10. The Janiculum is one of the hills of Rome. The Via Vitellia is the highway referred to.

11. Perhaps the nation in Cilicia (Asia Minor) also known as the Cietae. A Roman army from Syria fought them in the 30s A.D.

12. Location of Tiberius' favorite villa, where the emperor was rumored to indulge in "unnatural vices."

13. Tax gatherers.

14. Light-armed infantry skirmishers.

15. The knobs at the centers of the shield. Caesar = the emperor (here and elsewhere).

16. Kikkar: a Jewish gold coin. Obol: a Greek coin of low denomination.

17. "Agalah" ("cart, chariot") was the Hebrew name for the Big Dipper; Algol is a bright star in Perseus; Mira is a star in the constellation Cetus.

18. *Algum* or *almug*: a tree mentioned in the Old Testament; perhaps sandalwood.

19. Roman-style dining couch.

20. The Latinized name given at the time to Edom (see Note 7).

21. Greek-style short mantle fastened at one shoulder.

22. A Latin quotation from the first-century B.C. philosophical poet Lucretius: "[The lifeless body] neither grows, nor does one see it lasting after death."

23. Greek names of receptacles: "from the storage jars into the mixing bowls."

24. Jewish political enemies of Herod Antipas's house.

25. A close friend and adviser of the first Roman emperor, Augustus, and the patron of the poet Horace.

26. An allusion to the boar that killed Adonis, originally a Phoenician vegetation god, identified by Aulus with the Greco-Roman god of wine.

27. A god said to be once worshipped with human sacrifices in the vicinity of Jerusalem.

28. Greek-style women's upper garment, resembling a shawl.

29. Discovered at Mycenae in Greece the year before the story was written.

30. Cybele: a goddess of Asia Minor. Patera: a Roman saucer-shaped drinking vessel.

31. Psyche (Greek: "soul") was the wife of Eros (Cupid), whom she sought everywhere after he deserted her for disobeying him. Butterflies are an emblem of the soul, and there is a genus of moths called *Psyche*.

32. A type of Phoenician flute.

33. A magical spinning top.
34. Tambourines.
35. Enemies or threats to the house of Herod. (Zosimus = Soemus?)

Zola, "L'attaque du moulin"

1. More literally, he had drawn a bad lottery number; this was the military-draft method at the time.
2. August 25, the day on which King Louis IX, later canonized, died in 1270.
3. The emperor was Napoléon III. The Franco-Prussian War broke out on July 19, 1870.

Maupassant, "Mademoiselle Perle"

On Twelfth Night celebrations, see the Introduction.
1. Small towns in different parts of France: Provence, Normandy, and Lorraine, respectively.
2. This observatory, founded in 1667, is on the Left Bank, some-what south of the Jardin du Luxembourg, but the reference may be more specifically to the residential area around the Jardins de l'Observatoire, immediately to the south of the Luxembourg.
3. Eminently respectable, government-subsidized theaters.
4. The Assumption of the Virgin, a major holiday in Catholic countries.
5. The sophisticated, worldly sections of Paris on the Right Bank (*boulevardier* = man about town).
6. This northern part of Vietnam was conquered by the French between 1882 and 1885 and then administered as a protectorate.
7. Fictitious? According to an official listing of French *communes*, there are three places in France called Rouy, but none with the appendage "le-Tors." If the Rouy in the *département* of Nièvre (central France) is meant, that region has landscape like that described in the story.
8. The French word abbreviated out of modesty is *con*.

A CATALOG OF SELECTED DOVER
BOOKS IN ALL FIELDS OF INTEREST

CONCERNING THE SPIRITUAL IN ART, Wassily Kandinsky. Pioneering work by father of abstract art. Thoughts on color theory, nature of art. Analysis of earlier masters. 12 illustrations. 80pp. of text. 5⅜ x 8½. 23411-8 Pa. $4.95

ANIMALS: 1,419 Copyright-Free Illustrations of Mammals, Birds, Fish, Insects, etc., Jim Harter (ed.). Clear wood engravings present, in extremely lifelike poses, over 1,000 species of animals. One of the most extensive pictorial sourcebooks of its kind. Captions. Index. 284pp. 9 x 12. 23766-4 Pa. $14.95

CELTIC ART: The Methods of Construction, George Bain. Simple geometric techniques for making Celtic interlacements, spirals, Kells-type initials, animals, humans, etc. Over 500 illustrations. 160pp. 9 x 12. (USO) 22923-8 Pa. $9.95

AN ATLAS OF ANATOMY FOR ARTISTS, Fritz Schider. Most thorough reference work on art anatomy in the world. Hundreds of illustrations, including selections from works by Vesalius, Leonardo, Goya, Ingres, Michelangelo, others. 593 illustrations. 192pp. 7⅛ x 10¼. 20241-0 Pa. $9.95

CELTIC HAND STROKE-BY-STROKE (Irish Half-Uncial from "The Book of Kells"): An Arthur Baker Calligraphy Manual, Arthur Baker. Complete guide to creating each letter of the alphabet in distinctive Celtic manner. Covers hand position, strokes, pens, inks, paper, more. Illustrated. 48pp. 8¼ x 11. 24336-2 Pa. $3.95

EASY ORIGAMI, John Montroll. Charming collection of 32 projects (hat, cup, pelican, piano, swan, many more) specially designed for the novice origami hobbyist. Clearly illustrated easy-to-follow instructions insure that even beginning papercrafters will achieve successful results. 48pp. 8¼ x 11. 27298-2 Pa. $3.50

THE COMPLETE BOOK OF BIRDHOUSE CONSTRUCTION FOR WOODWORKERS, Scott D. Campbell. Detailed instructions, illustrations, tables. Also data on bird habitat and instinct patterns. Bibliography. 3 tables. 63 illustrations in 15 figures. 48pp. 5¼ x 8½. 24407-5 Pa. $2.50

BLOOMINGDALE'S ILLUSTRATED 1886 CATALOG: Fashions, Dry Goods and Housewares, Bloomingdale Brothers. Famed merchants' extremely rare catalog depicting about 1,700 products: clothing, housewares, firearms, dry goods, jewelry, more. Invaluable for dating, identifying vintage items. Also, copyright-free graphics for artists, designers. Co-published with Henry Ford Museum & Greenfield Village. 160pp. 8¼ x 11. 25780-0 Pa. $10.95

HISTORIC COSTUME IN PICTURES, Braun & Schneider. Over 1,450 costumed figures in clearly detailed engravings—from dawn of civilization to end of 19th century. Captions. Many folk costumes. 256pp. 8⅜ x 11¾. 23150-X Pa. $12.95

STICKLEY CRAFTSMAN FURNITURE CATALOGS, Gustav Stickley and L. & J. G. Stickley. Beautiful, functional furniture in two authentic catalogs from 1910. 594 illustrations, including 277 photos, show settles, rockers, armchairs, reclining chairs, bookcases, desks, tables. 183pp. 6½ x 9¼. 23838-5 Pa. $11.95

AMERICAN LOCOMOTIVES IN HISTORIC PHOTOGRAPHS: 1858 to 1949, Ron Ziel (ed.). A rare collection of 126 meticulously detailed official photographs, called "builder portraits," of American locomotives that majestically chronicle the rise of steam locomotive power in America. Introduction. Detailed captions. xi + 129pp. 9 x 12. 27393-8 Pa. $13.95

AMERICA'S LIGHTHOUSES: An Illustrated History, Francis Ross Holland, Jr. Delightfully written, profusely illustrated fact-filled survey of over 200 American lighthouses since 1716. History, anecdotes, technological advances, more. 240pp. 8 x 10¾. 25576-X Pa. $12.95

TOWARDS A NEW ARCHITECTURE, Le Corbusier. Pioneering manifesto by founder of "International School." Technical and aesthetic theories, views of industry, economics, relation of form to function, "mass-production split" and much more. Profusely illustrated. 320pp. 6⅛ x 9¼. (USO) 25023-7 Pa. $9.95

HOW THE OTHER HALF LIVES, Jacob Riis. Famous journalistic record, exposing poverty and degradation of New York slums around 1900, by major social reformer. 100 striking and influential photographs. 233pp. 10 x 7⅞. 22012-5 Pa. $11.95

FRUIT KEY AND TWIG KEY TO TREES AND SHRUBS, William M. Harlow. One of the handiest and most widely used identification aids. Fruit key covers 120 deciduous and evergreen species; twig key 160 deciduous species. Easily used. Over 300 photographs. 126pp. 5⅜ x 8½. 20511-8 Pa. $3.95

COMMON BIRD SONGS, Dr. Donald J. Borror. Songs of 60 most common U.S. birds: robins, sparrows, cardinals, bluejays, finches, more—arranged in order of increasing complexity. Up to 9 variations of songs of each species. Cassette and manual 99911-4 $8.95

ORCHIDS AS HOUSE PLANTS, Rebecca Tyson Northen. Grow cattleyas and many other kinds of orchids–in a window, in a case, or under artificial light. 63 illustrations. 148pp. 5⅜ x 8½. 23261-1 Pa. $5.95

MONSTER MAZES, Dave Phillips. Masterful mazes at four levels of difficulty. Avoid deadly perils and evil creatures to find magical treasures. Solutions for all 32 exciting illustrated puzzles. 48pp. 8¼ x 11. 26005-4 Pa. $2.95

MOZART'S DON GIOVANNI (DOVER OPERA LIBRETTO SERIES), Wolfgang Amadeus Mozart. Introduced and translated by Ellen H. Bleiler. Standard Italian libretto, with complete English translation. Convenient and thoroughly portable–an ideal companion for reading along with a recording or the performance itself. Introduction. List of characters. Plot summary. 121pp. 5¼ x 8½. 24944-1 Pa. $3.95

TECHNICAL MANUAL AND DICTIONARY OF CLASSICAL BALLET, Gail Grant. Defines, explains, comments on steps, movements, poses and concepts. 15-page pictorial section. Basic book for student, viewer. 127pp. 5⅜ x 8½. 21843-0 Pa. $4.95

THE CLARINET AND CLARINET PLAYING, David Pino. Lively, comprehensive work features suggestions about technique, musicianship, and musical interpretation, as well as guidelines for teaching, making your own reeds, and preparing for public performance. Includes an intriguing look at clarinet history. "A godsend," The Clarinet, Journal of the International Clarinet Society. Appendixes. 7 illus. 320pp. 5⅜ x 8½. 40270-3 Pa. $9.95

HOLLYWOOD GLAMOR PORTRAITS, John Kobal (ed.). 145 photos from 1926-49. Harlow, Gable, Bogart, Bacall; 94 stars in all. Full background on photographers, technical aspects. 160pp. 8⅜ x 11¼. 23352-9 Pa. $12.95

THE ANNOTATED CASEY AT THE BAT: A Collection of Ballads about the Mighty Casey/Third, Revised Edition, Martin Gardner (ed.). Amusing sequels and parodies of one of America's best-loved poems: Casey's Revenge, Why Casey Whiffed, Casey's Sister at the Bat, others. 256pp. 5⅜ x 8½. 28598-7 Pa. $8.95

THE RAVEN AND OTHER FAVORITE POEMS, Edgar Allan Poe. Over 40 of the author's most memorable poems: "The Bells," "Ulalume," "Israfel," "To Helen," "The Conqueror Worm," "Eldorado," "Annabel Lee," many more. Alphabetic lists of titles and first lines. 64pp. 5 5/16 x 8¼. 26685-0 Pa. $1.00

PERSONAL MEMOIRS OF U. S. GRANT, Ulysses Simpson Grant. Intelligent, deeply moving firsthand account of Civil War campaigns, considered by many the finest military memoirs ever written. Includes letters, historic photographs, maps and more. 528pp. 6⅛ x 9¼. 28587-1 Pa. $12.95

ANCIENT EGYPTIAN MATERIALS AND INDUSTRIES, A. Lucas and J. Harris. Fascinating, comprehensive, thoroughly documented text describes this ancient civilization's vast resources and the processes that incorporated them in daily life, including the use of animal products, building materials, cosmetics, perfumes and incense, fibers, glazed ware, glass and its manufacture, materials used in the mummification process, and much more. 544pp. 6⅛ x 9¼. (USO) 40446-3 Pa. $16.95

RUSSIAN STORIES/PYCCKNE PACCKA3bl: A Dual-Language Book, edited by Gleb Struve. Twelve tales by such masters as Chekhov, Tolstoy, Dostoevsky, Pushkin, others. Excellent word-for-word English translations on facing pages, plus teaching and study aids, Russian/English vocabulary, biographical/critical introductions, more. 416pp. 5⅜ x 8½. 26244-8 Pa. $9.95

PHILADELPHIA THEN AND NOW: 60 Sites Photographed in the Past and Present, Kenneth Finkel and Susan Oyama. Rare photographs of City Hall, Logan Square, Independence Hall, Betsy Ross House, other landmarks juxtaposed with contemporary views. Captures changing face of historic city. Introduction. Captions. 128pp. 8¼ x 11. 25790-8 Pa. $9.95

AIA ARCHITECTURAL GUIDE TO NASSAU AND SUFFOLK COUNTIES, LONG ISLAND, The American Institute of Architects, Long Island Chapter, and the Society for the Preservation of Long Island Antiquities. Comprehensive, well-researched and generously illustrated volume brings to life over three centuries of Long Island's great architectural heritage. More than 240 photographs with authoritative, extensively detailed captions. 176pp. 8¼ x 11. 26946-9 Pa. $14.95

NORTH AMERICAN INDIAN LIFE: Customs and Traditions of 23 Tribes, Elsie Clews Parsons (ed.). 27 fictionalized essays by noted anthropologists examine religion, customs, government, additional facets of life among the Winnebago, Crow, Zuni, Eskimo, other tribes. 480pp. 6⅛ x 9¼. 27377-6 Pa. $10.95

FRANK LLOYD WRIGHT'S DANA HOUSE, Donald Hoffmann. Pictorial essay of residential masterpiece with over 160 interior and exterior photos, plans, elevations, sketches and studies. 128pp. 9¼ x 10¾.   29120-0 Pa. $12.95

THE MALE AND FEMALE FIGURE IN MOTION: 60 Classic Photographic Sequences, Eadweard Muybridge. 60 true-action photographs of men and women walking, running, climbing, bending, turning, etc., reproduced from rare 19th-century masterpiece. vi + 121pp. 9 x 12.   24745-7 Pa. $10.95

1001 QUESTIONS ANSWERED ABOUT THE SEASHORE, N. J. Berrill and Jacquelyn Berrill. Queries answered about dolphins, sea snails, sponges, starfish, fishes, shore birds, many others. Covers appearance, breeding, growth, feeding, much more. 305pp. 5¼ x 8¼.   23366-9 Pa. $9.95

ATTRACTING BIRDS TO YOUR YARD, William J. Weber. Easy-to-follow guide offers advice on how to attract the greatest diversity of birds: birdhouses, feeders, water and waterers, much more. 96pp. 5³⁄₁₆ x 8¼.   28927-3 Pa. $2.50

MEDICINAL AND OTHER USES OF NORTH AMERICAN PLANTS: A Historical Survey with Special Reference to the Eastern Indian Tribes, Charlotte Erichsen-Brown. Chronological historical citations document 500 years of usage of plants, trees, shrubs native to eastern Canada, northeastern U.S. Also complete identifying information. 343 illustrations. 544pp. 6½ x 9¼.   25951-X Pa. $12.95

STORYBOOK MAZES, Dave Phillips. 23 stories and mazes on two-page spreads: Wizard of Oz, Treasure Island, Robin Hood, etc. Solutions. 64pp. 8¼ x 11.
                    23628-5 Pa. $2.95

AMERICAN NEGRO SONGS: 230 Folk Songs and Spirituals, Religious and Secular, John W. Work. This authoritative study traces the African influences of songs sung and played by black Americans at work, in church, and as entertainment. The author discusses the lyric significance of such songs as "Swing Low, Sweet Chariot," "John Henry," and others and offers the words and music for 230 songs. Bibliography. Index of Song Titles. 272pp. 6½ x 9¼.   40271-1 Pa. $9.95

MOVIE-STAR PORTRAITS OF THE FORTIES, John Kobal (ed.). 163 glamor, studio photos of 106 stars of the 1940s: Rita Hayworth, Ava Gardner, Marlon Brando, Clark Gable, many more. 176pp. 8⅜ x 11¼.   23546-7 Pa. $14.95

BENCHLEY LOST AND FOUND, Robert Benchley. Finest humor from early 30s, about pet peeves, child psychologists, post office and others. Mostly unavailable elsewhere. 73 illustrations by Peter Arno and others. 183pp. 5⅜ x 8½. 22410-4 Pa. $6.95

YEKL and THE IMPORTED BRIDEGROOM AND OTHER STORIES OF YIDDISH NEW YORK, Abraham Cahan. Film Hester Street based on Yekl (1896). Novel, other stories among first about Jewish immigrants on N.Y.'s East Side. 240pp. 5⅜ x 8½.   22427-9 Pa. $6.95

SELECTED POEMS, Walt Whitman. Generous sampling from *Leaves of Grass*. Twenty-four poems include "I Hear America Singing," "Song of the Open Road," "I Sing the Body Electric," "When Lilacs Last in the Dooryard Bloom'd," "O Captain! My Captain!"—all reprinted from an authoritative edition. Lists of titles and first lines. 128pp. 5³⁄₁₆ x 8¼.   26878-0 Pa. $1.00

THE BEST TALES OF HOFFMANN, E. T. A. Hoffmann. 10 of Hoffmann's most important stories: "Nutcracker and the King of Mice," "The Golden Flowerpot," etc. 458pp. 5⅜ x 8½. 21793-0 Pa. $9.95

FROM FETISH TO GOD IN ANCIENT EGYPT, E. A. Wallis Budge. Rich detailed survey of Egyptian conception of "God" and gods, magic, cult of animals, Osiris, more. Also, superb English translations of hymns and legends. 240 illustrations. 545pp. 5⅜ x 8½. 25803-3 Pa. $13.95

FRENCH STORIES/CONTES FRANÇAIS: A Dual-Language Book, Wallace Fowlie. Ten stories by French masters, Voltaire to Camus: "Micromegas" by Voltaire; "The Atheist's Mass" by Balzac; "Minuet" by de Maupassant; "The Guest" by Camus, six more. Excellent English translations on facing pages. Also French-English vocabulary list, exercises, more. 352pp. 5⅜ x 8½. 26443-2 Pa. $9.95

CHICAGO AT THE TURN OF THE CENTURY IN PHOTOGRAPHS: 122 Historic Views from the Collections of the Chicago Historical Society, Larry A. Viskochil. Rare large-format prints offer detailed views of City Hall, State Street, the Loop, Hull House, Union Station, many other landmarks, circa 1904-1913. Introduction. Captions. Maps. 144pp. 9⅜ x 12¼. 24656-6 Pa. $12.95

OLD BROOKLYN IN EARLY PHOTOGRAPHS, 1865-1929, William Lee Younger. Luna Park, Gravesend race track, construction of Grand Army Plaza, moving of Hotel Brighton, etc. 157 previously unpublished photographs. 165pp. 8⅞ x 11¾. 23587-4 Pa. $13.95

THE MYTHS OF THE NORTH AMERICAN INDIANS, Lewis Spence. Rich anthology of the myths and legends of the Algonquins, Iroquois, Pawnees and Sioux, prefaced by an extensive historical and ethnological commentary. 36 illustrations. 480pp. 5⅜ x 8½. 25967-6 Pa. $10.95

AN ENCYCLOPEDIA OF BATTLES: Accounts of Over 1,560 Battles from 1479 B.C. to the Present, David Eggenberger. Essential details of every major battle in recorded history from the first battle of Megiddo in 1479 B.C. to Grenada in 1984. List of Battle Maps. New Appendix covering the years 1967-1984. Index. 99 illustrations. 544pp. 6½ x 9¼. 24913-1 Pa. $16.95

SAILING ALONE AROUND THE WORLD, Captain Joshua Slocum. First man to sail around the world, alone, in small boat. One of great feats of seamanship told in delightful manner. 67 illustrations. 294pp. 5⅜ x 8½. 20326-3 Pa. $6.95

ANARCHISM AND OTHER ESSAYS, Emma Goldman. Powerful, penetrating, prophetic essays on direct action, role of minorities, prison reform, puritan hypocrisy, violence, etc. 271pp. 5⅜ x 8½. 22484-8 Pa. $7.95

MYTHS OF THE HINDUS AND BUDDHISTS, Ananda K. Coomaraswamy and Sister Nivedita. Great stories of the epics; deeds of Krishna, Shiva, taken from puranas, Vedas, folk tales; etc. 32 illustrations. 400pp. 5⅜ x 8½. 21759-0 Pa. $12.95

THE TRAUMA OF BIRTH, Otto Rank. Rank's controversial thesis that anxiety neurosis is caused by profound psychological trauma which occurs at birth. 256pp. 5⅜ x 8½. 27974-X Pa. $7.95

A THEOLOGICO-POLITICAL TREATISE, Benedict Spinoza. Also contains unfinished Political Treatise. Great classic on religious liberty, theory of government on common consent. R. Elwes translation. Total of 421pp. 5⅜ x 8½. 20249-6 Pa. $9.95

MY BONDAGE AND MY FREEDOM, Frederick Douglass. Born a slave, Douglass became outspoken force in antislavery movement. The best of Douglass' autobiographies. Graphic description of slave life. 464pp. 5⅜ x 8½. 22457-0 Pa. $8.95

FOLLOWING THE EQUATOR: A Journey Around the World, Mark Twain. Fascinating humorous account of 1897 voyage to Hawaii, Australia, India, New Zealand, etc. Ironic, bemused reports on peoples, customs, climate, flora and fauna, politics, much more. 197 illustrations. 720pp. 5⅜ x 8½. 26113-1 Pa. $15.95

THE PEOPLE CALLED SHAKERS, Edward D. Andrews. Definitive study of Shakers: origins, beliefs, practices, dances, social organization, furniture and crafts, etc. 33 illustrations. 351pp. 5⅜ x 8½. 21081-2 Pa. $8.95

THE MYTHS OF GREECE AND ROME, H. A. Guerber. A classic of mythology, generously illustrated, long prized for its simple, graphic, accurate retelling of the principal myths of Greece and Rome, and for its commentary on their origins and significance. With 64 illustrations by Michelangelo, Raphael, Titian, Rubens, Canova, Bernini and others. 480pp. 5⅜ x 8½. 27584-1 Pa. $9.95

PSYCHOLOGY OF MUSIC, Carl E. Seashore. Classic work discusses music as a medium from psychological viewpoint. Clear treatment of physical acoustics, auditory apparatus, sound perception, development of musical skills, nature of musical feeling, host of other topics. 88 figures. 408pp. 5⅜ x 8½. 21851-1 Pa. $11.95

THE PHILOSOPHY OF HISTORY, Georg W. Hegel. Great classic of Western thought develops concept that history is not chance but rational process, the evolution of freedom. 457pp. 5⅜ x 8½. 20112-0 Pa. $9.95

THE BOOK OF TEA, Kakuzo Okakura. Minor classic of the Orient: entertaining, charming explanation, interpretation of traditional Japanese culture in terms of tea ceremony. 94pp. 5⅜ x 8½. 20070-1 Pa. $3.95

LIFE IN ANCIENT EGYPT, Adolf Erman. Fullest, most thorough, detailed older account with much not in more recent books, domestic life, religion, magic, medicine, commerce, much more. Many illustrations reproduce tomb paintings, carvings, hieroglyphs, etc. 597pp. 5⅜ x 8½. 22632-8 Pa. $12.95

SUNDIALS, Their Theory and Construction, Albert Waugh. Far and away the best, most thorough coverage of ideas, mathematics concerned, types, construction, adjusting anywhere. Simple, nontechnical treatment allows even children to build several of these dials. Over 100 illustrations. 230pp. 5⅜ x 8½. 22947-5 Pa. $8.95

THEORETICAL HYDRODYNAMICS, L. M. Milne-Thomson. Classic exposition of the mathematical theory of fluid motion, applicable to both hydrodynamics and aerodynamics. Over 600 exercises. 768pp. 6⅛ x 9¼. 68970-0 Pa. $20.95

SONGS OF EXPERIENCE: Facsimile Reproduction with 26 Plates in Full Color, William Blake. 26 full-color plates from a rare 1826 edition. Includes "TheTyger," "London," "Holy Thursday," and other poems. Printed text of poems. 48pp. 5¼ x 7. 24636-1 Pa. $4.95

OLD-TIME VIGNETTES IN FULL COLOR, Carol Belanger Grafton (ed.). Over 390 charming, often sentimental illustrations, selected from archives of Victorian graphics—pretty women posing, children playing, food, flowers, kittens and puppies, smiling cherubs, birds and butterflies, much more. All copyright-free. 48pp. 9¼ x 12¼. 27269-9 Pa. $7.95

PERSPECTIVE FOR ARTISTS, Rex Vicat Cole. Depth, perspective of sky and sea, shadows, much more, not usually covered. 391 diagrams, 81 reproductions of drawings and paintings. 279pp. 5⅜ x 8½. 22487-2 Pa. $7.95

DRAWING THE LIVING FIGURE, Joseph Sheppard. Innovative approach to artistic anatomy focuses on specifics of surface anatomy, rather than muscles and bones. Over 170 drawings of live models in front, back and side views, and in widely varying poses. Accompanying diagrams. 177 illustrations. Introduction. Index. 144pp. 8⅜ x11¼. 26723-7 Pa. $8.95

GOTHIC AND OLD ENGLISH ALPHABETS: 100 Complete Fonts, Dan X. Solo. Add power, elegance to posters, signs, other graphics with 100 stunning copyright-free alphabets: Blackstone, Dolbey, Germania, 97 more–including many lower-case, numerals, punctuation marks. 104pp. 8⅛ x 11. 24695-7 Pa. $8.95

HOW TO DO BEADWORK, Mary White. Fundamental book on craft from simple projects to five-bead chains and woven works. 106 illustrations. 142pp. 5⅜ x 8. 20697-1 Pa. $5.95

THE BOOK OF WOOD CARVING, Charles Marshall Sayers. Finest book for beginners discusses fundamentals and offers 34 designs. "Absolutely first rate . . . well thought out and well executed."–E. J. Tangerman. 118pp. 7¾ x 10⅝. 23654-4 Pa. $7.95

ILLUSTRATED CATALOG OF CIVIL WAR MILITARY GOODS: Union Army Weapons, Insignia, Uniform Accessories, and Other Equipment, Schuyler, Hartley, and Graham. Rare, profusely illustrated 1846 catalog includes Union Army uniform and dress regulations, arms and ammunition, coats, insignia, flags, swords, rifles, etc. 226 illustrations. 160pp. 9 x 12. 24939-5 Pa. $10.95

WOMEN'S FASHIONS OF THE EARLY 1900s: An Unabridged Republication of "New York Fashions, 1909," National Cloak & Suit Co. Rare catalog of mail-order fashions documents women's and children's clothing styles shortly after the turn of the century. Captions offer full descriptions, prices. Invaluable resource for fashion, costume historians. Approximately 725 illustrations. 128pp. 8⅜ x 11¼. 27276-1 Pa. $11.95

THE 1912 AND 1915 GUSTAV STICKLEY FURNITURE CATALOGS, Gustav Stickley. With over 200 detailed illustrations and descriptions, these two catalogs are essential reading and reference materials and identification guides for Stickley furniture. Captions cite materials, dimensions and prices. 112pp. 6½ x 9¼. 26676-1 Pa. $9.95

EARLY AMERICAN LOCOMOTIVES, John H. White, Jr. Finest locomotive engravings from early 19th century: historical (1804–74), main-line (after 1870), special, foreign, etc. 147 plates. 142pp. 11⅜ x 8¼. 22772-3 Pa. $10.95

THE TALL SHIPS OF TODAY IN PHOTOGRAPHS, Frank O. Braynard. Lavishly illustrated tribute to nearly 100 majestic contemporary sailing vessels: Amerigo Vespucci, Clearwater, Constitution, Eagle, Mayflower, Sea Cloud, Victory, many more. Authoritative captions provide statistics, background on each ship. 190 black-and-white photographs and illustrations. Introduction. 128pp. 8⅞ x 11¾. 27163-3 Pa. $14.95

LITTLE BOOK OF EARLY AMERICAN CRAFTS AND TRADES, Peter Stockham (ed.). 1807 children's book explains crafts and trades: baker, hatter, cooper, potter, and many others. 23 copperplate illustrations. 140pp. 4⅝ x 6.
23336-7 Pa. $4.95

VICTORIAN FASHIONS AND COSTUMES FROM HARPER'S BAZAR, 1867–1898, Stella Blum (ed.). Day costumes, evening wear, sports clothes, shoes, hats, other accessories in over 1,000 detailed engravings. 320pp. 9⅜ x 12¼.
22990-4 Pa. $15.95

GUSTAV STICKLEY, THE CRAFTSMAN, Mary Ann Smith. Superb study surveys broad scope of Stickley's achievement, especially in architecture. Design philosophy, rise and fall of the Craftsman empire, descriptions and floor plans for many Craftsman houses, more. 86 black-and-white halftones. 31 line illustrations. Introduction 208pp. 6½ x 9¼.
27210-9 Pa. $9.95

THE LONG ISLAND RAIL ROAD IN EARLY PHOTOGRAPHS, Ron Ziel. Over 220 rare photos, informative text document origin (1844) and development of rail service on Long Island. Vintage views of early trains, locomotives, stations, passengers, crews, much more. Captions. 8⅞ x 11¾.
26301-0 Pa. $13.95

VOYAGE OF THE LIBERDADE, Joshua Slocum. Great 19th-century mariner's thrilling, first-hand account of the wreck of his ship off South America, the 35-foot boat he built from the wreckage, and its remarkable voyage home. 128pp. 5⅜ x 8½.
40022-0 Pa. $4.95

TEN BOOKS ON ARCHITECTURE, Vitruvius. The most important book ever written on architecture. Early Roman aesthetics, technology, classical orders, site selection, all other aspects. Morgan translation. 331pp. 5⅜ x 8½. 20645-9 Pa. $8.95

THE HUMAN FIGURE IN MOTION, Eadweard Muybridge. More than 4,500 stopped-action photos, in action series, showing undraped men, women, children jumping, lying down, throwing, sitting, wrestling, carrying, etc. 390pp. 7⅞ x 10⅝.
20204-6 Clothbd. $27.95

TREES OF THE EASTERN AND CENTRAL UNITED STATES AND CANADA, William M. Harlow. Best one-volume guide to 140 trees. Full descriptions, woodlore, range, etc. Over 600 illustrations. Handy size. 288pp. 4½ x 6⅜.
20395-6 Pa. $6.95

SONGS OF WESTERN BIRDS, Dr. Donald J. Borror. Complete song and call repertoire of 60 western species, including flycatchers, juncoes, cactus wrens, many more–includes fully illustrated booklet. Cassette and manual 99913-0 $8.95

GROWING AND USING HERBS AND SPICES, Milo Miloradovich. Versatile handbook provides all the information needed for cultivation and use of all the herbs and spices available in North America. 4 illustrations. Index. Glossary. 236pp. 5⅜ x 8½.
25058-X Pa. $7.95

BIG BOOK OF MAZES AND LABYRINTHS, Walter Shepherd. 50 mazes and labyrinths in all–classical, solid, ripple, and more–in one great volume. Perfect inexpensive puzzler for clever youngsters. Full solutions. 112pp. 8⅛ x 11.
22951-3 Pa. $5.95

PIANO TUNING, J. Cree Fischer. Clearest, best book for beginner, amateur. Simple repairs, raising dropped notes, tuning by easy method of flattened fifths. No previous skills needed. 4 illustrations. 201pp. 5⅜ x 8½. 23267-0 Pa. $6.95

HINTS TO SINGERS, Lillian Nordica. Selecting the right teacher, developing confidence, overcoming stage fright, and many other important skills receive thoughtful discussion in this indispensible guide, written by a world-famous diva of four decades' experience. 96pp. 5³/₈ x 8¹/₂. 40094-8 Pa. $4.95

THE COMPLETE NONSENSE OF EDWARD LEAR, Edward Lear. All nonsense limericks, zany alphabets, Owl and Pussycat, songs, nonsense botany, etc., illustrated by Lear. Total of 320pp. 5⅜ x 8½. (USO) 20167-8 Pa. $7.95

VICTORIAN PARLOUR POETRY: An Annotated Anthology, Michael R. Turner. 117 gems by Longfellow, Tennyson, Browning, many lesser-known poets. "The Village Blacksmith," "Curfew Must Not Ring Tonight," "Only a Baby Small," dozens more, often difficult to find elsewhere. Index of poets, titles, first lines. xxiii + 325pp. 5⅜ x 8¼. 27044-0 Pa. $8.95

DUBLINERS, James Joyce. Fifteen stories offer vivid, tightly focused observations of the lives of Dublin's poorer classes. At least one, "The Dead," is considered a masterpiece. Reprinted complete and unabridged from standard edition. 160pp. 5³/₁₆ x 8¼. 26870-5 Pa. $1.00

GREAT WEIRD TALES: 14 Stories by Lovecraft, Blackwood, Machen and Others, S. T. Joshi (ed.). 14 spellbinding tales, including "The Sin Eater," by Fiona McLeod, "The Eye Above the Mantel," by Frank Belknap Long, as well as renowned works by R. H. Barlow, Lord Dunsany, Arthur Machen, W. C. Morrow and eight other masters of the genre. 256pp. 5⅜ x 8½. (USO) 40436-6 Pa. $8.95

THE BOOK OF THE SACRED MAGIC OF ABRAMELIN THE MAGE, translated by S. MacGregor Mathers. Medieval manuscript of ceremonial magic. Basic document in Aleister Crowley, Golden Dawn groups. 268pp. 5⅜ x 8½. 23211-5 Pa. $9.95

NEW RUSSIAN-ENGLISH AND ENGLISH-RUSSIAN DICTIONARY, M. A. O'Brien. This is a remarkably handy Russian dictionary, containing a surprising amount of information, including over 70,000 entries. 366pp. 4½ x 6¼. 20208-9 Pa. $10.95

HISTORIC HOMES OF THE AMERICAN PRESIDENTS, Second, Revised Edition, Irvin Haas. A traveler's guide to American Presidential homes, most open to the public, depicting and describing homes occupied by every American President from George Washington to George Bush. With visiting hours, admission charges, travel routes. 175 photographs. Index. 160pp. 8¼ x 11. 26751-2 Pa. $11.95

NEW YORK IN THE FORTIES, Andreas Feininger. 162 brilliant photographs by the well-known photographer, formerly with *Life* magazine. Commuters, shoppers, Times Square at night, much else from city at its peak. Captions by John von Hartz. 181pp. 9¼ x 10¾. 23585-8 Pa. $13.95

INDIAN SIGN LANGUAGE, William Tomkins. Over 525 signs developed by Sioux and other tribes. Written instructions and diagrams. Also 290 pictographs. 111pp. 6⅛ x 9¼. 22029-X Pa. $3.95

ANATOMY: A Complete Guide for Artists, Joseph Sheppard. A master of figure drawing shows artists how to render human anatomy convincingly. Over 460 illustrations. 224pp. 8⅜ x 11¼. 27279-6 Pa. $11.95

MEDIEVAL CALLIGRAPHY: Its History and Technique, Marc Drogin. Spirited history, comprehensive instruction manual covers 13 styles (ca. 4th century thru 15th). Excellent photographs; directions for duplicating medieval techniques with modern tools. 224pp. 8⅜ x 11¼. 26142-5 Pa. $12.95

DRIED FLOWERS: How to Prepare Them, Sarah Whitlock and Martha Rankin. Complete instructions on how to use silica gel, meal and borax, perlite aggregate, sand and borax, glycerine and water to create attractive permanent flower arrangements. 12 illustrations. 32pp. 5⅜ x 8½. 21802-3 Pa. $1.00

EASY-TO-MAKE BIRD FEEDERS FOR WOODWORKERS, Scott D. Campbell. Detailed, simple-to-use guide for designing, constructing, caring for and using feeders. Text, illustrations for 12 classic and contemporary designs. 96pp. 5⅜ x 8½. 25847-5 Pa. $3.95

SCOTTISH WONDER TALES FROM MYTH AND LEGEND, Donald A. Mackenzie. 16 lively tales tell of giants rumbling down mountainsides, of a magic wand that turns stone pillars into warriors, of gods and goddesses, evil hags, powerful forces and more. 240pp. 5⅜ x 8½. 29677-6 Pa. $6.95

THE HISTORY OF UNDERCLOTHES, C. Willett Cunnington and Phyllis Cunnington. Fascinating, well-documented survey covering six centuries of English undergarments, enhanced with over 100 illustrations: 12th-century laced-up bodice, footed long drawers (1795), 19th-century bustles, 19th-century corsets for men, Victorian "bust improvers," much more. 272pp. 5⅜ x 8¼. 27124-2 Pa. $9.95

ARTS AND CRAFTS FURNITURE: The Complete Brooks Catalog of 1912, Brooks Manufacturing Co. Photos and detailed descriptions of more than 150 now very collectible furniture designs from the Arts and Crafts movement depict davenports, settees, buffets, desks, tables, chairs, bedsteads, dressers and more, all built of solid, quarter-sawed oak. Invaluable for students and enthusiasts of antiques, Americana and the decorative arts. 80pp. 6½ x 9¼. 27471-3 Pa. $8.95

WILBUR AND ORVILLE: A Biography of the Wright Brothers, Fred Howard. Definitive, crisply written study tells the full story of the brothers' lives and work. A vividly written biography, unparalleled in scope and color, that also captures the spirit of an extraordinary era. 560pp. 6⅛ x 9¼. 40297-5 Pa. $17.95

THE ARTS OF THE SAILOR: Knotting, Splicing and Ropework, Hervey Garrett Smith. Indispensable shipboard reference covers tools, basic knots and useful hitches; handsewing and canvas work, more. Over 100 illustrations. Delightful reading for sea lovers. 256pp. 5⅜ x 8½. 26440-8 Pa. $8.95

FRANK LLOYD WRIGHT'S FALLINGWATER: The House and Its History, Second, Revised Edition, Donald Hoffmann. A total revision—both in text and illustrations—of the standard document on Fallingwater, the boldest, most personal architectural statement of Wright's mature years, updated with valuable new material from the recently opened Frank Lloyd Wright Archives. "Fascinating"—*The New York Times.* 116 illustrations. 128pp. 9¼ x 10¾. 27430-6 Pa. $12.95

PHOTOGRAPHIC SKETCHBOOK OF THE CIVIL WAR, Alexander Gardner. 100 photos taken on field during the Civil War. Famous shots of Manassas Harper's Ferry, Lincoln, Richmond, slave pens, etc. 244pp. 10⅝ x 8¼.   22731-6 Pa. $10.95

FIVE ACRES AND INDEPENDENCE, Maurice G. Kains. Great back-to-the-land classic explains basics of self-sufficient farming. The one book to get. 95 illustrations. 397pp. 5⅜ x 8½.   20974-1 Pa. $7.95

SONGS OF EASTERN BIRDS, Dr. Donald J. Borror. Songs and calls of 60 species most common to eastern U.S.: warblers, woodpeckers, flycatchers, thrushes, larks, many more in high-quality recording.   Cassette and manual 99912-2 $9.95

A MODERN HERBAL, Margaret Grieve. Much the fullest, most exact, most useful compilation of herbal material. Gigantic alphabetical encyclopedia, from aconite to zedoary, gives botanical information, medical properties, folklore, economic uses, much else. Indispensable to serious reader. 161 illustrations. 888pp. 6½ x 9¼. 2-vol. set. (USO)   Vol. I: 22798-7 Pa. $9.95
Vol. II: 22799-5 Pa. $9.95

HIDDEN TREASURE MAZE BOOK, Dave Phillips. Solve 34 challenging mazes accompanied by heroic tales of adventure. Evil dragons, people-eating plants, blood-thirsty giants, many more dangerous adversaries lurk at every twist and turn. 34 mazes, stories, solutions. 48pp. 8¼ x 11.   24566-7 Pa. $2.95

LETTERS OF W. A. MOZART, Wolfgang A. Mozart. Remarkable letters show bawdy wit, humor, imagination, musical insights, contemporary musical world; includes some letters from Leopold Mozart. 276pp. 5⅜ x 8½.   22859-2 Pa. $7.95

BASIC PRINCIPLES OF CLASSICAL BALLET, Agrippina Vaganova. Great Russian theoretician, teacher explains methods for teaching classical ballet. 118 illustrations. 175pp. 5⅜ x 8½.   22036-2 Pa. $5.95

THE JUMPING FROG, Mark Twain. Revenge edition. The original story of The Celebrated Jumping Frog of Calaveras County, a hapless French translation, and Twain's hilarious "retranslation" from the French. 12 illustrations. 66pp. 5⅜ x 8½.   22686-7 Pa. $3.95

BEST REMEMBERED POEMS, Martin Gardner (ed.). The 126 poems in this superb collection of 19th- and 20th-century British and American verse range from Shelley's "To a Skylark" to the impassioned "Renascence" of Edna St. Vincent Millay and to Edward Lear's whimsical "The Owl and the Pussycat." 224pp. 5⅜ x 8½.   27165-X Pa. $5.95

COMPLETE SONNETS, William Shakespeare. Over 150 exquisite poems deal with love, friendship, the tyranny of time, beauty's evanescence, death and other themes in language of remarkable power, precision and beauty. Glossary of archaic terms. 80pp. 5³⁄₁₆ x 8¼.   26686-9 Pa. $1.00

BODIES IN A BOOKSHOP, R. T. Campbell. Challenging mystery of blackmail and murder with ingenious plot and superbly drawn characters. In the best tradition of British suspense fiction. 192pp. 5⅜ x 8½.   24720-1 Pa. $6.95

THE WIT AND HUMOR OF OSCAR WILDE, Alvin Redman (ed.). More than 1,000 ripostes, paradoxes, wisecracks: Work is the curse of the drinking classes; I can resist everything except temptation; etc. 258pp. 5⅜ x 8½. 20602-5 Pa. $6.95

SHAKESPEARE LEXICON AND QUOTATION DICTIONARY, Alexander Schmidt. Full definitions, locations, shades of meaning in every word in plays and poems. More than 50,000 exact quotations. 1,485pp. 6½ x 9¼. 2-vol. set.
Vol. 1: 22726-X Pa. $17.95
Vol. 2: 22727-8 Pa. $17.95

SELECTED POEMS, Emily Dickinson. Over 100 best-known, best-loved poems by one of America's foremost poets, reprinted from authoritative early editions. No comparable edition at this price. Index of first lines. 64pp. 5³⁄₁₆ x 8¼. 26466-1 Pa. $1.00

THE INSIDIOUS DR. FU-MANCHU, Sax Rohmer. The first of the popular mystery series introduces a pair of English detectives to their archnemesis, the diabolical Dr. Fu-Manchu. Flavorful atmosphere, fast-paced action, and colorful characters enliven this classic of the genre. 208pp. 5³⁄₁₆ x 8¼. 29898-1 Pa. $2.00

THE MALLEUS MALEFICARUM OF KRAMER AND SPRENGER, translated by Montague Summers. Full text of most important witchhunter's "bible," used by both Catholics and Protestants. 278pp. 6⅝ x 10. 22802-9 Pa. $12.95

SPANISH STORIES/CUENTOS ESPAÑOLES: A Dual-Language Book, Angel Flores (ed.). Unique format offers 13 great stories in Spanish by Cervantes, Borges, others. Faithful English translations on facing pages. 352pp. 5⅜ x 8½. 25399-6 Pa. $8.95

GARDEN CITY, LONG ISLAND, IN EARLY PHOTOGRAPHS, 1869–1919, Mildred H. Smith. Handsome treasury of 118 vintage pictures, accompanied by carefully researched captions, document the Garden City Hotel fire (1899), the Vanderbilt Cup Race (1908), the first airmail flight departing from the Nassau Boulevard Aerodrome (1911), and much more. 96pp. 8⁷⁄₈ x 11³⁄₄. 40669-5 Pa. $12.95

OLD QUEENS, N.Y., IN EARLY PHOTOGRAPHS, Vincent F. Seyfried and William Asadorian. Over 160 rare photographs of Maspeth, Jamaica, Jackson Heights, and other areas. Vintage views of DeWitt Clinton mansion, 1939 World's Fair and more. Captions. 192pp. 8⅞ x 11. 26358-4 Pa. $12.95

CAPTURED BY THE INDIANS: 15 Firsthand Accounts, 1750-1870, Frederick Drimmer. Astounding true historical accounts of grisly torture, bloody conflicts, relentless pursuits, miraculous escapes and more, by people who lived to tell the tale. 384pp. 5⅜ x 8½. 24901-8 Pa. $8.95

THE WORLD'S GREAT SPEECHES (Fourth Enlarged Edition), Lewis Copeland, Lawrence W. Lamm, and Stephen J. McKenna. Nearly 300 speeches provide public speakers with a wealth of updated quotes and inspiration–from Pericles' funeral oration and William Jennings Bryan's "Cross of Gold Speech" to Malcolm X's powerful words on the Black Revolution and Earl of Spenser's tribute to his sister, Diana, Princess of Wales. 944pp. 5⅜ x 8⅜. 40903-1 Pa. $15.95

THE BOOK OF THE SWORD, Sir Richard F. Burton. Great Victorian scholar/adventurer's eloquent, erudite history of the "queen of weapons"–from prehistory to early Roman Empire. Evolution and development of early swords, variations (sabre, broadsword, cutlass, scimitar, etc.), much more. 336pp. 6⅛ x 9¼. 25434-8 Pa. $9.95

AUTOBIOGRAPHY: The Story of My Experiments with Truth, Mohandas K. Gandhi. Boyhood, legal studies, purification, the growth of the Satyagraha (nonviolent protest) movement. Critical, inspiring work of the man responsible for the freedom of India. 480pp. 5⅜ x 8½. (USO) 24593-4 Pa. $8.95

CELTIC MYTHS AND LEGENDS, T. W. Rolleston. Masterful retelling of Irish and Welsh stories and tales. Cuchulain, King Arthur, Deirdre, the Grail, many more. First paperback edition. 58 full-page illustrations. 512pp. 5⅜ x 8½. 26507-2 Pa. $9.95

THE PRINCIPLES OF PSYCHOLOGY, William James. Famous long course complete, unabridged. Stream of thought, time perception, memory, experimental methods; great work decades ahead of its time. 94 figures. 1,391pp. 5⅜ x 8½. 2-vol. set.
Vol. I: 20381-6 Pa. $13.95
Vol. II: 20382-4 Pa. $14.95

THE WORLD AS WILL AND REPRESENTATION, Arthur Schopenhauer. Definitive English translation of Schopenhauer's life work, correcting more than 1,000 errors, omissions in earlier translations. Translated by E. F. J. Payne. Total of 1,269pp. 5⅜ x 8½. 2-vol. set. Vol. 1: 21761-2 Pa. $12.95
Vol. 2: 21762-0 Pa. $12.95

MAGIC AND MYSTERY IN TIBET, Madame Alexandra David-Neel. Experiences among lamas, magicians, sages, sorcerers, Bonpa wizards. A true psychic discovery. 32 illustrations. 321pp. 5⅜ x 8½. (USO) 22682-4 Pa. $9.95

THE EGYPTIAN BOOK OF THE DEAD, E. A. Wallis Budge. Complete reproduction of Ani's papyrus, finest ever found. Full hieroglyphic text, interlinear transliteration, word-for-word translation, smooth translation. 533pp. 6½ x 9¼.
21866-X Pa. $11.95

MATHEMATICS FOR THE NONMATHEMATICIAN, Morris Kline. Detailed, college-level treatment of mathematics in cultural and historical context, with numerous exercises. Recommended Reading Lists. Tables. Numerous figures. 641pp. 5⅜ x 8½.
24823-2 Pa. $11.95

PROBABILISTIC METHODS IN THE THEORY OF STRUCTURES, Isaac Elishakoff. Well-written introduction covers the elements of the theory of probability from two or more random variables, the reliability of such multivariable structures, the theory of random function, Monte Carlo methods of treating problems incapable of exact solution, and more. Examples. 502pp. 5³/₈ x 8¹/₂. 40691-1 Pa. $16.95

THE RIME OF THE ANCIENT MARINER, Gustave Doré, S. T. Coleridge. Doré's finest work; 34 plates capture moods, subtleties of poem. Flawless full-size reproductions printed on facing pages with authoritative text of poem. "Beautiful. Simply beautiful."–*Publisher's Weekly*. 77pp. 9¼ x 12. 22305-1 Pa. $7.95

NORTH AMERICAN INDIAN DESIGNS FOR ARTISTS AND CRAFTSPEOPLE, Eva Wilson. Over 360 authentic copyright-free designs adapted from Navajo blankets, Hopi pottery, Sioux buffalo hides, more. Geometrics, symbolic figures, plant and animal motifs, etc. 128pp. 8⅜ x 11. (EUK) 25341-4 Pa. $8.95

SCULPTURE: Principles and Practice, Louis Slobodkin. Step-by-step approach to clay, plaster, metals, stone; classical and modern. 253 drawings, photos. 255pp. 8⅛ x 11.
22960-2 Pa. $11.95

CATALOG OF DOVER BOOKS

THE INFLUENCE OF SEA POWER UPON HISTORY, 1660–1783, A. T. Mahan. Influential classic of naval history and tactics still used as text in war colleges. First paperback edition. 4 maps. 24 battle plans. 640pp. 5⅜ x 8½. 25509-3 Pa. $14.95

THE STORY OF THE TITANIC AS TOLD BY ITS SURVIVORS, Jack Winocour (ed.). What it was really like. Panic, despair, shocking inefficiency, and a little heroism. More thrilling than any fictional account. 26 illustrations. 320pp. 5⅜ x 8½. 20610-6 Pa. $8.95

FAIRY AND FOLK TALES OF THE IRISH PEASANTRY, William Butler Yeats (ed.). Treasury of 64 tales from the twilight world of Celtic myth and legend: "The Soul Cages," "The Kildare Pooka," "King O'Toole and his Goose," many more. Introduction and Notes by W. B. Yeats. 352pp. 5⅜ x 8½. 26941-8 Pa. $8.95

BUDDHIST MAHAYANA TEXTS, E. B. Cowell and Others (eds.). Superb, accurate translations of basic documents in Mahayana Buddhism, highly important in history of religions. The Buddha-karita of Asvaghosha, Larger Sukhavativyuha, more. 448pp. 5⅜ x 8½. 25552-2 Pa. $12.95

ONE TWO THREE . . . INFINITY: Facts and Speculations of Science, George Gamow. Great physicist's fascinating, readable overview of contemporary science: number theory, relativity, fourth dimension, entropy, genes, atomic structure, much more. 128 illustrations. Index. 352pp. 5⅜ x 8½. 25664-2 Pa. $8.95

EXPERIMENTATION AND MEASUREMENT, W. J. Youden. Introductory manual explains laws of measurement in simple terms and offers tips for achieving accuracy and minimizing errors. Mathematics of measurement, use of instruments, experimenting with machines. 1994 edition. Foreword. Preface. Introduction. Epilogue. Selected Readings. Glossary. Index. Tables and figures. 128pp. 5⅜ x 8½. 40451-X Pa. $6.95

DALÍ ON MODERN ART: The Cuckolds of Antiquated Modern Art, Salvador Dalí. Influential painter skewers modern art and its practitioners. Outrageous evaluations of Picasso, Cézanne, Turner, more. 15 renderings of paintings discussed. 44 calligraphic decorations by Dalí. 96pp. 5⅜ x 8½. (USO) 29220-7 Pa. $5.95

ANTIQUE PLAYING CARDS: A Pictorial History, Henry René D'Allemagne. Over 900 elaborate, decorative images from rare playing cards (14th–20th centuries): Bacchus, death, dancing dogs, hunting scenes, royal coats of arms, players cheating, much more. 96pp. 9¼ x 12¼. 29265-7 Pa. $12.95

MAKING FURNITURE MASTERPIECES: 30 Projects with Measured Drawings, Franklin H. Gottshall. Step-by-step instructions, illustrations for constructing handsome, useful pieces, among them a Sheraton desk, Chippendale chair, Spanish desk, Queen Anne table and a William and Mary dressing mirror. 224pp. 8⅛ x 11¼. 29338-6 Pa. $13.95

THE FOSSIL BOOK: A Record of Prehistoric Life, Patricia V. Rich et al. Profusely illustrated definitive guide covers everything from single-celled organisms and dinosaurs to birds and mammals and the interplay between climate and man. Over 1,500 illustrations. 760pp. 7½ x 10⅝. 29371-8 Pa. $29.95

Prices subject to change without notice.

Available at your book dealer or write for free catalog to Dept. GI, Dover Publications, Inc., 31 East 2nd St., Mineola, N.Y. 11501. Dover publishes more than 500 books each year on science, elementary and advanced mathematics, biology, music, art, literary history, social sciences and other areas.